ABOUT THE AUTHOR

David Chadwick is an acclaimed author, historian and award-winning journalist whose work includes *Liberty Bazaar*, his debut novel, and *High Seas to Home*, an historical account of the Battle of the Atlantic. David uses his experiences reporting politics, crime and business to inform his fiction. He divides his time between Greater Manchester and southern Spain.

ALSO BY DAVID CHADWICK

Fiction

Liberty Bazaar

Non-fiction

High Seas to Home – Daily Despatches from a Frigate at War
(with Shirley Morgan and Allan Seabridge)

Short stories

Panopticon (edited with Nicky Harlow)

Weird Love (edited with Nicky Harlow)

To Zahreen

TIN SOLDIERS

With love and thanks for
47 years (and counting!)
of cherished friendship

Dave x.

DAVID CHADWICK

Matador
Unit E2 Airfield Business Park,
Harrison Road, Market Harborough,
Leicestershire. LE16 7UL
Tel: 0116 2792299
Email: books@troubador.co.uk
Web: www.troubador.co.uk/matador
Twitter: @matadorbooks

ISBN 978 1803136 387

British Library Cataloguing in Publication Data.
A catalogue record for this book is available from the British Library.

PPrinted and bound in Great Britain by 4edge Limited
Typeset in 11pt Minion Pro by Troubador Publishing Ltd, Leicester, UK

Matador is an imprint of Troubador Publishing Ltd

PRAISE FOR DAVID CHADWICK

'Offbeat, refreshingly absorbing … twisty and well-realized … Features impeccable research'

— *Kirkus Reviews* (starred review)

'A compelling story with a profound moral dimension – and a political page-turner that transcends the genre of historical fiction'

— Faber Prize winner Livi Michael

'First class storytelling. An addictive novel with a tremendous feel for its time and settings – lived out by characters with real passion and true human complexity'

— Paul Du Noyer, founding editor of *MOJO*

'Chadwick shares that light touch intensity of the king of this genre, John le Carré … the claustrophobia … the intrigue, the rules of engagement and the double dealing'

— Michael Taylor, *The Marple Leaf*

'Much to please both thinker and those demanding entertainment.'

— *The Book Bag*, five star review

'Chadwick pens a story with precision and poise'

— *Readers' Favorite*, five star review

For my sons Jacob and Sammy with love.

ONE

Wednesday May 13, 1970

The battle honours of the Fighting 55th were carved on the façade of the regimental armoury in Manhattan. Gettysburg to Normandy, you name it. But one engagement damn certain never to appear was Ramskill University Campus. There, six days ago, National Guardsmen of the 55th fired on students protesting America's invasion of Cambodia. They left three dead, a half dozen wounded, and a real bad taste.

This was the unit I was about to join as I headed for the armoury building at East 14th Street and 3rd Avenue. It was an elegant Beaux-Arts structure dating back to 1907, with oriel windows and an American eagle carved over a high arched entrance.

I reported to the reception desk and was shown to the office of Colonel Philip Sheridan Riley II, who had commanded the Guard at Ramskill.

Riley was a big framed, fleshy faced man with bristly grey hair. Wide-spaced eyes and flared nostrils over a cinderblock jaw made me think of an aggressive bull hippo. Glancing at the five decks of medal ribbons on his class A uniform coat, I guessed he'd be early fifties and had served in World War II, or Korea, or both.

He gave me a frosty look as I stood in front of his desk. Portraits of previous regimental commanders gazed from dark panel walls. A bust of George Washington stood by one window; Old Glory and the New York State colours hung from poles by another. The place smelled of pre-Depression affluence – beeswax and brass polish, cigar smoke and a hint of decanted brandy.

There was no visitor chair, which came as no surprise. I didn't expect cigars or brandy either.

This was because Colonel Riley was the opposite of happy. First, his promotion to brigadier general had been put on hold following the Ramskill incident; and second, he'd gotten stuck with me.

'So, Captain Appalachia is back.' He talked as if this was some kind of reunion, even though we'd never met. 'The hillbilly hero has returned.'

It seemed Riley was the worst sort of snob. Then again, maybe he was the best: I knew exactly where I stood with him, even if it was eyeball-deep in shit. 'But you're not a captain any more, and you're not a hero, are you?'

I kept my tone even. 'Not if you say so, Colonel.'

He looked down at a typewritten sheet on his desk. 'Says here you quit Vietnam and came back to the States for personal reasons; that you still want to serve and believe enlisting in the National Guard is the most appropriate way of doing so.'

He pushed the document to one side and looked at me straight. 'I heard a different version from a pal in Saigon. Want to know what he said?'

I said nothing.

'He told me you developed a mile-wide yellow streak and withdrew your Green Berets in an act of gross cowardice that exposed a whole infantry company to enemy fire and cost the lives of two dozen of our boys.'

He went quiet for a stretched-out moment, but kept his eyes on mine. 'That true?'

I didn't blink, didn't break the stare. I could do this all day. 'I'm not at liberty to comment, Colonel.'

He made a throaty-nasal noise someplace between a growl and a snort. 'Sure you're not. In my opinion, the whole disgraceful affair should be all over the TV and newspapers.'

He leaned back in his chair. 'You got anything to say about that?'

'No, Colonel, I don't.'

He shoved stubby fingers through his scrubbing-brush hair, as if he couldn't understand my refusal to get provoked. Then he changed his approach. 'I know you have friends in high places – in particular General Laurence Westerby. Amazing what a friend like that can do. I guess it wouldn't be so good for morale if the US Army court martialled a Medal of Honor recipient, so Westerby decided to keep a lid on this. What was the deal? You left quietly and no one pressed charges?'

'There was no deal, Colonel.'

'The hell there wasn't.' He banged a stumpy-fist on the desk. 'Up to me you'd have been stripped of that Medal of Honor, tried, convicted and locked up in Leavenworth already.'

He appeared to realize he was the one who'd gotten stoked, and pulled his crap together. 'Luckily for you, Tyler, it's not up to me.'

He moved the document back to the centre of his desk. 'This order has come direct from Almerin O'Hara, New York National Guard adjutant general, who I happen to know served in World War II with your pal Westerby. It says I have to accept you on my strength as a private first class.'

He looked at me for a response.

'Honoured to enlist, Colonel.'

I hadn't said what I assumed he wanted me to, so he said it for me. 'Bit of a come-down from Special Forces captain to National Guard grunt, wouldn't you say?'

'No I wouldn't, Colonel. We all have a part to play serving the country.'

He looked at me for a long time, as if unsure whether I was dicking with him. Finally, he made a knowing expression, like he'd just worked out what had *really* gone on. 'Westerby tried to get you into my unit without loss of rank, didn't he? But every friendship has its limits and the idea of having a chickenshit officer on his hands must have stuck in O'Hara's craw.'

Again, the long pause, the searchlight gaze. 'Well?'

'I wouldn't know anything about that, Colonel.'

He stood up and moved in slow, heavy strides to my side.

I kept my eyes front, face expressionless.

He leaned close to my ear. 'I know how you saved Westerby's ass from the Viet Cong; how he swung you your ridiculous field commission as payback. But you were never a real officer. You were never one of us. And now you're back where you belong. Only you don't belong – not in my command. No place for cowards in the 55th. You understand?'

I didn't blink. 'Yes, Colonel.'

He returned to his chair and changed his tone yet again.

I got the impression he'd grown bored with trying to rile me. 'You'll have heard all about the events up at Ramskill Campus?'

I said I had. The whole country had, the whole planet.

'Some folks are calling it the Ramskill Massacre.' He swivelled his chair so he was facing away from me. 'What do you think of that?'

I told him I thought it was unfortunate. Which was an understatement. Coming three days after four students were killed by the National Guard at Kent State University in Ohio, the Ramskill shootings had also been dubbed Kent State II.

'It's a goddam travesty,' he said. 'My boys were faced with ruthless, fanatical and highly organized commie agitators. They got inside kids' heads, got 'em tossing Molotov cocktails, hurling rocks, burning down buildings.'

I knew Riley had deployed more than twelve hundred guardsmen that day, comprising both battalions of the 55th Infantry, plus elements of an armoured cavalry squadron. However, only twelve soldiers had been involved in the shooting. They belonged to Bravo Company, 2nd battalion, headquartered at Ramskill – the company I was joining.

'We came under sniper fire too.' He swung his chair back to face me. His look was someplace between anger and anguish. 'That was why my boys returned fire.'

But this wasn't what I heard. I was a reporter before I was a soldier, and now I was both, which meant I had a sharp nose for bullshit. Newspaper copy from Ramskill confirmed students had thrown stones and Molotovs at the guardsmen as well as torching buildings. I had no doubt the guardsmen had come under intense and prolonged provocation, but there was no credible evidence of sniper fire.

Clearly, though, now was not a good time to tell Riley what I'd heard.

'Did you know one of the fatalities was the son of a congresswoman?' He shook his head and exhaled through his big nostrils. 'What thoroughly rotten luck.'

He was referring to Boyd Brigstock, a twenty-year-old sophomore whose mom was a leading House Democrat. And it was as if this *thoroughly rotten luck* had been visited specifically on Colonel Riley, that *his* bum deal totally eclipsed that of the smart young man left lying in a pool of himself on a campus parking lot. Or, for that matter, the gross misfortune of the two professors – Oleg Bobkov and Gordon Richardson – who also died that day, even though they had nothing to do with the protest.

Riley picked up a pencil and held one end in his right hand, the other in his left. 'It's all grist to the mill of those paranoid loony tunes and their fairy stories about a police state and a tyrant in the White House.'

There was no shortage of conspiracy theories, this much was true. And Richard Nixon was at the centre of most of them. But this was the age of crazy, a time when paranoia was often justified and some conspiracy theories were lame compared with the shit that was really going down.

'This country is facing a crisis unprecedented in modern times,' he said. 'Sooner or later, one side is going to break – and it won't be us.'

I watched his pencil bow, then snap in two.

He seemed to remember my presence and gave me an offended look, like I'd been snooping on his private thoughts.

'You better be real careful up at Ramskill,' he said. 'Last thing I want is somebody like you with a point to prove. You're not in Vietnam now and you can't John Wayne yourself out of trouble. Step out of line just once and I'll come down on you so hard you'll wish you were back with the Viet Cong. You hear me, Private Tyler?'

'I hear you, Colonel.'

TWO

I was walking from my apartment in the East Village toward the Fillmore East on 2nd Avenue when I first noticed the junkie. He was sitting on the sidewalk, propped against a fire hydrant. He looked dazed and defeated – a knocked down boxer waiting out a count that never got to ten. His face was scooped out, hair matted, eyes half-lit. Whatever planet he was on, it wasn't this one. He'd scrawled *Viet vet – please help* on a scrap of cardboard that lay alongside a military beret. A half-assed Samaritan dropped a dime in the beret and the bum mumbled an approximation of thanks.

As I got closer I noticed a tattoo on the guy's bare forearm depicting the head of a bald eagle and scroll that said *101st Airborne, 1967.* I'd served in the *101st*, before transferring to 5th Special Forces so I tossed two quarters into the beret as I went by. If he noticed my generosity, he didn't show it.

I crossed the street at East 6th and headed for the Fillmore. I didn't need to be in Ramskill until the following morning and couldn't imagine a better way of spending the evening than with Jefferson Airplane. The concert hall was jumping. The Airplane laid down some righteous sounds. And for a couple of hours I reconnected brain circuits broken in early childhood, restored amputated emotion. I felt normal, just like everyone else in there – or leastways what I thought normal felt like. Rock and roll could do that.

When the gig ended I went to Gem Spa, a 24-hour news stand on 2nd Avenue where you could get the best New York egg cream soda I ever drank. I found a spot nearby and sipped the drink from a Coke-style glass. It didn't contain eggs or cream; just milk, seltzer, and chocolate syrup. But it did come with a time machine. Taste memory flipped me right back to the mid-50s when I used to come here as a teenager on a Saturday night looking for girls and trouble.

By 1970 the East Village was a whole other scene. It was still a tough part of town, but an influx of bohemians, priced out of Greenwich Village by spiralling rents, brought a more civilized vibe.

So why did I get the feeling I was being watched? Not tailed, so much as observed. And not out of hostility so much as curiosity. I looked around but saw nothing untoward. And since I didn't detect any threat, I didn't look any closer.

Then I clocked a small crowd gathered around the junkie I'd seen earlier, the down-and-out Vietnam veteran. He was sitting in the same place on the sidewalk, oblivious to the half-dozen youths surrounding him. One of them kicked him in the thigh. I heard him yowl. A chorus of laughter went up from the others. The guy doing the kicking made a grab for the junkie's beret, which I remembered contained the cash he'd bagged. Junkie may have been spaced, but not so much that he'd let these guys take his cash. He clutched the beret to his chest, told them to shove off.

Seemed the area hadn't gotten so civilized after all.

I finished my egg cream and crossed 2nd Avenue.

Elbowing my way through the horseshoe of youths, I stepped in front of the aggressor as he was about to deliver another kick.

He was an Hispanic dude in stylish jeans and a tight white T that showed off a muscular physique. Long black hair was pushed behind his ears, resting on his shoulders. Dark eyes gleamed faint in the dark. Height and build were similar to mine – around six feet one and 180 pounds.

'You should back off, man.' I tried to sound reasonable. 'Can't you see this guy has nothing worth taking?'

White T's eyes narrowed. 'Who the hell are you?'

'Somebody who doesn't want trouble.' I produced a five dollar bill from my wallet and offered it to him. 'Take this and move on – you won't find half of that in this guy's hat.'

White T took the five spot and shoved it in his pocket. 'Guess I'll take your money *and* his.'

I made a disappointed sigh. It didn't have to be like this. But I'd known the likely outcome all along because back in the day I'd also been a Lower East Side punk.

I gave him a don't-be-an-asshole look. 'That's not the deal.'

White T's right hand went behind his back and he pulled a cutthroat razor. Flicking out the blade, he held it level with my face.

'Man, I'm gonna cut you so bad your own mama won't recognize you.'

I tried one last time. 'You should put that thing away. You're five bucks ahead – why not take it as a win?'

White T frowned. Seemed he couldn't accept that I wasn't scared.

Truth was I didn't get scared because I had what you might

call a fear bypass. But that didn't mean I felt nothing at all and it sure didn't make me blasé about violent confrontations. And if five years in Vietnam taught me anything it was to take nothing at face value. Including clowns like this. *Especially* clowns like this.

I saw his neck muscles tense.

We'd done talking. Silence hung mean.

But not for long.

He came at me fast, blade slashing right to left. This wasn't about speed, though, it was about anticipation. I got a fix on the razor, then I hit the back of his hand with my left palm and the inside of his wrist with my right. The double impact sprung the razor from his grip. It went spinning to the ground. In the same movement, I stepped forward and landed a head butt that crunched his nose in a gory spatter. He staggered back and hit the sidewalk clutching his face. It wasn't the smartest play – even without the blade White T might have hit me with his free hand. But it *was* spectacular – and that was exactly what I wanted.

Because although there was strength in numbers, there was weakness too – a tendency to step back and let another guy step up. My calculation was that the sight of White T going down so hard would make the others hesitate. They'd look around, waiting for somebody else to take a shot.

The logic worked. If the rest of the group had been thinking of piling in after White T, they weren't any longer. They backed off, two of them dragging him to his feet, his mashed nose in need of urgent medical attention.

I picked up the razor and folded the blade back into the handle, then tossed it to one of the retreating punks. He caught it with fumbling fingers.

‘If I were you,’ I said. ‘I’d stick to shaving with that thing.’

I turned back to the junkie who’d been watching the show from his ringside seat on the sidewalk. I saw red-veined eyes and a narrow stubbly face with caved-in cheeks.

‘Thanks, man. I owe you.’ He spoke as if there was a snowball’s chance in hell of him ever being in a position to return the favour.

But I dug that he needed a little dignity, so I took his hand and hauled him to his feet.

‘You got someplace to go?’

He told me he’d been crashing at a flophouse on the Bowery. I knew exactly the type of place he meant because I used to go looking for my mom in them. They reeked of piss and vomit and rancid booze. Every morning it was someone’s job to check nobody had died in the night. But they were better than sleeping on the street, especially in the winter. I even thought about escorting this guy to his flop and taking a look around, maybe finding my mom. It was a ridiculous idea, I knew that. She’d resisted my attempts to get her sober for years before I went to Vietnam. That had been five years ago and the life expectancy of an alcoholic on the Bowery was nowhere near that long.

So I said, ‘You should go there right away. Those guys might circle back.’

I took out another five spot and tucked it in the breast pocket of his ragged suit coat. There was no point telling him to buy himself a square meal because we both knew my donation was headed straight to a liquor store cash register or the pocket of some drug dealer.

He thanked me again then shuffled off into the grainy stew of urine-yellow street lights and gaudy neon scrawls. I watched until he was a smudge, then nothing. For a moment he might have been a grunt fading into triple canopy jungle mist.

I lit a Camel and set off back my place, contemplating the three very different individuals I'd encountered that day: Colonel Riley, the junkie, and White T. I figured I'd gotten Riley pegged, which was useful – the others too for that matter, even if it was of no use whatsoever.

I was dead wrong about two of the three though.

THREE

Next morning I rented a Buick Skylark and took the Bronx River Parkway from New York City to White Plains. Then I followed country roads through white-fenced pasture and broadleaved woodland to Ramskill. The place was thirty miles north of Manhattan and the Skylark ate this up in less than forty-five minutes.

I was on my way to take up three jobs in Ramskill, which meant I'd have my work cut out. Along with part-time soldiering with the National Guard, I was covering Ramskill for my old paper, the *New York Examiner*, and on top of that, I had to deliver a series of seminars at the university's Journalism School. This freaked me out in a way the Viet Cong never did. See, I never graduated high school, still less J-school. In fact, the only education I got was from my adoptive mom and present-day city editor, Maggie Call. She hauled me off the streets of Brooklyn when I was a teenage delinquent and taught me the basics of reporting. Later, I started work as a freelance for the *Examiner*, then got a training contract and eventually a staff job. But I wasn't a proper reporter in much the same way as I wasn't a proper officer. In fact, I wasn't even a proper New Yorker – I spent the first fourteen years of my life in a West Virginia coal-mining town. Most of the time, being an outsider didn't bother me. Occasionally – like now – it could be a problem.

I took my foot off the gas as I entered the outskirts of Ramskill. I'd been expecting a quaint little town – a folksy Americana stereotype. What I got was somewhat different. Main Street looked more like Pleiku after Charlie swung by with a bunch of rocket-propelled grenades. Store windows had been boarded up and slogans sprayed on buildings and sidewalks – *Kill the Pigs, Nixon is a Nazi* and *Hands off Cambodia*, that sort of stuff. The banks seemed to have been singled out for special treatment. One was being re-glazed; another having anti-capitalism graffiti scrubbed off its façade; another still reduced to charcoal and rubble. Elsewhere, an auto repair shop had been vandalized, cars on the forecourt overturned and burned out. Townsfolk watched me drive by with sidelong glances. There was a highly visible police presence too. On street corners, state troopers stood by their cruisers in groups, as if it wasn't safe to get separated.

I thought about the work I needed to do as a reporter. A newspaper like the *Examiner* was supposed to be a community talking to itself and it seemed Ramskill had plenty to say. But the conversation wasn't neighbourly chatter, it was paranoid whispering.

I passed City Hall at the corner of Main Street and Independence Avenue, then continued through an industrial area and across a bridge spanning the railroad. North of the tracks, the real estate got more shabby, the businesses more focused on manufacturing and downmarket retail.

Ramskill Armoury, two miles north of mid-town, was an imposing two-storey affair, significantly bigger than regimental headquarters in Manhattan and much newer – the modernist design was clean and functional. But for the Civil war-era cannon at the gate, it could have passed as a high school or a corporate head office.

My outfit shared the premises with other National Guard units – armoured cavalry, artillery, signals, engineers, medics, bandsmen and more. You wouldn't have thought so as a burly master sergeant came striding across the parking lot like he owned the place.

'You Tyler?'

I said I was and he told me he was Master Sergeant Bohannon.

He looked me up and down, as if I was a piece of shit. Then he told me this was just what he considered me to be. He knew why I'd quit the Green Berets and been sent home and he also knew there was no place for me in Bravo Company. But orders were orders and that was that.

I said nothing and took a closer look at the guy who had clearly made it his business to make mine as difficult as possible.

It wasn't often I found myself looking up at people, but Bohannon was a good two inches taller, perhaps six, three. He was much heavier too – around 240 pounds, most of it muscle. He'd be a tough customer in a brawl and I sensed he was already getting his rocks off at the prospect of taking me on. He'd clearly had a lot of work done on his face, though the surgery had been drastic rather than plastic: A white diagonal scar ran from his hairline to his jaw and his punched-flat nose had been broken in at least two places. Pale green eyes, buzz-cut ginger hair, and a pale complexion underscored the Irish descent his surname suggested. I guessed he'd be mid-thirties

– a shade too old for the Vietnam draft; a tad too young to have served in Korea. Most guys would have admitted this was a lucky break, but I'd bet my boots Bohannon told folks the opposite. He was a hard man and he'd want to give the impression he felt cheated out of fighting the good fight in a flat-out shooting war.

'You better come with me,' he said.

I followed him into the armoury and along a wide corridor to an office with a nameplate on the door that read: *Capt Edison Phipps, Commanding Officer, B Company.*

If Bohannon was a by-the-book military guy, Phipps was the opposite. Slouched in his chair with his feet on the desk, he was reading a paperback novel and smoking a cigarette. He was in civvies – purple psychedelic shirt, bellbottom pants and brown suede boots with elasticated sides. Light brown hair was fashionably cut, covering the tops of his ears and collar – way too long for Uncle Sam's book of rules. He was a good looking guy with deep blue eyes, an alabaster smile, and sun-tanned skin. Coming to his feet he walked around the desk, moving slow and lithe like a gymnast or maybe a fencer. All in all, Edison Phipps was some laid back cat – more like an Upper East Side socialite than a National Guard officer. I knew he was from an old-money, Ivy League background. Even so, I wasn't expecting this level of casualness.

'Welcome to Bravo Company.' His voice was relaxed as he extended a hand.

This was not what I was expecting. I wondered what Bohannon made of his chief's display of camaraderie.

'Master Sergeant Bohannon will show you the ropes but I like to greet our new recruits personally.' Phipps kept his eyes on mine. 'Especially when we get someone as highly experienced as you. These are tough times for my boys, what with the tragic events of last week. A fresh face is just what we need for morale.'

I thanked him and said I hoped I'd be useful to the company. But I was puzzled. Was Phipps being sarcastic? I couldn't believe he hadn't heard the scuttlebutt surrounding my return from Vietnam. I'd gotten it in the neck from Riley and Bohannon, so why was Phipps so cool about it? At that moment, I really wasn't sure who was more likely to be a problem, the bully-boy sergeant or the playboy captain. These men had been in command when soldiers of Bravo Company opened fire on the campus, killing three and wounding six more. The official line was no one had given the order to fire – the guardsmen perceived a threat in the chaos and reacted. But that didn't mean Phipps and Bohannon weren't responsible. Was one covering up for the other? Did they have each other's back? Or had they, too, gotten wrong-headed in the confusion? Whichever way you looked at this, it didn't look so good for Bravo Company.

Phipps went back to his desk chair. 'I gather you're going to be reporting for the *New York Examiner* as well as doing some teaching work at the university?'

I said yes to both.

Phipps turned to me with an expression that was solicitous rather than commanding. 'It goes without saying – but I gotta say it anyway – that any information you acquire while serving with the Guard can't be used in your paper. Leastways, not without the explicit written consent of myself and Colonel Riley. You OK with that?'

'Of course, Captain.'

He made a grateful nod. 'You should also know that all sorts of wild stories are flying around the campus. We're getting called Bloody Bravo and I have no doubt you'll hear much more and much worse. But we must keep in mind that a number of investigations are in progress – all involving Bravo Company – and we don't want to be accused of prejudicing the findings. So my advice would be to keep your ears open and your mouth shut – and take everything with a real big pinch of salt. That seem fair to you?'

I nodded yes.

'Splendid.' The wide smile returned. 'Then go collect your kit and I'll see you presently.'

I was leaving the armoury when I saw a slope-shouldered youth in a way-too-big uniform walking toward the doors I just came out of. As he got closer I made out pinched features and acne-pitted cheeks. He gave me a nervous glance, looked away, then at some indeterminate point over my shoulder. On his sleeve he wore the single chevron of a private first class – same rank as me. I guessed he'd be late teens, maybe twenty.

We met half way between the armoury and parking lot. I said, 'You in B Company?'

'Who wants to know?' His voice was a mix of anxious and aggressive.

'Wat Tyler. I just enlisted.' I held out my hand.

I was mildly surprised when the kid accepted the handshake. I felt narrow bony fingers and a clammy palm. 'Lenny Lesniak,' he said.

A shadow fell across his face as he realized he'd been fraternising with Bohannon's enemy. He pulled back his hand as if I just gave him an electric shock. 'Hold up a sec. You're the guy from Vietnam – the yeller-belly who got a hundred of our boys killed.'

I resisted a wry smile. The number had been two dozen according to Colonel Riley, but stories like this lost nothing in the telling.

'Hey, Lesniak, you slimy Polack runt!'

Bohannon was standing outside the building. 'Get your skinny ass in here right now.'

What little colour there was in Lesniak's face vanished.

'Be right with you, Sarge,' he said, and hurried toward Bohannon.

FOUR

I stowed my gear in the trunk of the rental car and drove back through midtown to the Belvedere Hotel, a modest place in downtown Ramskill where I took a room for the next seven nights. I'd been offered accommodation on campus, but wouldn't have felt comfortable. I was the *Examiner's* Ramskill reporter and didn't want to give the impression I was the university's mouthpiece. The husband-and-wife proprietors weren't in, but a clerk handled my registration and showed me to my room. It was a Spartan affair with a narrow squeaky bed, cracked wash basin and beat-up bureau. But it was cheap and centrally located, which was why I picked it.

Later that afternoon I went over to the campus. It was an impressive place: Sleek contemporary structures of concrete, steel and glass set among older, yellow-brick halls. A long driveway swept up to a grand colonial-style building with a domed clock tower that I understood to be Putney Hall, the university's administrative hub. Students moved in small groups across broad green spaces between buildings. Some sat on grassy banks or in the shade of trees, chatting, listening to transistor radios, reading books. I was surprised the university hadn't followed Kent State and shut down immediately after the shootings. I guessed the Ramskill authorities wanted to send out a business-as-normal message, even though the vibe in the city was anything but.

I parked on a lot outside Putney Hall. This was the spot where, one week ago, three people had been shot to death and a half dozen others wounded. A twelve-man squad from B Company had opened fire from outside Stanton Hall, a modern four storey building a little over a hundred yards from where I was standing. It was hard to imagine the chaos and the carnage, the anger and the panic because, right now, this place seemed the reverse of all those things. Then I saw a red cross spray-painted in a taped-off parking space, blue ones in other empty spaces, and yellow circles on the trunks of three big sycamores at the edge of the lot. The investigators must have colour-coded the bullet hits – red crosses for fatalities, blue for wounds, and yellow circles to indicate other places.

I went into Putney Hall, checked in at the front desk and headed for the Journalism School. This was one of two H-shaped buildings standing side by side on the northern side of the campus.

The office I was borrowing belonged to a professor on a three-month sabbatical to India. He'd left the place pretty much as if he'd gone to New York City for the weekend. I was fine with this, though not so much with his taste in decor. Instead of a pair of visitor seats, he had two beanbag chairs in a lime green and bright orange fabric. By the window I saw an African drum crafted from an old soy sauce barrel and painted in vivid colours. There was also a wind instrument with ethnic carvings that might have been an Australian didgeridoo, plus a stringed deal that looked like an Indian sitar. I was into all sorts of music, but I didn't want to imagine the sounds this ensemble might make.

I sat in the desk chair and looked through the window at the practice field. A few kids were messing around with a Frisbee, others with a soccer ball.

'You must be Wat Tyler.'

I looked up at the woman who had entered my office. She was something to see: Long-limbed and fine-boned with angular features and rust-red hair falling sheer to her shoulders. Her eyes were light blue, complexion lightly freckled. It was a look I recognized from my youth among the hill folks of West Virginia, though her silk paisley pattern blouse and black suit pants were a little too fashionable for a college professor, and way too fashionable for a hillbilly girl. She'd be about thirty – same as me.

'I'm JoBeth Medlock.' Her smile revealed white, slightly uneven teeth. 'I have the office next door. I got a temporary gig, like you.'

I mirrored the smile. 'Judging by that twang, I'd say you were from the Mountain State, also like me.'

'Of course,' she said. 'You're from Fayetteville.'

I frowned. 'How do you know that?'

Her smile stayed in place. 'I did my homework.'

'And where do *you* call home?'

'I was born and raised in Beckley. Haven't called it home in a while though.'

'So we're practically kin.' I wasn't being altogether facetious. Beckley and Fayetteville were coal mining towns separated by a twenty mile stretch of Route 19. And in those close-knit Appalachian communities the gene pool was pretty self-contained.

'And also practically neighbours – I gather you have a place in the East Village. I live in Greenwich – when I'm not up here in Ramskill.'

'You sure did do your homework.' I tried to shield my surprise. If she knew this much about me, she'd certainly have picked up the rumours surrounding my hasty departure from Vietnam. After all, that's exactly what reporters were paid to do. Yet she didn't appear to be judging me, one way or the other. More unusual still, she wasn't even curious. Maybe she was being open-minded, or just polite.

'You'll be telling me next we work for the same paper. You're not on the *Examiner* too, are you?'

She shook her head. 'I'm not a journalist.'

I made a curious expression. 'So what are you doing at the J-school?'

'I'm a lawyer. I run seminars on law for journalists – mainly defamation and contempt of court. Sort of stuff you need to know if you don't want to get your paper shut down.'

It made sense, although you didn't need to be a lawyer to teach reporters about libel legislation or how to protect their sources in a courtroom situation.

Regardless of her credentials, she seemed like a solid source of information and I asked her what she made of the situation in Ramskill.

She sat on one of the beanbags and gave me the same kind of look I was giving her: We were like two dogs going in circles to sniff each other's asses. After some time she said, 'I'd say Ramskill is a jittery and unpredictable place right now. The absence of arrests suggests the cops and feds haven't made a great deal of progress – though I must admit the picture is complicated. The city has a population of

21,000, the university has around 16,000 students, plus 750 faculty staff. The townspeople need the students to keep their business afloat and the students need the townsfolk for the goods and services they provide. You think they'd get along, but the tension had been getting worse well ahead of last week's shootings. Even the campus police and the city police are at loggerheads.'

It seemed absurd to have two separate police departments for one college town and I said so.

She made a gloomy expression. 'Add into that the state troopers, the National Guard, and the FBI and you got the ingredients for all sorts of crossed wires.'

'I sensed a bad vibe when I drove through town,' I said. 'Sounds like I underestimated just how ugly.'

'Wanna take a closer look?' She looked at me direct. 'We could grab something to eat while we're in town. I know a decent little bistro.'

I gave her a curious glance. Was she hitting on me? Then again, these were liberated times. Maybe she was just being friendly. Also, I needed help and I'd take it any way I could get it. So I said sure, I'd like that.

We took her Corvette Stingray ragtop and headed off campus to West Union Street, a broad boulevard where students came to drink, debate and date. Ten or twenty years ago it would have been a kitschy apple pie scene. Now, it was like a movie set where a historical film had gotten mixed up with a contemporary picture. Young guys were decked out in Victorian frock coats, Civil War tunics and Davy Crockett beaver-hats; hippie women wore Indian beads, headbands, buckskin coats. They intermingled with dudes in T shirts and jeans, girls in miniskirts and tank tops. On one street corner I saw a motorcycle gang hanging around outside an auto repair shop, ape-hanger Harleys parked up nearby.

She slowed down as we neared the centre and indicated a ramshackle clapboard dive named the Barricade.

'That's where the radical activists gather to plot the downfall of global capitalism over a few mugs of 3.2 beer. You'll also find leftist professors who wanna make the scene and shoot the shit. In their day-jobs they teach liberation math, physics, geography – even liberation journalism.'

'What's that?'

She shrugged. 'What's anything around here? It's the sound of something, not the substance that matters.'

Next we rolled past a smarter establishment with a Romanesque façade called The Toga Tavern. 'There you'll find the jocks – the athletes – along with the Greeks.'

She noticed my baffled expression.

There was no point bullshitting so I said, 'I never went to college.'

'No shame in that.' She gave me a kindly look. 'Greeks are fraternity, or frat men. They belong to societies with Greek letter names – like Epsilon Beta Pi. Sororities are the female equivalent.'

Next location on her guided tour was the Lincoln, a traditional brick-built hostelry with tables and benches on a tidy lawn out front. 'Here's where the straights come to play. They look and talk relatively ordinary and most are political moderates, but that doesn't mean they can't be roused.'

She stopped the car outside a large purple-painted shack named Rick O'Shea's, with a facia sign showing a bullet ricocheting off a brick wall. Strains of the Rolling Stones' *Gimme Shelter* were pumping out the open door and windows. 'This is the haunt of the freaks – they're the long-hairs, the beard boys, the no-bra girls, the way-outs. They do drugs, they do one another, and they do heavy rock – louder, the better.'

At least, though, I had something in common with one of these groups.

Then she added, 'The freaks tend to mix with the motorbike gangs and drug dealers, who are more often than not one and the same.'

I looked across the street at a bunch of state troopers standing by their cruiser. They were looking at the freaks and the freaks were looking at them. 'You think there's any chance things will settle down?'

She shook her head. 'That won't happen. Not here and not in the rest of the country.'

FIVE

I got back to my hotel shortly after 10.00pm and made my way across the lobby toward the stairs and a decent night's sleep. JoBeth Medlock had told me more about the university's strained relations with the city over dinner and I had a lot to think about – including JoBeth Medlock. I was usually good at reading people and the fact that I couldn't read her made her interesting.

My foot was on the first step when a strident female voice nailed me from the check-in desk.

'You must be Mr Tyler.'

I turned to see a matronly woman, maybe sixty, with wiry grey hair brushed back from a plump face. Horn-rimmed glasses rested on a bulbous nose and she gazed at me through heavy-lidded eyes. She was wearing a floral pattern polyester dress and a necklace of marble-sized pearls that were almost certainly plastic.

I realized she was one of the proprietors. 'You must be Mrs Vinson. Pleased to meet you.'

She called over her shoulder. 'Emmitt, our new guest just got back. You better get yourself out here.'

Her husband appeared almost immediately from an office

behind the desk. His features were long and narrow, skin creviced and droopy. His eyes, though, were bright blue and boyish, like some part of him forgot to grow old. His clothes were less formal than hers –plaid shirt and corduroy pants.

I told the husband I was pleased to meet him too.

He opened his mouth, but before he could speak, his wife said, 'We heard all about you from Gerry Bohannon.' She folded her forearms under her bosom. 'Can't say we like what we heard, although I guess your money's as good as anyone's.'

I said nothing – I had no doubt Bohannon was spreading the poison wherever he thought it would make most trouble for me.

I said good night and moved toward the stairs but Ma Vinson wasn't done.

'You're a reporter, ain't you?'

'Violet, this ain't no time to bother Mr Tyler about that stuff.' Emmitt Vinson made an imploring expression.

His wife ignored it. 'Newspapermen never sleep, or am I wrong Mr Tyler?'

I told her no, she wasn't wrong and asked if she had a story for me.

'Yes I do. If you're interested in psychos roaming the countryside committing horrible acts.'

'Now hold on, Violet, we don't know – '

'What have I told you about interrupting me, Emmitt?' She gave him a withering look. 'I was talking to Mr Tyler here.'

Funny, I thought, how fast I'd gone from yellow-bellied trash to respectable newspaper reporter. But I was interested in what she had to say – even if it did turn out to be bullshit – so I took out my notebook and asked what she knew.

She came a little closer. 'I heard Chip Amelsfort's sheepdog got stabbed to death and his ears cut off, over at Stony Edge Farm. That was just last night.'

I said, 'Any idea who might do that?'

'Why, it's them revolutionary bums from the campus there.' Violet Vinson said this as a statement of fact. 'Heartless SOBs. You ever seen a dog with no ears, Mr Tyler?'

I said no I hadn't.

But I had seen Viet Cong with no ears. Sometimes grunts cut them off for bodycount validation, or to wear on a string around their necks as trophies. I never tolerated the practice in any of my units, but I couldn't control the whole US military.

I thought about this some more. A lot of guys went to college after coming back from Vietnam, and some became radicals. But for a college student to go around hurting and mutilating animals in that way was a stretch and then some.

Emmitt had another try at finishing a sentence. 'We don't know that, Violet, and – '

'Folks are also talking about being watched, stalked,' his wife said. 'Like there's someone hiding in the shadows, waiting.'

I made a note of this too. Probably an over-reaction by nervous folks at a stressful time. But worth keeping in mind.

'You gonna run a story, Mr Tyler?' Now she was at my elbow.

I closed my notebook. 'Can't say for certain, Mrs Vinson, but I will look into it.'

One thing I was certain of though: JoBeth Medlock was dead right about the town-and-gown animosity.

SIX

I heard about the latest college shooting on a radio news bulletin early the next morning. Two kids killed and twelve injured shortly after midnight when police opened fire with shotguns during unrest at Jackson State College in Mississippi.

I skipped breakfast – and Violet Vinson – and headed for the *Examiner's* local office on foot. Coming seven days after the business at Ramskill and ten after Kent State, the Jackson shooting meant more trouble was inevitable.

Already, fresh graffiti had appeared on the buildings and sidewalks of West Union Street. There was the usual *Screw Nixon*, *Off the pigs*, *Burn the banks* stuff, but one aerosol artist posed the question everybody was asking: *Kent, Ramskill, Jackson – where next?*

A group of twenty or thirty placard-wielding students were chanting anti-government slogans outside the Barricade bar. Whether they'd been there all night or had gotten out of bed especially early was hard to tell, though my money was on the all-nighter. Ramskill cops and state troopers were assembled in small groups in parking lots and on street corners. Townsfolks went about their business warily. The proprietor of a hardware business was nailing plywood boards over his store window and a nearby druggist was following suit. The town was a landmine waiting to get stepped on.

The *Examiner's* office was a one-room deal located above a dry-cleaning place on Station Street. I had a desk, a typewriter, a phone and shared use of a rest room. But it was plenty to get the job done.

First call I made was to city hall. I wanted to know if City Mayor Milt McStay was planning to ask Governor Nelson Rockefeller to mobilize the National Guard again. McStay's office put out a statement about the mayor monitoring the situation while keeping in close touch with the governor and law enforcement chiefs. Next I called the city police department, the campus cops and the state police, but there was nothing from the overnight sheets. Then I talked to Maggie Call on the *Examiner's* city desk in Manhattan and gave her my take on reactions in Ramskill to the Jackson shootings. I didn't have much but even so she wanted a three paragraph holding piece which I filed right away.

Then I checked the mail and found the envelope Maggie had posted containing the *Examiner's* spread on the three people killed at Ramskill, along with the half dozen injured. I already knew none of the three fatalities had been involved in the protest, and had a little background on Boyd Brigstock, the twenty-year-old son of a Democratic congresswoman, whose death had been such *thoroughly rotten luck* for Colonel Riley's promotion prospects. The photo showed a handsome young man with even features and an engaging smile. He'd been in the second year of a civil engineering degree until a bullet went through his brain, right there on the parking lot.

Next I read about Gordon Richardson, aged thirty-eight, an English literature professor and gifted poet. Like rock music, poems were powerful medicine that could stimulate my suppressed emotions. I made myself a promise to look up Richardson's stuff. His picture showed a carefree sort of guy with an easy smile and curly blond hair. He'd been hit in the chest as he crossed the parking lot on his way to the faculty cafeteria for lunch and died on the operating table two hours later.

Finally, I came to Professor Oleg Bobkov, aged forty-three, a research scientist at the university's Biomedical Centre. He had a whole alphabet of qualifications I'd never heard of, though I had heard of the places where he earned them – Princeton, Yale, Berkeley and Oxford. He was a stringy-looking guy with delicate features, thick framed glasses, and a receded hairline that was barely visible on the horizon of his scalp. Like Boyd Brigstock, he'd taken a bullet to the head and died instantly, close to where Gordon Richardson got hit.

The *Examiner* had quoted family, friends and colleagues of all three victims, and among those in the Bobkov piece was Dr Loretta Hausinger, a member of his team at the biomedical place. She said what a great guy Bobkov was, and also talked about the important work he was doing. I decided to start by visiting her.

SEVEN

The Biomedical Centre was a glass-fronted building located in its own landscaped grounds on the eastern side of the campus. Gardeners worked in groups of three or four, pruning shrubs, mowing lawned areas, watering flower beds. Elsewhere, a bunch of workmen were fixing two barracks-like structures behind the main building that looked like hold-overs from World War II.

Inside, the parquet floor was so smooth I could see my own reflection. Even so, a worker was moving a buffing machine back and forth in a systematic operation. Nearby, another guy was using furniture polish on the wood surfaces in the reception area, and another still was up a ladder, cleaning the windows.

I'd called ahead to arrange my appointment and went to the reception desk, where a friendly clerk told me Hausinger would be with me directly.

She appeared a few minutes later, wearing a white lab coat.

I took her hand and saw a petite woman with a dark, sharp-cut bob, softened by attractive rounded features. Lucid brown eyes held mine and she made an accommodating smile. I guessed she'd be mid to late thirties.

'I gather you want to talk about Oleg,' she said.

'I'd like to write a piece about the professor and the other folks who died.'

She made a puzzled expression. 'But your paper already ran a story about Oleg. I was quoted in it.'

'I want to go deeper into the people behind the tragedy – their backgrounds, interests and achievements and ambitions, who they were as individuals.'

She considered the idea, then invited me into her office. I followed her through a door at the back of the reception area and along a strip-lit corridor with offices on either side. A guy with a bucket and mop was cleaning the linoleum floor, even though it looked pristine.

My host stopped beside him. 'You're doing a real good job, Andy. Keep it up.'

He looked up from his work with a self-conscious smile. He was a good-looking guy, tall and rangy with blond hair, intense blue eyes and a strong jawline. I'd have said he was a little younger than me – maybe twenty-seven or eight – and looked more like a singer in a rock band than a janitor.

I wondered too about the cleaning and polishing deal. Was the place being kept spotless for a reason? Did they experiment with infectious diseases? I made a mental note to ask Hausinger.

Farther along the corridor we passed an open door labelled 'Conference room' and I caught a glimpse of a big space with a dozen easy chairs arranged in a circle around a low table. Seemed even formal meetings here happened in a laid back setting.

Her office was right next door. She went to her desk and I sat in a visitor chair opposite. The office as a whole was more conservative than the J-school one I was borrowing and its contents said little about the occupant except that she was organized.

She offered me a drink and I said I could use a coffee. She spoke into an intercom and we made small talk until her secretary brought in the beverages.

Then she told me to fire away and I asked about her relationship with Bobkov.

She was happy to talk, but not so keen on saying much. They'd worked together for three years and she'd learned a lot because he was an outstanding scientist. He was a private guy who didn't socialize much, but was always a thoroughly supportive colleague. I asked about his outside interests and she said he didn't have any that she knew of. I enquired about his family: His folks emigrated to the States from Russia before the Bolshevik Revolution, but he never talked about them and she didn't know if he was still in touch, or where they lived.

I sipped my coffee and asked about his work at the Biomedical Centre.

She sipped hers and smiled. 'As director of research, Oleg supervised our work in pharmacology, psychology and physiology, along with elements of biochemistry, genetics, and molecular biology.'

This list of subjects wouldn't mean much to my readers so I probed a little deeper. 'What sort of practical applications might this work have?'

'Well, we research medicines and therapies that help people to cope better with stressful situations in the home and workplace.' She set down her coffee cup. 'I know this doesn't make great newspaper copy, but I'm not at liberty to discuss the details of what we do, and even if I was, it would be densely technical stuff.'

She was more forthcoming on her shock and sadness at the death of her boss, but at the end of the interview I realized I'd gotten a whole lot of very little.

She seemed to sense my disappointment. 'I do want to help,' she said as we walked back into the reception area. 'I do.'

I wondered, though. And I hoped I'd get more from the co-workers of Gordon Richardson in the English department.

EIGHT

The guy sitting on a beanbag chair in my office reminded me of Grigori Rasputin as a young man – long, centre-parted hair, dark eyes and a frizzy beard grown to his chest. A sinuous frame clad in a black shirt and jeans added to the prophetic look, which I was sure was carefully cultivated.

'I'm Corey Quilton.' He smiled, but didn't stand. 'I'm majoring in liberation journalism and I'm booked onto your seminars. Just dropped by to say hi.'

I didn't ask what liberation journalism was, or why he was thought it was OK to turn up in my office uninvited, though I did appreciate the friendly welcome.

'I totally dig what you did to get out of Vietnam. I'd have done the same – stuck it to the Man big time.' He took out a roll-your-own cigarette and lit it. 'Like Ali said, 'No Viet Cong ever called me nigger'.'

'No argument there,' I said. 'But nobody ever called you or me nigger either because we're not black.'

He made a bitter chuckle. 'Maybe not literally, but we're both slaves to the capitalist system just like our coloured brothers and sisters. We're the lumpen proletariat; and we're in bondage to the bourgeois bastards who run this country, its military, its education system, everything.'

Despite the Rasputin look, he didn't strike me as a son of the soil. But he'd obviously heard some version of the story about my departure from Vietnam and put his own gloss on it. It said a lot about the USA in that spring of 1970 that people like Riley and Bohannon saw me as a coward, while Corey Quilton thought I was a hero.

Me, I didn't believe in cowards or heroes, but this wasn't the time to debate it.

'Anyway,' he said, 'your name speaks for itself: Wat Tyler, leader of the English Peasant's Revolt, 1381. Your namesake was a solid proto-socialist.'

'Until he got betrayed and killed by the king's henchmen,' I said. 'But I'm not really like the original guy.' Yet in some ways I was. My dad's folks were poor West Virginians, and that made me a peasant of sorts. And he brought my mom over from Liverpool after World War II – and that made me half English. But the truth was that I picked up the name when a sloppy copy editor left the *l* out of Walt in my byline. A history professor saw it and wrote an amusing letter, congratulating my editor on hiring a medieval rebel. After that, everyone on the paper called me Wat, and I didn't complain because it was a cool moniker.

But I didn't tell Corey Quilton this. Until I knew the lay of the land I wanted to keep everybody onside. And if this meant him thinking I was on his, that was well and good. At least for now.

*

Corey Quilton might not have looked like a son of the soil, but Chip Amelsfort certainly did. Dirt was ingrained deep in the cracks and creases of his wrung out face; denim bib overalls were crusted with grime; and his rubber boots caked in ochre mud.

He didn't move as he watched me park on the road and walk up the clay track to his farm at Stony Edge, a mile or so outside Ramskill.

Keeping my eye on the 12-guage shotgun in the crook of his arm, I made a friendly smile. 'Expecting trouble, Mr Amelsfort?'

His flinty expression stayed that way. Narrow eyes moved a fraction as he looked me up and down. 'I got reason to, son.'

'So I heard.' I introduced myself, showed him my press card, and repeated what Violet Vinson told me happened to his sheepdog.

'If I ever catch them sons of bitches … '

'I'd like to run a story in the *Examiner*, Mr Amelsfort. Maybe help catch whoever did it.'

He shrugged his shoulders in a what-the-heck sort of way and walked over to a stone water trough between the farmhouse and barn.

'Did you report it to the police?'

'What's the point?' He propped the shotgun against the trough. 'They got enough on their plate already with all them idiot students running around starting fires and wrecking the city.'

This surprised me. 'So you don't think it was students that attacked your dog?'

'Her name was Bella.'

I took his point. Had a fondness for dogs myself. 'Mrs Vinson seemed to think Bella was attacked by revolutionary extremists.'

'Violet could be right, but it don't *feel* like students to me.' He took a clay pipe from his bib pocket, and put it between his teeth. 'Some of them kids on campus is crazy, that's for sure. But what they done to my Bella, that was downright deranged. Also, why should commie agitators do such a thing a poor dumb animal?'

'So who do you think was responsible?'

'Really, I don't know.' He scratched his head. 'I heard rumours about some research facility at the university where they do stuff to kids before they ship out to Vietnam.'

I gave him a hard look. 'What sort of stuff?'

'Mess with their heads. Make them more aggressive, less scared. Word is they go in as volunteers, but then get brainwashed and turned into killing machines. Like I say, though, it's just tittle-tattle.'

I thought about Loretta Hausinger. She never mentioned any sort of military research, but that wasn't surprising because if anything was going on, it would certainly be classified. And in any case, it was no secret that Uncle Sam was routinely dispensing all sorts of psychoactive shit to enhance combat performance. The US military had the best amphetamines on the planet. Other drugs were available too – stuff that could put you on another planet altogether.

'One thing I am sure about,' he said, gazing at the treeline. 'I seen somebody lurking on the land at the edge of my farm. I didn't get a real good look, but I'm pretty sure he was a black fella.'

This puzzled me. Ramskill had a significant number of black students – I'd seen them on campus. But I hadn't seen a single black face in any of the newspaper or television coverage of the unrest. Then again, the black watcher wasn't necessarily a student. He could have been one of the Vietnam draftees at the Biomedical place that Amelsfort had heard stories about.

Clearly he wouldn't know anything about that, so I said, 'Was this before Bella was attacked?'

'About a week before. And more than once – two, maybe three times.'

I followed his stare across the sheep meadow to the stand of oaks. 'This black guy, did he seem threatening?'

'Not so much threatening as watching. I got the feeling I was under surveillance.'

Odd, I thought, that Violet Vinson had reported similar stories of her neighbours claiming they'd been covertly observed. 'Any idea who the watcher might be?'

'No I don't. But I do have this.' He picked up his shotgun and slapped the stock with his palm. 'And I'll be good and ready if he makes one wrong move.'

*

It was late afternoon by the time I got back to town. I was tired and hungry, but something was eating me about Chip Amelsfort's story. So instead of returning to the hotel, I drove back to the Biomedical Centre.

Loretta Hausinger sounded like she meant it when she said she wanted to help. I wanted to see if this was true.

The gardeners had disappeared from the front of the centre. So too had the janitors from the inside. The receptionist was still at her desk, though, and I asked to see Hausinger.

She gave me an apologetic look. 'I'm sorry, sir, but Dr Hausinger has just gone into a departmental conference.'

I smiled. 'I don't mind waiting.'

'It could be a long time, sir. Those meetings often go on for hours. I could take a message and – '

The gunshots guillotined her voice.

I counted six reports as I moved through the reception area doors and along the corridor that I knew led to the conference room. I stopped where the corridor took a ninety degree turn and listened. Whoever was doing the shooting may well be looking for another target and I didn't want to hand him one.

But I heard nothing.

I peered around the corner.

Saw nothing

I headed for the conference room door, about fifty yards away. I halted outside, but I couldn't hear a sound.

So I took a chance and looked inside. First I saw two dead guys, both shot in the head from behind. They were slumped forward and sideways in their easy chairs, one leaning right, the other left. On the far side of the room a third man was lying on the floor, two gunshot wounds between his shoulder blades, a third to the back of his head. Looked as if he'd seen what happened to the other two and tried to get out the window. But it was closed and he hadn't gotten anywhere near it.

Then I saw Loretta Hausinger. She was lying face down with a bloody gash on one side of her head and a gunshot wound to her waist.

Unlike the others, though, she was breathing.

NINE

I scanned the room. It was clear. The shooter had obviously fled.

Loretta Hausinger made a feeble groan and rolled onto one side.

I crouched by her side and examined the head injury. Although nasty, it appeared superficial. I lifted her torn blouse from the gunshot wound and realized the bullet had passed through the abdominal oblique muscles, missing her gut by inches.

'You've been hit on the head and a bullet went through your side,' I said. 'But you're gonna be fine. You understand?'

She nodded and said yeah, she understood.

At this point, the receptionist arrived. Her complexion was leeched and I dug why. The room was a slaughterhouse.

I asked her if she'd called 911 and she said the cops and an ambulance were on their way.

I left Hausinger with the receptionist and went to look for the killer.

First thing I pegged was that Hausinger's office door was ajar.

I took a peek inside. Between the doorway and the

window, the place looked like a tornado just tracked through it. Everywhere else was untouched. Clearly the intruder beat a path to the window, opened it, and fled into the grounds.

Was this a lucky getaway? Or had he – or she – known the layout of the building and plotted an escape route in advance? I suspected the latter, but that would have to wait.

Outside I saw a twenty yard strip of lawn, then dense woodland. I climbed through the window and looked around. There were no tracks on the grass, but it was smooth and firm so this was no surprise. I moved a little way into the trees. No sign, no sound. The killer could have struck out in any direction, so I returned to the conference room as the wail of howlers grew louder.

Gene Ducey, the campus police chief, took me to his office to make a statement but there was very little I could tell him that he hadn't seen for himself. Ducey was ex-NYPD and had the direct manner you'd expect from a tough street cop. He was approaching retirement, balding, jowly and carrying too much gut-weight. But that didn't mean his law enforcement brain wasn't in good shape.

When he'd done taking my statement, I headed out of his office but he called from his desk. 'I heard stories about how you ended up coming back from Vietnam. Gotta say it don't sound good.'

I rolled my eyes and turned to face him. 'Let me guess: Gerry Bohannon.'

'Small town, gossip travels fast.' Ducey leaned back in his chair and gave me an inquisitive look. 'But you and me, we're New York City critters. So I asked around some old NYPD pals. They told me they trusted you as much as they'd trust any reporter – regardless of what happened. Or didn't happen.'

‘That’s good to hear,’ I said.

‘Doesn’t mean we’re buddies, Tyler. But it does mean I’ll keep an open mind. That sound fair?’

I nodded. ‘Can’t say fairer, chief.’

*

Back at my office in Ramskill, I called the city desk and told Maggie what happened. She asked me what I thought we should do and I gave this some thought.

The story we had in the bag was as strong as they came: Three professors shot to death and a fourth wounded at Ramskill University, just eight days after three people were killed and six injured on the same campus. We had nothing to link the two incidents although it was a fact that four of the six fatalities were faculty staff, as was Loretta Hausinger who had narrowly escaped with her life. True, conspiracy stories often sold papers better than hard news. What happened to Chip Amelsfort’s sheepdog was a fact. And I didn’t put those words about the Biomedical Centre into his mouth. On the flipside, there was no evidence linking the incident at his farm with the shootings at the centre. And the conspiracy theory went in a totally different direction if you listened to Violet Vinson, who was convinced radical students on mind-bending drugs were responsible. If we printed anything along those lines, another student riot would go from a distinct possibility to a nail-on certainty. There was also the credibility and reputation of the *Examiner* to consider.

So I said what I knew Maggie wanted and expected me to say: We should stick to the facts and look into the stories Amelsfort and Violet Vinson had heard. Maggie agreed and I filed a five-hundred word piece that would make an exclusive front-page lead for tomorrow's first edition. Sure, the *New York Times*, the *Post* and *Daily News* would get the story from various sources, as would the TV and radio stations. But I'd been there when it went down. My piece would be a first-hand account that we'd have to ourselves.

TEN

Next morning I went to the hospital to check on Hausinger. In view of what happened to her colleagues, Ducey had stationed an officer outside her room and called ahead to let him know I'd be visiting.

She was sitting up in bed, head bandaged, but looking surprisingly well considering her recent ordeal.

A doctor looked up from his clipboard, told me not to over-tax her, then left the room.

I pulled up a chair by her bed and we got through the pleasantries in short order.

Then I went straight to it, 'You had a close shave back there.'

She made a faint smile. 'If you hadn't gotten there when you did … '

But I wasn't sure my arrival had any effect on the shooter's decision to bolt. He fired six rounds, which suggested a six-shot revolver. He probably figured he could get the job done with six bullets but couldn't and didn't have time to reload. So making a run for it was probably his only option. That said, it wouldn't do my cause any harm if Hausinger wanted to cast me in the role of her saviour.

I said, 'Chief Ducey told me you didn't see the killer, but I'd be ever so grateful if you'd go through what happened again. Sometimes people recall stuff that wasn't immediately apparent. Details, sounds and smells, anything that wasn't as it should have been.'

'OK, since it's you who's asking ...' She hesitated.

I told her there was no hurry, no pressure. I appreciated this wouldn't be easy, but it was really important.

Her fingers gripped the bedsheets so tight her knuckles went pale. Then she started to recount her ordeal. 'I'd just walked into the room when the shooting started. The shots came from over my shoulder. The guy must have been concealed behind some file cabinets in the corner. All I saw was Carlos and Headley getting shot in the back of their heads. They kind of flipped forward, then went limp and their foreheads hit the table.'

She hesitated, placed a fist against her mouth. 'I saw it, but I didn't know it. Not in that moment. It was so tripped out, so unreal. Then Sandro was scrambling over the table. He was trying to reach the window, but he got hit in the back and went down. I'd started to turn when I was clubbed on the side of my head. Something heavy – Chief Ducey says it was likely the pistol. After that, everything is even more hazy. It all happened so fast, yet so slow. And my memory is messed up: Pin-sharp one moment, out of focus the next. I'm not sure if I can – '

I placed a hand on her arm. 'Take as much time as you need.'

She looked up at the ceiling, took a few breaths, then back at me. 'I remember falling to the floor. My head was hurting like hell. I felt like I was there in the room, but not in the room. I heard Sandro wailing. I looked through the table-legs and saw him on his belly, squirming, trying to crawl to the window. Then there was another shot and he went still. The shooter must have finished him off. It was all so … so callous …'

Her voice had gone flat, unemotional. Yet she was clearly distressed – agitated and frustrated, I thought, as she struggled to remember.

I poured her a glass of water from the jug on the nightstand.

She took a few small sips, more deep breaths. Then she seemed ready to go again. 'I heard footsteps on the carpet but I couldn't see any feet. And suddenly I sensed him right behind me, real close. There was a metallic click. That would have been the hammer on the revolver being drawn back. I remember thinking, 'This is it. This is the end. But it can't be the end because I got too much to do.' And I got angry because I realized I wasn't ready to die. I twisted sideways and tried to wriggle under the table. The gun went off and I felt a sting in my side. And then you were there, telling me I'd been hit in the head and shot in the side but that I was going to be fine.'

'You did well,' I said.

I meant it. This woman had salt.

She made a small smile. 'I survived, that's all.'

'What about the research programme your team was involved in? Will that survive?'

Her smile vanished. 'Four people from a five-strong team are dead. What do you think?'

'Surely you still have your database, test results, studies and reports?'

She shrugged. 'Without the knowledge and insight behind that stuff, we've lost months, maybe years. Maybe everything.'

'Can you think who might have done this?'

'No,' she said. 'I can't.'

A look of total weariness came over her. She turned her head and gazed, unblinking, through the window at the empty sky.

Time to call it a day – for now.

ELEVEN

It was mid-afternoon when I arrived at the Campus Police Department and asked to see Chief Ducey.

In town and on campus, the tension had ratcheted up another few notches. Question everybody was asking was: Who was responsible for the latest shooting? Some townsfolks blamed radical students. Others talked about the secret programme to brutalize Vietnam draftees that Chip Amelsfort mentioned. Truth was nobody knew the truth, and that scared people even more.

Ducey said he'd give me fair treatment and seemed as good as his word. I'd been waiting less than five minutes when I was shown into his office.

He leaned back and placed his hands behind his head, revealing big sweat patches under the arms of his uniform shirt. 'What can I do you for you, son?'

'There's a lot of bad feeling out there, Chief.' I took out my notebook. 'You confident your boys can keep a lid on it?'

He gave me a gimme-a-break look. 'On the record, of course I am. Off the record, I'm concerned.'

I scribbled a line of shorthand. 'Word at the Student Union is there'll be another show of force. The kids think the mayor has been talking to the governor about calling in the National Guard again.'

He took out a block of Red Man plug chewing tobacco and used his ochre-stained incisors to bite off a chunk. 'In that case, the kids know something I don't.'

I frowned. 'Wouldn't the mayor consult you if he was planning to take that sort of action?'

He made another longsuffering expression and I recalled what JoBeth Medlock told me about the rifts between the university authorities and the mayor; the campus cops and the city cops.

He used his tongue to push the wad of tobacco to one side of his mouth. 'What I can tell you is that I'm taking personal responsibility for the investigation into yesterday's homicides and attempted homicide.'

I made more notes. 'Any FBI involvement?'

'Murder isn't a federal offence. You know that.'

Of course I did. But this wasn't a straightforward homicide case. Three people had already been killed on campus by the National Guard and now four more had been shot, three fatally. There was no point pushing it though. Besides, the feds may well be in town already and Ducey's opposite number in the city police department keeping him in the dark.

Instead I asked if he had anything for me on the latest incident.

He opened a manila file on his desk and took out a pair of half-moon reading glasses. They seemed way too small for his big face and had the weird effect of magnifying the lower half of his mud-brown eyes.

He looked down at the folder. 'This here's the medical

examiner's initial findings, along with some information from the university press office.

'First victim was Dr Carlos Gonzalez, aged forty-seven. Press office says he was a distinguished pharmacologist from Detroit. Second guy: Dr Headley Reese, forty-two.' He scrunched up his brow as he read from the typewritten lines. 'A highly respected psychologist with a background in pharmacology. Home town, Fort Wayne, Indiana.'

He looked up, as if to make sure I was getting these long academic words. 'Then we got Dr Sandro Poole, thirty-eight. Apparently he was an experienced physiologist and biochemist, originally from Cedar Rapids, Iowa. All were single, all lived on campus.'

The only information he had about Loretta Hausinger was that she was also thirty-eight, a psychologist with experience in physiology, and lived on campus.

I asked, 'Anything on the murder weapon?'

He turned a page. 'We recovered six cartridges and the corresponding bullets that killed Doctors Gonzales, Reese and Poole and wounded Dr Hausinger. Lab report says they were fired from a Smith & Wesson .38 Police Special.'

I knew this was a highly accurate and powerful handgun. I imagined the murder scene and ran the math in my head. After taking out Gonzales and Reese point blank, the shooter used up three bullets – half his ammunition – on Poole as he tried to escape. Then he moved in to finish off Hausinger, who he'd apparently pistol-whipped to the floor. But he didn't anticipate her sudden movement and his last bullet clipped her side. The question that bothered me was why he didn't shoot her in the head as he had the other three? Sure, a bullet to the central body mass would probably prove fatal. But not necessarily. And it may not have killed her instantly. She could have been able to give vital information to first responders.

Also, why did the killer only have six rounds? Of course the answer could be simple: This was a poorly planned, or heat of the moment thing. The guy saw what he'd done and panicked. It takes nerve to kill people up close. Perhaps the shooter didn't have it. Or not enough.

But then he'd made a clean getaway – the only aspect of the hit that seemed to have been carried out efficiently.

There was other stuff that didn't add up. But running my concerns by Ducey would be futile. Whatever he was thinking, he wouldn't share it with me – even off the record. Not until he knew he could really trust me.

So I thanked him for his time and information and left the police station.

Walking across the open green spaces toward my office at the J-School, I chewed on what I knew.

What had Loretta Hausinger told me about her team's work: *We research medicines and therapies that help people to cope better with stressful situations in the home and workplace.* I didn't believe her woolly worded marketing spiel was anywhere close to what was really going on.

Nor did the folks in downtown Ramskill. They were convinced the Biomedical Centre was where *The Manchurian Candidate* met *The Island of Doctor Moreau.*

Perhaps they were right – or not entirely wrong.

Bottom line: Four scientists from a team of five had been shot dead in a little over a week, while Hausinger, the fifth, was lucky to be alive.

Yet the way the incident unfolded was puzzling, even contradictory.

It felt like a black ops hit – the work of the KGB. But those guys didn't mess around. They absolutely wouldn't have sent someone with a poor aim and no spare ammo. They'd have made damn sure all of them were dead.

Or would they?

What if the Soviets wanted to cover their tracks? What better way than making the work of a professional look like that of an amateur? Maybe Hausinger had been left alive as part of this misdirection – especially if eliminating the others would kill the research programme, or cause a critical delay.

Another puzzle: Why had Bobkov been eliminated eight days before the second attack? It was difficult to believe that the two events were unrelated. Yet it was just as difficult to see any sort of logic in the time-lapse.

Not knowing exactly what the scientists were working on made the problem even thornier. But if the research conflicted with the interests of powerful individuals or organizations, they could have been behind the shooting.

Hell, it could even have been a radical student group. That might explain why the hit had been so sloppy, yet the getaway so slick.

I thought about Corey Quilton, my welcoming Marxist buddy. He didn't look capable of what had gone down at the biomedical place. But experience told me murderers rarely looked like people imagined. See a killer up close, you see the guy on the street, the girl next door. And if Quilton hadn't done this himself, maybe he knew who did.

TWELVE

One advantage of a small town like Ramskill was that most places were an easy walk. So I left my car on the campus parking lot and set off back to my hotel on foot. Outside the university gates I had two choices: The main road, or a rocky trail that ran east through woodland and meadow. I was in no hurry so I followed the scenic route. It took me up a shallow hillside and past a small lake before turning back toward town, wheat fields on one side and a forest of aspen and dogwood on the other.

I'd been walking twenty minutes when I heard the gunfire.

Four shots fired fast, then a break, then four more, and another four.

I ran in the direction they were coming from, somewhere in the trees.

My first concern was that yesterday's shooter was back, that another three people – or more – were lying dead in the woods.

Then I saw Lenny Lesniak, the scrawny kid from Bravo Company. He was standing in a clearing holding a Browning Hi Power automatic pistol. Thirty feet away, a dozen tin cans had been arranged on a low bough. There were a lot of blond wood gashes where bullets had gouged out tree bark, but no sign of any tin cans on the ground nearby.

Lesniak turned to face me, pointing the gun at my head.

'What are you doing here?' His eyes were wide, face shiny with sweat.

And his gun-arm was shaking. He'd fired twelve rounds and hadn't hit any of the tin cans, but that didn't mean he couldn't hit me. I was a closer, bigger target. I figured he was firing 9mm ammunition, which meant he'd have one and possibly three bullets left, depending on his magazine capacity.

'Lower the gun, Lenny.' I kept my voice steady. 'You don't want to shoot me.'

'How do you know that, you piece of chickenshit?'

I made a friendly smile. 'You didn't want to shoot those cans, either. Otherwise you'd have hit them.'

I moved closer. If he pulled the trigger now, he couldn't miss. True, I didn't feel fear in the ordinary sense, but I sure recognized danger when I saw it. Yet there was opportunity here as well as risk.

'You shouldn't be here.' His voice was on-the-edge whiny. 'You shouldn't see me like this.'

'C'mon, Lenny, put the gun down.'

The barrel was wavering and quivering now, six feet from my head.

I could almost hear the wheels and sprockets turning inside Lenny's head. He screwed up his face, as if he was struggling to wring out a logical thought sequence.

Very slowly, he let the pistol fall to his side.

'You should go home, Lenny,' I said. 'And next time you need some practice, go to the armoury firing range.'

'I can't.' He looked at me, desperate. 'I can't let the master sergeant and the captain and the others see how I can't hit nothing no more.'

The way he said 'no more' made me think he'd hit something – or someone – at some time recently.

I said, 'You were in the squad that fired on the protestors, weren't you?'

He nodded, breathing deep, avoiding my gaze.

'What went down that day, Lenny?'

'Why should I tell you?'

'Why shouldn't you?' I added softly, 'Maybe I can help. Whatever shit you went through, you can be sure something similar happened in Vietnam.'

He took a while to think about my offer. Then he started talking, real slow at first, but quickly gathering pace. 'We was backed up against Stanton Hall. We had no place to go. They started coming toward us, then moving back, taunting us, like.' He sucked in a lungful of air. Now his words were coming in a torrent. 'Somebody shouted 'Here we come!' And they did. They came right at us. A lot of thoughts went through my head right then. Like: Are we gonna protect our lives? Are we gonna run? Are we gonna – '

He broke off, looked over my shoulder, at the ground, at the branches above, anywhere but at me.

'What happened, Lenny?' I kept my voice gentle.

'Those damn gas masks made it worse. A lot worse.'

This came left-field. The reports I'd read didn't mention the use of CS gas. I said so.

Lenny raised his slopey shoulders and dropped them again. 'We never got the order to lay down gas. We waited, waited, waited, but it never came. And we was wearing them masks the whole time. And that really sucked. It was a hot day – seventy-five degrees, more, and the sun was beating strong. Soon as I pulled that stinky rubber mask over my face I started sweating. Sweating real bad. I felt trapped in some misty tunnel. I couldn't see the guy next to me, and I couldn't see much in front. Just blurry shapes coming at me, shouting, screaming, throwing rocks. I had no idea what was happening.'

Gas masks could do that. In crowd-control situations they gave soldiers the advantage of looking mechanical, impersonal, anonymous. But the big disadvantage was that they made the wearer feel isolated, alone in a crowd. That made command and control more difficult. So why did Phipps or Bohannon order the squad to put on gas masks without deploying gas?

I carried on probing, 'Was that when the shooting started?'

Lenny shook his head no, then nodded yes. 'I dunno. Thought I did, then I wasn't so sure. The more I try to remember, the more fuzzy it gets.'

'But the shooting started after you received the order to open fire, right?'

'I forget, man.' He wiped globules of sweat from his brow with the back of his arm. 'It all happened in a blur. There was so much noise. You wouldn't believe the stuff we was getting called – and the girls was the worst. Pure hate, man. Real horrible shit. And suddenly everyone in the squad was shooting. So I started shooting. I thought they was gonna rip us to shreds.'

The kid was in a bad way, no argument there. But even confused information was useful, so I pressed him again. 'But you did shoot above their heads, didn't you?'

'I thought I did. But it was so crazy, man, so messed up.' By now Lenny was straight up freaked. His words came so quick that the one merged into the next. 'There were kids I was at grade school with. Kids who lived on the next street. Kids I worked with at the tyre factory. I fired in the air, I fired in the air – I just couldn't shoot 'em.'

I took a step closer. 'Why *should* you have shot them, Lenny? Why should anyone in your squad have shot them if you were ordered to fire over their heads?'

He looked at me for a long moment and I saw a change come over him. It was as if he'd become aware of his hysterical state and slammed the brakes on. 'I'm not sure of nothing, and that's God's honest truth. And you're right, man. I should go home.'

I realized pushing him any further at this point would just drive him deeper into his shell.

'I'll come with you,' I said. 'I was heading into town anyways.'

We walked without talking through the wood and down a steep slope to where the trail rejoined the main road on the outskirts of town.

After fifteen minutes of silence he gave me a sideways glance. I guessed he'd been doing some thinking along the way.

'Hey, man, I gotta say … ' He hesitated and made a goofy grin, like he knew what he wanted to say but couldn't get the words out. At last he shook his head and said, 'What you did back there, it took real balls.'

I shrugged.

'I don't think you're a chickenshit.' His tone was more measured now. 'Everybody has their breaking point, don't they? No shame in that. You reached yours someplace in Vietnam. I reached mine on campus nine days ago.'

I looked at him direct. 'You're not broken, Lenny. You need to get your head right, and that's easier said than done. But you will do it. And I'd be a damn sight more worried if you went through that experience and *didn't* react in some way. You dig?'

He said yeah, he dug.

Of course it was fine for me to talk. My problem with violence was I didn't have a problem. I never got a hard on for killing like some guys, but I hit the Viet Cong like I hit typewriter keys. I killed people in a way that wasn't normal. It was what I got paid for, my work, my craft even. Like rock music and poems, it kick-started idling emotions. But unlike listening to Bob Dylan or reading Hart Crane, the idea of jiving with death in order to feel normal was the definition of *ab*normal.

We went our separate ways at the corner of Washington and Independence streets.

After a few paces, he turned and said, 'Just so you know, the guys in B Company are all right. We're regular joes. We ain't fascist thugs and police state puppets like them campus kids say.'

I looked back at him. 'I'm sure of it, Lenny.'

'Some of those radicals, they're the true extremists. Guys from rich families like Corey Quilton, they're the ones breaking the law and throwing their weight around.'

Corey Quilton's name made me prick my ears. So my welcoming Marxist buddy was from privileged stock. This surprised me. Then it didn't.

I asked, 'What's Quilton been up to?'

‘What ain’t he been up to?’ Lenny rolled his eyes. ‘He threatened to get my old man fired from the Quilton tyre factory if I didn’t quit the Guard. I told him to stick it and nothing happened with my pop. But Corey’s a piece of work. I also heard he was riding Boyd Brigstock, the student who got shot to death on campus.’

I frowned. ‘Riding him how?’

‘Boyd was from a political family but refused to get involved with Corey’s crowd. Corey kept on at Boyd for not putting pressure on his mom – she’s a congresswoman, see? Corey wouldn’t let up. He called Boyd a traitor. And the worst of it is that Corey’s now shouting from the rooftops that Boyd died a socialist martyr.’

This was even more interesting than Quilton’s background. Of course I knew about Harriet Brigstock. She had a reputation as a left-leaning Democratic congresswoman. She was also in Manhattan as a representative to the UN Security Council, due to consider a Sino-Soviet-backed resolution calling on the USA to quit Cambodia.

I had to wonder if Corey Quilton was just full of shit, or a for-real revolutionary who’d stop at nothing to achieve what he wanted – whatever that was.

THIRTEEN

My opportunity to find out came all too soon.

Quilton was giving out on Marx's theory of dialectic materialism when I arrived at the seminar room on Monday morning. His Rasputin hair and frizzy beard looked at odds with his army surplus jacket. I guessed it was part of a Fidel Castro look.

He stopped talking and I felt everyone's eyes on me.

This was the moment I'd been dreading. I'd sooner have faced a battalion of North Vietnamese regulars than the college kids sitting in front of me with their bright-eyed expectations and their pens and notepads at the ready.

Then I remembered what Laurence Westerby told me the day after he got me boosted from master sergeant to captain: *You're the boss now and your people are your responsibility, so don't show self-doubt. First thing you should do is pick something you can do exceptionally well, and show them how they can improve the way they do it. They'll respect you for that, and you'll feel a lot more comfortable.* He was right. I spent little enough time in high school, never mind West Point. But I was a dab hand at stripping down an M16 rifle and reassembling it in the dark. So I did this wearing a blindfold in front of the guys in my new command. Then I offered a case of beer to anyone who could do it faster. When we were done, my beer money was still in my pocket and I felt a comforting sense of acceptance.

I did something similar now – something useful they could benefit from. I talked about the importance of accuracy to good journalism. Then I asked the first three rows to tell me their names, dropped each one in my short term memory box, and repeated them back – that was twenty kids I'd never seen before, and they were impressed. Next I promised to teach them the mnemonic trick at the next seminar, and that virtually guaranteed a full house for my second gig.

I went on to talk about what was a good story and what was a non-story, and how an apparent non-story could actually be a huge story. I used anecdotes, like a guy fresh out of J-school coming back from a civil rights demonstration to say there was no story because the police chief banned the protest – which of course turned it into a page one lead. After that, I started to wonder why I'd been so worried.

When the class was over, Corey Quilton was waiting for me in the corridor outside.

From what Lenny Lesniak told me, I thought he was a hypocrite and a bully. But if Quilton had been leaning on Boyd Brigstock to get to his congresswoman mom, I needed to find out more. Also, if Quilton really was a hardcore activist, he may have had a role in provoking the tension in town and on campus. Again, though, I needed to know more.

So I ambled over to where he was standing and returned his smile.

He told me he enjoyed my seminar and asked me some

halfway intelligent follow-up questions. Then he said he was heading back to the commune where he lived and asked if I wanted to join him for a joint. Normally I'd have said no, but this wasn't an option if I wanted to get a look closer look into his activities.

He lived in a place known as the Green House on Fenwick Street on the campus side of town. It was a big timber frame building with large bay windows and a steep-pitched roof. Inside, guys and girls moved around a living room full of mismatched furniture, rucked-up rugs and a colour TV tuned to *The Brady Bunch*.

'We call it a commune,' Quilton explained. 'But it's much more out there than the ones you get in California. Really, this is an experiment in group living. No rules, no routines, no hassle. Sweet anarchy.'

It didn't smell so sweet, though. Long abandoned plates of food, stale nicotine and unwashed bodies gave off a rank stink. Trash cans were brimming with fast food boxes, beer cans and candy wrappers.

He took me to what he called his space – one half of the master bedroom where a city hall-size American flag was hung upside down from ceiling grommets, acting as a room divider.

A double mattress was pushed against one wall and there was an ancient leatherette couch near the window. Stacked on the sill, I saw Herman Hesse's *Siddhartha* and Noam Chomsky's *American Power and the New Mandarins*, along with back copies of adult comics such as *Mother's Oats* and *Zap*. On the wall was a poster of Che Guevara in olive drabs and another showing two rhinos getting it on, with the caption: *Make love, not war*.

Inviting me to take a seat on the couch, he flopped on the mattress and started to roll a joint. 'So what do you think?'

'What about?'

'Everything. Anything.'

I considered his question. He was probing me as much as I was him. There was no point pretending I was a fellow traveller, but I could convince him I was a potential ally. So I laid out my revolutionary socialist credentials: How I'd read folks from Marx and Mao to Proudhon and Gramsci. How I'd experienced first-hand the social conditions in the coal towns of West Virginia and the slums of New York City. How I'd gotten to know a Viet Cong battalion commander during a temporary truce and came to respect his views on building a true socialist society. None of it was bullshit, which was important because I could tell that Quilton could tell.

'You got a real cool story there, Wat.' He inserted a roach into one end of the joint and examined it like it was a work of art. 'I also understand your city editor is Maggie Call, who is also your adoptive mom, and a solid-sent sister. Gotta say, I like the op-eds she writes on gay rights and sex equality.'

He was better informed than I thought. I hadn't wanted to bring Maggie into this because although she didn't hide her sexuality, she didn't advertize it either. But Quilton already knew all this so I let it play.

'You know what you should do?' He lit the joint and took a long pull. 'Call your press and TV contacts and throw your Medal of Honor into the Hudson. That would make one hell of a story.'

I accepted the joint and took a short toke at it. I thought cannabis was real take-it-or-leave-it stuff and I never understood why so many folks rated it. Place like this, though, you embraced it or you just didn't fit in.

'Why did they give you that medal anyway?'

I handed him the joint. 'Honestly? I don't know. An infantry company was in trouble and my unit went to get them out. I remember going in, but nothing about the action itself. Apparently I singlehandedly charged a VC strongpoint and drove them back. I think I went short-term crazy and that's why I can't recall anything.'

Another explanation was that some part of my emotional wiring was still sparking – that I could still get traumatized. For most guys this would be a serious worry. For me, it was a sign of hope. But I wasn't going to bare my soul to Corey Quilton.

He offered me another go on the joint. 'So when did your memory start working again?'

I declined the joint. 'Back in the chopper, when the firefight was over. I became aware of this trippy pink gunk stuck to my arms and chest. I recall a medic telling me it was skin and soft tissue from wounded grunts I brought back.'

He reclined on the mattress. 'That's good, man. You got that award for saving life, not taking it.'

I knew from the combat report that I'd also killed a good many Viet Cong, but I left Quilton with his assumptions.

Besides, I had some questions of my own.

'What's your story, Corey?'

He made a playful grin. 'I guess you know my family owns the tyre factory?'

I nodded.

'And I also guess you're wondering why I rejected all that?'

I was actually wondering why he was pretending to reject 'all that', but I just nodded again.

He picked the Chomsky book off the window sill and tossed it to me. 'That book changed how I saw America, it changed my life. Without Chomsky, I'd never have read Marx, or Rousseau or Bakunin.'

'Bakunin, was the guy who said 'The urge to destroy is also a creative urge', right?'

He gave me a sly wink. 'Spot on, comrade.'

'That why you want to destroy the university?'

'That's why I want to destroy the United States. It's why I joined SLUT.'

I didn't try to disguise my ignorance.

'Socialists for Liberation, Understanding and Tolerance.' He made an indulging smile. 'Cool acronym, huh?'

'Yeah, real cool. Was Boyd Brigstock a member?'

He chuckled at that. 'Boyd was a straight. He wasn't remotely interested in the revolution.'

I raised an eyebrow. 'So why pressure him to lobby his congresswoman mommy?'

'SLUT uses any and all means necessary.' He stubbed out the joint in a saucer-cum-ashtray. 'But, hey, it wasn't me who shot the kid.'

'You're one mean mother, Corey, aren't you?'

'I hope so, Wat. I really do.' He laughed, half serious, half flippant and somehow something else as well.

And he left me thinking here was a guy capable of anything and nothing and happy to keep me guessing.

FOURTEEN

The animal mutilator struck again in the night. This time the victim was Herbie, pet rabbit of nine-year-old Ramskill girl Carol Robbins. Herbie had been taken from his hutch at the rear of Carol's home on Henderson Street. His neck was broken, his ears were cut off and his remains left in the back yard. Carol was understandably traumatized when she found the poor critter.

I picked up the story from the city police overnight sheets and got there shortly after 9.00am. Carol's dad Marty met me at the door and showed me into the living room. He owned a downtown diner and had taken the morning off to be with his family. The little girl was upstairs in her room being comforted by her mom and I understood why Marty wanted to shield her from the press. He had, though, agreed to talk to me after the cops left.

'It was horrible,' he said, taking a seat beside me on the couch. 'Just horrible.'

I took out my notebook and asked him to go through what happened.

He made a helpless expression. He was a chubby guy in his early thirties, balding with a broad face and droopy eyelids. 'Carol went out to feed Herbie after breakfast. The scream she let out was truly terrifying.' He placed his hand over his eyes and shook his head, as if the memory was too painful. 'It'll stay with me the rest of my days.'

'Take your time, Mr Robbins, no hurry.' This wasn't true – I needed to file my story for the next edition – but pressing someone in this sort of situation would get me nowhere, except thrown out on the street.

At last he carried on, now with some determination in his voice. 'I rushed out and Carol was standing there, staring at Herbie. He was dangling from the clothesline, strung up by his hind legs. There was blood everywhere. *And no darned ears*.'

He looked at me, fierce-eyed. 'Who would do that?'

'Somebody disturbed. Whoever it was, though, I'm sure the cops will catch them soon.' I tried to sound confident, but I really wasn't so sure. 'What did you do next, Mr Robbins?'

I saw tears welling in his eyes. 'I took her in my arms and carried her inside and hugged her tight till she stopped screaming. Then I called the cops.'

'Did you see or hear anything suspicious last night? Anything at all out of the ordinary?'

He shook his head no.

'Any thoughts on who might be responsible?'

Angry emotions seemed to crowd his brow. 'I got thoughts all right, Mr Tyler, but you couldn't print 'em.'

I didn't want stuff I couldn't print, so I tried to coax him back onto a more newsworthy path. 'I get that you're upset, Mr Robbins. What parent wouldn't be? You heard what happened to Chip Amelsfort's sheepdog last week?'

'Who hasn't?'

'You think the two incidents might be connected?'

'You betcha.' He was getting more and more agitated. 'My next-door-neighbour's son served in Vietnam. He heard stories about GIs cutting off the ears of dead Viet Cong and I don't believe what happened here last night, and out at Chip's farm, are a coincidence.'

He hesitated again, as if working out whether he'd said too much or not enough.

He needed a nudge. 'What *do* you believe, Mr Robbins?'

He blinked a couple of times, then his words came hot and sharp. 'I'll tell you what I believe, Mr Tyler: I believe that biomedical place on campus is taking in so-called volunteers before they ship out to Vietnam. I believe they're being brainwashed, dehumanized, and turned into psychopaths. And I believe one of 'em has gone rogue. First, up at Chip's place. Now here. Where next?'

'I visited the Biomedical Centre only last week,' I said. 'And I didn't see any guys looking like Vietnam draftees.'

'Maybe they keep them someplace secret.'

I thought about the hold-over World War II buildings that looked a lot like army barracks. Was it possible they were being used to accommodate human lab rats?

'Something else I believe,' Marty Robbins said. 'Sooner or later, whoever's doing this won't stop at animals.'

'Can I quote you?'

'Please do.'

I made a tight smile. He just gave me my lead paragraph.

*

I went to Rick O'Shea's for an after-work beer. This was the place where the way-out dudes and no-bra girls hooked up with the motorcycle gangs and drug dealers. I didn't fit in, but I didn't fit in at any other place either. And at least Rick O'Shea's had a righteous juke box. Right now it was belting out Led Zeppelin's *Good Times Bad Times*.

I ordered a bottle of Ballantine's ale and found a table near the window where I could read the downstate edition of the *Examiner*.

The trouble by the juke box started when a burly biker with a *Waffen-SS* coalscuttle helmet started cussing because somebody knocked over his beer. I heard an apology from the guilty party and an offer to buy him another. I couldn't see this person but the voice sounded like a woman's or a youth's. Seemed the accident happened when the offender tried to pass between Coalscuttle and the juke box.

I came to my feet to get a better view. Clearly, Coalscuttle wasn't satisfied with a simple apology and replacement. He wanted more – and I suspected violent retribution was at the top of his list.

Moving a little closer, I realized the beer-spiller was female.

Closer still and I recognized JoBeth Medlock.

Coalscuttle was towering over her, one muscular arm leaning on the wall above her shoulder, hemming her in. I couldn't hear what he was saying because of the juke box music but the flecks of spit spraying from his mouth told me it was nothing nice. Medlock looked slight and small and utterly dominated by the mass of his frame.

I was getting ready to intervene when she slipped two fingers into the front pocket of his jeans and tugged his pelvis toward hers.

Not what I was expecting – not what Coalscuttle was expecting either.

In the same fluid movement, Medlock placed the heel of her free hand under his chin and levered him back, using the base of his spine as a fulcrum. For all his bulk, Coalscuttle was utterly helpless as she walked him backward across the bar room and out onto the street. On the sidewalk, she tugged his groin a little closer to hers, destroying his fragile equilibrium, and sent him sprawling to the ground.

The David and Goliath act brought a chorus of whistles and cheers from the crowd that followed Medlock and Coalscuttle outside. Even his biker buddies were laughing and, in the face of this humiliation, he took the only course available and beat it.

Only when she turned to go back into the bar did Medlock notice me.

'That was a neat move,' I said.

She pushed back strands of dark red hair from her angular features and made a so-what shrug.

'Get you a drink?' I asked.

She said she could use one and asked for a gin and tonic. I got another Ballantine's and we took seats at the table where I'd been reading the paper.

What she was doing in a dive like Rick O'Shea's was a puzzle. I tried a gentle probe. 'Didn't expect to find you in here.'

She sipped her drink and made a knowing smile. 'I could say the same.'

In other words, I should mind my own business.

I tried again, 'I'm into hard rock. Wouldn't have thought you were.'

'Why wouldn't you?'

Now she had me backed into a corner. Smart woman.

I said, 'Most women I know tend to like smoother sounds. Motown and Stax, that sort of stuff.'

'Do you like Motown and Stax?'

'Sure I do. I like most things.'

'Why shouldn't I?'

It was a good point. This line of questioning wasn't even getting me nowhere – I was going backward into a hole of my own digging.

So I was grateful when she switched the conversation. 'I gather you took a little heat from the university president as well as the city police chief over your piece in the *Examiner*.'

This was something of an understatement. The air of hostility and suspicion had gotten a good deal worse after my story about the animal mutilator's latest atrocity appeared above the fold on page one. Mess up a sheepdog, you're a grade A shit. Do the same to a little girl's bunny, you're an honest to gosh monster. What gave my piece its punch, though, was Marty Robbins' warning that the perpetrator would likely move on to a human victim. Maggie was happy enough because copies were flying off the newsstands. But Blair Murdoch, the university president, and Don Didrikson, the city police chief, were furious. They blamed me for pouring gasoline on the flames of 'town-and-gown' antagonism.

I explained how I'd been summoned to each of their offices and told how grossly irresponsible I'd been to report Marty's prediction.

She made a small grin. 'I bet those were the two most different dressing downs you ever had.'

She wasn't wrong. Murdoch, a sleek, fine-boned sophisticate with silver hair and stentorian voice, was courteous enough, but still left me in no doubt of his distaste for me and my kind – even though I was technically a faculty member. Didrikson, weasel-faced and wiry-built, had served his time as a Westchester Sheriff's deputy, and had the aggressiveness to prove it. As far as he was concerned, I was the craven yellow-belly in the gospel according to Gerry Bohannon. There'd been nothing subtle about the police chief's language.

I returned her smile. 'Different words, same message.' I glanced at the copy of the *Examiner* on the table, then back at her. 'You think I had it coming?'

She took a long look at me, like she was making up her mind about something. 'I get why Murdoch and Didrikson were angry, but I thought your piece was reasonable, even restrained. You could have reported the conspiracy stories linking the animal atrocities to the attack at the biomedical place, or the campus protest shootings. But you didn't.'

It was a fair assessment. Truth was I hadn't made those connections because I couldn't stand them up. The theories about brainwashed Vietnam draftees that Marty Robbins and Chip Amelsfort told me about needed investigating before I went public.

I sipped my drink and gave her a curious look. 'Do *you* think there are links?'

She sipped hers and gave me a frank one. 'I wouldn't be surprised. There's a lotta crazy crammed into a lotta heads on campus and downtown. Who knows whether Marty Robbins is right about the next victim being human, but if I was the city police chief, I'd be worried.'

I was aware, too, of Chip Amelsfort's claim that he'd seen a black guy lurking on the edge of his land, apparently watching him. Violet Vinson also said her neighbours had seen a watcher, although she never mentioned skin colour. So I asked Medlock what she thought about this.

'If you're asking if this stalker could be a black student, the answer is almost certainly not.'

I made a puzzled frown. 'Why do you say that? I've seen a lot of black students at Ramskill. Don't they have radical activists?'

'Sure they do. And they're as much into revolution as any of the whites. But they have a different agenda – for good reasons. They spell America with a KKK instead of a c. They advocate violence and regard all whites as direct or potential enemies. Of course they wanted a piece of the action when the rioting started, but not with white soldiers on campus. Way they see it, a white guy with a gun will shoot a black person for no reason or any reason. So they've been hunkering down. And after the cops shot and killed two black kids at Jackson State on Friday, you can see they have a point.'

Medlock was right. This also explained the absence of black faces in the newspaper and TV coverage of the Ramskill rioting.

She set her drink down. 'Talking about radical activists, I hear you met Corey Quilton.'

I made a wincing expression. 'Sounds like you've had the pleasure too.'

'His opener was that he thought I'd make an excellent SLUT. Funny, huh?'

'He's a funny guy, and not the laugh-a-minute kind.'

She asked me what I made of Quilton and I told her I couldn't decide if he was a pretentious prick or a dangerous prick or both.

'My money is on both,' she said. 'He's a virtuoso exhibitionist, but that doesn't mean he isn't a devious schemer. You should watch him.'

She said this in a way that made me wonder where she was coming from. Happy as I was to have a friendly face around, this woman was a puzzle. For somebody who arrived not long before I did, she knew an awful lot about the university and its politics. And, unlike most folks, she didn't regard me as either a lily liver pissant or an anti-war protest hero. My thoughts also returned to the question of what had brought her to Rick O'Shea's. Despite what she said, I was one hundred per cent certain it wasn't the music. Hell, the place was such a shit-hole that even a hard-bit rock and roll junkie like me wouldn't come back in a hurry.

So why *was* she there?

FIFTEEN

Next morning I went to Ramskill Armoury for a meeting with Captain Edison Phipps. He'd called me earlier to explain that an experienced sergeant had just left the company and he was promoting me to Bohannon's second in command, a boost that would put the three stripes of a buck sergeant on my uniform. Maybe Phipps wanted me in a place where Bohannon could keep an eye on me. Or, where I could keep an eye on Bohannon. Either way, Big Gerry was not going to be happy.

The moment I stepped into the building I realized this was the mother of understatements.

Bohannon was waiting in the drill hall as I headed for the captain's office on the opposite side.

He moved forward with purposeful strides and stopped right in front of me, blocking my way.

'You been stirring up all sorts of shit, ain't you? Writing them stories, talking to Lenny Lesniak.'

'Free country when I last checked.'

He puffed out his chest. 'Don't gimme backchat, you raisin-sack pansy-ass.'

'Let me past. I got an appointment with the captain.'

'He ain't here yet. That leaves just the two of us.'

He took a step closer. His bashed-up face loomed: The pale scar running in a ragged diagonal from his ginger hairline to his heavy jaw, the beat-flat nose, the green eyes, pupils dilated by adrenalin. I smelled beer and onions on his breath.

He was taller and heavier than me, and in good shape. But that didn't count for much without speed. Question was, how fast was he?

The answer wasn't long in coming.

His haymaker punch was powerful – I saw his fist curling toward me.

If he connected, I'd go down.

But he wasn't so quick.

One step back took me just out of range. Then I moved in with a jab to his solar plexus. I felt his hot booze and onion breath on my forearm as he folded forward.

Standing back, I watched him coughing and wheezing, head between his knees.

Now I had a decision to make: Finish him off, or give quarter to a guy who would neither give or expect it.

'Hey, guys!' Phipps came loping across the hall, arms outstretched in a what-the-hell? gesture. 'Pack that in would you?'

In a way it was helpful to have had the decision taken out of my hands. Trouble was the guy who took it might also decide to take me out of Bravo Company. I'd just struck a superior, and that was a deep serious offence. Some officers would order a summary court martial.

But Edison Phipps wasn't some officers. He gazed down at his elasticated suede boots as Bohannon got back on his feet.

Then he looked up and addressed the master sergeant, 'Want to tell me what happened just now, Gerry?'

'I was instructing Private Tyler on the gut punch, sir, and didn't tense my muscles in time. It was an accident.'

Phipps made a tolerant sigh. 'It's Sergeant Tyler from here on in, Gerry. Pete Hassler left the company last night. Wat here will replace him as second in command of your squad.'

'Captain, I'm not sure if …'

'If what, Gerry?' Phipps didn't raise his voice. 'If you got something to say, I'm here to listen.'

Bohannon's expression went stony. 'I ain't got nothing to say, Captain.'

Phipps turned his attention to me. 'How about you, Wat? You got anything to say'

I wasn't at all sure of Bohannon's motive. I was damn certain he wasn't lying for my benefit, but I saw no other option than to go along with him. I said, 'It happened like the master sergeant said, Captain.'

Phipps looked from Bohannon to me and back again. 'You two take me for a complete sucker?'

Bohannon said nothing. I said nothing.

At last Phipps scratched his head and spoke to both of us. 'Gerry, you can be a real hothead, you know? And Wat, you got to control yourself better. Just take it easy, will you? Darn it, the very last thing I need at a time like this is trouble among my senior guys. You dig?'

We nodded like scolded school kids.

'OK, I want you to shake hands and promise to put this *accident* behind you.'

Bohannon made a deep throaty cough as if he was forcing back words fighting to get out of his throat.

I made an accommodating grin and held out my hand.

Bohannon took it. I half expected him to try for a knuckle-crusher, but it never came. Instead he looked me in the eye, cold and hard. The adrenalin had subsided and his pupils were back to normal. I didn't have the slightest doubt, though, that Big Gerry was already planning his revenge.

SIXTEEN

Loretta Hausinger showed me into her apartment on the north side of the campus and I accepted her offer of coffee.

She went into the kitchen to make it and I looked around her living room. You can learn a lot about a person from their domestic arrangements and I was particularly interested in learning more about Hausinger. Unlike many of her colleagues, she displayed no signs of political affiliation – no Che Guevara or humping hippo posters on the walls, no trendy paperbacks on the shelves. Instead she had tasteful landscapes and leather-bound classics. The furniture was correspondingly conservative – nothing flashy or overstated. It was as if she didn't want the room to say anything at all. But even saying nothing says something.

She came through with two cups of coffee and we sat opposite each other on wing-backed armchairs.

'You're looking much better,' I said.

I wasn't just being kind. She still had a livid bruise above her temple and moved with some difficulty due to the gunshot wound. But the colour had returned to her face and her deep brown eyes seemed eager to engage. The hospital doctors must have been impressed by the speed of her recovery because they discharged her only five days after the shooting.

'Are they any closer to catching the person who did this?' She touched the bruise on her head.

'Chief Ducey says not.' I drank some coffee. It was strong and tasted good. 'He's puzzled and I get why. The shooting itself was messy – otherwise you wouldn't be here. Yet the getaway was perfect. No one saw anyone leave the building and there's no trace of an escape route. It's like he vanished into thin air.'

'The cops will catch him though, won't they?' She sounded anxious.

'Sure they will.' I wasn't sure at all though. With no description, no murder weapon, no clue as to motive, and no idea where the killer went, Ducey had his work cut out.

'You still can't think of anyone who might have done this? Anyone who had a reason for wanting to shut down your research work?'

She shook her head and sipped her coffee.

'Can you tell me anything about the guys who died – Gonzalez, Reese and Poole? The police press statement was very light on personal information.'

She made an apologetic expression. 'I hardly knew them and what I did know I didn't like. They operated as a men-only club and made it clear from the outset that they didn't like having a woman on the team. They were sexist boors, all of them. As you can imagine, we didn't socialise.'

'What about Oleg Bobkov? Did they get along with him?'

She shrugged. 'Better than with me. Oleg was our team leader, so they had to make an effort. He went for the occasional beer with them, but he was never in their little clique. Why do you ask?'

'I'm trying to establish a link between what went down at the Biomedical Centre and what happened to Bobkov.'

She frowned. 'So you don't think Oleg's death was an accident?'

'No I don't. I'm confident he was murdered.'

Her frown deepened. 'But how?'

I took out a Camel but didn't light it. 'I believe someone saw an opportunity to take him out in the chaos of the protest. This could have been done after the guardsmen opened fire. They discharged almost a hundred rounds, so one extra would have attracted zero attention. Or it could have been the other way around: The shot that killed Oleg could have spooked the guardsmen, causing them to start shooting. Also, there have been unconfirmed reports of a sniper on campus. Maybe the guardsmen thought the shot that hit the professor came from a sniper rifle aimed at them and *that* was why they opened fire. But whichever way this went down, the confusion of the demonstration and the presence of the guard would have provided ideal cover for anyone wanting to eliminate your friend.'

'What does Chief Ducey think?'

'He's playing his cards close to his chest and I don't blame him. You asked me what I thought and I told you. But it's just speculation.'

'It's credible speculation though.' She indicated my Camels. 'May I?'

I offered her the pack. She took one and I gave her a light, but held off lighting my own.

The delaying tactic was part of my plan to cut down on smoking. The longer I waited to light up, the fewer cigarettes I'd smoke in the course of a day. Or so I told myself.

I waited a few beats, then broached the subject I knew was going to be difficult. 'You should also be aware there are rumours in town.'

'There are always rumours in town.' She sounded weary.

She wouldn't want to hear this, but I had to push it. 'Folks are talking about Vietnam draftees volunteering for psychological re-adjustment at the Biomedical Centre. If you believe what you hear, it's part of a combat readiness preparation programme that desensitizes guys to extreme violence before they deploy.'

'That's baloney.'

I lit my cigarette. 'It gets worse. There's another story doing the rounds – an even more disturbing one.'

'That's baloney too.'

'You haven't heard it.'

'I don't need to.'

'Maybe you do, Loretta.' I injected a note of gravity into my tone and that got her attention.

She looked up from her cigarette. 'Go on.'

'You heard what happened with the sheepdog and the bunny?'

'I read your piece in the *Examiner*.'

'A lot of townsfolks are convinced the animals were attacked by somebody who underwent this alleged procedure, then went on the rampage.'

'That's utter nonsense.'

I raised an eyebrow. 'On the record?'

'If you want, yes.'

I made a note.

Another concern was Chip Amelsfort's report of a black guy observing him from the treeline at the edge of his farmland. Violet Vinson's neighbours had also talked of being surveilled from the shadows by a lone figure. Was this the same guy who attacked the animals? After what JoBeth Medlock told me about black students keeping a low profile during the unrest, I doubted the watcher was one of them. I hadn't seen any black folks at the biomedical place either, but this wasn't to say there weren't any. So I asked Hausinger.

'We have no black people at the centre at all.' She made a slightly sheepish expression. 'We're not racist or anything. We just never had any black people applying to work with us. Why do you ask?'

I saw no point holding out so I told her what Amelsfort told me.

She agreed this was a mystery, that the watcher could be behind the animal mutilation. But she insisted there was no way he was connected to the Biomedical Centre.

She took a long toke at her cigarette and blew the smoke toward the ceiling. When she spoke, her voice was exasperated. 'Maybe the Biomedical Centre could benefit from a public relations campaign because spinning crazy yarns about us seems to be a common pastime in town. It's true that some of the research work we do here includes behavioural pharmacology. But we're absolutely not creating monsters out of kids on their way to Vietnam – or people who go around snooping on farmers and townsfolks.'

It was interesting, I thought, that she was willing to be specific about what *wasn't* going on at the biomedical place, but not so much about what *was* being done there. I didn't want another recitation about how she and her team had been helping people to cope with stress and anxiety at home and in the work place and didn't press her.

So it came as some surprise when she broached the topic herself – from an entirely unexpected angle. 'My work means I have some understanding of the effect prolonged exposure to combat environments can have on soldiers – including people like you.'

I took a drag on my cigarette and sat back. There was a difficult silence but I let it play. She'd started down this path and I left her to continue.

After a time she said, 'I heard the stories about why you came back from Vietnam.'

She did listen to *some* rumours. But I didn't want to rub her the wrong way so I kept the thought to myself.

She shifted awkwardly on the edge of the chair. 'I really can sympathize, Wat. I totally get how you could have been a decorated war hero one day and lost your nerve the next.'

'I was never a hero,' I said. 'I just did my job. And I didn't lose my nerve. I didn't have one to lose.'

She gave me a perplexed look.

'I have attachment disorder. You'll have heard of that.'

'Yes indeed.' She took a few beats to process this information but quickly collected her thoughts. When she spoke again, she sounded intrigued. 'I'm familiar with John Bowlby's work on maternal deprivation. May I ask, what was your experience?'

I didn't usually talk about this. But I'd been through a lot with Hausinger in a short period and found it surprisingly easy to talk to her. Besides, she was a solid news source and it would pay to keep her sweet. So I told her how my childhood home was a scene of non-stop domestic violence. My dad never hurt me, but he beat my mom hard and often. She got so messed up, physically and mentally, that she couldn't take care of me. We never bonded when I was a baby and things went downhill from there.

Hausinger looked at me straight. 'You were in a war zone before you could talk, weren't you?'

'In a manner of speaking, I guess.' I rested my cigarette in the ashtray. 'My infant brain realized fear was futile and worse, so it developed in a way that stopped me getting scared in the first place.'

She leaned forward, resting her elbows on her knees. 'How did this affect you as you grew older?'

'I struggled to process feelings, especially anxiety. But I had a deficit on the positive side too – happiness, excitement, exhilaration were all muted and sometimes dialled down to zero. I still struggle.'

She made a kindly expression. 'You seem exceptionally well adjusted.'

I returned her gaze, still perplexed by how relaxed I was about revealing this stuff. Then I reminded myself that she was a psychologist. Getting guys like me to talk was part of her job. 'I had therapy when I was a teenager,' I said. 'My shrink worked with Bowlby and motherless kids in the aftermath of World War II and was using his ideas when most psychoanalysts were dismissing them as quackery. That helped a lot. But it was like learning a foreign language. When you learn as an infant, you grow up speaking the lingo like a native, right? But if you learn that same language later in life, you pick up an accent. It's a similar deal with feelings. Me, I feel with an accent.'

'You do it very well.' She leaned closer and her soft rounded features filled my vision. 'Really you do.'

There was a brief quiet. I wasn't good at taking compliments. So I just waited.

At last she leaned back and said, 'Can you tell me what *did* happen in Vietnam?'

Now we were back on safer ground. I picked up my cigarette and recited the bare bones of my story: I made a tactical decision based on information available. Our people took casualties, we had to withdraw. Superior officers questioned my judgment. I asked to come home, they agreed.

'You have good reason to be positive, Wat.'

'How so?'

'You can rationalize why you quit the army after all those years in Vietnam. You can accept it and move on. That's why you've been able to readjust, to function back home. Lots of people never do. In a way, they never come back.'

She was right. I thought about the junkie I saved from a kicking near Gem Spa newsstand, the guy with the 101st Airborne tattoo on his arm. I wondered what would become of that poor bastard and thousands like him. And I wondered which was worse, coming home in a body bag, or coming home in no fit state to do anything except drugs.

SEVENTEEN

I left Loretta Hausinger's apartment and walked over to the shallow grassy slope in front of Stanton Hall – the place where the National Guard had opened fire. Students were chatting and laughing as they moved in and out of the shiny modern building. Things seemed almost back to normal. Then I noticed two campus cops standing in the lobby, two more coming over from Putney Hall and realized *almost* was a way off *completely*.

I'd told Hausinger I thought Bobkov had probably been killed by an opportunist with a grudge and a gun who took advantage of the rioting. I wasn't discounting this theory, but I was also contemplating another: What if the professor had been shot as part of a planned hit? I knew from newspaper reports that he met his friend Gordon Richardson outside Putney a few minutes after 1.00pm every weekday, and they walked together across parking lot C to the faculty cafeteria on the east side of the campus. If Bobkov's movements were predictable, he'd have been easy meat for a professional assassin, even amid the chaos.

First, though, I wanted a clearer picture of exactly what the guardsmen would have seen when they started shooting.

I stood where they'd stood and looked around. The slightly elevated position on top of the slope meant they'd have had a view over the heads of the protest group immediately in front of them – the kids hurling rocks and abuse. They'd have seen Putney Hall to the left, parking lot C straight ahead, and the cafeteria building to the right.

I knew from Gene Ducey that ninety-six rounds were discharged by the guardsmen. All the cartridge cases were recovered but only twenty-seven bullets. These included the three rounds that killed Bobkov, Richardson and Boyd Brigstock, plus six bullets that hit the half dozen people who were wounded.

I started processing what else I knew.

The proportion of bullets recovered was small, but this was consistent with most of the guard having fired into the air, on trajectories that would have taken the rounds way outside the campus where they'd have been hard or impossible to find.

The magazine capacity of the Garand M1 rifle issued to the twelve-man squad was eight rounds, so each of the soldiers emptied the magazine in his gun. This included Bohannon, but not Phipps who carried a sidearm that remained in his holster. Both Phipps and Bohannon denied having given the order to open fire. They said this happened because their men thought they were in mortal danger and reacted.

Bohannon and the rest of his squad claimed they shot over the protesters' heads. But clearly one or more fired low. Possibly this was in panic, or by mistake. Possibly some of them thought they fired high, but actually fired low. Many, like Lenny Lesniak, were twenty-year-old 'weekend warriors', not battle-hardened grunts. This might explain the discrepancy.

But what if every guardsman really had told the truth? What if all of them really had fired high?

They couldn't have.

Couldn't they?

I took a few beats to let my brain do its thing: Contemplate crazy; wander into way-out and beyond. It came down to this: The guardsmen could only have been telling the truth if somebody else fired the fatal shots.

But who?

I considered the question from a different perspective.

Like the guardsmen, I was looking straight ahead.

What if I was looking in the wrong direction?

If there was a shooter – and this was a 72-point italic *if* – he must have taken up a position behind the guardsmen. Anywhere ahead, or on either side and there'd have been a risk of them seeing him.

I turned to face Stanton Hall. Could a sniper have positioned himself in one of the rooms? I took a dozen paces back from the building and scanned it top to bottom, right to left. I did this again, and again. But I saw nothing helpful. In theory the shots could have come from any of the north-facing classrooms in the four-storey structure.

This was when I noticed the wooden shack at the side of the main hall.

I moved closer. It seemed to have two floors with a tarpaper roof and was probably some sort of store room, perhaps for groundskeeping equipment. The paintwork was flaky, the windows coated in grime. Except for one – in an upstairs room looking out over the parking lot.

Around the back, I found a door. The hasp and staple

looked new and the wood above was splintered where screws had been prised from their holes. This place had been broken into, and recently. I took the set of picks from my pocket and opened the padlock.

Inside, the place was crammed with a sit-on lawn mower, pruning shears and wood saws, shovels, forks and plastic tubs of grass seed. Bare wood stairs ascended to a second floor and I went up them, wary of the ancient creaking timber under my feet. The room above was a dumping ground for disused gardening gear, along with old cans of paint and creosote.

I moved to the window – the one that stood out from the others because it wasn't opaque with grime. Close up I could see that someone had gone to the trouble of cleaning it – inside and out. The latch opened smoothly and the window swung outward, giving a clear view from Putney Hall across the parking lot to the cafeteria.

Perfect for a shooter aiming at the spot where Oleg Bobkov would have been.

I looked down at the wood flooring. It was covered in dust, except for an oblong area near the window that showed irregular clean patches and light scuff marks. Hard to tell what caused them, but my money was on a sniper lying in a prone firing position.

I searched the place for more tangible evidence but I couldn't see anything remotely incriminating. Then again, a seasoned sniper would have made absolutely certain he left no trace.

Yet he would have been in a hurry to get away.

And perhaps he wasn't such a shit-hot marksman.

Looking out across the parking lot, it was obvious that Gordon Richardson was standing so close to Bobkov that he must also have been hit by the sniper. My guess was that the shooter missed his mark – Bobkov – with his first shot and took out Richardson by accident. He then took a second shot which did kill Bobkov.

Two shots to nail one target was not the work of an expert.

Maybe the guy got flustered, made a mistake and left something behind.

I thought this more in hope than expectation, but it didn't stop me going down on my hands and knees and examining the timber boards close-up.

I covered every square inch of the floor space and found nothing. I moved the paint and creosote cans. Still nothing. Next I rummaged among the discarded gardening gear and gave up when I nicked my finger on a pair of rusty hedge clippers.

I decided to call it quits and headed back down the stairs. Half way down, a brief shaft of sunlight came through the upstairs window, reflecting a soft gleam near my right foot.

I looked closer.

My eyes locked on a small steel object lodged in a gap between the tread and the wall.

Stooping, I picked up a threaded steel cap with a shallow coned top. It was about an inch in diameter and a quarter inch deep, with a knurled circumference.

I turned it slowly between my fingers and pinned a serial number stamped onto the metal: A7575180.

I had a very good idea what it was, but I needed to be sure.

EIGHTEEN

I slathered mustard on my mashed potato knish and walked along the street to Junior High School 64 in the New Lots neighbourhood of Brooklyn. Built in the 1890s, the place had the gaunt and intimidating appearance of a penitentiary. It sure felt that way for the two years I went there after my mom brought me to New York City. There had been upsides, although not at school. As a hillbilly kid, I never belonged to the gangs of young blacks or Puerto Ricans, or tough ethnic whites. Once I showed I could handle myself in a street fight, my outsider status became an advantage: Because everybody knew I was in nobody's pocket, I became a useful go-between and eventually a deal-maker. All before I turned sixteen.

Of course I hadn't driven from Ramskill to Brooklyn to reminisce.

I finished my knish and headed for Pitkin and Shepherd Avenues. The place I was looking for was a row house on Shepherd with boarded-up first floor windows, worn-away paint and crumbling brick.

I pressed a buzzer and waited.

After some time I heard the gravelly voice of Titus Grundy. I said who I was and the intercom went dead. A few minutes later I heard a half dozen bolts and locks being opened and the door edged six inches ajar.

'Never thought I'd see you on my Goddamn doorstep.' Grundy looked me up and down and didn't seem particularly happy. He was a sinuous black guy, early forties, with narrow craggy features and eyes that somehow looked alert and drowsy. He'd been the operations sergeant in my first Green Beret team and also happened to be the best sniper I knew.

'Pleased to see you too, Titus.' I made an aw-shucks shrug. Grundy's nickname in country had been Grumpy and it wasn't difficult to get why. He didn't say much. When he did, he was usually blunt to the point of rudeness and beyond. But he was one hundred per cent solid and two hundred per cent knowledgeable about sniper stuff. 'You going to invite me in?'

'Looks like you invited yourself.'

He opened the door and I went into a dim lobby, then followed him up two flights of stairs. His gait was stiff and he paused every few steps – the result of a shrapnel wound that shattered his right leg three years ago and ended his army career.

When we reached the top, I asked. 'How's civilian life?'

'What do you think?' He turned to face me, grim-faced. He was wearing the same olive drab T and khaki pants that he'd have worn on a Special Forces strike force camp.

I said, 'You working?'

He made a dismissive shrug. 'Got a job at a gunsmith in mid-town Manhattan. Pay's decent and they treat me right. Ain't exactly the life, though.'

At least he'd gotten a life, which was a lot better than what some veterans ended up with. But I figured the last thing he wanted to hear was a count-your-blessings pep talk. Besides, I dug where he was coming from. From a key leadership role in a Green Beret A team to fixing firearms for regular joes could not have been an easy transition.

He showed me into his living room – a Spartan, tidy space that looked much like the senior NCO quarters he and I once shared. I guessed on one level, Grundy never made the transition at all.

He lit a cigarette. 'I heard you lost your captain bars and got sent home.'

'Where you hear that?'

'I keep in touch.'

'What do you think?'

'What you got to say about it?'

'Nothing.'

'Then that's what I think.' He didn't blink, didn't show any emotion at all.

This was the thing with Grundy – you'd get uncomplicated, unconditional loyalty without any sense that he liked you, or gave a damn about the consequences. Many Special Forces guys were unusual, but Grundy brought a whole new definition to the word.

He said, 'How are the guys?'

I gave him a resume. We'd lost four since Grundy rode the liftbird out.

He shook his head and we let the silence run, as if it would be disrespectful to talk too soon after I spoke those names.

At last, he said, 'Sonny still with you?'

He was referring to the team leader of our CIDG – Civilian Irregular Defense Group – strikers who we trained and fought with. As long range recon operators they were better than any Vietnamese army unit, North or South.

I nodded yes. 'Still never quits gabbing.'

'Well, tell the crazy little bastard to put a sock in it – from me.'

I said I would.

Sonny and his team were from an ethnic group called the Bru – hill people who'd gotten persecuted by Saigon just as much as Hanoi. Grundy identified with them in general and Sonny in particular, even though the two men were polar opposites: Sonny talked too much and Grundy hardly talked at all. I suspected Grundy's affinity with the Bru was down to his experience as a black American. But he'd never told me and I never asked.

He looked at me for a long moment. 'You always were good at handling Sonny's people.'

This was a rare compliment – hell, it was an unprecedented one. Truth was I treated the Bru, along with the Chung and the Tay, in the same way as the black, Puerto Rican and poor European street gangs in Brooklyn. We were all outsiders. I didn't belong to them, but I didn't belong to anyone else either. I showed them strength and a little respect and they responded.

I shrugged. 'Same mud, same blood.'

'I guess.' He flicked his cigarette ash into a trash can and gave me a meaningful look. 'But you ain't here to talk about the old days.'

'I need your help, Titus.'

'How's that?'

I handed him the steel cap I found on the stairway. 'Know what that is?'

He gave me a pained look. 'Don't you?'

I knew it was the protective cover for an adjustment knob on a sniper scope, certainly US army issue, probably World War II-era. The cap would have to be removed to turn a dial that aligned the scope with the rifle barrel. What I needed to find out was what type of scope and which rifle.

I said, 'I need to know *exactly* what it is.'

He placed his cigarette in an ashtray and examined the serial number stamped on the conical steel top. 'This belongs to a Lyman M82 scope for the Garand M1C. It was adopted as the army's standard sniper rifle in 1944 but never saw active service until Korea.'

This told me a lot: The regular Garand M1 was the rifle issued to the National Guard at Ramskill.

But it didn't tell me enough.

I said, 'I never came across a scope with a threaded cap like this. Unscrewing it to make your adjustments, then screwing it back on must have been a pain in the ass.'

He nodded. 'The army eventually replaced it with a flip-up version on the M1D, but that wasn't until the early 50s. Shooters using the screw cap could have dropped the damn thing, even lost it.'

He gave me a knowing look. 'That how you came by it?'

I nodded yes. 'I'm looking into the possibility of a shooter using an M1C today. Would that be viable?'

He resumed his smoke. 'Viable, sure. But if you're asking me if anyone would pick out an M1C ahead of a more modern weapon, the answer is absolutely not. Accuracy has improved massively since they were issued.'

'What if you had no choice – if you *had* to use an M1C?'

He skewered me with those dopey-agile eyes. 'We talking about an experienced marksman here?'

I said nothing, which he took to mean yes.

'In that case, I'd be confident of a hit. But I wouldn't be as confident as I'd like to be. I mean, why take even the smallest risk?'

The answer was because the M1C sniper at Ramskill fired the same ammo as the National Guard guys firing the standard M1 Garand. He fired from the same position, in the same direction. In this way, his shots would have gone unnoticed. Nobody would suspect Bobkov had been assassinated. And the Guard would take the heat.

Grundy was right, though: Using the obsolescent MIC rather than a newer, better gun would have entailed some margin for error. Knowing this, I was sure Gordon Richardson died because he was standing too close to the mark, Oleg Bobkov. And the shooter made no mistake with his second shot.

Did the same guy also kill Boyd Brigstock? He was in a different part of the parking lot and my gut assessment was that it would have been possible, but extremely difficult. Truth was, it was too soon to tell. But it sure wasn't too late.

Outside Grundy's place I found a pay phone.

I made a call, then another.

NINETEEN

My first phone call got me into the United Nations headquarters building at 42nd Street and 1st Avenue. It was an impressive piece of post-war real estate with its glass-fronted Secretariat skyscraper rising above the elegant curves of the General Assembly Building, Conference Centre and Hammarskjöld Library.

I went in through the 1st Avenue entrance and presented my credentials at Security Council reception.

Major General Laurence Westerby was waiting for me in a meeting room near the main chamber.

He ushered me into the room and closed the door. 'Good of you to swing by, Wat.'

'Good of you to see me, General.'

'You sure haven't been hanging around, have you?'

'You don't pay me to hang around.'

I took a seat opposite him at one end of a conference table.

He was a tall willowy guy with graceful good looks and an easy manner. Back-lit blue eyes and a limelight smile made people around him feel relaxed and confident. He was forty-eight, but looked younger and it was easy to see why the media called him the Hollywood General. He claimed to hate the showbiz moniker, but this never stopped him making the most of it to push his agenda everyplace from the boonies of Vietnam to the committee rooms of the Pentagon. Among other things, he was in New York to brief our guy on the UN's Military Staff Committee on the situation in Cambodia.

I was among the other things.

He leaned back in his seat and crossed one leg over the other. 'So your cover story did the trick?'

'Like a dream. With very few exceptions, I'm either an anti-war protest hero or a despicable yellow-belly.'

'It's astonishing.' He made a grim smile. 'I gave a set of unembellished facts in strict confidence to a half dozen people here in New York. Within twenty-four hours each one of them was spinning his own yarn to a whole bunch of other people.'

I wasn't surprised, though I was surprised that Westerby was. Maybe he'd regarded some of those six guys as trustworthy and was disappointed when they let him down.

The facts he mentioned were basically what I told Loretta Hausinger: I made a tough but necessary decision to withdraw my unit. As a result, the infantry battalion we were shielding took heavy casualties. Its commanding officer was angry and he did question my judgment. But he never alleged dereliction or cowardice, still less called for a court martial. Later, Westerby briefed me on this mission which involved me asking to return to the States, which I did. Everything else, from Gerry Bohannon's version to Corey Quilton's was self-interested fiction.

Westerby stood up and went to a coffee percolator. He poured himself a cup and asked me if I wanted one. It looked like molasses, but I accepted his offer.

When he sat back down, his manner seemed more

upbeat. 'I talked with Rockefeller and O'Hara this morning. They agree your latest discovery means you should press on with even greater urgency.'

The people he'd spoken to were New York National Guard Adjutant General Almerin O'Hara and Governor Nelson Rockefeller. O'Hara was an old friend of Westerby's and my mission was his idea in the first place. He and the governor wanted an inside investigation into the role of the guard in the Ramskill shooting, but this required a complete outsider. O'Hara contacted Westerby and Westerby contacted me. Technically I was on detached duty as a member of Westerby's staff.

I wasn't altogether happy with the way this was going – did O'Hara and Rockefeller think I could simply put my foot on the gas and deliver a result overnight?

I said, 'Of course I'll do what I can, General. But you know this sort of work takes time. And I'm only one guy.'

He gave me one of his retina-melting smiles. 'How about I team you up with a partner?'

I was even less happy the way this was going. 'You also know I prefer to operate alone.'

'Then I'd need to make it an order.' He raised his palms upward in a what-can-I-say? gesture. 'The Department of Justice also has an investigator in Ramskill. Washington is insisting the two of you work together. It does make sense, Wat. I mean, you wouldn't want to risk getting your wires crossed, would you?'

He went to an intercom handset on the wall and spoke into it.

I shouldn't have been surprised when JoBeth Medlock appeared in the doorway.

*

Two hours later I was looking at her across a table in the India Pavilion at 325 East 54th Street. We were there because she offered me dinner at a restaurant of my choice as a goodwill gesture, and I loved food from the sub-continent. I could have hit her bank balance by picking a fancier place, but I also had an interest in maintaining a working relationship. And although the Pavilion was small and unfussy, it was as good as any Indian in New York.

She'd entered Westerby's room expecting me to be pissed off about being blindsided. And I was. At the same time, though, I had to admit she was good at her job. Not once had I imagined she was anyone other than who she claimed to be.

Westerby explained that she was an assistant US attorney for the Southern District of New York, with federal jurisdiction including Manhattan and Westchester County, where Ramskill was located. The FBI didn't recruit female agents in 1970, though she'd received Bureau training at Quantico and had extensive experience of undercover work for the Department of Justice. According to Westerby, she'd been tipped off by her bosses about my arrival in Ramskill, but told to keep quiet about her own activities until they came to an understanding with O'Hara and Rockefeller. This 'understanding' meant we were now partners and expected to share all our intelligence. Westerby had delivered our side of the deal by telling Medlock everything I'd uncovered. In return I got to know what she'd found out, which was nothing I didn't already know or couldn't have guessed. This irked me somewhat, though I appreciated she didn't have the military knowledge or direct line into the National Guard that I did.

On the plus side, she had the authority to request a firearms laboratory test to establish whether the two rounds that killed Bobkov and Richardson had come from any of the twelve rifles issued to the guardsmen who opened fire. If my deductions were correct, those shots had come from the sniper's M1C, so there would be no match with the National Guard weapons. Medlock also agreed to run similar tests on the bullet that took out Boyd Brigstock, although I doubted this was a sniper round. Taking out Bobkov with an antiquated M1C seemed problematic enough for the shooter without adding the Brigstock kid to his hit list. Moreover, Bobkov and Richardson's movements were predictable – they always crossed the parking lot on their way to lunch soon after 1.00pm – whereas Brigstock had been there purely by chance.

I waited while a waiter served a plate of poppadoms and a selection of relishes on a tray of small glass dishes.

When he went away, I said, 'So you weren't at Rick O'Shea's for the hard rock after all.'

'I was there to meet a contact – one of Corey Quilton's fellow travellers from SLUT. But he must have gotten spooked because he never showed.'

I felt her watching me as I broke off a piece of poppadom and dipped it in some mango chutney.

When I looked up, she was smiling. 'But I do like Led Zeppelin and The Doors as well as Motown and Stax.'

I returned her smile. There was a lot to like about Medlock. Her dark red hair and sloping features were attractive, though not in an obvious sort of way. She was clearly smart and a cool operator – especially the way she handled the biker with the Nazi helmet.

Then I remembered the sense of being watched, or rather

studied, after I left the Jefferson Airplane concert. And I realized something else about her.

I gave her a direct look. 'You were tailing me that night I went to the Fillmore East, weren't you?'

She used her tongue to push her poppadom to one side of her mouth. 'You did a good thing saving that junkie from those toughs.'

'That's kind of you,' I said, 'but why were you surveilling me?'

She poured us both a glass of water from the jug on the table. 'I was aware you'd arrived in New York City. I was in Lower Manhattan anyway, and I decided to do a little homework. I like to know who I'm dealing with.'

'And?'

'And I'm cool about working with you.'

Maybe she was. This would explain why she'd been so friendly when I arrived on campus. It also told me why the FBI presence was so low-key. Of course Medlock wasn't an agent, but she'd certainly be liaising with the Bureau. No doubt her skills and connections would be useful, but I was still unhappy about her having known so much about me before I knew anything about her.

When the main course had been served, she said, 'Westerby speaks very highly of you. What's the deal with the two of you?'

I forked a chunk of tandoori chicken, then chewed on the food and the question. I had nothing to hide and what she was asking about had already been reported in the newspapers, so I went ahead and told her. 'His chopper was shot down deep in enemy territory during the Tet Offensive and my A-team was sent to find him before Charlie did. We located him but lost some guys in a firefight, including our CO. I was the unit's master sergeant so this left me in charge. After two weeks playing cat and mouse with Charlie, we got him back in one piece. Anyways, he was impressed with the way I handled the operation and wanted me in command of my own unit. He pulled some strings in Saigon and Washington and soon after that I got a direct commission to captain.'

She gave me an inquisitive look. 'Master sergeant to captain? That's got to be highly unusual.'

'Nobody was more surprised than me. To my knowledge it only happened once before in Vietnam when they boosted a special warfare expert called Dick Meadows. That was when it hit me that what Westerby wants, Westerby gets.'

She dipped her nan bread in some dopiaza sauce and gave me a shrewd look. 'It didn't end there, though, did it? You must have continued to work for him?'

This was a quid pro quo I wasn't going to tell her about – at least not yet. I was never in Westerby's pocket, but unlike a lot of West Point officers, I was happy to take on operations that required an unorthodox approach. This usually meant tossing the rule book, crossing the line between risky and crazy. I also did my fair share of black ops. But I wasn't going to tell her this either.

Instead I said, 'Fifth Special Forces Group isn't attached to any one corps or division, so I've never been under his command. Having said that, my unit has completed a number of missions that Leaping Larry had an interest in.'

'Leaping Larry?'

I took a sip of water. 'He's an energetic and dynamic commander. Never stays put and always takes the fight to the enemy. Hence, Leaping Larry.'

‘I’m told he also gets called the Hollywood General.’

‘He likes Leaping Larry better.’

When the waiter had cleared away our main course stuff, I decided it was time for me to get some information about her.

She was forthcoming enough: She went to college in Philadelphia and graduated in law before joining a small firm in the city. She grew tired of criminal defence work and joined the district attorney’s office, working with law enforcement officers to secure a number of high profile convictions. Then, after a stint at the Department of Justice in DC, she got her current job as an assistant US attorney in the Southern District of New York.

She talked freely and enthusiastically about her work and I got the impression she was not only good at what she did, but deeply committed to it.

So why did I get the sense she was holding something back?

TWENTY

The second phone call I made outside Titus Grundy's place got me a meeting with Maggie Call, my city editor.

We met at my apartment on East 7th Street, midway between Avenues A and B in the East Village neighbourhood of Alphabet City. I'd gone out for some cigarettes and when I returned she was waiting on the stoop, watching kids play stickball in Tomkins Square Park. I stopped on the top step and we stared at each other for a stretched-out moment. Then she made a small smile and put her arms out. We hugged long and hard. We hadn't seen one another since I was in New York two years ago and it felt like forever. See, Maggie wasn't just my boss and she wasn't just my adoptive mom. She was my first and only safe haven. The one person on the planet I could absolutely rely on, trust with anything, beyond question and without hesitation. For this reason, I'd told her about my latest mission from the get go. And in any case, I couldn't have asked her for the Ramskill reporter job without being honest about why I really wanted it.

She pushed me back to take a good look at me, and I looked into her slightly misty blue eyes.

She was slim, with keen features and a stylish pixie haircut. At forty-nine, she'd been a leading light in the

Women's Liberation and Gay Rights movements for many years, although she didn't seem particularly radical in a charcoal pantsuit and white blouse.

We told each other how well we looked, then went up to my place on the second floor. Maggie called it my Batcave because I'd paid a small fortune for a security features that included a reinforced door with special locks and steel window shutters that I rolled down when I wasn't home. The protection was for my stereo sound system and record collection, which were the most precious things I owned.

She gazed at the long wall of floor-to-ceiling vinyl in the living room. 'You seriously need to sort this room out, Wat. You can't possibly have listened to all these records.'

This was true. And although it was my ambition to try, I bought new music much faster than I could listen to the stuff already on my shelves. I had studio albums, live recordings and no end of bootlegs. The whole collection was kept alphabetically, from the Ad Libs to the Zombies, then chronologically in line with the release date of each album.

On the face of it, I was a lost-cause music geek but Maggie knew why I hoarded and cherished these records. Before she entered my life, music was the nearest thing I had to a safe haven. It went right back to the days when my mom played country radio songs extra loud to disguise the beating heading her way when my dad came home drunk. Curled in bed, I wrapped myself in harmony and rhythm while I heard and didn't hear the thumps and thuds and screams downstairs. I escaped to Burl Ives' *Big Rock Candy Mountain* and Jimmy Wakely's *Oklahoma Hills* and Hank Williams' *Lost Highway* and anyplace else conjured by a song that wasn't the place I really was. Then, when I was old enough to buy my own records, possessing music was a way of possessing myself, of making my refuge physical.

We sat on the couch.

I took out a Camel, but didn't light it. 'I guess you want to know what happened with Lawrence Westerby?'

'Not as much as I want to know how you've been.'

'Fine,' I said. 'I've been fine.'

She was having none of this. 'You've been *too* fine. That was always the problem, wasn't it?'

'It's not a problem in Vietnam.'

'Isn't it?' She gave me an X-ray look. 'You've been out there way too long. You should come home. You've done your damn duty in spades.'

We both knew I hadn't stayed in the Nasty so long because of duty or patriotism. I got a jolt out of the action that was part and parcel of special warfare. I'd started to understand that this wasn't healthy, but I wasn't ready to give it up. Not just yet.

I tried to placate her. 'I'm home now, aren't I?'

'For how long?' Maggie was a tough woman but I sensed she was on the edge. 'I want you home for good – and not in a goddamn body bag.'

I placed the cigarette in my mouth but still held back from lighting it. 'That won't happen, Maggie. I'm good at what I do.'

'That's what scares me the most.'

There was a paralyzed silence. We loved each other as much as any mother and son, but we weren't so good at showing emotion.

She was first to recover. 'You could spend some time looking for your mom. You could go down to West Virginia and look up your dad.'

I gave her a sour look. 'What makes you think I want to do either of those things?'

'Your mom could still be alive. Your dad could have turned his life around.'

'I'm pretty certain she isn't and he hasn't. Besides, I really don't care.'

She made a quizzical expression.

I maintained a blank one.

But she'd set me thinking.

I didn't blame my mom for taking me from West Virginia to New York City. But I did blame her for hitting skid alley as soon as we got here. She was on the Bowery sucking canned heat while I was ducking school and running wild. She saved us from my dad but she couldn't save me from herself. I kept on at her to quit boozing. I kept on at her for months, years. But she wouldn't listen. In the end I gave up trying.

'Maybe you don't care,' Maggie said. 'But you are curious. When you left for Vietnam, you were someplace between blame and guilt over what happened with your mom. I don't believe you ever resolved that.'

'I don't need to. Not any longer.'

She went into the kitchen and filled the kettle from the faucet. When she came back she said, 'How long is it since you saw your dad?'

'I care even less about him.'

My dad had been beating my mom since before I was born, though he never laid a finger on me. In his lighter moods, he'd play with me, take me fishing or hiking. One time he snuck me down the coal mine where he worked and told me with a proud smile that I could follow in his footsteps. But that never happened. My dad died the day he got laid off at the mine. He kept on breathing, but everything vital stayed a thousand feet under the earth. Even as a kid I saw the wrongness of that hard-living guy with his bodybuilder physique moping about the house while my mom became the breadwinner, sewing garments in a sweatshop for not much more than nothing. Soon after that, my dad started beating her oftener and harder. He'd have killed her if she hadn't left him.

'I haven't been back to Fayetteville since 1954,' I said. 'And don't intend to.'

Maggie was like a dog with a bone. 'You should think about it.'

Finally I lit my cigarette. 'If you're trying to give me incentives to quit Vietnam, it's not working. I'd sooner stay there forever than go back to that shitty little coal town.'

'Maybe you could go back with JoBeth Medlock. I gather she's from the next town down.'

She ambushed me there, no argument. I tried to hide my surprise.

'How do you know where she's from?'

'I pulled an archive clip.'

'Wait a minute.' I gave her a suspicious frown. 'How do you know who she is?'

Maggie smiled. 'Geraldine Gomez pinned the pair of you at the India Pavilion last night. She recognized your date from a feature we ran last month about the US Attorney's Office.' Maggie made a teasing expression. 'Geraldine told me you didn't notice her because you were so into your friend.'

Geraldine was a hawk-eyed gossip columnist who made a handsome living from chronicling the tittle-tattle of Manhattan society.

I took a long drag on my cigarette. 'I got to hand it to you, Maggie, nothing happens in this town without you getting to know real fast.' I was a little irritated at having been clocked by Geraldine, but at least the mention of JoBeth brought us back to the reason we were having this meeting: The Ramskill shootings.

I explained that JoBeth wasn't a date but my new partner. Then I brought Maggie up to speed on the meeting with Westerby and the latest developments at Ramskill.

'You can't say you don't need the help,' she said. 'And your new partner is a resourceful operator. I read the clips. She's led some major investigations and prosecuted an impressive list of convictions.' She gave me a mischievous glance. 'I saw her picture too, which may explain why Geraldine thought you were on a date.'

I ignored the jibe. But I did make a mental note to check out the *Examiner's* archive. I was convinced there was more to JoBeth Medlock than met the eye. Maybe the clippings would give me a hint.

She went back to the kitchen and returned with two cups of Earl Grey tea, which she knew I liked. 'So, have the pair of you come up with any sort of working theory?'

I accepted my tea from her and took a drink. 'We think Oleg Bobkov was the sniper's mark; Gordon Richardson became collateral when the shooter missed with his first shot; but he made sure of Bobkov with his second. It's also possible, but highly unlikely that the shooter hit Boyd Brigstock as well. But we'll have a better idea when those test results come back.'

She swallowed some Earl Grey. 'You know, of course, that the Brigstock boy's mom is an ambitious House Democrat?'

I nodded. 'The family background was in the clips you mailed me.'

She placed her cup on the low table. 'What wasn't in those clips is a story that broke this morning. The Soviets have called for an emergency session of the Security Council over the invasion of Cambodia. The council will convene sometime next week and Harriet Brigstock will attend as a congressional representative. She has considerable influence on Capitol Hill and will certainly have something to say on Cambodia.'

I stubbed out my cigarette and told her about Corey Quilton and SLUT, in particular how he'd admitted pressing Boyd Brigstock to lobby his mom about pulling out of Cambodia.

'You think this guy Quilton was trying to intimidate Boyd?'

'He makes no bones about it. Then again, he makes no bones about wanting to destroy the university, kill all cops, and tear down every capitalist institution in the country.'

'Small ambitions then.'

'Question is, how much of it is hot air. Ramskill campus is full of radical posturing. Some of it's part of a genuine desire to build a fairer world; some is pretentious bullshit; and some is malicious and violent. What we should be asking is whether Corey Quilton, or somebody like him, was capable of shooting Boyd Brigstock to get to his mom?'

'How would that tie in with Bobkov and the incident at the Biomedical Centre?'

I shrugged. 'I really don't know. Maybe there is no tie-in. But the Boyd Brigstock angle is worth looking into.'

She finished her tea. 'Then perhaps you and your new partner should be talking to Harriet Brigstock.'

TWENTY-ONE

I rendezvoused with JoBeth at the flagpole in Battery Park. We had a quarter of an hour to spare so we walked to the waterfront. The morning was hazy, with faint dazzles playing lazy on the sullen water of the Upper Bay. Out past the fortress-like Immigrant Building on Ellis Island, I could make out the Statue of Liberty, a pale green stab on the skyline.

She leaned on the iron railing and gave me a sideways look. We'd discussed what we were about to do on the phone and I sensed the reservations she expressed earlier hadn't gone away. Just the opposite.

'Boyd Brigstock as the sniper's main target doesn't stack up,' she said. 'Not alongside Oleg Bobkov's death and the homicides at the biomedical place. They must be linked, but I can't see any sort of connection with the Brigstock kid.'

'There might not be one. We could be looking at two totally unrelated incidents, but we'll know more when we get the results from the firearms lab.' I threw her an inquisitive glance. 'When's that likely to be?'

She waggled a downturned palm. 'How long is a bit of string? Right now the guns are being held in the campus police evidence room. Your pal Gene Ducey won't turn them over to the FBI without a judicial order. And guess what, my people are still trying to get hold of a judge.'

A Liberty Island visitor ferry was leaving the jetty and I waited until the noise of its engines subsided. 'In that case, where's the harm in looking at the Brigstock situation while we wait? If it's a dead end, fine. We can put it down as a tragic accident and move on.'

'OK,' she said. 'So tell me what you got on Harriet Brigstock.'

I watched the visitor ferry as it butted across the grey water. 'Aged fifty-one and the Democratic representative for New York's 18th congressional district since 1957. Sits on a number of committees including House Appropriations, Armed Services and Oversight. Her politics are left-leaning, but she's no radical. Came up in a poor neighbourhood in Brooklyn and married into money. Widowed eight years ago when her husband George died of a heart attack. She's now the sole proprietor of the family business – a substantial insurance brokerage specialising in marine commerce.'

'Losing her only son must have hit her particularly hard.'

'You'd think so. But Harriet Brigstock is tough. I was a crime reporter before Vietnam, so I didn't have much to do with her, but the newsroom scuttlebutt said she was she was an old-school, streetfighting politician.'

'She'll have enemies then.'

'Lots. Vocal supporter of civil rights, organized labour, women's equality, and gay rights. On the flipside, she's an outspoken critic of the arms race, the Washington lobbying system and big corporations with their snouts in the taxpayer trough. She's pissed off a lot of folks for a lot of years.'

Medlock glanced round as a bunch of saffron-robed

Hare Krishnan monks rolled past, apparently on their way to the ferry terminal. When they were gone, she turned back to me. 'I guess it's time to go.'

We walked away from the waterfront toward Bowling Green and the southern end of Broadway.

'One other thing,' I said. 'She has a special dislike for reporters and lawyers.'

'This won't be an easy conversation, will it?'

'No it won't.'

*

It wasn't.

This much became clear when we were shown into the offices of Brigstock Marine Insurance at 26 Broadway – a massive neoclassical building with a curved façade that followed the arc of the street. It was known as the Rockefeller address until the Rockefellers decamped in 1933, and this slender link proved our only asset.

'I agreed to see you as a courtesy to the governor,' the congresswoman said. 'Nelson Rockefeller is a personal friend. But I'm a busy woman. You got five minutes and I'll throw you out the moment I smell bullshit.'

She was a short tubby woman with a helmet of stiff blonde hair and a rutted face that made her look a good few years older than she was. Her eyes were small and darting, constantly alert. She lit a new cigarette from the butt of an old one and I got a glimpse of nicotine-yellow teeth. Her nylon skirt suit was crumpled and cookie crumbs were lodged in the creases. All told, she did not look a picture of health.

We followed her from the reception area into her office – a big space with stylish décor and furniture that seemed at odds with its frowzy occupant. In some ways I was surprised she was back at work so soon after the death of her only son. In some ways, though, I wasn't. I'd seen this sort of reaction in the Nasty. Someone's close buddy would field a big one and they'd carry on as if nothing happened. Maybe it was denial, maybe the distraction of routine, maybe something of both.

She sat in a swivel chair behind a leather topped desk and gestured for us to sit in the two visitor seats opposite. 'The governor told me you're investigating the death of my son. What do you want from me?'

JoBeth spoke up first. 'We believe there may be suspicious circumstances surrounding Boyd's death.'

'I've been through all this with the FBI and the local police – the guy on campus and the city cop.' Harriet Brigstock sounded bored and frustrated. 'I have nothing to tell you that I didn't already tell them.'

I said, 'You heard of an organisation called SLUT, ma'am? It stands for Socialists for Liberation, Understanding and Tolerance –'

'I know what it stands for, son. They're just a bunch of spoiled kids full of hot air looking for attention.'

'We know from the leader of their Ramskill chapter that they were putting pressure on Boyd. They wanted him to get you to about withdrawing from Cambodia.'

She gave me a strangely amused look. 'You think I'd have taken political advice from Boyd?'

I wasn't going to get distracted. 'That's not the issue, ma'am. The issue is whether the SLUT people *thought* you might.'

'How can you take those folks seriously? Boyd shouldn't have. I mean they're –'

'Did they threaten him?'

I was surprised at JoBeth's intervention – and so was Brigstock.

The congresswoman said nothing. She stared back at JoBeth, face blank. The only parts of her that moved were the never-still eyes. I sensed she was deciding whether to give us a straight answer or have us tossed onto the street.

JoBeth took another swing, 'Did SLUT threaten *you*?'

That landed a hit, no question. Never thought I'd see this hard-bit politico with the wind taken out of her sails, but that's exactly what Medlock had done.

'Now look, Miss Medlow, I know you have a job to do but – '

'Med*lock*. And please answer my question.' My partner had Brigstock pinned to the wall, and she wasn't going to let go.

And I thought, wow, this is something.

When the congresswoman spoke again, her voice was sapped, her expression weary. 'Over the years I've ruffled enough feathers to supply a pillow factory. So I'm used to threats. I get them every week, sometimes every day. But if I let them get in the way of my work I'd never get anything done. Compared to some of the threats I've received these SLUT kids are lame.'

I sensed JoBeth needed support. 'Maybe they are, ma'am. But Miss Medlock and I really believe you should at least consider the possibility that they're not.'

I waited for a reaction, but Brigstock said nothing so I pressed on. 'How does this sound for the *Examiner's* next lead story: "The son of a congressional representative to the UN Security Council was shot dead after being hounded to influence his mother by revolutionary activists. The death of Boyd Brigstock on Ramskill University Campus followed a series of threats against him and his congresswoman mom, by extreme left wing group SLUT."'

I let the words hang.

Then I said, 'Doesn't sound so lame to me, ma'am. I'm sorry, but something stinks about the way Boyd died. You need to talk to us. Tell us what you didn't tell the Bureau and local law enforcement.'

She leaned to one side and opened a drawer in her desk, producing a scruffy sheet of notepaper and shoving it across the desk.

JoBeth picked it up and held it so we could both read it. The message had been typed using an old ribbon that produced faint, fuzzy-edged letters. It was headed SLUT – Socialists for Liberation, Understanding and Tolerance. Underneath this, it read: *Your son Boyd is known to us. He is in danger. For his sake you must do everything in your power at the UN Security Council to end Nixon's unlawful invasion of Cambodia and get US troops out of Vietnam*. There was no signature, no date.

'Clever,' JoBeth said. 'The message is clear but the threat is veiled.'

Brigstock lit another cigarette. 'That's why I didn't tell anybody.'

But she sounded as if she was trying to convince herself rather than JoBeth or me.

'This Security Council meeting,' I said. 'What's going to happen?'

'Nothing that's not totally predictable.' She took a drag

on her cigarette and exhaled slow so the smoke curled out from her mouth and nostrils. 'The Soviets and the Chinese will produce a draft resolution calling for us to get out of Cambodia; we'll use our veto; nothing will change in Indochina.'

'So what's the point of the Security Council convening at all?' I realized this came over as naive, but I wanted Brigstock to reach her own conclusion.

'A Security Council session is a global platform,' she said. 'The meetings are used for the purpose of international public relations. Typically, the people tabling a resolution look like the good guys, and those vetoing it are the black hats.'

'And in this case?'

'There may be a perception among certain members of the international community that the Soviets and Chinese are trying to thwart an act of naked aggression by the US against a small country like Cambodia.'

'So would it be fair to say the rhetoric of the meeting will likely affect international relations? For example, the Soviets and Chinese will gain influence in some countries – especially non-aligned ones – while the stock of the US will probably fall?'

She examined her half-smoked cigarette and nodded.

I gave her another nudge. 'What if an American representative to the Security Council publicly supported the Sino-Soviet draft resolution?'

She made a hacking laugh. 'Look, son, I may be against invading Cambodia and sure, the war in Vietnam can't end soon enough. But I'm not going to break ranks by endorsing a propaganda stunt by our strategic enemies.'

'What if you did?' I leaned forward. 'What if you spoke

up in favour of the Sino-Soviet resolution? At the Security Council meeting, or afterward on the steps of the UN building, or in my newspaper office?'

'That would never happen.'

'Indulge me, ma'am.'

She smoked her cigarette almost to the filter and used it to light a fresh one. Then she looked from me to JoBeth and back again. 'There'd be hell to pay. Opposing Cambodia in Congress is one thing. Actively siding with the communist powers at the UN would be the end of my career. Having said that, I'd be a hero in Peking and Moscow – the Ruskies might even give me the Order of Lenin.'

I said, 'They probably would.'

Brigstock was starting to sound tetchy again. 'But this is all absurdly hypothetical.'

I sat back. 'It is to you and us. But think about it from the perspective of SLUT. They know you as a firebrand left-of-centre Democrat. They know you don't agree with Cambodia. And they know you lost your son when the establishment cracked down on a protest against Nixon's invasion of that country. On Planet SLUT, that's a perfect cocktail for pressuring you to go rogue and damn the consequences.'

The dark darty eyes were back in action. 'What the hell are you suggesting?'

I said, 'If somebody from SLUT had gotten hold of a sniper rifle and took up a position close to the National Guard, they could have shot your son and made it look like the soldiers did it. From SLUT's point of view, that might be enough to push you over the edge – particularly in tandem with their little notes of encouragement.'

She said nothing.

JoBeth took over with the questions. 'Did you receive anything from SLUT after Boyd died?'

The congresswoman made a resigned expression, took out another sheet of paper and slid it across the desk.

JoBeth placed it on her knee so we could both read it. Again, it was headed SLUT and was written in the same faded type as the earlier note: *Your son has been murdered by Nixon's fascist state. We feel your pain. We rage against this injustice. Do what's right by him. Go to the Security Council and get the USA out of Cambodia.* As with the previous letter there was no signature and no date.

'There have been more like it.' The congresswoman looked miserable. 'They started arriving the day after Boyd was killed and they haven't stopped.'

'As a mother, that must be tough to deal with,' JoBeth said.

Brigstock stabbed out her cigarette in a congested ashtray. She was angry again, but this time not with JoBeth and me. 'I deal with their stuff – along with the other crap I get from scores of other loony tunes – by *not* dealing with it. By ignoring it and getting on with my work.'

She looked at JoBeth. 'But you're right. It is tough. I lost my only son two weeks ago and these bastards are trying to make political capital out of it.'

For the first time the politician fell away, laying bare the face of a grieving mother.

We came in here as a longshot. But after what Harriet Brigstock revealed, the idea that Corey Quilton and SLUT were involved in Boyd's death seemed seriously plausible.

TWENTY-TWO

I met JoBeth at O. Henry's Steakhouse at West 4th Street and 6th Avenue in Greenwich Village and we got an outdoor table under a candy-stripe canopy. The early evening was warm and it was fun to watch the bohemian street scene. My plan was to repay her for buying me dinner at the India Pavilion, but she wouldn't hear of it so we ended up going Dutch.

After leaving Harriet Brigstock's office, I'd spent the rest of the day talking to Westerby and Maggie, while JoBeth reported back to the US Attorney's office. We all agreed the congresswoman's disclosures meant the death of her son and the possible involvement of SLUT needed further investigation. Of course Maggie was also aware of the news angle I'd suggested to Harriet Brigstock. But she always said getting a story right trumped getting it first and she didn't deviate from this. In return, Westerby and JoBeth agreed I'd get to write an exclusive when we had control of the facts.

We'd finished our coffee and I was about to ask if she wanted a refill when I pinned the stocky guy in the worsted business suit hustling along the opposite sidewalk. Something familiar about his gait made me look again, closer.

'What's *he* doing here?'

I must have said this out loud because in my peripheral vision I noticed JoBeth throw me a funny look.

I did a double-take. But there was no mistaking that heavy hippo head with its small ears and cinderblock jaw. Colonel Philip Sheridan Riley II was the very last person I'd have expected to see in the hip and happening environs of Greenwich. For a chunky fella, he was slaloming with surprising agility along the crowded sidewalk, his tie flapping loose over his shoulder. This urgency tweaked my curiosity.

Without really thinking, I took out my wallet, slapped a ten spot on the table and took off after him.

'Where the hell are you going?' JoBeth was at my side.

I was struggling to keep pace with the big man. If it hadn't been for the coat and tie in the sea of denim and psychedelic paisley, I'd have lost him.

'See the big guy up ahead in a suit and tie?'

She bobbed along next to me. 'Just about. What about him?'

'He's the colonel commanding the 55th Infantry Regiment – the senior National Guard officer at Ramskill Campus on the day of the shootings.'

'Why are we following him?'

'I don't know. Something odd is going down. He's an establishment square in the most anti-establishment part of the city.'

'It's a free country.'

'Call it instinct.' I was getting irritated by this distraction. 'I can see you back at O. Henry's if you want.'

She tugged my sleeve. 'I want to come along, but let's do this right. I'm assuming you've met him and therefore he could make you.'

'True, but he's in too much of a hurry to look over his shoulder.'

'Even so, better if I take the lead. You can follow behind.'

This made sense. And I didn't need convincing about her tradecraft because she'd already surveilled me without my knowing. So I did what she said and dropped back fifteen yards.

I could no longer eyeball Riley but tracked JoBeth as she turned left into Jones Street. This was the place where *The Freewheelin' Bob Dylan* album cover had been photographed in '63. A couple were posing for a photo as Dylan and Suze Rotolo, his then-girlfriend, as the three of us intruded in their painstakingly framed shot. The guy taking the picture called me an asshole and came after me, waving his camera. I quickened my pace. Last thing I needed now was a bust up on Bob Dylan Boulevard. I called a hurried apology over my shoulder and, thankfully, the girl pulled him back.

JoBeth stopped at the corner with Bleecker Street, and I hung back. I guessed Riley had paused, possibly trying to get his bearings in what was probably unfamiliar territory.

The other possibility was that he'd made JoBeth.

The odds were slim. Even so …

I counted to ten. Still no movement.

She glanced over her shoulder and made an I-dunno shrug.

Then she was moving again, along Bleecker and across the 7th Avenue intersection. Our weird little procession moved quickly to Bleecker and Grove, where the mystery tour ended.

JoBeth beckoned me to join her. From where we stood on the street corner, we could see Riley standing on the sidewalk outside Luciano's Coal Oven. I'd known the place well since the late 50s. It was a pizza restaurant with well-worn wooden booths, kooky paintings and a jazz trio hunkered down in one corner – and absolutely not the sort of place I'd have expected Riley to visit.

He continued hanging around outside, looking every inch a fish out of water. For guys like Riley, the generation gap was a chasm. He must have had a powerful reason to cross it.

JoBeth touched my arm. 'Looks like he's got a date.'

I saw a slim east Asian woman, early to mid-twenties, cross the street and approach Riley with her arms outstretched. He returned the gesture and they embraced.

They went into the restaurant. We kept our distance.

A few minutes later we saw them being shown to a cosy window booth. He reached out and took her hand. They chatted and laughed. Wine was served, they chinked glasses.

This was mindblowing.

Colonel Philip Sheridan Riley II, married with two grown up kids, was apparently having an affair with a woman who must have been half his age or younger.

JoBeth looked at me hard. 'What do you think this means?'

'I don't know, but it wouldn't go down too well with his wife and daughters.'

She guided me back down the street, out of Riley's line of sight. 'After Ramskill, I can't imagine the governor being too impressed either. That girl may well have been born and raised in the USA, but what if she's a Chinese national? Vietnamese? Hell, she could even be Cambodian.'

She wasn't wrong. There could be an innocent explanation, though I couldn't imagine what it might be.

'This is something else we need to look into some more,'

she said. 'But there's nothing we can do right now. They could be in there for hours.'

'So what do we do?'

She smiled. 'Wanna catch some live music? I know some people who might get us in someplace in Greenwich.'

*

We went to see Joni Mitchell play the Bitter End at 147 Bleecker Street.

It was one of the hottest venues in town and by the time we arrived the place was jumping. Capacity was only 230, but big name artists loved the intimate space, the audience interaction and the righteous acoustics.

We got drinks at the bar and found a table near the front. Joni was in great voice, her songs juicing up the part of my brain that ran on fumes most of the time. When she took a break, we got a double round of drinks, and when she finished her encore, we got more drinks, and more.

Fair to say that by the time we left, we were loaded.

JoBeth linked her arm through mine as I walked her back to her place, a half mile away on Christopher Street.

I waited while she rummaged in her purse for her key. When she found it, she opened the front door and looked over her shoulder, 'Want to come up?'

I said sure.

We rode an old-style cage elevator up to her fourth floor apartment. The living room was tastefully furnished with a mid-blue fabric couch and armchairs, Turkish carpet on wooden flooring, and a lot of potted plants – yucca, Chinese pancake, asplenium, even a Tonkin maple.

'Should we continue were we left off?' She produced Joni's *Ladies of the Canyon* album.

I said yeah, and she placed the record on the turntable of her stereo system.

'You know you'll need to find this guy a home outdoors at some point?' I rubbed the Tonkin maple's thick waxy leaves. 'Could grow up to forty feet.'

She crossed the room as *Morning Morgantown* filled it. The song title was somewhat at odds with the time of day, but it still sounded good.

A puzzled frown wrinkled her brow. 'How come you know that?'

'I know a lot about plants – especially in Indochina. Spend as much time as I do in the boonies of Vietnam, you get to know them on first name terms.'

She was standing real close and I picked up scents of apricot and musky vanilla. 'I like it that you know strange stuff. I think it's cool.'

'I like it that you're the opposite of cool.'

Our faces were less than twelve inches apart. I saw tiny gold flecks in her pale eyes.

She made a playful expression. 'So what does that make me?'

'Hot.'

She edged nearer then stopped, her mouth a few inches from mine. 'Too hot to touch?'

'Only one way to know.'

I locked my lips on hers. She kissed me back, fierce and wanting.

We got each other's clothes off without breaking the kiss, then she led me into her room and we tumbled together onto the bed. We'd had a good deal to drink, but not enough to numb our senses. We went to it sharp and agile and unrelenting. Then we did it again, and again, finally falling away, lying on our backs and gazing at the dim outline of the ceiling.

'You OK?' she asked.

'Yeah.' I took her hand and pulled her close so her head was resting on my chest.

'Me too,' she said.

TWENTY-THREE

I drove back to Ramskill early the next morning. JoBeth had some business to take care of in Manhattan and said she'd see me the next day on campus.

I was travelling against the rush-hour traffic so the journey was easy.

I wasn't though.

She'd made pancakes for breakfast and we chatted as we ate, parting with a kiss. On the face of it, we were upbeat about what happened the previous night. We agreed it had been a blast and that we needed to do it again soon. But neither of us suggested a date. Maybe we felt a little awkward because we had to work together.

Maybe it was something else that neither of us wanted to talk about.

For my part, I honestly didn't know what wasn't right, only that something wasn't. My track record for relationships wasn't great. In fact, my track record just wasn't. Most of the time I did one night stands and I'd never seen any woman longer than a few weeks, which I put down to my attachment issues. I really liked JoBeth. Maybe I liked her too much and on a subconscious level didn't want to make her another casualty of my emotional failings.

I sensed there was something on her side too but there was nothing I could do, at least for now.

I spent the rest of the day preparing for my next seminar, which would undoubtedly bring me back into contact with Corey Quilton. I asked about him around the Journalism Department and the feedback from other teachers was unanimous: He was a disruptive pain in the ass. One frustrated professor told me Quilton was an exceptionally bright PhD student who tailored his academic work to suit the needs of SLUT. When his revolutionary commitments were demanding, he only registered for one course – last semester this had been in basket-weaving, which he attended one day a week. In this way, he boosted his free time while retaining his rights as a student to move freely around the campus.

This was useful information. It reflected the depth of Quilton's commitment, showed he was a true believer, a flat out zealot. Question then became: What *wouldn't* he do for the cause? Enlist an assassin to zap Boyd Brigstock? Or even pull the trigger himself?

This was another question that would have to wait.

In the meantime, I went back to my hotel, freshened up and snuck out again without encountering the formidable Violet Vinson or her downtrodden husband.

I spent a couple of hours in a friendly bar on the edge of town, drinking beer, reading the newspapers, and listening to radio coverage of the New York Yankees game against the Detroit Tigers.

I was on my way back to the hotel when I spotted the slim figure moving toward a pony in a small paddock next to a family home. The pony was standing at the gate, as if it was used to getting petted by passers-by.

It was almost dark and the absence of street lights made it difficult to make out any detail, but as I got closer I saw the guy was wearing dark pants, a roll neck sweater and a wool hat.

Something about the way he was closing in on the pony snagged my attention.

Something told me he wasn't going to feed it carrots.

I moved closer still. As a Special Forces operator, stealth was totally my bag. But somehow he sensed my presence and wheeled around.

The stand-off was just long enough for me to realize he was black.

Then he came at me with fast, efficient strikes aimed at my head. I'd been expecting him to run, not fight and the onslaught took me by surprise. All I could do was block the meaty blows he threw at me. I backed off, the sides of my forearms sore from parrying, but without serious injury. I circled back and forth, weighing him up, seeking an opportunity of my own. I spotted one when he glanced sideways, as if looking for an avenue of retreat, and launched a T-kick to his thigh. I felt the sole of my foot connect, but he'd seen it coming and pivoted to reduce the impact. If I hurt him, he didn't show it. Just the reverse. He stepped up and levelled a corkscrew punch at my jaw. The guy was quick, no argument. But in that moment I forced my brain to slow right down. I leaned left, watched his gloved fist shoot past my head with two inches to spare. He was right at the end of his reach and this exposed his wrist between the glove and the cuff of his sweater.

Something was wrong. Skin on his wrist was white. But the guy was black. It didn't compute.

I countered with a strike with the heel of my right hand. He anticipated and ducked, but not quite enough. My blow glanced off his brow, knocking the wool hat off his head as he staggered back. I pressed my advantage, throwing myself on top of him and wrestled him to the ground. We landed on a soft grassy patch near the paddock fence, rolling over and over. This close it was impossible to land targeted strikes, but it didn't stop him trying. I felt his fists hammering the side of my head. I rammed my brow against his cheekbone. It was a half-assed head butt but it did give me some relief from the short punches.

And it opened up a truly weird sight: His face was black but his ear was white.

Just as shocking, the top third of it was missing. Moonlight played briefly on serrated scar tissue where the flesh had been hacked or bitten off.

Then he wriggled to one side and slammed his knee into my side. Half-winded, I couldn't keep hold of him. In a New York second he was on his feet, running with a limp into the night. I came to my feet, wheezing, but just couldn't get enough air into my lungs to go after him.

*

Next morning I woke up with painful bumps on the side of my head that made me wince when I ran a comb through my hair. My forearms were sore too where I'd blocked those blows. I swallowed a couple of aspirin and went downstairs for some breakfast.

For once I was glad to see Violet Vinson. As she stood by my table, pouring me a cup of coffee, I asked her about the snooper her neighbours had spotted. I was particularly keen to find out if they noticed any details.

She stood back, holding the Pyrex coffee jug and looking at the ceiling. After some time she said, 'As I recall, Bill Schwartz told me the fella was tall and slim, dressed in dark clothes. His wife thought he was wearing some sort of hat – baseball cap or some suchlike. George and Martha Braddock said the same. But Herb Granger, he reckoned the guy was short and squat. Then again, Herb's short sighted and his memory ain't so good. So I took that with a pinch of salt.'

'Apart from hanging around in the shadows, did this guy threaten your neighbours in any way?'

She shrugged. 'I guess not. In fact, when Bill Schwartz tried to approach him, he backed away fast and disappeared into the woods.'

'Do you know anyone who felt they were being observed, but didn't actually see the guy?'

She nodded vigorously. 'A whole bunch of people said exactly that. Sometimes they heard something, but most of the time they just got this strange sense of someone watching them.'

I said this information was very helpful and thanked her for it.

From the kitchen I heard her husband Emmitt calling for help with the breakfast orders.

Violet ignored him. 'You think this watcher fella is the animal killer, Mr Tyler?'

'I don't know, Mrs Vinson. It's possible.'

'But you're going to write something in the paper?'

'When I've got the facts together, yes.'

She was on her way back to the kitchen when a fresh

thought seemed to enter her head. Half turning, she said, 'Oh, and Nora Stewart said this man had a dark complexion. She wondered if he was a negro.'

This was even more interesting – though not surprising. I was fairly sure Nora Stewart – and probably the others – had seen the same guy I encountered last night. I was also confident this was the individual Chip Amelsfort had glimpsed on the treeline near his farm.

One thing I was certain of: He wasn't black. He was wearing camouflage greasepaint similar to the stuff I daubed on my face for Green Beret night ops. Of course this didn't necessarily mean he had a military background. This became much more likely though when you considered his close quarter fighting skills and the highly attuned hearing that told him I was coming up behind him. But why was a fella with special warfare training sneaking around the outskirts of Ramskill at dusk?

The obvious answer was that he was the animal mutilator. Seeing him closing in on the pony attracted my attention in the first place. Something else: Part of his ear had been severed. From what I'd seen, it had been hacked or bitten off in some savage encounter, quite possibly in Vietnam. Maybe he was the type of guy who collected the ears of dead Viet Cong. Maybe one VC fighter saw him picking up trophies and gave him some of the same. Maybe he'd been traumatized by his disfigurement and developed a crazy compulsion to saw off the ears of animals. First he targeted the sheepdog, then the bunny, then the pony. Sure, I'd stopped him getting to the third critter, but if Marty Robbins was right, sooner or later he'd move to a human victim.

This was where the theory fell short. Because, despite his

fighting skills, his first instinct had been to get away from me. This was also apparently the case when Violet's neighbour Bill Schwartz tried to approach him. Nor had he made any sort of threatening move against any of Violet's other neighbours, or for that matter, Chip Amelsfort. In my experience somebody with a sharp knife and a thirst for blood wouldn't carve open animals but run away from human confrontation. Thinking back to last night, everything the guy did was designed to facilitate a getaway. True, he came at me first. But my guess was that if I'd gone down, he'd have bugged out. Having said that, it wasn't something I'd have wanted to put to the test.

Then there were Violet's neighbours who had a sense of being watched. My gut told me they *were* being watched. The guy must have been moving around the fringes of the town and nearby farms for some time. Mostly, no one saw him and when he was spotted, he backed off. This wasn't the behaviour of a sadistic slasher, rather a reconnaissance specialist.

But why would anyone in their right mind want to reconnoitre the outskirts of Ramskill?

Perhaps that was it: The guy wasn't in his right mind.

So what next?

I ate my breakfast and decided to pay Loretta Hausinger another visit.

TWENTY-FOUR

I called at her campus apartment and a neighbour told me she was back at work. I shouldn't have been surprised. Hausinger was one of the most cussedly determined people I ever came across.

I walked to the Biomed Centre and was approaching the shimmering glass fronted structure when I noticed a dozen men standing in front of the World War II hold-over buildings down the side. They had been painted purple and mauve since I was last here, but if the zany colour scheme was intended to make them looks less like military barracks, it hadn't worked. The guys were equally out of whack with their surroundings. Two were wearing bib overalls, the rest jeans and T-shirts, but they all had a lean, haggard appearance. Most had whiskers, but I got the impression they just hadn't shaved rather than grown a beard. Others had long hair, though it wasn't the look of cultivated dishevelment you saw among the hippies at Rick O'Shea's. More like they couldn't be assed visiting a barber. Difficult to tell ages among all those beards and shaggy manes, though I guessed they were late twenties, early thirties. They were smoking and drinking cans of soda, but there was no joshing or banter. They talked with straight faces, in low voices.

And they reminded me more of prisoners in the exercise yard than workers who just knocked off for their lunch break.

I thought of the rumours I heard from Chip Amelsfort and Violet Vinson – about draftees coming here to get turned into combat-hardened killing machines. But if there was one thing these guys were not, it was raw recruits heading into Vietnam.

One of them was gazing in my direction, as if trying to figure out if he knew me. I looked back at him but he turned away. He was more emaciated than the others, a little shorter. Perhaps we'd met sometime, though I couldn't place him and he didn't seemed eager to engage in any sort of conversation.

I went into the main building and asked for Loretta Hausinger, who appeared a few minutes later and showed me to her office.

'You don't let the grass grow,' I said. 'I'm surprised the doctors have allowed you to start working again.'

She gave me a starchy smile. 'I don't need their permission. Besides, I am a doctor myself, remember?'

I felt like saying, *Yeah, but you're not a trauma surgeon.* But there was no point so I kept schtum.

Instead, I told her what happened last night.

She made an expression of mock reproach. 'Sounds like you had quite an ordeal, Wat. Are the doctors happy for *you* to work?'

Touché, I thought. But I wasn't going to get distracted from the purpose of my visit.

'You're sure the guy I tangled with couldn't have come from this place?'

She gave me a tut-tut look. 'You been listening to that scuttlebutt in Ramskill again?'

I raised an eyebrow. 'You haven't answered my question.'

She made a long exasperated sigh. 'Yes, Wat, I am sure. One hundred per cent sure. Does *that* answer your question?'

'And you never came across a guy with part of his ear missing?'

'Never.'

I held her gaze. 'On my way into the building, I saw a bunch of guys outside those wooden hold-over buildings. Who are they?'

She gave me a you-gotta-be-kidding-me look. 'You think you were attacked by one of our janitors? A mop and bucket guy? Or maybe a lawnmower man?'

I said nothing, waited.

'You're serious aren't you?' There was a note of incredulity in her voice.

'They didn't look like janitors or groundskeepers.'

She gave me a challenging stare. 'What exactly do janitors and groundskeepers look like?'

I was getting a little irritated by this verbal fencing, but I kept my voice friendly. 'I'll tell you what they *don't* look like, Loretta. They don't look like a bunch of ex-cons.'

'OK, Wat, you got me.' She held up her hands in a gesture of sarcastic surrender. 'The centre has been operating an enlightened recruitment policy for some time. We employ homeless people, folks down on their uppers. And, yes, sometimes some of them have served time.'

She looked at me aggressively. 'Is that so difficult for you to accept?'

I cast my mind back to my first visit to the Biomedical Centre and remembered Hausinger speaking to a janitor, telling him what an excellent job he'd done. That wasn't how you'd expect a research scientist to talk to somebody cleaning the floor. She might have passed the time of day, sure. But I recalled an almost maternal concern about the work he'd done. This rehabilitation employment programme would explain it.

'No, Loretta, it isn't difficult for me at all.' I gave her an olive-branch smile. 'I dig your altruistic attitude. You also give them accommodation in those old buildings?'

She nodded yes. 'They're usually off the street so they need a roof over their heads. But those hold-overs are only a half-way house arrangement. As soon as they have enough money saved, they move into their own places in the community.'

Gotta say, I felt kind of ashamed that I'd regarded this an act of philanthropy as suspicious. It was too bad more employers didn't adopt a similar approach.

'I think I owe you an apology,' I said.

'Accepted.' She smiled. 'On one condition.'

I told her to name it.

Her smile widened. 'Dinner tonight. You pick up the tab.'

*

The place she picked was a soft-lit bistro with a Mediterranean vibe called Le Lavendou on the south side of the city centre.

We were shown to a table in a discreet corner and studied the menu.

Loretta looked cool in an ivory crochet knit dress and I was glad I made an effort by putting on a silk shirt and smart bellbottom pants. I'd put more thought into this than usual because I wasn't sure whether this was meant to be a date or just a friendly meal out. I also wondered how it might look if we bumped into JoBeth. The one night stand at her place wasn't exactly a commitment, but nor was it nothing.

After some time she looked up from the menu card. 'Any more news on Chief Ducey's investigation?'

I told her no, Ducey was still struggling to make progress.

She nodded and her eyes returned to the menu. She seemed anxious for the cops to make an arrest and I got why: There was a real possibility the killer would come back to finish the job.

The waiter returned and we ordered a bottle of house white and asked for the French onion soup to start. For the entrée, I ordered sea bass with sauté potatoes and mixed vegetables, while she opted for the swordfish steak in lemon butter with Niçoise salad.

When the wine had been served she took a big swallow and peered at me over the glass. 'This is the first time I've had a night out since I left the hospital.'

'Then let's drink to that.' I chinked my glass against hers.

She drank more wine and kept her eyes on mine. 'Thanks for coming, Wat. I feel safer when you're around.'

I said I was happy to be here. Clearly she'd cast me in the role of her protector. After my intervention in the shooting at the Biomedical Centre, this was understandable. But it wasn't a real solution. I couldn't be with her every time she went outside her apartment.

'You know Gene Ducey's offer of police protection still stands? You should think about it.'

She shook her head no and took another large gulp of wine. 'I couldn't work with the cops following me everywhere. I couldn't relax.'

Yet she didn't seem particularly relaxed, even with me there. Why else was she knocking back the vino?

I didn't want her half-cut before the soup arrived so I tried to distract her. 'You never told me much about yourself. You're from Cleveland, right? You got family there?'

'Both my parents are retired now. Dad was a dentist, Mom never worked.'

'Brothers and sisters?'

'A brother. He died.'

'I'm sorry. He must have been young.'

'He was.'

This conversation was going no place good so I said I was sorry, I didn't mean to pry.

Another mouthful of wine went the way of the rest. Fortunately the waiter came with the soup and this at least put her booze consumption on hold.

We got through the soup without speaking.

When the dishes had been cleared, she said, 'You weren't prying. It was a natural question. My brother killed himself. And yes, he was young – twenty-eight.'

This bushwhacked me, no argument. What to say? I said nothing, let her fill the silence.

'Peter was quite a bit older than me, but we'd always been close. I was a heartbroken twelve-year-old when he enlisted in the Marines in 1942. I was even more heartbroken when he came home three years later because he wasn't the brother I waved off at the train station.'

I watched her swallow more wine. 'War can do that to people.'

'Peter had become a tortured soul. Agitated, depressed, volatile, unable to concentrate. He wouldn't talk to me or

Mom or Dad or anybody. Whatever version of hell was in his head, he just bottled it up. It got so bad that he couldn't hold his job down. He started drinking, getting into bar fights. Then in 1948, when I was fifteen, he shot himself in the head.'

'That must have been horrible.'

She took a toke at the cigarette, but left the wine glass alone.

'Was that why you became a psychologist?'

She nodded yes. 'I knew then that I had to help people like Peter. I've devoted my life to working with folks with mental health problems.'

'Including veterans with combat fatigue?'

She stubbed out the cigarette. 'These days it's known as acute environmental reaction.'

That stacked up in a way only the US military could make it stack up. Tell a kid's parents their boy is suffering from shell-shock, they'll worry themselves to death. Feed them some wordy euphemism that could mean almost anything, they won't worry so much. That was the theory, yet in some ways the verbal camouflage sounded more sinister than what it was meant to conceal.

But at least I was making progress. For the first time, Loretta had admitted there was a military dimension to her work. Leastways she hadn't denied it.

The conversation was cut short when the waiter brought the main course.

Then the one thing I was hoping wouldn't happen, happened.

JoBeth walked into the bistro with a group of people I recognized from the J-School.

She was looking straight at me.

TWENTY-FIVE

I caught up with JoBeth the following morning as she walked from the parking lot to the J-School. We exchanged pleasantries and then got locked in an awkward silence. I guessed she was making the same calculations I was: Take the bull by the horns, or refuse to acknowledge the bull existed.

I went the bovine route. 'Last night with Loretta Hausinger, that wasn't a date.'

She carried on walking toward the building. 'Why are you telling me this, Wat?'

'Just to be clear.'

'It's none of my business.'

'It's *our* business, though – yours and mine. Unless our bosses have decided otherwise, we're partners, remember?'

She stopped outside the main entrance and gave me a look someplace between puzzled and amused.

I said, 'Taking her to dinner was part of the investigation.'

She made a small smile and I got the impression she was enjoying this. 'You seemed to be investigating her real hard. Get anything useful?'

'As it happens, yeah.'

I told her about my tussle with the guy with the mutilated ear and my subsequent conversation with Loretta.

'I'm glad you're OK, Wat, really I am. And whoever this stalker is, we need to catch him.' Her expression was more friendly now. 'But you don't seem to have got much from Hausinger.'

'I'm sure her research work is related to the military.'

'She told you that?'

'Not in so many words. But she heard the rumours about me losing my shit in Vietnam and showed a sympathetic professional interest. And she became a psychologist in the first place because she wanted to help people like her brother, who took his life due to combat fatigue.'

'It's something to take on board,' she said. 'But we'll need to dig deeper.'

We went through the main doors and up the stairs.

At the top I asked, 'How about you? Did you get anything?'

'Sure did.' She beckoned me into her office. 'Wanna see what I brought back from Manhattan?'

I followed her inside and closed the door.

She produced a manila file from her brief case and handed it to me. 'The FBI lab came back with the firearms test results. You can digest the details at your leisure, but the headline is that none of the bullets that killed Oleg Bobkov and Gordon Richardson were from any of the twelve rifles issued to the National Guard squad that opened fire.'

This was what I'd been hoping for and it came as something of a relief. The cap from the obsolete sniper scope I found in the groundskeeper shack was compelling but not concrete evidence. It was probably manufactured more than twenty years ago and could have gotten to the place I found it in any one of a number of ways. And it could have lain there for years, decades even.

'So the sniper theory holds up,' I said.

'It's looking that way.'

The tone of her voice told me there was more to come – and that it wasn't necessarily good news.

'The lab also confirmed none of the National Guard rifles were used to shoot Boyd Brigstock. But – and this is really, really far-out – that the fatal round was *not* fired from the same gun that killed Bobkov and Richardson.'

I gave her a sharp look. Never saw this coming.

'So what do you figure?' I said.

She threw me a you-tell-me look.

I started thinking aloud. 'Either we're looking at a pair of snipers firing from the same position, which raises all sorts of questions. Or two shooters were operating independently, each with a different target, each unaware of the other's presence. And that raises even more questions. In fact, I can't imagine how it would be possible. What are the chances of two separate hits going down at exactly the same time and in exactly the same place?'

'Astronomical,' she said. 'And then some.'

I chewed on this some more. 'Another alternative is one sniper, two rifles.'

'That really would be stupid crazy.'

'Stupid crazy is the order of the day,' I said. 'Unless the whole idea was to leave us unable to figure out who was shooting who and why.'

She perched on the corner of her desk and made a worried frown. 'What really concerns me is the resources that must have been put into this. A few days back our only theory was some of the guardsmen fired low, probably without intending to. Now we're looking at the assassination of two entirely different individuals – Oleg Bobkov and Boyd Brigstock – for motives that must also have been entirely different.'

'Not to mention the triple homicide and attempted murder at the biomedical place,' I said. 'That's got to be linked to Bobkov's death. Whoever was behind that has taken out four members of a five-strong research team and narrowly missed a full house.'

She walked around the desk and sat in the leather chair. 'Tell me what you're thinking?'

'The KGB is the most obvious possibility.'

'But why would the Soviets want Boyd Brigstock dead?'

'They probably wouldn't. But SLUT might.'

'So, what? The KGB subcontracted the work to Corey Quilton? He took out Bobkov, then used the opportunity to shoot the Brigstock boy and pressure his mom into breaking ranks over Cambodia? If it worked, that would be a big win for the Soviets at the Security Council.'

'It's a massive *if*,' I said. 'You heard what Harriet Brigstock said about career suicide if she sided with the Russians at the UN. And to combine two diverse operations would be flat out bizarre. Especially for the KGB. Those guys are meticulous. They leave nothing to chance. Farming out important work to amateurs absolutely isn't their bag.'

'It would explain a lot though.'

I looked at my watch. 'Look, I have a seminar in fifteen minutes. Wanna hook up for lunch?'

She shook her head. 'I got stuff to do. Mind if I take a rain check?'

I made an even smile. 'Of course not.'

*

My seminar on developing news sources went well. Quilton wasn't there so there were no interruptions, which helped a lot. On the other hand, I'd been hoping to ask him about those notes from SLUT to Harriet Brigstock – before and after her son's death. That would have to wait.

I grabbed a sandwich and can of soda for lunch, ate on the grass in front of the J-School, then walked to the human resources department in Putney Hall. A friendly young clerk with thick-lens glasses and a pimply complexion greeted me at the front desk. I told him who I was and asked if I could look at the employment records for the Biomedical Centre.

Ever so respectfully, he told me the records were confidential. This was what I expected, but it was worth asking.

I was turning toward the door when he added, 'I couldn't have helped you anyway, sir. See, the Biomedical Centre recruits its own staff and keeps its own records.'

I looked back. 'Would that include janitorial and groundskeeping workers?'

The clerk nodded. 'As far as I know, sir, they handle all their hiring internally.'

I recalled what Hausinger said about the Biomedical Centre's right-on recruitment policy of giving jobs to homeless folks and those down on their luck. And I started thinking about fresh possibilities.

At the centre I asked the receptionist for Loretta, but she wasn't there. This was what I expected because she told me last night she had an eighty mile drive to a symposium at Princeton University. I asked to use the restroom and was handed a temporary pass allowing me into the office area where the staff facilities were located.

Next I went back to my office and waited.

By 6.30pm, the campus was quiet and I made my way back to the biomedical place, moving along the right side of the building to the men's restroom window, which I'd left a half inch ajar. It was six feet above the ground and a tight squeeze, but after an uncomfortable few minutes wriggling and twisting I got through.

The administration office was right next to the men's restroom. The door was locked but easy enough to open with my lock picks. Once inside, I looked along the rows of metal file cabinets until I found one marked Staff Records. The file cabinet lock presented a bigger challenge than the one on the door – until I spotted a row of keys with colour-coded plastic fobs hanging from hooks behind the manager's desk. Each one housed a cardboard tab on which some diligent worker had written which lock the key was for.

Moments later I slid open the Staff Records cabinet.

The janitorial staff files were at the back of the lowest drawer and I counted twenty. Sitting on the floor, with my back against the next cabinet, I started looking through each one.

A mugshot of the worker was glued to the top right corner of his file and I recognised some of the guys I'd seen yesterday outside the hold-over buildings. Loretta was right about their backgrounds – many had been homeless, most had registered for benefits, and all had had his fair share of bad luck.

But Loretta *hadn't* told me one crucial fact.

It didn't hit me immediately. But after I'd scanned the

first five files, the pattern began to emerge. I screwed up my brow, went back to the first file to check I hadn't misread it. Then, the second and back through to the fifth.

No mistake: They'd all served in the Nasty.

I'd looked at another nineteen files. Each one contained details of a veteran who'd fallen on hard times after coming back from Vietnam.

I flipped open the last of the twenty files, knowing what to expect.

But I didn't expect what I saw. I looked closer, closer still, even closer than that, until my nose was almost touching the photo. There was no doubt though: I was looking at a mugshot of a guy who'd lost part of his right ear – the guy I'd fought near the pony paddock.

TWENTY-SIX

Another disturbing awareness materialized.

I'd seen the guy before I fought him.

Way before.

He was a handsome fella with thick fair hair, azure eyes and smooth features. A glance at the details on his job application form told me he was twenty-eight. And he looked more like a singer in a rock band than a janitor. Even as the notion came to mind I realized I'd thought it before. I was looking at the cleaner Loretta talked to when she showed me to her office the first time I visited the biomedical place. I hadn't noticed part of his ear was missing, but then I was looking at him from the opposite side. I recalled her making a special point of praising his work. I recalled thinking how unusual that was. Looking back, it was more like the concern a doctor might show for a patient. Then I remembered how old Loretta's brother was when he committed suicide, three years after the end of World War II. Like this guy, he was twenty-eight.

I thought again.

And I wondered if her concern was more sisterly than doctorly.

It also occurred to me that Loretta had lied to my face when I asked her if she knew a guy with a mutilated ear.

This shocked me. I didn't trust people easily, but I thought I could trust her. Seemed I couldn't have been more wrong.

The name of the guy whose file I was reading was Andy Stuivermans. I looked again at his personnel record, this time paying closer attention to the detail. He served in Vietnam as an Army Ranger, mustering out as a sergeant first class with the Silver Star after three tours. I was even more surprised to read that he was born and raised in New Lots, Brooklyn. He and I would have been youths in the same neighbourhood. He even went to Junior High School 64, just like me. Unlike me, though, Stuivermans went on to graduate high school – something of an achievement for any kid from that part of Brooklyn. I read more: Before Vietnam, it seemed he had a bright future as an electrical engineer, working for a local company. Under the section headed: Hobbies and interests, he'd listed playing guitar and singing in a rock band. He even gave its name: The Rockaways, which I thought was a cool play on words because it referenced the style of music as well as a local Brooklyn beach called Rockaway. I noticed there was no home address, no next-of-kin, no references, and no mention of any employment after he returned from Vietnam six months ago.

I sat there for a while with my back against the file cabinet, turning over the implications of what I just discovered. What it came down to was too many questions and not enough answers. Hell, I had even less than not enough – I had no answers at all.

I needed to get some, fast.

*

JoBeth opened the door to her campus apartment and looked at me warily, as if I'd been drinking and had gotten into some sort of trouble.

I couldn't blame her. I'd ripped my shirt climbing back out of the restroom window and hustled across the campus to her place so I must have looked somewhat sweaty and dishevelled.

I said we had to talk, right now.

She seemed to get the urgency in my tone and showed me in. She got two beers from the refrigerator and I drunk mine down in one then told her what I'd found in the Biomedical Centre personnel files.

She looked at me appalled. 'You can't just break into places, Wat.'

'I just did.'

'But we can't use anything you found as evidence. You should know that much.'

'Sure I do. But if you were to establish probable cause, we could go back later with a search warrant. And in the meantime, we *can* use the information.' I was keen to find out how her prosecutor's mind interpreted my discoveries. 'So what are your thoughts?'

She made a resigned sigh, finished her own beer and brought two more. 'Well, you seem to have identified the guy you tussled with on Sunday night. And he's very likely the stalker the farmer and townsfolks have been talking about. Whether he's the animal mutilator is another matter.'

'The way he was going at that pony, he wasn't planning to stroke it.'

She gave me a dubious look. 'You'd never make that stand up in court. You wouldn't even make it stand up in a news story. I mean, he had no weapon. If he did, surely he'd have used it on you. And at the point the fight started, he wasn't breaking any laws. He could even claim you attacked him.'

She had a point. 'OK, so let's broaden this out. What do those employment records tell us about what's happening at the Biomedical Centre?'

She sipped her beer. 'Unless Loretta Hausinger and her colleagues have a good reason for hiring down-and-outs specifically with a Vietnam background, it seems you were right about there being some military dimension to the work they're doing. We should talk to Hausinger. Maybe she'll be more forthcoming if you threaten to go to Chief Ducey – or even run a news story.'

'She's at some academic function in Princeton and not expected back until tomorrow.'

'Then we wait.'

She walked to the window, as if the pacing would help her to think. 'You said Andy Stuivermans was a Ranger – they're an elite infantry unit, aren't they?'

I nodded. 'In some ways they're similar to Special Forces, in particular, the long range recon patrols they carry out. They're tough guys and slick operators. My guess is the face camo, the dark outfit and the twilight scouting around the edge of town was somehow linked to his activities in Vietnam.'

'You think he's unbalanced?'

'Well, that sure isn't how most folks would spend their spare time.'

I thought of the phrase Loretta had used, the euphemism

for combat fatigue: *Acute environmental reaction*. Was Andy Stuivermans suffering from this?

She said, 'What about the other veterans? Did they have any special warfare training like Stuivermans?'

I shook my head no. 'They all served in combat – bloody actions and close quarter fighting. Also, I'm sure they could handle themselves in any given military situation. But Stuivermans is the stand-out guy. Silver Star, sergeant first class, three tours of duty as a Ranger. In Vietnam he'd have been a distinguished and respected soldier. But it all seems to have turned sour when he came home.'

She gave me a piercing look. 'Something you have very recent experience of.'

I shrugged.

She kept her gaze on me. 'Did any of that stuff make *you* feel bitter, angry, resentful?'

'It's different for me. I'm operating under a cover story.'

'Even so.'

I thought about it. 'Yeah. I guess it did. Especially having people like Riley and Bohannon running their mouths about shit they have no comprehension of.'

And I thought if they could get under my skin, with my emotional anaesthetic, what might people like that do to a more sensitive soul?

Her gaze didn't waver. 'You think Stuivermans was the shooter at the Biomedical Centre?'

'It's possible, even likely. He had a good reason to be in the area at the time. And his Ranger smarts would explain how he got away without leaving a trace. But it wouldn't explain the botched hit. A guy with his experience would have taken out all four people in that room in very short order.'

'Nor, presumably, would he have gone in with just six rounds.'

'I'm not so sure about that. Guy like him, he wouldn't necessarily have needed six. Four marks at close range, he could probably have taken them all out with just as many bullets.'

I frowned.

I frowned harder.

She gave me a curious look. 'What is it?'

Part of me hesitated – the part that still wanted to trust Loretta, at least give her the chance to put her side of the story. But she lost her right to my trust when she denied knowing anybody with a mutilated ear. So I went ahead and laid down my thoughts. 'Perhaps the hit wasn't botched,' I said. 'Perhaps Stuivermans had more ammo, possibly more than one gun.'

'How do you figure that?'

I reminded her how Loretta's brother's suicide spurred her to become a psychologist. I recounted how she'd seemed unusually close to Stuivermans when she'd praised his work as a janitor. And I explained that Peter Hausinger was twenty-eight when he died – Stuivermans' age right now.

JoBeth drank some beer slowly, as if imbibing this information at the same time. At last she said, 'So you think there may have been some brother/sister-type relationship between Hausinger and Stuivermans?'

'Yes I do.'

'And what? He dusted the other three scientists in that conference room, but couldn't go through with killing his sister figure?'

'Worth exploring, wouldn't you say?'

She finished her beer. 'Could Stuivermans have hesitated at the crucial moment, wounding Hausinger instead of killing her? Then lost his nerve completely and bolted?'

'It's possible,' I said. This was pure spitballing, but I often found it helped tease out different ideas and fresh perspectives. 'A variation is that Loretta tried to stop Stuivermans killing the other three and got shot by accident, possibly in some sort of struggle for control of the gun. That might also account for her head wound. She could have fallen down and knocked her head on the table.'

JoBeth crushed her beer can and tossed it in the trash. 'But why would Stuivermans kill the other scientists – Gonzalez, Reese and Poole – in front of Hausinger?'

I gave this some thought. 'What if she wasn't meant to see any of it? She could have walked into that room when she was supposed to be someplace else.'

JoBeth wasn't convinced. 'Covering up a triple homicide would be way beyond the pale. I simply can't imagine someone like Hausinger doing that.'

'I agree it's difficult to swallow. But we should keep in mind that Loretta was devastated by her brother's death. She was only fifteen at the time, but maybe she blamed herself, or thought she should have stopped him. Having failed to save Peter, she might see it as her duty to save Andy.'

'OK,' she said. 'But even if that's true, it doesn't tell us why Stuivermans – or anybody else – wanted Gonzalez, Reese and Poole dead?'

I gave her a direct look. 'Possibly it was the same reason why somebody wanted Oleg Bobkov dead.'

She nodded slowly, then said what I was thinking, 'Could Stuivermans have been the sniper? Could he have shot

Bobkov, then gone into that conference room a week later to finish off the other three?'

'Given his Ranger skills, absolutely.'

She returned to the window, looked out across the campus. 'It still wouldn't explain why.'

'True, but at least we have some new facts and theories to work with.'

She turned back to face me. 'So what next?'

'We wait for Loretta to come back. In the meantime, you could find out if Stuivermans has a rap sheet and I could check out his military record.'

She said she could do this and we agreed to meet again later the next day in hopes of questioning Loretta.

She showed me out and we stood either side of the threshold facing one another.

The tension between us was tripwire-taut.

I didn't know what to say. I didn't know what not to say.

She grabbed a fistful of my shirt, pulled me against her and kissed me long and hard on the mouth.

Then pushed me away.

'I really like you, Wat.' She made a small smile. 'But I don't want to repeat the mistake we made on Sunday.'

I placed one hand on the doorframe and leaned toward her. 'You don't think it was a mistake, though, do you?'

Her smile widened, just a fraction. 'OK, it wasn't a mistake. But it *was* mistimed.'

'It didn't feel that way.'

The smile went away. 'Maybe not. But there's stuff about me you don't know – that you don't want to know, that nobody would.'

'Try me.'

‘I can’t. Not now. Not yet.’ She pushed her fingers through her dark red hair and gave me an imploring look. ‘Look, leave it for now. We’ll talk tomorrow, OK?’

TWENTY-SEVEN

I went to see Loretta late the following morning but she hadn't returned from Princeton. It was a two-hour drive on Interstate 95 so this wasn't surprising. I told the Biomedical Centre receptionist I'd come back later.

Next I called Westerby and updated him, then I called Maggie and did the same. Leaping Larry wouldn't have been happy about that, but if anything happened to me I couldn't necessarily depend on him to give Maggie the whole picture. Sure, he always had my back, but he was a political critter and his first loyalty was always going to be to his own ambition.

He agreed that I should look at Stuivermans' 201 file, the military personnel record that detailed his service history. One of Westerby's contacts at the Pentagon pulled the file and read me the gist on the phone. I wasn't surprised when I heard Stuivermans had sniper training.

Within a few minutes of hanging up with the Pentagon guy, JoBeth called. Stuivermans did have a rap sheet and she'd driven to Manhattan to look at it. All the offences were minor misdemeanours -intoxicated in a public place, disorderly conduct, vandalism. According to the NYPD cops JoBeth talked to, his military record had enabled him to dodge jail time, but he was just one more bust away from stir. No wonder he hadn't worked since he came back from Vietnam. We agreed to do more digging.

I was on my way back to find Loretta when I heard a shout from the student union and saw Corey Quilton jogging toward me.

'How you been, man?' He grinned like we were big buddies. 'Sorry I missed your seminar.'

'Revolution got in the way, did it?'

He fell in step at my side. 'That a negative vibe I detect?'

'That SLUT stuff you sent to Congresswoman Brigstock didn't exactly give off a positive vibe.'

'Hey, I was just doing my job.'

I stopped and turned to him. 'She showed me those notes you sent – and don't deny it was you.'

He shrugged. 'I'm not.'

He had a lotta gall, no argument there.

'In your first note,' I said, 'you claimed Boyd was in danger. How did you know that?'

'We're all in danger, man.' His attitude stayed breezy. 'From Nixon, from the pigs, from the FBI, the CIA, from the whole apparatus of state repression.'

I gave him a hard look. 'Did you or your pals at SLUT have anything to do with Boyd's death?'

'We were right here on campus sticking it to the Man when those National Guard stormtroopers opened fire. So I guess, yeah, we did have something to do with Boyd's death.'

'They opened fire because your people provoked them.'

'We were exercising our constitutional right to protest.'

'You know I'm in the National Guard? What do you think about that?'

'You demonstrated your credentials when you quit Vietnam.' He gave me a sly wink. 'I know you're working some angle.'

I set off walking again. The guy was a puzzle for sure. Was he really smart or really dumb? Full of poison or full of shit? And why did he seem so determined to be my buddy? If I told him I was J Edgar Hoover's favourite nephew, he'd still say I was pulling some deep cover revolutionary stunt.

He bobbed along at my side. 'I'm right, aren't I?'

'Why did you badger Harriet Brigstock after her son died? She showed me the second note you sent – the one alleging Boyd was murdered by the state?'

'But he *was* murdered by the state, wasn't he? That note was a gesture of solidarity, a call to arms – to do something at the Security Council about our illegal invasion of Cambodia.'

I reached the entrance to the Biomedical Centre and turned to go inside.

Over my shoulder I said, 'You're all heart, Corey.'

'Catch you later, Wat.' There was a note of enthusiasm, even excitement in his voice. '*Vive la révolution*!'

*

I was back in my office in the J-school when I got the call to report to Ramskill Armoury. More trouble had started downtown when a group of student protesters pelted state troopers with abuse and rotten fruit. Now I dug why Quilton had been so excited. He must have known something like this was about to happen.

Loretta still hadn't returned from Princeton, which was surprising and a little worrying. But I had other stuff on my mind as I drove around town, rather than through it, to the armoury.

I collected an M1 and ammunition from the armourer and joined the other guys of Bravo Company by the jeeps on the parking lot.

Phipps had been detained in Manhattan and his lieutenants had already deployed their platoons, which left Bohannon in charge of the headquarters unit. As a newly minted buck sergeant, I was his second-in-command.

He watched me approach with a leering smile. 'Good of you to join us, Sergeant Tyler.'

I ignored the jibe.

'Now that we're all here,' he said. 'This is the deal. Mayor McStay has declared martial law and ordered all students to leave the city. We have orders to – '

'The mayor has imposed martial law?' I frowned. 'I'm pretty sure he can't do that.'

'Well I'm pretty sure he just fucking did.' Bohannon seemed to be enjoying this. 'You wanna take it up with the state authorities, Tyler? Or maybe call the White House?'

Again, I said nothing.

Bohannon's gaze returned to the men of Bravo Company. 'As I was saying, we have orders to report to command headquarters in Conroy Park. So if it's all right with the attorney general here' – another glance in my direction – 'we'll mount up and ride in.'

I climbed into the lead jeep with Bohannon.

We drove south toward the city centre but hadn't got very far when we came up behind a slow-moving convoy of six armoured personnel carriers – APCs – with the insignia of the 102nd Cavalry. As we passed them I heard the rattle and squeak of drive sprockets and idler wheels, the crunch of heavy steel tracks on the road surface. Each APC mounted a .50-caliber machine-turret and two armour-shielded M60 machine-guns. In its belly, eleven soldiers were ready to debark from the rear hatch.

I saw townsfolks looking on with blank expressions. APCs weren't tanks but put them on the streets of an American city and the psychological effect would be much the same. Then there was the whup-whup-whup of a helicopter overhead – the only noise I knew that could make me feel drowsy and nervy at the same time. I looked up and saw it bank and hover over the city centre.

We arrived on the north side of Conroy Park five minutes later without having seen a single protester. Normally the park was an open green space with a sport field and fenced off play area for kids. Now it was milling with National Guard soldiers, surrounded by jeeps and 2.5-ton troop transport trucks. APCs stood at each street corner and a command tent had been pitched near the entrance.

I followed Bohannon toward a bunch of officers standing outside the tent. I was looking out for Colonel Riley, but he didn't seem to be there. The guy in command, a portly one star general, was deep in conversation with a bird colonel, two light colonels and several majors. They had a street plan of Ramskill laid out on a jeep hood and were poring over it like they were about to storm Omaha Beach. Milt McStay, the mayor, and Don Didrikson, the city police chief, were standing nearby, along with a captain from the state highway patrol.

We reported to a captain on the HQ staff who told us we were under the command of Brigadier General Justin Young.

Our orders were to take up a position at the corner of West Union and Station Streets and prevent the demonstrators gathered there from moving toward city hall.

Bohannon seemed cool with this and turned back to our jeep.

I stayed with the captain. 'How many students are we looking at, sir?'

He made an uncertain expression. 'We had reports of thousands.'

I found this difficult to believe. 'We just came in from Ramskill Armoury and didn't see any at all.'

I heard Bohannon breathing frustratedly right behind me.

The captain shrugged. 'Maybe they saw you coming and got off the street.'

This was the opposite of what juiced up activists would have done. But I needed information and the best way to get it was to play along with the captain. 'With General Young in command, sir, I'm sure we can handle those kids easy enough, whatever their numbers. Let 'em come, that's what I say.'

This did the trick. The captain made a comradely smile. 'That's the spirit, Sergeant. And you can rest assured those commies won't know what hit 'em if they try anything. We got both battalions of the 55th, a full armoured cavalry troop from the 102nd, and air support in spades.'

I thought, wow. That was close to fifteen hundred men and thirty armoured vehicles, not to mention the whirlybirds overhead. Significantly more firepower than the state authorities had sent here three weeks ago when the shooting started.

I saluted the captain and followed Bohannon back to our

jeep. The drive to West Union and Station took less than two minutes, though we needn't have hurried. The two dozen protesters had laid down their placards and were drinking beer outside a bar.

I turned to Bohannon. 'Looks like General Young got bad intel.'

He ignored me, climbed out of the jeep and surveyed the street scene. True enough, some stores had boarded up their windows and there had been minor acts of vandalism. Also, fresh graffiti had appeared on walls and sidewalks. But this was not a situation that required a military solution.

Bohannon had other ideas. Instead of having us wait by our vehicles, he ordered the platoon to form up with fixed bayonets.

I approached the master sergeant and spoke softly. The man was a knucklehead for sure, but I didn't want the others to hear me questioning his decision. 'Right now there's no problem. But if we fix bayonets, there sure as hell will be. They'll see it as an act of provocation.'

His eyes narrowed to venomous slits. 'Screw you, Tyler. We ain't here to pacify a bunch of socialist deviants.'

'We were ordered to contain a bunch of kids, not incite a riot.' I indicated the protesters at the nearest bar. 'They're busy drinking beer. We should leave them to it.'

'Your point is noted, Sergeant Tyler. Now fix your goddamn bayonet and take up your position.'

He strode along the line of soldiers as they formed up across the width of the street, nodding approvingly as the bayonets gleamed in the afternoon sunlight.

I followed and placed myself in front of him. 'This isn't the Alamo, Bohannon, and they aren't the enemy.'

'I'm in command here, Tyler. You follow my orders or this time you *will* face a court martial.'

I was about to tell him nothing would make me happier when the first volley of rocks rained down on us.

Glancing over my shoulder, I saw the beer-drinkers had given up boozing and taken up their placards. Right along the street, kids were emerging from bars and cafés, their faces angry, their mood ugly. Soon after that, the chanting started: *Soldiers off our streets; Off the pigs; Fuck the Man.*

A Molotov came in. It fell ten feet to my right, exploding in an orange fireball that sent the men nearby scurrying from the burning gasoline.

A cheer went up from the protesters. More rocks. More chanting.

Another Molotov fell dangerously close to the line of guardsmen.

More and more kids were coming onto the street. They gathered in a ragged phalanx and moved in our direction, liquored up, fired up and ready to call whatever bluff we put up.

Toward the back of the crowd I saw Corey Quilton. He was in his element, shouting, instructions to comrades at various locations behind the protesters, directing them toward us like sheepdogs manoeuvring sheep into a pen.

Silently cursing Bohannon, I fixed my own bayonet and prepared to meet the slogan-chanters. They stopped about three feet from our line, throwing insults, spitting phlegm. On the upside, they were too close to hurl Molotovs or rocks.

I glanced to my right. A lard-faced guy with scarlet zits and wispy blond sideburns was gripping his rifle so hard it was trembling. To my left, Lenny Lesniak looked anxious, but seemed to be holding it together.

'We're gonna be fine, boys,' I said. 'No need to do anything silly. No need for anybody to get hurt.'

In the crowd facing us, I recognised faces I knew – a guy from my seminar group, a girl who'd sat next to him, an instructor from the Journalism School. I recalled what Lenny told me about the day of the shootings. *There were kids I was at grade school with. Kids who lived on the next street. Kids I worked with at the tyre factory.* And I felt some of his inner conflict. In Vietnam, it was different. I was a soldier, nothing else. Here I was a reporter in a soldier's uniform and I couldn't escape a sense of moral contradiction.

A girl with long dark hair and an embroidered smock came toward me and reached out to place the stem of a flower in my rifle barrel. I'd seen pictures of this at other protests and knew the girl wasn't a threat.

But the zitty guy next to me didn't. His bayonet thrust flashed in my peripheral sight. The blade sank into the girl's arm before I could stop it.

She let out a shriek. Blood pulsed from her bicep. The kids around her gasped, fell back a few feet. The girl sank to her knees, bleeding, sobbing.

I placed my rifle on the ground behind me and crouched at her side, unfastening the belt around my waist.

I said, 'Give me your arm.'

She looked at me like I was from outer space. Her face was drained of colour, eyes wide, jaw loose. She looked at the wound, then away, then back at the wound, and back and forth, over and over. I'd seen this reaction in country when the brain refused to accept what had happened to the body.

'We gotta stop the bleeding.' I said. 'Let me see your arm.'

I grabbed her forearm, pushed away her smock sleeve

and wrapped the belt around the flesh under her armpit. Then I pulled it tight and fastened it in a tourniquet. Her blood was thick and warm between my fingers, but much less of it was coming from the wound.

'What's your name?'

'Sally, Sally Newchurch.'

'OK, Sally. You're gonna be fine, but we gotta get you to the hospital.'

Ignoring the jeering, the spittle, the shoves, I scooped her up and carried her toward a restaurant behind the line of soldiers. It was closed, but a middle aged woman inside saw me coming with the wounded girl and opened the door.

I asked her to call 911 and guided Sally to a chair. With her arm rested on a table, I made sure the tourniquet was still tight and looked into her scared-shitless eyes.

'The ambulance will be here very soon. In the meantime, you gotta stay real still, can you do that, Sally?'

She nodded. 'Will you stay with me?'

'Sure I will.'

The restaurant owner came back. The ambulance was on its way.

'What's your name?' Her voice had the detached flatness of somebody in shock and her expressionless face told the same story.

'Wat,' I said. 'Wat Tyler.'

She gripped my shoulder with her free hand. 'Thanks for pulling me out of there.'

I made a reassuring smile – despite the shock she was showing some awareness. I told her she was welcome.

Outside, the yelling and chanting had gotten louder, angrier. I glanced through the window and saw Bohannon pacing back and forth behind the line of guardsmen. The protesters were pressed close to the guard, bayonet tips inches from their faces. It was a standoff that couldn't last.

I needed to be there, but I just promised Sally I wouldn't leave her.

We waited, waited.

Finally the ambulance arrived, its siren drowning out the chants, flashing red lights distracting the demonstrators.

A few seconds later a red Oldsmobile 442 came barrelling along the street and parked outside a boarded up bank. Captain Edison Phipps climbed from the driver's seat, fastening his uniform collar as he hurried toward his overstretched command.

TWENTY-EIGHT

With Sally in the ambulance, I went to join Phipps and Bohannon.

The captain watched me coming, head cocked to one side, hands on hips in the way of a sport coach unhappy with a player's performance. As I drew near, he addressed me and Bohannon jointly, 'What do the pair of you have to say for yourselves? The captain on General Young's staff told me the situation here was under control.'

I watched the ambulance drive away. 'It was, Captain. Then we arrived.'

Bohannon said this was bullshit. He told Phipps the protesters were out in greater numbers than General Young had been led to believe, that they came right at us and he ordered the platoon to fix bayonets in response.

I waited him out, then gave my version, including how we narrowly avoided another student fatality after Sally Newchurch got bayoneted.

'I asked you two to work together.' Phipps made a *come on, guys* expression. 'Yet you, Gerry, tell me one thing and you, Wat, say exactly the opposite. What's a guy to do?'

'We should fall back, sir,' I said. 'Before somebody gets badly injured or worse.'

Phipps looked at Bohannon. 'Gerry?'

'I say we lay down gas, sir. That'll send 'em packing.'

Phipps ran his fingers through his dark bouffant mane. He was holding his steel combat helmet in his other hand, as if wearing it might make his hair go flat and wreck the look. 'We're in a tight spot here, guys, a really tight spot.'

I said nothing but I thought a lot of things. More than anything, I thought Phipps represented the worst kind of leadership: None at all. Somehow – unbelievably – Phipps' leadership was even worse than Bohannon's. The master sergeant's plan was the wrong one, but at least he had one.

I looked back at the restaurant, then Phipps. 'I need to make a call, sir.'

Bohannon laughed. 'Lemme guess, the Pentagon?'

I kept my face straight. 'In a manner of speaking, Gerry, yes.'

I turned to Phipps. 'Captain, at the very least you gotta stop this escalating. If more kids get hurt, there'll be hell to pay. And not just here in Ramskill.'

I hadn't wanted to place this much pressure on such inadequate shoulders, but Phipps needed to understand.

He took a few beats, then he looked at me straight, 'Make your call, Wat. But make it quick. If you haven't come back with a better idea in fifteen minutes, I'm gonna have to go with Gerry's idea and put down gas.'

I hurried to the restaurant and slipped the longsuffering owner a five-spot for using her phone – I didn't have the time to mess around with a payphone.

I called Laurence Westerby.

His secretary said he was in a Security Council session.

I asked her to pull him out.

She told me that wasn't possible.

I said if she didn't, the Security Council would have a new item at the very top of its agenda.

She put me on hold.

I looked through the window. Outside the protesters were still pushed close to the soldiers. I imagined the zit-faced kid who panicked and stabbed Sally. I imagined Lenny, just about keeping his shit together. I imagined the other kids in uniform with their rifles and bayonets, their through-the-roof anxiety and their twitchy trigger-fingers.

I looked at my watch. Three minutes had passed since I left Phipps – another twelve and he'd start laying down tear gas and there'd be bloody chaos.

I watched the second hand ticking away vital seconds.

Somewhere distant I heard the noise of shattering glass. A wild cheer.

I pictured Quilton spurring violence on one side; Bohannon doing the same on the other.

Hell, they might have been on the same team.

Eight minutes left on my watch.

Finally, Westerby came on the line. I gave him a situation report and asked him to get an urgent message to Almerin O'Hara, the New York National Guard adjutant general.

'What's your message, Wat?'

'All National Guard units to pull back immediately to General Young's HQ in Conlon Park. APCs off the streets, whirlybirds on the ground.'

'That's some message.' Westerby was used to taking unexpected developments in his stride, but even he was momentarily floored. Eventually, he said, 'O'Hara's a tough cookie. I know what his concern will be – withdrawing in that way would look like weakness.'

I stifled my exasperation. 'What it *won't* look like, General, is yet more blood on American streets. Protesters *and* guardsmen. The people who stand to gain from this are the extremists – radicals and reactionaries. I got two of them right outside – Corey Quilton and Gerry Bohannon. And there are people like them right across the country. This place goes up, everyplace else will follow real fast.'

He told me to leave it with him and hung up.

Another glance at my watch told me Westerby had five minutes to convince O'Hara.

I thanked the restaurant owner for the use of her phone and went back onto the street.

Phipps did not look in a good way. He had Bohannon shouting into one ear and a voice from his walkie-talkie going into the other.

He saw me coming and looked up like a drowning man hoping for a lifeline.

I said, 'We need to hold steady, Captain.'

He gave me a bewildered look. 'Who did you call? Are they sending reinforcements?'

'We'll receive fresh orders soon, sir. We need to be patient.'

'That how you handled the Viet Cong, Tyler?' Bohannon gave me a sneering look. 'With a little patience?'

'Sometimes, yeah.' I wasn't being facetious.

The master sergeant turned back to Phipps. 'We gotta lay down gas, sir. We gotta do it right now. We ain't got no time for this softly, softly shit. We ain't got – '

'Shut the fuck up, Gerry.'

In that tripped-out instant I saw something I'd never seen before in Edison Phipps –authority. Bohannon backed off. Just as quickly, Phipps the ditherer returned. He gave Bohannon an apologetic grin. 'Hey, sorry about that, Gerry.'

The big man shrugged. 'Ain't no problem, Captain.'

Phipps looked at me, his beseeching expression in place. 'How long now, Wat? That help you mentioned, those fresh orders?'

I said, 'Very soon, Captain.'

But I wasn't at all sure. What would O'Hara make of my admittedly odd request? True, he was said to be a reasonable man. True, he'd asked Westerby for help and Westerby asked for mine. But this had turned into a political snake-pit. And I knew from hard experience that disaster often followed when political considerations dictated military decisions.

A Molotov exploded close to where we were standing. Then a second and a third. We dodged between the leaping orange flame.

Quilton and his fellow travellers had almost certainly spotted the three of us behind the line of soldiers, figured out we were the leaders and lobbed the Molotovs in our direction.

'What's going on?' Phipps seemed confused. 'What just happened?'

I noticed he still had his helmet in his hand and told him to put it on his head before another salvo came over. Somewhat reluctantly, he did.

'Captain, we really gotta do something.' Bohannon's features were animated, though his tone was more respectful.

Phipps turned to me with a deflated look. 'Sorry, Wat. Whatever you were hoping for isn't gonna happen. We need to –'

He seemed to become aware of another voice coming through his walkie-talkie. Placing it against his ear, he walked away, nodding, listening.

When he turned back he looked like a man relieved of a massive burden. 'That was General Young himself. We got those fresh orders, Wat. We're withdrawing to Conlon Park.'

TWENTY-NINE

I met JoBeth in the Lincoln Tavern on West Union Street. This was the haunt of the straights – the politically moderate students who represented the majority of the kids at Ramskill. Like other student bars, the Lincoln had been left alone by the rioters. Whether capitalism should be reformed or destroyed may have been debatable. Taking out popular student watering holes absolutely wasn't.

After hanging around Conlon Park for four hours, Bravo Company got stood down along with most of the National Guard units. The drive back to the armoury had been weird. I rode in the lead jeep with Phipps and Bohannon and nobody said a word. I sensed tension between the captain and master sergeant that hadn't been apparent before. Bohannon seemed unusually cagey. Phipps looked lost in thought. And me, I was content to watch the pair of them stew. Later I went to the J-School and called Westerby. He confirmed the decision to withdraw had worked. Deprived of a target, the protesters broke a few more windows, aerosoled a few more graffiti, then went to celebrate their victory over the Man. Finally, I called Maggie and filed my story: A seven hundred-word, first-person piece for the front page of the final edition. I wrote it off the top of my head and didn't stop until I typed *-30-* to indicate the end of the piece. It was times like this when journalism really did it for me. I was never more alive than in that moment of hammering slick, fast words onto a blank page. Like rock music and poetry, it rekindled extinguished sensation, put me in touch with who I wanted to be. Or at least who I thought I wanted to be.

JoBeth sipped her beer and asked about Sally Newchurch.

I told her I'd just called the hospital and the doctors said she'd be fine. The wound needed a dozen stitches, but the surgery had gone well and they expected to send Sally home later in the week.

JoBeth gave me a lopsided smile. 'You did good, Wat. Corey Quilton certainly thinks so. He's giving out that you're subverting the establishment from within *and* looking out for the kids it wants to repress.'

I gave her a put-upon look. 'What do I need to do to get in Quilton's *bad* books?'

'I'd say that's *Mission: Impossible*. Anyway, we should count our blessings. We need to keep tabs on him and you being his buddy makes it so much easier.'

She was right about that. She'd watched the trouble developing on West Main Street as an observer for the US Attorney's Office and identified Quilton as a controlling influence. And if he was pulling strings at today's confrontation, it was likely he'd done the same during the protest that ended in the deaths of three people.

'Quilton might have been the star of the show this afternoon,' I said. 'But he couldn't have done it without the help and support of Gerry Bohannon.'

She gave this a little thought. 'I agree up to a point. The

main issue, though, is that your unit was only there as part of the ultimate exercise in overkill. The FBI counted no more than a couple of hundred protestors on the streets at any one time – until the National Guard rolled into town. That brought the kids out in their thousands.'

I took out a Camel but held off lighting it in line with my strategy to reduce the number of cigarettes I smoked. 'What's the feeling on campus?'

She glanced around the students in the tavern – mainly straights, but I saw a few Greeks and jocks, even a handful of freaks. I was becoming something of an expert in identifying student types.

'These kids aren't activists or revolutionaries, but they are pissed off big time.' There was more than a hint of vexation in her voice. 'They wouldn't have supported the protests on campus, or trashing downtown businesses. But they don't get why the tanks had to come, or soldiers with rifles and bayonets had to come. They don't get why guys with bullhorns were strutting around, ordering them off the streets, or why military helicopters were circling overhead.'

I put the cigarette between my lips, held off lighting it for a few more minutes. 'So how would you summarize what went down today?'

She set her beer on the table. 'Too many sledge hammers, not enough nuts. Hell, there were *no* nuts. It was difficult to believe I was in America. How was today allowed to happen, Wat?'

I drank some of my own beer. 'Scuttlebutt says Mayor McStay imposed martial law, then called in the guard.'

'That's absurd,' she said. 'Milt McStay doesn't have lawful authority to do either of those things.'

'But today's shitshow wasn't about reality. It was about perception – or rather misperception.' The craving for nicotine finally got the better of me and I lit my cigarette. 'From what I can gather, McStay started drinking early and got real stoked when he saw a bunch of kids vandalizing a bank. Upshot was he went on local radio and *threatened* to ask the governor for martial law and soldiers. Not surprisingly, the request got turned down.'

She finished her beer. 'So how come the National Guard ended up in Ramskill?'

I tapped my cigarette in the ashtray. 'A lot of folks from downtown called the station, saying they supported the idea and McStay realized he had a gallery to play to. So he made a second request, massively exaggerating the numbers of protesters. Apparently, Rockefeller agreed to a strictly limited deployment, but somewhere along the line – and don't ask me how – this was misinterpreted as the exact opposite. Westerby tells me they're still trying to find out how it all went wrong, but it's looking like political opportunism from McStay, combined the mother of communications breakdowns between the governor's people and the National Guard brass.'

'You believe that?'

I made a weary expression. 'I don't know what to believe. Maybe some hawkish types in the state government, or the National Guard wanted to provoke a showdown. But a high-level screw-up is also plausible. Either way the damage is done.'

She reached for her beer glass, brushing her arm against mine. 'Get you another?'

Was there a hint of a come-on? Or was I misreading her?

But I couldn't stay. I had to get my car from the armoury and any more to drink would put me at risk of copping a driving under the influence rap.

I took a cab to the big building at Main and Jefferson and was walking toward my rented Buick Skylark when I noticed a light on in one of the offices. No doubt someone working late, but I was curious to find out who.

I tried the main doors and was surprised to find them unlocked. I made my way across the drill hall to the office area. One of the doors was open and a wedge of light spilled onto the linoleum floor of the corridor.

I heard Bohannon's voice but no other. For a few seconds I thought he was talking to himself. Then I realized he was on the phone.

The door was eighteen inches ajar and I peeked through the aperture. The master sergeant was hunched over a desk with his back to me. Nobody else was in the room.

I pulled back – if he glanced up at the window in front of his desk, he'd see my reflection in the glass.

But I could hear him well enough from the corridor.

There was no way I could make out what the person at the other end of the line was saying. But the voice was male and he was angry. When he spoke, the receiver made a buzzing sound like it was loaded with riled hornets.

Bohannon was struggling to get a word in. When he did, he got cut short.

Seemed the conversation was about the shootings on May 7.

After a particularly stretched out tirade, Bohannon found an opening. 'Look, I really don't know what the Polack kid saw. But he had his gas mask on and it happened real fast.'

More heated language.

'Yes, he probably did see something. I'm just saying he couldn't have seen much.'

Still more chastening words.

'You don't need to worry. I'll make sure he keeps his mouth shut.'

Yet another venomous salvo.

Bohannon sounded like a scolded child. 'Of course I won't do anything stupid.'

I thought about what I'd heard. There were only two guys of Polish descent in Bravo Company. One was in his late thirties and would never be considered a kid. The other was Lenny Lesniak, aged twenty. Seemed Lenny knew more about what went down that afternoon than he'd told me.

Finally the other guy seemed to relent. His voice softened, the receiver stopped fizzing.

Bohannon made a tired sigh. 'Yes I'm sure about that. Captain Phipps saw nothing. He might as well not have been there. As usual, he left the decision-making to me.'

The softly spoken words continued and somehow they were more menacing than the ranting.

Especially when Bohannon said, 'Leave Tyler to me.'

THIRTY

It seemed Marty Robbins was right when he predicted the animal mutilator would move to human victims. Nineteen-year-old national guardsman Harold Kapp lost part of his left ear after he was set upon outside his home in Ramskill, late at night.

And it seemed Gerry Bohannon *had* been talking about Lenny Lesniak when he told the guy on the phone he'd 'make sure the kid keeps his mouth shut'. Bohannon had not, though, been able to keep himself from doing 'anything stupid' because Lenny had been found outside his parents' place following a savage beating.

I say *it seemed* because I wasn't at all sure about very much anymore. Nothing was straightforward and everything had at least two convincing explanations – none of them welcome.

See, when I first heard what happened to Harold, I was confident it was the work of Andy Stuivermans. Then I discovered Harold was the kid who bayoneted Sally Newchurch when she tried to place a flower in the barrel of my rifle. So it was also possible that Harold had been the victim of a revenge attack by Sally's boyfriend, or brother, or pop, or somebody from SLUT.

And although I still believed Bohannon was responsible for putting Lenny in the hospital, I couldn't discount the idea that Lenny had been assaulted by the same individual who took a blade to Harold's ear. That incident happened shortly after 10.00pm. Fifteen minutes later and two hundred yards away, Lenny was taken down.

As if the water wasn't muddy enough, both Harold and Lenny said they'd been approached from behind. And both were serving in the National Guard. Gerry Bohannon could have been behind both attacks. So could Andy Stuivermans. Or neither of them could have been involved in either.

Don Didrikson, the city police chief, said he wasn't ruling anything out and I didn't blame him. I wrote a piece along those lines and filed my copy ahead of the first edition deadline.

Next, I called the Biomedical Centre. The receptionist told me Loretta had taken a vacation and didn't know when she was expected back. This was downright concerning. And it made me wonder if Loretta was shielding Stuivermans. It seemed crazy, but crazy had gotten to be commonplace in Ramskill.

There was nothing I could do to locate Loretta or Stuivermans, so I turned my attention to Lenny and Harold. They'd both been taken to Ramskill Hospital, but the doctors there decided Harold needed specialist surgery and sent him with part of his ear in an ice-box to a dedicated unit in Manhattan. Lenny was still being treated in Ramskill so I drove to the hospital and asked to see him.

He agreed to talk, but on the understanding that our conversation was not for publication. This was too bad, though right then I needed information more than I needed news copy.

I found him sitting up in bed. He'd suffered concussion and three cracked ribs, along with cuts and bruises to his face. Both eyes were black, the flesh around one so swollen it was almost shut. His right cheekbone was red raw and his upper lip, fat.

I asked him how he was feeling and he said like shit. Then I went straight to it and asked who did it.

'I dunno, Wat. Bastard came at me from behind.'

'I think you do know, Lenny. I think we both know.'

The kid didn't react.

'It was Gerry Bohannon, wasn't it?'

Blank face.

I pushed on. I didn't want to do this to a traumatized kid, but couldn't see any other way. 'I was at the armoury last night and overheard Gerry on the phone to some guy. I heard Gerry say he'd make damn sure you kept your mouth shut. That was why he beat you up, wasn't it?'

He nodded.

I perched on the end of the bed. 'Tell me what happened.'

He hesitated, which was entirely understandable.

I tried to sound reassuring. 'Listen, pal, Bohannon is finished. He won't come after you again. I promise.'

He reached for the water jug on the nightstand, wincing as he poured himself a drink.

Then he took a sip and sat back against his pillows. 'I got a visit on Wednesday from the FBI. I didn't say nothing I hadn't told them or the campus cops already. But Gerry found out they'd been at my place. He got it into his head that I ratted him out, or I was cutting some sort of deal.'

This explained the conversation between Bohannon and the other guy, and it confirmed that Lenny knew more than he'd previously admitted about the day Bobkov, Boyd Brigstock and the others died. But I'd need to coax this out of him.

'Bohannon didn't come at you from behind, did he, Lenny? I think he confronted you about that visit from the feds.'

He drank a little more water. 'Gerry had this crazy look in his eyes. He said I had to tell him what I told the feds and he wouldn't believe me when I said I'd told them nothing.'

I edged a little further along the bed so we could talk more quietly. 'Was that why he attacked you? Because you couldn't tell him stuff you never said?'

Lenny went quiet and I let the silence play. I wanted to give him time to realize I was his best and safest way out of this.

After some while, I said, 'What really happened that day those folks got shot?'

He thought about it, then made a weary shrug, like he was fed up with pretending.

'It was like I said before. We was trapped against the building and the protesters was throwing rocks at us, screaming all sorts of shit. We really was scared for our lives.'

'I totally believe that, Lenny. But something else happened, didn't it? Something that shouldn't have happened.'

More silence. Again, I waited it out. This had to come from Lenny.

At last he gave me a forlorn look. 'We *was* ordered to fire. The order came from Gerry. He told us to shoot over the protesters' heads. And that's what we thought we was doing. But it was so confusing. Protesters everywhere. Coming at us, running away, coming at us again. And then we had them gas masks on so it was even harder to see what was going on.'

I started to realize why the squad had been told to wear gas masks even though no gas was laid down. It was to stop the soldiers seeing something.

Something vital.

But what?

I said nothing, gave Lenny the time he needed.

He gazed at his half-drunk glass of water. 'I wish this was beer. Better still, whiskey. I could use a shot of something strong.'

'You're doing well, Lenny.'

Without looking up from the glass, he said, 'I emptied my magazine real fast. Eight rounds. *Blam, blam, blam.* I was panicking, I admit it. I fired much faster than the other guys. I was trying to get a fresh clip from my pouch and I turned away from the protesters so I could concentrate better. That was when I saw Gerry.'

Another pause, fresh hesitation. I sensed Lenny was at a point of no return.

I gave him a nudge. 'What was Gerry doing?'

'He was firing into the kids.'

'Did you see if he hit anyone?'

He looked at me, fierce and angry. 'No I didn't. But he was definitely shooting low. He was taking aim, slow and careful – the exact opposite of what I did. He was running a bead, then firing, then finding another target and so on. I just stood there and watched. Then he turned and saw me watching.'

Poor kid, I thought. Psychopathic bully like Bohannon, the pressure he'd have put on Lenny to keep schtum would have been unbearable.

'You're gonna be fine, Lenny.' I tried to sound reassuring.

Yet pinning anything on Big Gerry wouldn't be easy. Dollars to dimes the rounds that hit the six wounded people were from the M1 he'd been issued with. But he was a slippery character. Maybe he'd claim he accidentally picked up a different rifle after one of the other guys put it down in the chaos and confusion. Maybe he'd think of some other way out.

What was bothering me most, though, was the FBI lab report that concluded none of the rifles used by Bravo Company had fired any of the fatal shots. I'd have bet my boots Bohannon was one of the shooters who killed Oleg Bobkov and Gordon Richardson, or Boyd Brigstock. Seemed I'd have been walking home barefoot.

Lenny must have noticed my consternation. He asked what was wrong.

I saw no good reason not to, so I told him.

Then he said, 'Gerry wasn't firing an M1 from the armoury.'

I looked at him sharp. 'What *was* he firing?'

'His own gun.'

I spoke slow, to make absolutely sure I fully grasped what Lenny was telling me. 'You're saying Gerry Bohannon took along a personal weapon instead of the M1 he should have been carrying?'

Lenny nodded yes. 'It was his daddy's rifle from World War II.'

'What happened to the one he took from the armoury?'

'He left it in his locker.'

This was mindblowing. 'Had he done this before?'

'Not that I know about.'

'Any idea where his daddy's old rifle is now?'

'Gerry keeps it at home.'

'Did any of the other guys know about this rifle swap?'

'I don't think so. We'd left the armoury and I needed to go back inside to use the john. I was walking by the lockers when I saw him switch the guns.'

'So you're the only member of the squad who knew he was using his own M1 and the only one who saw him aim and fire it into the protesters?'

Lenny nodded yes.

'Where was Phipps while this was going down?'

He made a bitter laugh. 'Where he always is. Nowhere to be seen. Our unit is really Gerry's unit. That's why we all do what Gerry tells us. Phipps, he's pathetic.'

No argument there.

I took a few beats to process what I just learned, but the upshot wasn't encouraging. There was no corroborative evidence to back up what Lenny told me. That meant no probable cause for the cops or the feds to get a search warrant. And without seizing the M1 from Bohannon's home, it would be impossible to make any of this stand up in court, or anyplace else.

THIRTY-ONE

Storm clouds rolled over the Catskill Mountains, shedding their load east of the Hudson. The rain came down hard, piercing the air with jagged spears. They rippled in the gauzy light and sizzled on the sidewalk, giving the impression downtown Ramskill was on a TV set with a bad picture and poor sound quality. On the plus side, the deluge was keeping the kids off the streets.

JoBeth was waiting for me in a diner on Washington Street. The front window was misted-up, reducing the folks on the sidewalk to blurry shapes. The place smelled of damp clothes and fried food.

Over a burger and fries, I caught her up on the latest developments.

After hearing what Lenny told me, she agreed Bohannon had almost certainly killed and wounded people on campus. Of course this was major progress, though we still had no clue who the second shooter was. And there had to be a second shooter because the rifle used to eliminate the two professors was not the same as the gun that killed Boyd Brigstock. Either that or Bohannon used two different rifles – his own and another M1, also not from the armoury.

The practicalities of the master sergeant carrying two rifles without anyone noticing virtually ruled this out. The idea of him also firing two different guns in the same ninety-second timeframe totally ruled it out.

There was a break in the conversation and she looked at me over the island of condiments on the table. 'You got something else on your mind, haven't you?'

I sat back. 'Nothing that isn't already on yours. I think it's more and more possible that Corey Quilton was working with Gerry Bohannon.'

She stirred sugar into her coffee and took a swallow. 'It's a reasonable working hypothesis. So how would this partnership have worked?'

I placed my pack of Camels on the table but didn't take one. 'We both saw Quilton stoking up the protesters on West Main Street. You described him as a controlling influence and I think that's spot on. Then Bohannon rolls up and immediately orders the guys to fix bayonets. This might have been down to plain stupidity, or it might have been a calculated act of provocation, or both, but the outcome was the same. And it didn't stop there. Even after Phipps arrived, Bohannon carried on urging him to take the most extreme decisions, right up until we got the order to pull back. I thought at the time Quilton and Bohannon might have been on the same team, but it was nothing more than an ironic observation. Looking back, it doesn't seem so whimsical.'

She placed her elbows on the table and rested her chin between interlocked fingers. 'And what? They'd come up with some sort of deal to serve both their agendas?'

'Stacks up, whichever way you look at it.'

'And you think this pact might have been in place before the campus shootings?'

'Again, it stacks up. Who benefited? On Planet Gerry and on Planet Corey, both of them.'

She finished her coffee and looked at me straight. 'Could Quilton have been the second shooter?'

I shook my head no. 'I checked out his alibi and it's solid. He was right in the centre of the protest, no doubt about it. But that's exactly where he'd have been most effective – the field marshal directing his troops.'

I paused, allowing my thoughts a little time to crystallize. 'Lenny talked about the protesters throwing stones and abuse at the soldiers before they surged forward and pulled back. Apparently they did more taunting, more rock-throwing, then repeated the advance and withdrawal procedure. The way Lenny described it made it sound like a tactical manoeuvre, and it probably was. The stone-throwing and name-calling, that was the equivalent of an artillery barrage to soften up the target; the rush toward the guard, that would have had the same shock effect as an infantry charge. You saw for yourself how Quilton was working the demonstrators on Wednesday.'

'Sounds plausible,' she said. 'We should pursue it.'

She waited while the waitress came over and refilled her coffee cup. 'Do the city cops have anything further on the attack on Harold Kapp?'

'Nothing – all I got was officialese from the press office about pursuing a number of leads. I know zero isn't a number, but I don't think Chief Didrikson does.' Didrikson didn't like me, probably because his campus cop rival Gene Ducey did. This may have accounted for him going through the press office rather than talking to me direct. But in any case I didn't expect any arrests any time soon. Lenny was refusing to press charges because it would be his word against Bohannon's; and Harold was sticking to his story about having been attacked from behind, which was probably true.

She said, 'What do *you* think?'

'It's possible Bohannon was behind both attacks, but I don't think it's likely.' I took a cigarette from the pack but didn't light it. My delaying exercise seemed to be working. I was beginning to believe my smoking habit was as much about the cigarette ritual as a nicotine-addiction.

'So you figure it's a coincidence that they're both National Guard guys and they live in the same neighbourhood?'

'Don't you?'

She nodded. 'The ear thing has got to put Stuivermans front and centre. First the sheepdog, then the bunny, now this. A Vietnam veteran whose own ear got mutilated, and who may have collected Viet Cong ears as trophies. And who has the special operations experience to pull off that stalker stuff.'

I was at the point when I really wanted to smoke my cigarette, but held off for just a few more minutes. 'The attack on Harold Kapp could be revenge for him sticking his bayonet into Sally Newchurch's arm.'

She raised an eyebrow. 'By Corey Quilton?'

'More likely one of his minions. Or Sally's family or friends. The ear thing could have been an accident, or deliberate misdirection – make it seem like a copycat attack linked to the sheepdog and the bunny.'

'I still think Stuivermans is the most likely.'

'On balance, I agree.'

‘Then the next question is: Was Stuivermans also the second shooter?’

I put the smoke between my lips and toyed with my lighter. ‘And the question after that is: Did Stuivermans act alone, or was he Bohannon’s partner?’

She made a dubious expression. ‘As well as Quilton?’

‘I don’t know. I’d never have put Bohannon, Quilton and Stuivermans together. But I’m sure those three are somehow connected to everything that’s gone down here: The campus shootings, the Biomedical Centre homicides, the ongoing tensions, and the ear-attacks.’

She signalled the waitress to bring our check. ‘We need to get more on Andy Stuivermans. And his sister-figure, Loretta Hausinger. She still on vacation?’

I said she was.

‘Then let’s go see the top man at the university. Maybe President Murdoch can shed light on the activities at the Biomedical Centre.’

I slid my cigarette back into the pack, congratulated myself for having not smoked it, and followed her from the diner.

Outside, the rain had let up but Ramskill city centre had not been cleansed of its sins, or its sinners. They were back on the streets, eyeing one another with mutual hostility in their blue uniforms, blue jeans and blue business suits.

THIRTY-TWO

Ramskill University President Blair Murdoch looked up from his desk as JoBeth and I were shown into his office in Putney Hall.

Murdoch was every inch the wise old head. A horsey face was dominated by a long nose and broad mouth that formed an inverted T. Wiry silver hair was combed back from a prominent brow and his grey eyes had a look of constant curiosity. He was wearing a poorly-fitted herringbone sport jacket with a knitted vest and a carelessly knotted tie. I'd say he was late-sixties or early seventies. Behind him, a pair of ceiling-high book cases were crammed with hefty volumes, which were also stacked on every horizontal surface. The antique rug was threadbare and I felt it slide on the wooden flooring as I moved toward the visitor chairs. It was as if, despite his lofty position, the guy had never really left the confines of the medieval nook at Oxford, where he began his rise to academic recognition.

'It's so good of you to call by,' he said, even though we asked for the meeting. He spoke with a mid-Atlantic accent that left me unsure whether he was an American who spent a lot of his life in Britain, or the other way around.

He started off by apologising to me for what he described as his 'unwarrantedly short manner' when we last talked. That had been after I wrote the story about Marty Robbins' warning that a human victim would be next after the ears were cut off his daughter's bunny.

'It seems you were entirely correct to run your story, Mr Tyler,' he said. 'Mr Robbins' prediction was, sadly, all too accurate.'

I said it was easy to be wise in retrospect and assured him Harold Kapp was in good hands at the New York specialist unit where his severed ear had been successfully sewn back on.

'I also owe you a debt of thanks.' Murdoch took out a pipe and started filling the bowl with tobacco from a leather pouch. 'Sally Newchurch, whose life you undoubtedly saved on Wednesday, is my niece. I can't begin to tell you how grateful we all are.'

I said I was glad to hear Sally had been sent home from the hospital and asked him if he could help us with some questions.

He raised an eyebrow. 'Are you asking as faculty staff or undercover investigators?'

I glanced at JoBeth and she made a little shrug.

Murdoch went on, 'I received a call this morning from the governor's mansion and another from the US Attorney's Office for the Southern District of New York. Both callers asked me to cooperate with your enquiries.'

JoBeth said, 'Does it matter whether we're asking as staff members or investigators?'

Murdoch made a slightly offended expression and I could tell from his tone that it wasn't for effect. 'As a matter of fact, it does, Miss Medlock. You see, contrary to the outpourings of some organisations in Ramskill, this university is not a subsidiary of the state government or an obedient servant of Richard Nixon. So, if it's all the same to you, I'd prefer you to ask your questions strictly as faculty members.'

I could see the old boy had a point. 'Very well, sir, as a member of your academic staff, I'd like to ask you about SLUT.'

'What about SLUT?' He ignited the tobacco in his pipe and briefly disappeared in a cloud of fumes.

'I understand its members want to put you in front of a firing squad, destroy the university, and incite popular rebellion against the federal government.'

His mournful face emerged from the smoky fug like a pike fish in murky water. 'You omitted to include calling for the random assassination of all campus police officers, threatening to blow up, or burn down university real estate, and declaring that any disciplinary measures taken against SLUT members would be regarded as, in their own words, 'An act of war.''

JoBeth said, '*Is* any action being taken against SLUT?'

Murdoch gazed down into his smouldering pipe bowl. 'We tried to ban the organisation from campus two years ago, but they took us to court and we've been mired in a law suit ever since. In the meantime, they enjoy full student rights and privileges.'

'You heard of Corey Quilton?' I asked.

He made a baleful expression. 'Who in Ramskill hasn't?'

'Do you regard him as a threat?'

'I do. The axiom that 'the end justifies the means' could have been written for Mr Quilton. He's exceptionally bright, malicious and manipulative.'

I glanced at JoBeth and she at me and I suspected we were thinking the same thing: This was further evidence that Corey Quilton wouldn't think twice about getting into bed with Gerry Bohannon, or Andy Stuivermans, or anybody else if he thought it would promote the revolution.

'We're also interested in the Biomedical Centre,' JoBeth said. 'Can you tell us anything about the activities Oleg Bobkov and his team were undertaking?'

He shook his head. 'No I cannot – in the sense that I'm not able to because I don't possess that information. What I can tell you is that the project had been receiving substantial funding from an anonymous donor in Manhattan.'

JoBeth frowned. 'Is that usual?'

'Absolutely not.' His pipe had gone out and he struck a match to re-light it. 'It only recently came to my attention that certain members of the university's board of trustees have bypassed my office to accept this financial contribution and approve Bobkov's programme.'

'Can they do that, sir?' I couldn't keep the astonishment from my voice.

'To the extent that they *have* done it, yes, Mr Tyler, it would appear so.' Again, he was lost in a wreath of tobacco fumes. As they dispersed, he said, 'Were their actions legal? That's a question I'm currently trying to establish, although my view is that this was entirely outside their powers as trustees.'

I asked, 'Can you tell us who these individuals are?'

He made an apologetic smile. 'Not without prejudicing the internal enquiry I instigated last week. The names of the nine trustees are on public record, but I'm still trying to establish who was involved and who was not, so it would be wrong of me to go into any more detail at this stage.'

I asked about the amount of the funding and got the same negative response.

But I sensed this was worth a little more probing. 'Would I be wrong, sir, to believe that the figure is a six-figure sum?'

He shook his head no.

'Five figures?'

He shook his head again. 'You went in the wrong direction, Mr Tyler.'

So we were talking seven figures – at least one million dollars. Possibly many millions.

I pressed on. 'How does this number compare with the Biomedical Centre's overall annual budget?'

'That, too, is on the public record. But as you're clearly looking for a little context, it would be fair to say that the value of Professor Bobkov's extra funding is significantly greater than the annual budget for all the centre's other activities combined.'

JoBeth wafted pipe smoke from her face. 'Do you have any reason to believe this covert finance was connected to the death of Professor Bobkov and the murder of three of his research team?'

'I'm afraid I don't.' Murdoch rested his pipe in an ashtray. 'I am, however, in regular contact with Chief Ducey and will ask him to alert you of any developments.'

It seemed we weren't going to get anything further from this conversation, so we thanked the old boy for his time and left the building.

Outside, we took a seat on a bench facing Stanton Hall, the shiny new building where the guys of Bravo Company fired on the protesters. Murdoch's disclosure of the secret funding for Bobkov's work was a major breakthrough. We knew a million bucks – and probably more – had been back-channelled into the programme. But we still didn't know what the programme involved and the one person who could tell us – Loretta Hausinger – was still absent, apparently having taken an unexpected vacation.

'We need to revisit the biomedical place,' JoBeth said. 'We need to talk to those guys you saw last time you went there.'

'You think they'll talk?'

She got up and started walking toward the Biomedical building. 'No harm asking.'

*

JoBeth was right about no harm asking, though the answer to our questions was unanimous silence.

The janitors and groundskeepers had gathered as usual after work outside the hold-over buildings where they were billeted. They smoked cigarettes and popped cans of soda, talking in low tones among themselves. When they saw us coming, they regarding us like deer being stalked by a pair of wolves.

Nobody was willing to talk, yet this said a lot. It told us that whatever was going on here was anything but normal. Ask a bunch of New Yorkers about their day and the usual problem is getting them to shut up. Not these people. It was also telling that they all had the same stock response, 'Sorry, Mister, I got nothing to say.' This meant they'd learned those words by rote. They'd also learned how to behave in this sort of situation: No hint of discourtesy, no eye-contact, just a stonewall refusal to engage.

Clearly this was a futile exercise so we called it quits.

Back at the J-school, I declined JoBeth's offer of a lift back to my hotel. I wanted to stretch my legs and set off along the country route where I'd encountered Lenny Lesniak practising his marksmanship.

I knew I'd picked up a tail soon after leaving the main road. Whoever was following me took care to stay out of sight, ducking behind a shrub or a tree whenever I glanced over my shoulder. But I could hear their footfalls and even caught a scent – an odd mix of disinfectant and nicotine.

After a half mile I grew tired of this and waited at a sharp jink in the path.

I didn't have long to wait. The scrawny figure appeared from around the bend and was clearly surprised when he saw me standing there.

'Help you with anything?' I asked.

I took in pale, pinched features and hollowed out cheeks. I'd seen this guy before but I couldn't recall where.

He said, 'You don't remember me, do you?'

Then I recognized him. He'd had a haircut and a shave and sobered up since I'd last seen him near Gem Spa newsstand on 2nd Avenue after the Jefferson Airplane concert. The tattoo on his forearm told me I wasn't mistaken. It showed the head of a bald eagle and scroll that read *101st Airborne, 1967*. This was the junkie I rescued from the street gang the night I arrived in Manhattan.

But I'd also seen him more recently: He was among the janitors hanging around outside the Biomedical Centre when I went there four days ago. He'd been clocking me and looked away fast when he realized I was looking back.

'I'm Kevin Jacks.' His smile revealed chipped and broken teeth. 'You saved my ass a couple of weeks back.'

He extended his hand. His fingers felt like corn stalks wrapped in toilet paper. 'Wat Tyler,' I said.

'Sorry I couldn't talk in front of the other guys. We've been given strict orders. But I figure I can help you.'

'Help me how?'

'You're looking for Andy Stuivermans,' he said. 'I know where he is.'

THIRTY-THREE

I asked, 'Where is that?'

He said, 'New York City.'

My hopes went off a cliff. 'It's a big place, Kevin. Can you be a little more specific?'

He shrugged. 'Possibly the East Village; possibly New Lots, Brooklyn.'

I gave him a disbelieving look. Was he putting me on? New Lots was the place I went to junior high, the East Village where my apartment was. If Kevin Jacks was right, Stuivermans was on my old stamping ground.

'Why would Andy go to those places?'

'He comes from New Lots. He had a girl in the East Village.'

'Why are you telling me this?'

'I'm worried about him, man. The guy needs help.'

'You and Andy are buddies?'

'Kinda. Got a smoke?'

I gave him a Camel and lit it for him. We walked over to a tree stump and sat down.

'We only knew one another a couple of weeks, but we hit it off straight away. See, we were both sergeants in the Nam, we both split with our girlfriends after we came home, and we both wound up on the Bowery. He showed me the ropes when I arrived here, took me under his wing. He's been here a long time, longer than any of us.'

'Why are you worried about him? Why does he need help?'

He sucked in cigarette smoke, held it for a few seconds, then exhaled slowly. 'He's been going out at night like he was on recce missions back in the Circus. He puts on dark clothes and paints his face with boot polish, then disappears. Sometimes for a couple of hours, sometimes all night.'

I thought about the twilight stalker and the ear mutilator.

I asked Kevin how he knew about Stuivermans' nocturnal activities.

'We bunk together,' he said. 'That's how it works at the research place. They pair you up and it's two to a room.'

'So, what, you see him prepping, going out and coming back?'

'I don't always see him come in. Not if he stays out all night. But sometimes I'm still awake when he gets back.'

'What do you make of this behaviour?'

He made a what-do-I-know? expression. 'It's way-out, man. When I asked him, he told me he wanted to stay sharp, keep an eye on things around the campus and around the city. He'd come out with paranoid stuff like 'You can never be too careful with Nixon' and 'Lord knows what kinda shit is going down that we never know about'.'

He took a long toke at the Camel, then looked at me straight. 'I dig that paranoid shit, man. I been there myself. But what Andy was doing, that was way beyond anything I ever got up to.'

I took out a cigarette myself and went through my routine

of not lighting it. 'Did Andy ever come back with blood on him?'

Kevin shook his head no. He did it instantly and instinctively. I didn't know if I could trust the guy, but his response seemed genuine.

Which made it puzzling as well as revealing. You couldn't do those things to the sheepdog, the bunny and Harold Kapp without getting covered in blood. So it seemed likely that Stuivermans was the stalker, but the ear slasher was a different person – even though Stuivermans was linked to this very specific type of mutilation by dint of his own disfigured ear. And while this fresh information was useful, it threw up a whole bunch of extra questions.

I rolled the cigarette between my fingers. 'You and Andy, did you talk much about the Circus?'

'Sure we did. That was part of the problem. Sometimes we didn't talk about nothing else. And sometimes Andy talked about the place like we never left, like Charlie was right outside the door.'

I could relate to that. I didn't feel fear like ordinary folks, but that didn't make me oblivious to danger. Even now, after three weeks back in the US, I'd sometimes catch myself reacting to a car backfiring or footsteps behind me. As I did when Kevin started tailing me along the path.

He studied the glowing tip of his cigarette. 'There was one time though, a few days ago, when he'd gotten hurt in some kind of fight.'

'Hurt how?'

'Nothing bad. Sore thigh and a bruised cheekbone – oh, and a sort of graze on his forehead.'

Any doubt that Stuivermans was the guy I fought near

the pony paddock vanished. Kevin had just described exactly where my blows landed. And I had to admit he'd given as good as he'd gotten.

I said, 'Did this happen on Monday night?'

He looked at me strange. 'How do you know that?'

'Somebody reported an incident on the edge of town,' I said. 'Two guys brawling, no one badly injured.'

At least the last part was true.

I wanted to find out more about the biomedical place, so I asked him how he'd ended up there after I'd hauled him out of the shit at Gem Spa.

He tossed is cigarette butt on the grass and crushed it under his shoe. 'Scuttlebutt on the Bowery said there was this research programme in Ramskill. Vietnam veterans only. They was screening guys at their campus in Lower Manhattan so I decided to take a look. My background checked out but they insisted on me sobering up and no drink or drugs on the programme. I had no money anyways, so I agreed to do the cold turkey and wound up here.'

'What's the deal?'

'They pay ten bucks a day, plus bed and board in return for taking some pills every day. You also gotta let them do tests – blood, urine, sight, and how you react to different images and sounds. And you gotta do a group session once a day – kinda like Alcoholics Anonymous. Apart from that, we have to do janitor work and groundskeeping – but nothing too heavy.'

I lit my cigarette. 'These pills they give you, what are they for?'

'Dunno, man. I asked, but they said if they told me it could skew the results. And they guaranteed I'd come to no harm.'

'Are all the guys in your group taking pills?'

He nodded.

'Including Andy?'

'Yeah.'

'Andy didn't come to no harm, though, did he?'

He looked at my cigarette. His mind wasn't difficult to read and I gave him another.

'That's why I wanted to tell you this stuff.' He sucked on the Camel. 'I'm scared he's gonna do something stupid. On top of that fight on Monday, Andy got into another the next day, and another. Then, two nights ago, he bugged out and hasn't come back.'

'You been OK with the pills?'

'So far.'

'What about the other guys?'

'Some don't seem affected at all. Others go weird. Andy went the most weird, but a good number get antsy, snappy, violent. They go quiet, then pick a fight for no reason.'

'How many people on the programme? Two dozen?'

'Thirty. Platoon-size, that's what they said.'

This figured. They were recruiting veterans and accommodating them in barracks-like buildings. For some reason they wanted to maintain a military-like structure, possibly to promote a sense of discipline and routine. I said, 'At a guess, how many guys would you say have been affected by the pills?'

He inhaled a lungful of nicotine and took a few beats to consider the question. 'Maybe four or five.'

'So most aren't affected, but a significant minority have been?'

'I guess.'

This also figured. Those sorts of proportions might correspond to a control group comprising half the contingent. They'd get fed placebos while an experimental group representing the other half would be given whatever was being tested. I guessed this was some sort of psychotropic substance that influenced or altered an aspect of their combat experience.

'How did you get along with the scientists on the research team?'

'They were all dead by the time I arrived. Except Dr Hausinger. I got along with her fine.'

'Did Andy get along with her?'

'He sure did. Had a thing for her. And from what I could make out, she had a thing for him too. That was how the fights started. One of the guys would make a crack about her and Andy went ape. But she disappeared on Monday and Andy cut out a couple of days after that.'

'Could he have gone to meet up with Dr Hausinger?'

'It's possible. But the last thing he said to me was that she'd left us to stew, he'd had enough of the place and he was going home. That's why I think he's in the East Village or New Lots.'

I handed him the rest of my Camels, told him he'd been a big help and asked for one last favour.

When I'd told him what I wanted he looked a little dubious.

I said I'd bring more cigarettes and he said sure, why not?

As he moved off back toward the campus, I recalled what he said after the incident at Gem Spa, about him owing me. Back then I'd thought there was no chance at all of him ever being in a position to make good on that debt.

Now, I thought just how wrong I'd been.

THIRTY-FOUR

When Kevin made the all-clear sign, I followed JoBeth from the shrubbery, across the grass and into the hold-over building.

The clandestine stuff was more than a little ridiculous but Kevin didn't want his buddies to think he was a snitch. We could have gotten permission to enter the building from Blair Murdoch, but he would have been obligated to keep Chief Ducey in the loop. And although I got along well enough the campus cop, I wanted to keep what Kevin had told me between JoBeth and me.

The other guys were working on the opposite side of the Biomedical Centre, so we had an opportunity to search the room shared by Andy Stuivermans and Kevin without them knowing. This was the favour I'd asked of him – and, of course, he got a ten-pack box of Camels as a bonus.

We followed him along a narrow hallway, flanked by plywood walls, and into a room on the right. There was a single bed on either side, with a nightstand and bureau next to each bed.

'I'll leave you to it.' Kevin was antsy and went to keep watch in case any of the others came back early.

The room was squared away, which was what I expected for two veterans living in an army-type environment. They each had one poster – Kevin's was Raquel Welch in *One Million Years BC* and Stuivermans had a cool picture of Jimi Hendrix at Woodstock last year.

He'd left a copy of Allen Ginsberg's *Kaddish and Other Poems* on the nightstand, along with underground newspapers including the *Village Voice* and the *East Village Other*.

So the guy had good taste in literature as well as music. And the more I thought about it, the more the guy I was chasing reminded me of me.

I picked up the Ginsberg poetry book and opened it. There was an inscription on the title page: *Andy, Come back to me safe and sound, with much love, Erikka.*

He'd come back all right, but he wasn't safe and he wasn't sound.

JoBeth was at my side. 'What do you make of it?'

'Looks like a gift before he deployed to Vietnam,' I said. 'That would make it a cherished possession. I'd say he left in a hurry.'

She bit her lip. 'Unless he left in a rage, or after having some sort of breakdown.'

She leafed through a copy of the *East Village Other*, then a mimeographed poetry anthology called *Off-Beat*. 'He's not your average down and out, is he? Music, poetry, culture? This may explain why he got along so well with an intellectual like Hausinger.'

'Also, the underground magazines chime with what Kevin thinks – that Andy went back to Lower Manhattan.'

She tossed the magazine back onto the nightstand. 'Could this Erikka be the girlfriend he broke up with?'

'I'd say so. Remember his personnel file? No home address, no next-of-kin, no references, and no mention of any employment after he got back from Vietnam.'

'You think he could have gone to look for her? To make up?'

'Gotta be a possibility.'

I started going through the bureau and found more evidence of a hasty departure: The top two drawers were filled with T-shirts, Levi jeans, socks and underwear. Maybe he'd taken some clothes with him, though, because the bottom drawer was empty except for a lining of old newspaper pages. I was about to close it when I noticed a grainy picture of someone who looked vaguely familiar.

I looked again.

It was Harriet Brigstock. The photo had been taken when she was much younger, but I was sure it was her. The cutline confirmed this.

I looked closer.

The date at top of the page read *June 15, 1955*. I realized the newspaper page wasn't being used as a lining for the drawer, it was stored there. And there was other material – whole pages, plus clippings of individual articles.

The publication dates ranged from 1954 to 1956, and the clips were from different papers. But they had one element in common: Harriet Brigstock.

'Over here,' I said. 'I got something.'

We took the yellowed articles from the drawer and laid them flat on the bed.

The one with the photo of Harriet Brigstock was about a controversial plan to rezone a residential area in New Lots for industrial development. Brigstock had been a member of the city council's land use committee that greenlit the proposals, despite fierce opposition from local residents. They rejected Brigstock's claims that rezoning would lead to slum clearance, better housing and jobs for local people.

I remembered the redevelopment project – and the shitstorm surrounding it.

Another clipping on the bed included a photo of guys in hard hats with bulldozers and a wrecking ball in the background. This was about the demolition of tenement blocks on a site where developers wanted to build a new manufacturing plant. Other stories reported mass protests by residents.

But it was the first two paragraphs of the final piece, dated September 20, 1955, that reached out from the page and grabbed me by the throat:

A widow took her own life after she and her children were evicted from their home due to a controversial redevelopment project in New Lots, an inquest heard.

Agnes Stuivermans (37) left a note alleging the rezoning of residential land for industrial use had made her family homeless and resulted in her sons Andrew (13) and Herbert (11) being taken into care.

THIRTY-FIVE

We drove down to Manhattan first thing the next morning.

The implications of what we found in Andy Stuivermans' bureau were still ricocheting around my head and I guessed it was the same for JoBeth.

Judging by those clippings, the guy had a deep-rooted and obsessive grudge against Harriet Brigstock. He blamed her for his mom's suicide and the destruction of his family.

This created more questions than I could handle and I had to put the brakes on my thought process. As I saw it, there were two key questions. First: Did Stuivermans shoot Brigstock's son as payback for what he believed she'd done to *his* family? And second: Did Stuivermans leave Ramskill to complete his mission by killing the congresswoman?

We already knew she was in Manhattan for the Security Council session. And I'd just learned from Maggie that she'd also agreed to speak at a rally protesting the invasion of Cambodia, due to take place the day before. This added opportunity to a clear motive of revenge. Did he have the means to murder Harriet Brigstock? Three tours in Vietnam as a Ranger didn't leave this in much doubt.

Yet there was so much we didn't know. A few old news

stories at the bottom of a drawer didn't make Andy Stuivermans a murderer. Nor did his nocturnal stalking activity. True, the matter of his disfigured ear and the ear-related attacks were more disturbing. But the more I thought about this, the more I suspected somebody else carried out those attacks.

JoBeth glanced at me from the passenger seat. 'What I don't get is why he'd wait so long for his revenge.'

This was a problem I'd been wrestling with too. I told her what I thought, 'He was only thirteen when his mom took her life. For a lot of years, he simply wouldn't have been able to do very much – except nurse his hate for the woman he blamed.'

She wasn't convinced. 'But none of that stopped him graduating high school and going on to qualify as an electronic engineer. There was no suggestion of him doing anything unbalanced – just the opposite.'

'Until he came back from the Circus,' I said. 'Long range reconnaissance ops can mess with your head. And you get a lot of time to brood.'

She'd clearly anticipated this. 'And yet he also succeeded in Vietnam. Joined an elite unit, became a senior leader, won the Silver Star.'

'Sure. But to do those things he had to be effective in the field. In the context of Vietnam, that usually means killing folks. OK, you can argue that he was killing the enemy. But one enemy can sometimes morph into a different enemy.'

'Even back home?'

'Especially back home. According to his buddy Kevin, he broke up with his girlfriend and ended up with a booze problem bad enough to put him on Skid Row. More time to brood, more time for all that resentment to fester.'

I saw her make a knowing nod. 'And of course, we have no idea what kind of shit they were feeding him at the biomedical place.'

'We need to find him,' I said. 'Before he finds Harriet Brigstock.'

We arrived in New York City in less than an hour and parked outside my apartment on East 7th Street.

Stuivermans' personnel file said he had no family or home address in New Lots, so we started our search in the East Village. This meant looking up some of my old contacts and I gotta say this freaked me out. Seeing those faces and places from the past, I felt like I was tracing my own life, chasing myself. We visited the Sagamore Cafeteria and the Dom on St Mark's Place, then Club 82 on East 4th Street and Ratner's kosher dairy restaurant on 2nd Avenue. And a whole bunch of other spots. We drew a blank, though we managed to grab some righteous cheese blintzes and coffee at Ratner's. Next we went deep into the Lower East Side. Unlike the East Village, the area hadn't benefited from an influx of bohemians. The farther south we went, the more extreme the poverty. Each block was a run-down, beat-up microcosm of some part of Poland or Ukraine or some eastern European Jewish community. We went into some tough areas and managed to emerge without getting mugged. Even so, we drew another blank. Then we moved to Greenwich Village. Our problem there wasn't muggers, it was tourists cramming the streets. We swung by the White Horse Tavern and the Cedar Tavern, the Café Wha? and the Gaslight Café, the Back Fence and the San Remo. We swung by more places, and more. But again, we drew a blank.

We paused for a late afternoon break at a coffee shop on Waverly Place.

‘We can’t carry on like this,’ she said. ‘We need to be more focused, more specific.’

I gave her a weary look and said I couldn’t agree more.

‘This used to be your beat too,’ she said. ‘What sort of places would *you* hang out? And what about this Erikka? Let’s run with the assumption that she was his long-time girlfriend and they split fairly recently.’

I sipped my coffee. ‘She inscribed that poetry book for him. That tells us they’re both book worms.’

I thought back to the other stuff we found on the nightstand – the *Village Voice* and the *East Village Other* and the mimeographed poetry magazine *Off-Beat*.

‘The only places in New York City you could snag those literary titles he left at Ramskill are the underground bookstores. We could try the 8th Street Bookshop and the Paperbook Gallery here in Greenwich. Also, the Peace Eye in the East Village.’

We finished our coffee and checked out the bookstores. We told folks we were trying to find Andy Stuivermans because his pal Kevin Jacks said he was in the area. In addition, we name-dropped his old rock and roll band, the Rockaways in hopes that somebody may have heard them, or knew any of the other band members. And we mentioned Erikka. Not having a last name made this a longshot, although the way she spelled her first name with two ks was helpful. Folks were friendly, but we still drew a blank.

By the time we’d visited a half dozen outlets, the evening rush hour was in full swing. JoBeth said she needed to talk to her boss and suggested we meet up again later in the evening.

This was a welcome development because the next place

to visit was the Bowery and I wanted to go alone. I told JoBeth it would be easier if just one of us talked to the bums. I also told myself that. I even half believed it.

THIRTY-SIX

The Bowery was a place of ghosts for me, but unlike in the East Village they didn't conjure happy memories. They lingered in doorways and on street corners, reeking of piss and puke and the garbage they rooted through. They'd shit themselves but were too blitzed to clean up. Their faces were caked in dried blood from injuries in binges they couldn't recall. They stole from each other without blinking, then shared their luck when somebody panhandled his way to a bottle of something. They sold their blood to the hospitals to buy booze, then ended up back at the hospital needing a transfusion.

I knew these ghosts well because my mom had been one of them.

And though I was looking for Andy Stuivermans, I was also looking for Jean Tyler. Because despite my emotional impairment, despite the near-zero chances of my mom surviving another five years on the Bowery, I was still in the pincers of dogged guilt and ridiculous hope.

I asked in the liquor stores and the second-hand stores, the shabby cafés and the Three-Sixteens – church missions with John 3:16 over the door – the line that said *For God so loved the world that He sent His only begotten son …*

I asked if anyone had seen Andy Stuivermans but I didn't need to ask about my mom. She'd have been easy enough to spot because the population of Skid Row was almost exclusively male. There had even been a ludicrous suggestion of a link between alcoholism and homosexuality. I knew it was ludicrous because getting laid was absolutely the last thing on the minds of these people.

But nobody had seen or heard of Stuivermans and I didn't see a single female down-and-out.

Next I visited some flophouses. They were much less in demand in the spring than the winter, but Stuivermans had been getting ten bucks a day at the biomedical place so he could afford a roof over his head.

The places I went to varied massively. The cheapest comprised a dormitory with bare wood flooring and rows of perished rubber sleeping mats. If folks had any possessions they could store them in metal cages at one end of the dorm. The stench trapped inside was actually worse than on the street. There was a sign in the hallway to the washroom and toilet, but I heard the sound of retching and didn't go any nearer.

In some of the more upmarket places, fifty cents got you a tiny cubicle just big enough for a bed, a bucket and a chair. I tried my luck in one called the Bright Day Hotel. An odour of sour sweat and booze pervaded the lobby, but the other Bowery smells seemed to have stopped at the entrance. If Stuivermans had fallen off the wagon but not yet hit rock bottom, this was the kind of place he might spend a few dollars.

I approached a bored looking clerk sitting at a cash register behind a steel-barred hatch. Overhead was a sign saying *No welfare customers – Cash only*.

I asked about Stuivermans and he said he hadn't seen him. I wasn't allowed upstairs to talk to the residents, but this changed when I pushed a dollar between the metal bars.

This was happy hour in the Bowery dives, so the Bright Day was largely empty. In one room, though, I found a bare-chested guy wearing suit pants, suspenders and a purple fedora that looked weirdly new. He was sitting on his bed sucking a quarter pint of vodka. He glanced up, nervy-aggressive. Looked sixty, probably forty.

He hadn't seen Stuivermans before or after I placed a one-spot on his bed.

I was on my way out when he said, 'You're the second person today asking about a guy like that.'

I stopped, turned back.

'Who else has been asking?'

'This chick.'

'What did she looked like?'

I saw the dollar signs in his eyes and took out another buck.

'Pretty, slim, blonde hair to her shoulders. Twenties, I guess.'

He reached for the bill but I held onto it.

'What was she wearing?'

He thought about this. 'One of them fringed buckskin jackets, the type hippies wear. Indian bead designs on the chest. And a peace sign on the collar.'

I let him take the money. Odds on this was Erikka, and odds on she was looking for Stuivermans in the same places I was. I decided to look again at the spots I'd already been to with JoBeth. Maybe our paths would cross.

Outside, I headed back in the direction of Houston Street.

The female derelict was dead ahead with her back to me.

I thought I recognised something in the chicken-bone limbs and spiderweb hair. The tatty cotton dress was two sizes too big and her heels lifted out of her torn canvas tennis shoes with every step.

She almost vanished into the sidewalk crowd.

I went after her. I hustled. Got close.

Same height, same build.

Surely not after all this time.

I shouted, 'Mom!'

She didn't hear.

I tapped her shoulder and she turned around.

She had the same unplugged eyes, same crepe paper skin, same slack gape.

But this wasn't my mom. I had a good idea how five years on the Bowery might change a person and the one thing it wouldn't do was make them look less dreadful than they used to. Because wrecked as she was, this woman seemed in much better shape than my mom was when I last saw her in the summer of '65.

I said, 'Sorry, ma'am. Thought you were somebody else.'

'Spare a dime?' One arm came up in an automatic movement, palm outstretched.

I gave her a dollar and realized I had to get out of there before I parted with my sanity as well as my money.

*

Logic told me the chances of me finding the girl described by the guy with the bare chest and purple fedora were remote. But that evening I wasn't doing so well with logical thinking.

So I spent three hours revisiting the spots I'd been to with JoBeth. Fringed buckskin coats were all the rage in 1970 and there was no shortage of young women wearing them. Not surprisingly, none checked the boxes Fedora had given me. Some came close, though, and on a couple of occasions I had to extricate myself from difficult situations when these girls and their boyfriends saw me looking at them.

After three hours of futile buckskin-hunting I was dead beat, weary and frustrated. But the Turntable record store on 8th Street was just a few blocks away from JoBeth's place on Christopher Street.

I went inside. It was almost 8.30pm but the place was still busy. The long racks of vinyl brought back memories of days and nights spent in pursuit of a rare import or bootleg. Whatever I wanted, the Turntable was always a rich vein.

On the off chance, I sauntered over to the R section of second hand records and looked up The Rockaways. Maybe they'd cut their own record and if so I was interested in hearing it.

There was no album.

But there was a girl in a buckskin coat flicking through the records on the aisle facing me.

I clocked rounded features, blonde hair to her shoulders, Indian-style embroidery and a peace symbol on the lapel.

I said, 'Erikka?'

THIRTY-SEVEN

She looked up and I saw curious blue eyes, an expression that started off friendly but soon switched to suspicious.

'I'm sorry,' she said. 'I don't recall where we met.'

'We didn't.' There was no point bullshitting because there were too many ways this could go south. And gaining her trust was going to be crucial.

'So how did you know who I was?'

'Through Andy. He is – or was – your boyfriend, right?'

'How do you know Andy?'

'I don't – not directly. I'm from Ramskill University, where Andy was working until a few days ago.'

She frowned. 'Who are you?'

'My name is Wat. Wat Tyler. I'm a teacher at Ramskill and also a reporter for the *Examiner*.'

There was a slightly alarmed note in her voice. 'Did you follow me here?'

'No I didn't.'

'Then how did you know where to find me?'

'I didn't know.' I made a you-got-me-there shrug. 'I was browsing the records, then I looked up and there you were.'

Her frowned deepened.

I said, 'Listen, Erikka, we both want the same thing – to find Andy.'

She didn't seem at all reassured by this.

I kept my voice level, 'I think you've been looking in the same places as me. A guy at the Bright Day Hotel on the Bowery told me a young blonde woman wearing a buckskin jacket with a peace symbol on the collar had been asking about Andy not long before I arrived. Then I saw you here in the store. But I wasn't sure it was you. When I called your name, I was just playing a hunch.'

I sensed she was about to bolt, or call the manager.

Which gave me an idea.

I glanced over to the sales counter and realized the idea was solid.

'Hey, Brian!'

An overweight guy with a sparse comb-over and a droopy black moustache turned away from a pile of records on the counter. Brian Kaminski looked hot and bothered – and significantly older than when I last visited his store five years ago.

I raised my voice so he could hear better. 'Spare a minute?'

Brian gave me an irritated look and came waddling over to where we were standing. 'What is it, Wat? Can't you see I'm busy?'

He seemed to notice Erikka for the first time. 'This guy bothering you, Miss?'

She made a non-committal shrug.

'Brian, you need to tell Erikka here who I am.'

He ran his fingers through the thin strands on his sweaty scalp. 'Well, Wat, you used to be a regular customer here, and you used to work on the *Examiner*. But you ain't bought a record from me for years. So you gotta be going someplace else. And I ain't seen your name in the paper either, so you must be working someplace else.'

'I've been in Vietnam for five years.' I tried to keep the exasperation from my tone. 'I did tell you before I left.'

'Don't recall. Lotta kids went to Vietnam.' He spoke without a hint of apology, but that was Brian all over. He turned away and headed back to the counter. Over his shoulder, he said to Erikka, 'Wat's a solid sender – even if he has been buying records someplace else.'

I said to her, 'Brian's sense of time is all messed up. I really have been in Vietnam.'

'OK, I get that you're not a weirdo.' Now she was looking at me with a different sort of curiosity. 'But why are you looking for Andy?'

'It's not straightforward,' I said. 'Let me buy you a drink. There's a place across the street.'

We went to the bar and found a quiet corner.

'OK, you got my attention,' she said. 'Tell me what this is all about.'

I told her the truth. Well, most of it. I didn't explicitly say Stuivermans was a suspect in the campus shooting, or the triple homicide at the biomedical place. But she was a smart kid and joined up the dots.

'Andy's not been right since Vietnam. I get that more than anybody. But he's not a murderer.' She drank some beer and gave me a hard look.

I held her eyes. 'But you can see why law enforcement might think he's in the frame. That's why I need to find him – why I need your help.'

She gave me an odd kind of look. 'You remind me of him. Look like him too. It's not obvious at first, but there's a definite connection. Different life, you could have been brothers.'

This didn't sound like a compliment – more of a perturbed observation and I didn't know how to take it. I'd realized some time ago that the pair of us had led strangely parallel lives and the idea fazed me a little. Maybe it was because if his life had turned to shit, who was to say mine wouldn't follow suit? Right then, though, I needed Erikka to co-operate. So I said, 'Different life, we could have been friends. We went to the same junior high in New Lots, we dig the same music and we did similar stuff in Vietnam.'

'Vietnam's the difference.' She gave me an angry-sad look. 'Vietnam fucked Andy up, whereas you're together.'

'I'm not as together as you might think,' I said. 'So what was Andy like before the war?'

'Happy. Confident. Comfortable in his own skin. That was rare for a New Lots kid who spent time in the care system. But he was a special guy. We graduated together and he became an electrical engineer. He was good at his work too. His bosses told him had a great future.'

'When did you two get together?'

'High school. It was like we were made for one another. We loved literature and poetry in particular. The beats, but also Shakespeare and the metaphysical guys, the romantics, Walt Whitman and TS Eliot. And music. We went to concerts together here in Manhattan. When he formed the Rockaways, he wrote the lyrics as well as the music.'

'That's a real cool name for a rock band.'

'They made some real cool sounds. Played school and community halls, a couple of small venues in Greenwich.

There was even talk of a record deal. Andy and I had our lives in front of us. We were gonna get married, have kids, get a dog – Andy loved dogs. He wanted a beagle. Then Vietnam happened. Every time he came home between tours I saw less and less of the man I knew, the boy I loved. It was like he'd gotten addicted to that damn war. When he finally mustered out, he was a different guy.'

'Different how?'

She set down her beer. 'Bad tempered. Irritable. Couldn't concentrate. They no longer had an opening at his old company and the only work he could get was casual labour. Then Herbie, his younger brother got killed in the Mekong Delta. That hit Andy right between the eyes. He felt he was responsible. Andy was drinking more and more. And he started taking amphetamines. He'd also tried to resurrect the Rockaways, but he couldn't get along with the other guys and they broke up. Not long after that, he and I broke up.'

'I'm sorry to hear that, Erikka.'

She looked at me, foggy-eyed. 'Andy made a success of his life against all the odds, but it still wasn't good enough. They wouldn't let him make it. They got him in the end. That's the way of things, I guess.'

I agreed it was a screwed-up world, that Andy got a shitty deal. Then I said, 'This grudge Andy had for Harriet Brigstock, was that a thing before he went to Vietnam?'

She nodded yes. 'He'd always hated the Brigstock woman. Can't say I blamed him. That rezoning scheme she was pushing took a wrecking ball to the tenements where he grew up. You know how folks in that part of Brooklyn used to watch out for each other. Anyway, his friends and neighbours got scattered to the wind. Those jobs Brigstock promised never materialized. Andy and Herbie eventually lost their mom and ended up in care.'

'Did this resentment of Brigstock get any worse after he mustered out?'

Another morose nod. 'It went from an occasional bee in his bonnet to a real obsession.'

There was a brief quiet, then she looked up, angry and defiant. 'But he wouldn't kill her if that's that you're thinking.'

'I wasn't thinking that.'

But I was.

I asked another tough question, 'Did he get the ear wound in Vietnam?'

She shook her head, even made a brief smile. 'That happened in a street fight when we were sixteen. We saw this old boy getting mugged in East Flatbush and Andy stepped in. The mugger pulled a switchblade and Andy took a swipe intended for the old guy.'

This surprised me. I thought again about a number of assumptions, in particular the ear-related attacks on the sheepdog and the bunny and Harold Kapp.

I had one last question, 'Why did you start looking for him?'

She raised her shoulders and let them drop. 'Guilt. Maybe if I'd been a little more understanding, a little more ...'

'None of what happened is your fault.' I reached out and gripped her hands. 'And it's not too late. You can still help him. *We* can still help him.'

I searched my pockets and found a calling card. 'If you find Andy, tell him I want to talk – that's all. On the phone, face-to-face, anywhere he likes. Would you do that?'

She said she would, although I seriously doubted he'd ever get in touch with me. Even so, a slim chance was better than no chance.

THIRTY-EIGHT

I arrived at JoBeth's place on Christopher Street an hour late. This was fine, though, because so did she. We approached from opposite ends of the street and met at the front door.

She pretended a stern expression. 'What's your excuse?'

'Bet it's better than yours.'

'We'll see.' She opened the front door and we rode the cage elevator up to her apartment.

She offered me a drink and I said I could use a stiff bourbon. She poured one for me and one for herself, then joined me on the couch.

'You go first.' she said.

I took a big swallow of whiskey and lit a cigarette – I was done with the delaying tactic, at least for now – then told her what happened with Erikka.

'Good work,' she said. 'And not a bad excuse for getting here late.'

'Wanna tell me yours?'

'Wanna refill?'

I said sure and sat back while she told me.

'I started looking into the background of your National Guard boss, Colonel Philip Riley.' She kicked off her shoes and massaged one foot, then the other. 'He served in World War II, but only the last few months. Most of his active duty was in Korea. This got me wondering if the Asian girl we saw him with is the bait in a honey trap. If an affair like that came out it would ruin him. His wife would likely file for divorce and he'd have a lot of explaining to do with his family. That's not to mention the end of his career in the National Guard as well as in his day job – senior partner at a corporate and commercial law firm in the financial district.'

I took out another Camel, but this time refrained from lighting it. 'That would make him easy meat for any blackmailer or shakedown artist.'

She nodded. 'Or somebody with an interest in provoking trouble at Ramskill: The pro-war faction or the anti-war faction; the North Vietnamese or the Soviets; or pick your own three-letter federal agency. Riley could have been blackmailed into sanctioning the shootings as well as handling the cover-up.'

I gave her an appreciative look. She was a smart cookie, no argument. 'So, what have you been up to?'

She took a drink. 'I waited outside his office and tailed him to Wall Street subway station. He took the 5 train to East 23rd Street and walked three blocks to Grammercy Park. No surprise when he met the Asian girl. From there, they walked arm-in-arm to a swish French restaurant at 21st and 3rd.'

She paused to drink more bourbon and her expression changed from animated to puzzled. 'I have to say, though, that for a guy having an affair with a woman half his age, he was a surprisingly easy mark. No awareness of risk whatsoever, not even the odd glance over his shoulder.'

I shrugged. 'Maybe he's gotten complacent.'

'Or maybe he wants to get caught. Some guys do. They can't take the pressure any more. They just want it to be over.' An edge in her voice told me she was talking from experience.

She moved on quickly, as if she regretted touching on the subject. 'I hope you're not pissed off. I thought it better to go after Riley on my own. Like we agreed last time we tailed him, he'd have made you the moment he saw you.'

I gave her a laid-back smile. 'Why should I be pissed off? I did my own thing too.'

She drank more bourbon. Boy, she was getting through it. 'Anyway, I decided we need some help. We can't be in New York City *and* Ramskill at the same time, right? So I requested FBI surveillance of Riley.'

The need for nicotine finally got the better of me and I lit my cigarette. 'Makes sense I guess – unless J Edgar's boys are behind the unrest at Ramskill.'

She finished her drink. 'Let's park the paranoia for the time being. In fact, let's park everything.'

This was fine with me. She fixed more drinks and put John Coltrane's *Blue Train* on the turntable. I was cool with a little jazz and we leaned back on the couch, nursing our tumblers and soaking up the sounds.

Pretty soon the whiskey started smoothing out the wrinkles of the day. The hectic world outside receded and we leaned into one another, shoulder-to-shoulder.

After a while, I reached out, took her hand and turned to face her.

She looked knockout sexy.

Moving toward me, she kissed my mouth, slow yet eager. I kissed her back, just as slow, just as eager. She stood up, pulled me to my feet and led me into the bedroom. By the time we hit the sheets my dick was fully mobilized and it soon became clear she was in a similar state of readiness. We got it on with restrained urgency, stretching the moment, making it last, building little by little to urgent urgency, climaxing in a hot blast of need and desire.

After, we lay back, just breathing.

When we'd cooled off I said, 'You all right?'

'Uh huh.'

She snuggled her head under my chin and placed her arm across my chest. Her hair was smooth against my skin and smelled faintly of jasmine and vetiver.

'If you want, we can talk about those things you think I might not want to know.'

She made a faint groan. 'Can we talk another time?'

'Absolutely.' I kissed the top of her head.

'It's just that … '

'We don't need to talk at all,' I said. 'Not if – '

'I used to be a criminal defence attorney in Philadelphia.' She spoke quietly but insistently and without lifting her head from under my jaw. 'Then I got a guy acquitted on a murder charge and he killed three more people two hours after walking out the court room.'

I stroked her hair. 'Hey, that was your job. If you didn't do it, somebody else – '

'I thought I was such a damn good advocate.' She went on talking, almost to herself. I sensed she'd been steeling herself for this moment for a very long time. 'Then I hated myself for what I did because, deep down, I knew all along the guy was guilty. That was why I became a prosecutor. I told myself I needed a new direction. But I was really just running away. That's one thing I know for sure I'm good at.'

I said nothing, gave her some time. She wanted to say her piece and didn't need any pearl-of-wisdom interjections from me.

'My plan when I was a high school senior was to practise law in West Virginia: Graduate from a big city law school, then go back home to Beckley. But I never did go back.'

She readjusted her head slightly, sucked in a lungful of air, as if to ready herself for another hurdle. 'See, my daddy was an accountant at one of the big coal mines and my momma, she stayed home. I realized something was wrong when I smelled perfume on him –Momma never cared for that sort of thing. Anyway, I tailed him after work one evening and he led me straight to where his mistress lived. She was just three years older than me. What was worse, *I* knew *he* knew I was following him. And I knew he didn't care.'

'That's why you thought Riley wanted to get caught, isn't it?'

She nodded yes. 'This mistress, she was twenty-one and real pretty. She wouldn't normally have looked twice at my dad. But he was splashing the cash bigtime. Whatever she wanted, she got. But he was spending money that didn't belong to him. He was embezzling the coal mine.'

She paused again and I thought it was curious how she'd strayed back into her West Virginia accent. The way she was talking, she might never have left those dirty old coal towns. I wondered if I did the same sometimes.

'Daddy got arrested the day Momma was told by her sister about his mistress. Upshot was Daddy went to jail, Momma went to a psychiatric hospital and JoBeth went to study law in Philadelphia, never to return.'

She made a wistful sigh. 'How awful is that?'

'I never went back either.'

'You had good reason to stay away. The only reason I did was because I couldn't grow a spine. I couldn't face the shame.'

'You were young and alone. You could face those people now, though.'

'No point. My mom died in the psych clinic and my dad never got in touch when he came out of prison. He just vanished off the face of the earth. Then again, I didn't make any great effort to find him.'

'Maybe one day.'

'Maybe never.'

'I thought that for five years. But today, when I went looking for Andy Stuivermans on the Bowery, I was also looking for my mom. Never thought I'd ever do that, even if it was an utterly forlorn hope. She was in a dreadful state when I went to Vietnam. I'm pretty certain she's dead.'

'She could have quit the booze.'

'Highly unlikely, but possible.'

'So you could still find her – maybe one day.'

'And you could still find your dad – maybe one day.'

'I'd need to stop running first. Running from my dad, and my mom, and running from those poor people in Philly who got shot to death because I'd just gotten an acquittal for the psychopath who killed them. And, of course, running from myself.'

I placed my fingers under her chin and lifted her head up so she was looking straight at me. 'You can stop running here,' I said. 'You can stop running now.'

She made a faint smile. 'We could go back to West Virginia together – maybe one day.'

I kissed her lips. ‘I’d love to do that.’

I meant it too. Which was as close to a commitment as I’d ever come.

THIRTY-NINE

Harriet Brigstock saw us at her apartment in the Dakota building on the corner of West 72nd Street and Central Park West. Located on the seventh floor, the place was lavishly furnished and afforded panoramic views across the park. As with her office at 26 Broadway, it was a none-too-subtle statement that said: Look how far this girl from a Brooklyn slum has come.

Yet her creviced complexion and dumpy frame looked one hundred per cent Brownsville and zero per cent Upper West Side.

We followed her into her living room and sat facing her on soft leather armchairs.

'What is it this time?' She didn't sound especially pleased to see us, though at least we didn't get the flat out rude treatment she gave us last time we saw her.

JoBeth took the lead. 'Our investigations suggest you may be in danger from a former special operations soldier with a deep-seated grudge against you. We think he might have used a sniper rifle to shoot your son, and suspect he's come to Manhattan looking for you.'

'What grudge?'

I told her how the rezoning project had led to the razing

of Andy Stuivermans' old community, his mom's suicide and he and his brother going into care.

She lit a cigarette and her hyperactive eyes narrowed. 'Why would he want to shoot my son? Boyd never did anything to hurt him.'

I said, 'Maybe he wants to destroy your family step by step – in the way he believes you destroyed his.'

She blew out a jet of blue-tinged tobacco fumes. 'That New Lots programme was a bad deal for everyone – I got taken for a ride too. And I understand why this boy would be angry. But I didn't force his momma to do what she did. I didn't put him into a foster home.'

JoBeth leaned forward. 'Ma'am, you should know that this guy Andy Stuivermans isn't in a stable state of mind. He seems to be suffering from an extreme form of combat fatigue. In addition, if our source is correct, he's been used as a lab rat for the development of a new drug at the Biomedical Centre up at Ramskill. Our source believes Stuivermans' condition has been made much worse by whatever it is he's been taking.'

Brigstock frowned, but seemed more concerned with the research activities than the danger posed by a sniper with a score to settle. 'What sort of drug are we looking at here?'

'We don't know,' JoBeth said. 'We're still trying to get to the bottom of what's been going on at the biomedical place.'

'Well, keep me informed would you?' The congresswoman gave each of us a direct look, then did her thing with lighting a fresh cigarette from the butt of the one she just smoked.

I gave her a stern look. 'We'll let you know if anything turns up, ma'am. But in the meantime you need to be real careful. This fella Stuivermans is a serious threat.'

She made an almost careless shrug. 'I can't just shut up shop, Mr Tyler. I got a busy schedule – commitments I can't go back on, events that can't be cancelled, promises I can't break.'

'We understand that, ma'am,' I said. 'All we're suggesting is that you don't paint a target on your back. For example, speaking at the rally in Washington Square isn't a good idea.'

This seemed to amuse her. 'I'm afraid it's exactly the opposite. As we discussed when we talked last time, I can't go rogue and support the Sino-Soviet resolution to the Security Council. But I can – and must – make my views known at the demonstration beforehand.'

I tried to keep the frustration from my voice. 'You'll be extremely vulnerable, ma'am, especially to a sniper. You really shouldn't do it.'

She made an uncompromising expression. 'Your concerns are noted, Mr Tyler. But I really have to do it.'

JoBeth and I glanced at one another and tacitly agreed there was no point dragging this out.

We thanked Brigstock for her time and drove back to JoBeth's place.

As the apartment door closed behind us, she kissed me long and lazy and suggested putting the investigation to the back of our minds until tomorrow. Gotta say, this was not in the least bit difficult.

FORTY

Next morning I went into the *Examiner* office and updated Maggie on the investigation. There was nothing we could report since the attacks on Lenny Lesniak and Harold Kapp so we agreed to see how the week played out.

When I came out of the conference room I picked up a phone message from Ramskill University President Blair Murdoch. He'd called half an hour ago and said he wanted to meet urgently, although he didn't say why. Nor would he elaborate when I returned the call: It was a confidential issue that could only be discussed face to face. I reached JoBeth at the US Attorney's office but she was due to go into a meeting with her boss. We agreed that I'd see Murdoch alone and touch base with her later that day on campus.

I drove back to Ramskill and found the president in his big untidy office.

'So good of you to come, my boy.' He came to his feet, shook my hand, and indicated the chair in front of his desk.

I apologised for JoBeth's absence and told him she'd be on campus just as soon as she could. In the meantime, I was keen to find out why he wanted to see us.

'In the circumstances, *wanted* isn't the word I'd have

chosen.' He gave me a rheumy look and pushed a manila envelope across the inlaid leather surface of his desk. 'I'm sure you'll agree when you see the contents.'

I picked up the envelope and pulled out a selection of seven by five inch colour photos. They showed Oleg Bobkov and Gordon Richardson kissing, embracing and touching. The settings seemed to be in their offices, or at their apartments. Some showed them semi-clad, others naked.

'I received those images in the post this morning.' Murdoch rubbed the bridge of his nose, as if massaging a headache. 'In light of your concerns about the way Bobkov and Richardson died, I thought you should see them at once.'

I looked at the postmark, which showed the envelope had been mailed in Ramskill on Friday. It had been addressed to Murdoch in double spaced type and with STRICTLY PRIVATE AND CONFIDENTIAL typed in red capitals in the top left corner.

I said, 'Do you have any idea at all who might have sent these?'

'None whatever.' He made a dismal shrug. 'That was why I called you.'

I looked again at the images and considered what I knew. It had been obvious since the get-go that Bobkov and Richardson were close – they lunched together every weekday and this was what made Bobkov a predictable target. Clearly, though, these photos put their friendship in a totally different light.

I wondered too if it might explain *why* they were shot. See, gay rights was very much in its infancy in 1970. Sure, we'd had the Stonewall riots in Greenwich Village the previous June, but not much had changed since and there was still a very long road ahead. Maggie was a leading figure in the New York City gay rights movement so I knew just how tough it was to be gay or lesbian back then. A lot of folks considered homosexuality to be a sin, an obscenity, and worse, a threat. Homosexuals were often the victims of vicious beatings. Some of them died as a result. I'd never come across a gay assassination, although looking at these images made me wonder. Take a violent bigot like Gerry Bohannon, for example. I doubted he'd think twice if he saw a couple of fags in his crosshairs and thought he wouldn't get caught. Maybe Bobkov's death wasn't linked to his work. Maybe he and Richardson had been killed just because they were gay.

There was another possibility.

I glanced at Murdoch, who was busy filling his pipe. 'Do you think Bobkov or Richardson, or both were being blackmailed?'

He looked up from his task. 'I'd be surprised if they weren't. Why else would these photographs have been taken?'

'Were either of them wealthy? Or were from wealthy families?'

'I didn't know either of them personally, though I understand Bobkov's parents were penniless immigrants from Russia and Richardson was from a comfortable middle class family, but not a rich one. I'll look into their files and let you know if I come up with anything.'

'I'd be grateful, sir.' I made an apologetic smile. 'I think we both know, though, that any blackmail activity would almost certainly have related to the work Bobkov was doing at the Biomedical Centre.'

He made an equally apologetic one. 'And I think we both

know, Mr Tyler, that I can't disclose details of the internal enquiry into the unorthodox funding of Bobkov's programme that is currently underway. Of course I will make you aware of its findings at the earliest possible opportunity.'

I nodded. This was exactly what I was expecting. Even so, it was important to raise the issue. Something else was bothering me. 'Why do you think these pictures were sent to you now, when they're both dead and buried?'

He sucked on his pipe and blew out a dense tobacco cloud. 'It could be an attempt to blackmail *me*.'

This threw me, gotta say. 'You, sir? I don't understand.'

'Acts of homosexuality among faculty staff is dismissible misconduct. You don't reach my years without realizing that it's been going on since the dawn of time and my attitude has always been to turn a blind eye. However, if a homosexual relationship between two senior professors became public, it could seriously damage the university's reputation. Some parents might ask themselves if Ramskill was the sort of institution their offspring should be attending. Some young people might wonder if they should come here.'

'But you haven't received any sort of blackmail demand?'

He shook his head.

I thought about this a little more. 'Another possibility is that the people who sent these pictures are behind the assassination of Bobkov – as well as the covert funding programme you're probing.' I held up my hand to acknowledge the protest I sensed was on his lips. 'I accept you can't comment on this, sir, but knowing what I do, I'd say it's entirely plausible that any conspiracy against Bobkov would benefit not only from his death, but also using his private life to trash his scientific reputation.'

'As president of this university, I couldn't speculate.' He peered through a haze of pipe smoke and gave me a knowing look. 'However, as a private individual, I'd say you may well be onto something – particularly in the absence of any sort of financial demand.'

This was as much as I was going to get from Murdoch, but it was good enough. What worried me most was that the architects of this conspiracy had the power not only to put Bobkov in the grave, but also to stop him speaking from beyond it. Wreck somebody's personal legacy, you'll wreck their professional one as well.

I had one last question. 'May I ask, sir, what you intend to do with the pictures?'

'Eventually, burn the damn things.' He took the prints back and returned them to the envelope. 'But for the present, I'll keep them safe.'

Of course, whoever sent the prints would still have the negatives. But Murdoch seemed to have plenty on his plate without me adding to it, so I kept schtum, thanked him for his help and left.

FORTY-ONE

I met JoBeth for lunch at a diner in downtown Ramskill and we traded the intel we'd picked up that morning.

I started by outlining my meeting with Murdoch and she agreed the photos of Bobkov and Richardson were more likely to do with trashing the former's reputation than extorting money from the university.

When the waitress had done clearing the table, JoBeth told me what she'd been up to in Manhattan. 'I was curious about why Harriet Brigstock wanted us to keep her up to date on what's been happening at the biomedical place. So I checked out her recent activities and discovered she's chairing a congressional investigation into pharmacological research practices. Seems she's been going after large pharmaceutical companies accused of cutting corners on research and development. She's made some big claims and some big enemies.'

I stirred some creamer into my coffee. 'Including the people backing Bobkov's research?'

'Gotta be a strong possibility.' Glancing through the diner window, she watched a group of placard-toting students march past chanting abuse about Richard Nixon, the cops, and capitalism. As they moved along the sidewalk and the noise subsided, she continued. 'I also looked at the Ramskill University board of trustees – as Murdoch said, their names are on the public record and we know some of them supported the dubious funding programme. Trouble is, none appear to have any connections to the pharmaceutical industry, or the military, or any other sector that might have an interest. I've asked my FBI pals to run more detailed background checks, but for the time being we're flying blind.'

'You think these people are a direct threat to Brigstock?'

'Yes I do. If she's jeopardizing a seven-figure investment they'll do everything in their power to protect it. And given the way they bypassed Murdoch, I'd say they have an awful lot of power.'

'Can't fault your logic,' I said. 'But surely Andy Stuivermans is the most obvious danger.'

She drained her coffee cup. 'Agreed. But if we can believe Stuivermans has been working with Gerry Bohannon; and Bohannon has been working with Corey Judson; then it follows that these folks with upwards of a million bucks on the line could be in hock with any one of them, any two, or all three.'

I gave her a longsuffering look. 'You got any other uplifting theories?'

'No more theories. But I do have some very interesting information about your boss Colonel Riley.'

She waited while the waitress refilled out coffee cups. Then she said, 'The FBI surveillance gave us an instant return. They tailed Riley to another meet with the Asian girl. This time it was at a hotel in the theatre district.'

I rolled my eyes. 'Just can't keep his hands off her, can he?'

She didn't comment. 'They didn't stay long – just a couple of drinks – then the feds followed her to an apartment building in Chelsea. They made some discreet enquiries and identified her as a Korean national called Park Ahnjong. And get this: She just completed a PhD in biochemistry at a school affiliated to Columbia University.'

This blew me away. We'd been working on the assumption that Riley was having an affair with a waitress or maybe a bank clerk. Our reasoning was that she'd have been impressed by his wealth and willingness to spend some of it on her. But that reasoning didn't work so well with a doctoral graduate with Ivy League connections.

JoBeth watched the astonishment register on my face, then hit me again, 'And get this too: She recently became an intern at a big pharmaceutical company in Manhattan called Kershaw Lefevre Laboratories.'

Getting blown away was becoming routine. I said, 'We need to find out if Riley has connections to Kershaw Lefevre. And if Kershaw Lefevre has any connections to the Biomedical Centre.'

She nodded. 'We need to talk to Riley.'

I agreed. 'And we need to find Loretta Hausinger. She's the key to what's being going at the biomedical place.'

JoBeth looked doubtful. 'She hasn't been seen for nearly a week. Either she doesn't want to be found or something's happened to her.'

'She's not dead,' I said.

She gave me a puzzled look. 'How do you know that?'

'I don't. Not for sure. After what happened to the other people in her team and her own narrow escape, she should be dead. But she's smart and resourceful and involved in all of this in ways we don't yet know about. She could know where Andy Stuivermans is. She may even be with him.'

'So how can we find her?'

I had to admit I didn't have an answer. Not right then anyway.

FORTY-TWO

My lock picks got me into Loretta's campus apartment without a hitch.

JoBeth didn't know what I was up to and I had no intention of enlightening her because I knew what her objections would be. But I wasn't a federal prosecutor so I didn't need to worry about illegal searches or contaminated evidence. What I did need to worry about was finding Loretta. Although I thought she was still alive, I was acutely aware that this could change any moment.

I started my search in the living room but found nothing useful. Checking out the dining area, bedroom and bathroom didn't prove any more fruitful – except for some prescription migraine pills I'd have expected her to bring if she was planning a vacation.

I hit pay dirt, though, when I went into the kitchen. A beef stew had been left in a Pyrex dish next to the stove, along with some potatoes in a pan of water, ready for boiling. After a week in the hot weather the stew had dried out and was giving off a rancid odour. Nearby, the spuds had started to disintegrate, turning the water murky grey. The migraine pills may had been an oversight, the food, never. Wherever she'd ended up after her symposium at Princeton, Loretta had every intention of coming home that evening to eat the stuff she'd prepared.

Problem was, I was no nearer to finding out where she'd gone.

Until I noticed the picture postcard among a number of snapshots and written reminders pinned to a cork board. The postcard depicted a scenic view across woodland toward a broad stretch of water. And it had been placed right in the centre of the board in the way folks did with stuff that conjured happy memories.

I took the postcard and flipped it over. The handwriting was neat and well punctuated. It didn't say much but what it did say was useful: *Dear Loretta, It was so lovely to welcome you to Foxley Farm last week. Pocantico is such a lovely little lake and the cabin is there for you to use whenever you need a break – although please note we'll be in Europe until mid-June. With all our love, Rachael and Bob.*

Pocantico Lake was a favourite spot for hikers and anglers, about a half hour drive from Ramskill. It was remote, but not too far from the beaten track. An ideal location for somebody with a headful of trouble who wanted to disappear. It was exactly the sort of place I'd choose to lay low.

I returned the postcard to the cork board and was on my way out of the apartment when I heard the sirens.

*

Three fire engines came barrelling through the campus gates and headed for the Biomedical Centre. A pillar of dark smoke was coiling over the treeline as I hustled in that direction.

When I got there, the right side of the building was in the grasp of big orange flames. They punched out through broken windows, lapping the external walls and spreading fast toward the main entrance.

I saw Gene Ducey arrive along with a convoy of campus police cars and a couple of ambulances.

Outside the hold-over buildings, I pinned Kevin Jacks and some of the other janitors.

He nodded in the direction of the bushes and headed off as if he was going to take a leak.

I got his drift – he didn't want the others to see him talking to an outsider – and I circled around the back of the building.

Kevin was waiting in a small clearing behind a clump of rhododendrons.

I gave him a Camel, a light and asked him if anyone was still in the building.

He took a long drag on the cigarette and shook his head. 'All our guys are accounted for and I overheard one of the professors telling the fire chief everybody was out.'

I asked if he knew how the blaze started.

'I spotted a fire in one of the labs in the research area,' he said. 'I was cleaning the hallway outside, smelled the smoke and there it was. But another guy says he saw the conference room burning at around the same time. We both tried to use foam extinguishers, but it was no use and we called 911.'

'Any flammable substances in the lab?'

He made a what-do-I-know? expression. 'They keep all sorts of stuff in there.'

'Did you see anyone hanging around the building? Anything at all suspicious?'

He said no, nothing.

I had my doubts though that this was a coincidence. Because if this was pure bad luck, this had to be the most dangerous place to work in New York State. Four out of a five-strong research team murdered, the fifth cheating death by a whisker, and now the building ravaged by fire. And if it wasn't a coincidence, who was responsible? Corey Quilton and SLUT had to be in the frame. They'd torched other university buildings as well as downtown businesses. So why not the biomedical place?

Then again, if the motive for killing Bobkov and the others was to stop their programme, whoever was responsible would also benefit from the physical destruction of the research facility. But who were these people? For reasons I couldn't begin to fathom, their interests seemed to be diametrically opposed to those of the folks covertly funding the research project. Another possibility was Andy Stuivermans. Maybe he never went to Manhattan. Maybe he'd been in Ramskill the whole time, waiting for this opportunity.

I was walking back to the J-School when I heard Gene Ducey call my name.

The campus police chief detached himself from a group of firefighters and came hurrying toward me.

'You see Corey Quilton today?'

I raised an eyebrow. 'Should I have?'

He made a wry smile. 'Word on the ground is you're his hero. The guy who stuck it to the Man in the Nam, saviour of Sally Newchurch after she got bayoneted.'

'I'm nobody's hero,' I said. 'Especially not Quilton's. But he does consider me useful right now. You think he started the fire?'

Ducey made a dubious expression. 'You know I can't

speculate. But he is a person of interest and I do need to talk to him.'

'OK,' I said, 'I'll let you know if I see him.'

*

I saw Corey Quilton a half hour later, but I didn't call Ducey – there was no point. Quilton was leaving the Barricade bar as I drove by on my way out of town. He made a friendly wave as I went past and I gave him a brief nod. He could have been anywhere by the time I parked up and got through to Ducey on a payphone.

My destination was Pocantico Lake where I hoped to find Loretta Hausinger. Of course there was a better than even chance she wasn't going to be there, but the most I had to lose was an hour's driving time for the round trip.

I'd pegged the light grey Chevrolet Corvair in my rearview soon after I left Ramskill. I started getting suspicious when it was still there as I exited Route 9A and went east on 117. I slowed, the Corvair slowed; I accelerated, so did the Corvair. This was becoming tedious, so I pulled onto the shoulder and waited to see what my tail would do. The Corvair lost some speed but went straight past. Craning my neck, I glimpsed an elderly guy wearing glasses and a plaid shirt. Looks could be deceptive – especially fleeting ones – but he didn't look like the kind of individual who would pose any sort of threat.

I sat there a few beats wondering if paranoia had gotten the better of me. The old boy could have been driving the same route at the same speed for perfectly innocent reasons. He could be on his way to visit his grandkids, going fishing, returning home from a shopping trip. Anything.

I resumed my journey and turned left onto Bedford Road, then right onto Old Sleepy Hollow Road. Nothing behind me except a white panel van that soon turned onto a farm track. A half mile farther I turned right onto Pocantico Lake Road, a narrow country lane that took me through arable pasture and woodland to Foxley Farm. Its days in the agriculture business were long gone and the old yellow brick farmhouse had been converted into a luxury retreat with a swimming pool, landscaped garden and stable block.

The lane petered out and became a dirt track that ran into a broad stretch of woodland. I left my car at the farmhouse and followed the trail into the welcome shade of red oak, sycamore and bitternut hickory. After two hundred yards I saw the deep blue water of the lake glimmering in the mesh of leaves and branches.

Ten seconds later, a log cabin on the lakeside came into view.

Ten seconds after that I heard the slide of an automatic pistol being racked.

FORTY-THREE

'I didn't know you could handle one of those things,' I said.

I heard Loretta's sneakers crunching dry twigs as she came out of the foliage and moved in front of me. 'There a lot about me you don't know,' she said.

'Am I supposed to put my hands up?'

She lowered the handgun. 'This wouldn't have been necessary if I'd known you were coming.'

'I'd have called ahead,' I said. 'But you haven't been easy to find.'

'Well, you found me.' She started walking toward a wooden landing stage on the lake shore.

I went with her. 'Somebody torched the Biomedical Centre this morning.'

She didn't seem surprised and I had to wonder why. This place was less than a half hour drive from Ramskill so she was close enough to have started the fire and gotten back here well ahead of my arrival.

She seemed to sense my suspicion. 'You think I did it?'

'Honestly, Loretta, after all the stuff that's gone down recently, I have no clue what to think.'

'You and me both.' She made a wan smile. 'But I didn't put a match to the Biomedical Centre.' She gave me a direct look. 'In fact, I'm fairly certain I was meant to die in that fire.'

I frowned. 'Come again?'

'I should have been in the building this morning. I called in yesterday afternoon and told them I was planning to return to work today.' She ran her fingers through her hair in an agitated motion. 'I was actually getting into my car. But I lost my nerve and stayed away. If I hadn't, I may well be dead right now. '

I kept my eyes on hers. 'Why would you lose your nerve?'

She broke the eye contact and gazed across the still surface of the lake. 'I saw some guys working on the telephone wires yesterday. I'd gotten it into my head that they were tapping the phone up at the farmhouse. Paranoid, right? Anyway, by lunchtime I'd thought it through and convinced myself I'd been out here on my own too long and was getting hysterical.'

She turned back to face me. 'Then you got here and told me what happened. This is going to sound weird, but I knew what you were going to say. I knew they planned for me to die in that damn building.'

She scanned my face, as if looking for a reaction.

I kept my expression blank though. I wasn't sure if I could trust her. And if she'd been in this place alone for a week, I wasn't sure she could trust herself. I asked, 'Who are *they*?'

'The people behind the programme.' She said this as if it should have been obvious to me. 'They're shutting up shop because it's all turned sour and they want to start over someplace else. They'll have taken the research findings and physical evidence – the pharmacological product and lab equipment – then burned what was left.'

She gave me a despairing look. 'Don't you see, Wat? I was part of what was left.'

But I couldn't see, at least not right then.

'Are you saying they were trying to finish the job they started when Gonzales, Reese and Poole were killed?'

'No. That was something different. That wasn't them.'

'Then who?'

She walked to the end of the landing stage and looked down at the water, gloomy green in the shadow of the tree boughs.

I moved to her side. She knew much more about the shooting than she'd admitted, and I was sure she'd been covering up for Andy Stuivermans. I was through with the bullshit so I went straight to it. 'You were there, weren't you, when Andy shot those guys? What happened? You tried to grab the gun and got shot in the struggle?'

She kept her eyes on the water. 'I was there, yes. But Andy didn't shoot them. He wasn't even in the building.'

'Then who was the shooter?' I kept my voice level, even though my mind was racing to process this. 'You must have seen him.'

'No I didn't,' she said. 'Because I was the shooter.'

FORTY-FOUR

This didn't compute. Yet it totally computed.

Loretta moved from the landing stage into the shade of a big oak with roots half in and half out of the water. 'If I tell you what happened, it's just between the two of us, right? You can't go to the cops, you can't print anything. Do we have a deal?'

I didn't see that I had a choice so I agreed.

She placed her palms on the sides of her head and shut her eyes as if trying to funnel skittering thoughts into some sort of order. At last she seemed satisfied and started talking. 'When we started out on this project, Oleg and I had noble intentions and lofty hopes. Even after those three sexist assholes were brought in, we made significant progress in the right direction.'

'Which was what?'

At first she seemed narked by my interruption, then appeared to realize I needed some context. 'We called it psycho-pharmacological realignment. The aim was to re-sensitize veterans brutalized by the experience of combat.' She made a humourless laugh. 'What's so goddamn ironic is that we were doing the exact opposite of what the local rumour mill was pumping out. We weren't *de*humanizing raw recruits and sending them into a war zone; we were taking guys out of the war zone and *re*humanizing them.'

She took a seat on a dense root that snaked from the base of the oak and vanished under the water. 'Our programme was designed to enable veterans to hold down jobs, keep their marriages together, stay out of jail. We thought we could help them to put all that horror behind them – to lead prosperous, productive lives. We developed a synthetic anti-psychotic by synthesizing various substances including mescaline, chlorpromazine and psilocybin. Our product was codenamed MPQ-13 and the early lab work was encouraging. Then we moved onto the testing phase.'

I sat beside her and took out a Camel. 'So that was why you were recruiting veterans off the streets of New York City?'

'We had no shortage of volunteers.' She looked at my cigarette. 'May I have one?'

I offered her the pack and a light. I held off lighting mine though.

'So what happened with the tests?'

She took a toke at the cigarette. 'Initial outcomes were positive. Too positive. In retrospect, we were naive. We told our backers way too soon. But we were excited. We thought we were making genuine, sustainable progress. Looking back, though, this was the point where we lost control. Expectations were raised and substantial resources redirected from other areas. Our project went from an obscure side-show to a big money investment with all sorts of unrealistic claims attached to it.'

She went quiet and looked out across the lake. A sudden gust veered from the opposite side, destroying the mirror surface with a succession of fitful shivers.

I didn't press her. I played with my unlit cigarette and waited.

'Then we encountered problems. Some test subjects started reacting badly to MPQ-13. Not only did it not help them, it made their condition substantially worse.'

'Like Andy Stuivermans?'

'Yes,' she said, 'like Andy.'

She sucked in more cigarette smoke. 'Despite our evidence, the backers were determined to push ahead. They dismissed our concerns. They insisted almost all test subjects benefited and the small minority who didn't could be screened out of the process. And they trivialized the adverse effects we were reporting.'

I lit my own cigarette. 'Money and morality never did make good bedfellows.'

She flung me an angry stare. 'They were obsessed with getting the drug licensed and into production before somebody did something crazy – like ending the war in Vietnam.'

It wasn't hard to imagine where this obsession came from. These people had clearly invested heavily. They'd expect a big return – and soon. If the war did end, demand for the product would nosedive. And with mounting pressure at home – not least on Ramskill campus – there was always a possibility that this could happen. I was keen to know who Loretta's backers were, but she started talking again before I could ask.

'They talked to the five of us as a team and at first we stood firm. Then they approached us separately. I was offered a highly paid job with lucrative share options. I said no and so did Oleg. But pretty soon it became clear that Gonzales, Reese and Poole had sold out. Oleg was furious. MPQ-13 was his baby, his responsibility. He pleaded with the Gang of Three as we called them, but they weren't listening. He pleaded with our backers, with the same result. Then he threatened to go public. He gave them seven days to reconsider and three days later he was shot to death on campus.'

I said, 'You should have told me earlier.'

'I didn't know if I could trust you.' She crushed her cigarette butt under her sneaker. 'I didn't think I could trust anybody.'

She looked along the shoreline. A heron was wading the shallows, looking for prey. When she spoke again, she sounded strangely relaxed. 'I had to stop the programme at all costs. But I'd seen what happened to Oleg. So I needed to think of another way. And I found one. I got hold of a handgun, went into the conference room and shot them all.'

There was a long quiet.

I waited.

The heron stabbed its long beak into the water and came up with a shimmering eel.

I waited some more.

At last she said, 'I shot Gonzales and Reese in the head, close up. Poole was more messy. He saw what happened and tried to get out through the window.' By now I detected an edge of tension in her voice. 'I put two rounds in his back, but he still wouldn't go down. He just wouldn't die. So I walked across the room and fired one through his head.'

The heron flapped into the air, wheeled across the lake.

She watched it vanish behind the treeline. 'People say you always have choices, but I couldn't see one that didn't end in me doing what I did. Those men I killed were about to betray every medical, scientific and professional ethic. Andy and the others who reacted badly were just the beginning. If MPQ-13 went into full production there'd be thousands more like them. That's not to mention the people they'd harm due to their condition being made worse. I simply couldn't live with that knowledge.'

I got why she didn't like those guys, but gunning them down in cold blood was a whole other deal. I tried to imagine the scene: Loretta standing there with the gun, Carlos Gonzales and Headley Reese slumped over the conference table, blood-matted hair on the backs of their heads; Sandro Poole, face down on the floor, bullet holes his back and skull, one arm reaching toward the window.

But what I couldn't imagine was how Loretta got shot.

Did Poole manage to put up a fight? Maybe he made a desperate lunge for the gun and it went off in the tussle, hitting her in the flank. Maybe he turned and ran for the window and that was when she put those rounds into him. But if this was what happened, why hadn't she told me? She'd explained everything else, so why she was she holding back on this.

Then I began to realize what had gone down.

Perceptions unthinkable moments ago suddenly slotted together.

Contradiction became clarification.

I saw everything at once, the whole scene.

And I thought: *Wow*.

It was like looking at the jungle floor at your feet and seeing nothing but ground cover and rotting vegetation. You'd see an ochre patch you thought was a leaf; then a darker spot you took to be shade. Then you looked again.

Then you saw him. You saw his flat head and tarry eyes, the black and tawny bands on his body. You were looking at the two-step snake that was never there, but was always there. If he bit you, you'd get more than two steps before you died but not much farther. And if he didn't, you'd be counting this as the luckiest break you ever got.

Right now, I considered Loretta Hausinger to be much more lethal than any two-step snake.

I said, 'You shot yourself, didn't you?'

Her expression was unreadable. 'That was the toughest part. I knew it was impossible to go against them without getting what Oleg got. I needed to make them think I was a victim too. So I pointed the gun at my side and pulled the trigger.'

It sounded crazy. It *was* crazy. That was why it worked.

'That must have hurt like hell,' I said.

She winced and touched her side. 'I never expected so much pain. I don't know how I found the strength to go through with the rest of my plan. It was just a few seconds but it felt like forever. I was shaking from the shock. I thought I was going to pass out. I thought I was bleeding to death. But I managed to place the gun in the file cabinet right next to me and shut it before you arrived.'

I indicated the cut on her forehead. 'Was that self-inflicted too?'

She grimaced. 'It happened when I fell over and banged my head on the chair. It worked out well, though, didn't it? Along with the bullet hole in my side, nobody thought for a second that I'd done those things to myself.'

'No wonder there was no trace of a getaway.' I didn't even try to hide my fascination. 'Presumably you left your office window open to suggest that was the way this fictional hitman left the building?'

She nodded yes.

It was damn clever, I thought. And it must have taken real grit.

'Of course there was a risk the gun might be found,' she said. 'But I was prepared to bet nobody would think the shooter left it in the room. Therefore nobody would look. And I was right. After I left the hospital I recovered the gun and disposed of it.'

'You're some operator,' I said.

She looked at me hard. 'I'm not looking for compliments, Wat.'

I looked at her, just as hard. I thought again of the two-step snake. 'That wasn't a compliment, Loretta.'

There was another tense interlude. A pair of swifts skimmed over the water, jinking at impossible angles, hunting invisible insects.

At length I said, 'Who are the people backing the project?'

She asked for another cigarette and I handed her one. I was going to take one for myself but I desisted.

'They're from a big pharmaceuticals company called Kershaw Lefevre Laboratories.'

I didn't think there could be anything left to shock me.

This did though.

Absolutely it did.

I recalled Park Ahnjong, the Korean girl with the PhD in biochemistry, who Colonel Riley was seeing. She was an intern at Kershaw Lefevre.

I wasn't sure just then how she and Riley were linked to this defective super drug, MPQ-13. But I was certain they were.

‘You should also know there are people at the Pentagon,’ she said.

‘There are always people at the Pentagon.’

‘You shouldn’t be so cocky –’

The bullet fizzed over her head, missing by inches, embedding itself in the bark of the big oak.

I threw myself at her and we tumbled to the ground behind the trunk.

I pressed my body on top of hers as a long burst of automatic fire struck the tree, showering us in bark and chips of wood.

Peeking above a root, I saw movement on the opposite bank. The gunman was on his way around the shoreline. Pocantico was not a big lake and he’d be close enough to get more shots away all too soon.

I dragged her to her feet and tugged her toward the farmhouse. ‘We gotta leave,’ I said. ‘Right now.’

FORTY-FIVE

We reached my Skylark before the gunman could get another shot away. I bundled Loretta into the back and told her to lie on the floor until I said otherwise.

Then I spun the car around and floored the gas until I came to Old Sleepy Hollow Road. There were no other vehicles in sight so I drove fast back to Beech Hill Road, then went west on Route 117 – I didn't want to go anywhere near Ramskill. At US9 I turned south for New York City.

Frequent glances in my rear view told me we were safe – for now, anyway – and I told Loretta she could come up from the floor.

'You OK?' I said.

'A bit shaken up, but in one piece.' She climbed into the front passenger seat. 'You?'

I said I was fine.

'Where are we going?'

I checked the speedo and slowed down a little. Last thing we needed right now was getting pulled over by the highway patrol. 'As far from Foxley Farm and Ramskill as we can get.'

'Then what?'

'I'm working on it.'

For a few minutes we said nothing, watched the tree-lined highway roll by.

She broke the silence. 'Who do you think was doing the shooting back there?'

I shrugged. 'I was hoping you could tell me.'

'I've never been shot at before.' She made a weak smile. 'Except by myself.'

I kept the mood light. 'Not many people can say that.'

The truth was that I was almost certainly responsible for what happened back at the lakeside and I was angry with myself.

Clearly I *had* been tailed by the old boy in the Chevy Corvair – if he actually was an old boy – and the guy in the white panel van, and maybe even the cattle truck that drove past the entrance to Foxley Farm. How could I have been so sloppy? I'd never have made that mistake in country. But this wasn't in country. This was in downstate New York. And maybe I was being too harsh on myself.

There was another possibility. Maybe whoever tried to kill Loretta already knew she was there at the lake and I got there minutes ahead of him. If that was so, I wasn't to blame and may well have saved her life – for real this time.

When I told her I didn't know who shot at her, I wasn't being totally upfront because I didn't want to upset her any more than she already was. And I didn't want an argument. From what she said earlier, she was still loyal to Andy Stuivermans and would reject any suggestion that he fired those shots. But I was wondering if he'd been playing her all along. If he never went to New York City. If he started the Biomedical Centre fire, then followed me to the lake.

Another candidate was Gerry Bohannon. Another still,

Corey Quilton or one of his SLUT comrades. And if SLUT was involved with the KGB, nothing was off the table.

Yet whoever it was wasn't a great marksman. Those rounds had been fired from an assault rifle at a range of around 150 yards. For anyone with experience of that type of weapon, Loretta would not have been a difficult target. And instead of taking his time with a second shot, the shooter panicked, peppering the general area with automatic fire in hopes of a lucky hit. This tended to rule out Stuivermans – a Ranger simply wouldn't have missed in the first place. Except Stuivermans wasn't a Ranger any more. He was a derelict with a serious psychological problem.

The miss and the hasty switch to automatic fire would also rule out direct KGB involvement, though not necessarily Quilton or a fellow traveller. He saw me driving out of town. He could have gotten his buddies to tail me. On the face of it they were a bunch of anarchistic lefties who weren't very organized. But I knew from what I'd seen of their activities just how organized they really were. Then there was Bohannon. On his own, he wasn't smart or skilful enough to have pulled off anything like this. But who said he was on his own?

A further possibility was that I'd been tailed by a gunman sent to eliminate Loretta by the Pentagon untouchables she'd mentioned, or by a rogue individual within Kershaw Lefevre Laboratories. Hell, Riley himself could have been giving the orders. I had evidence linking him to the pharmaceutical business via his Korean girl, Park Ahnjong. Maybe he held shares in the company and had connections to the directors. Maybe Park Ahnjong was a North Korean or Chinese illegal. Maybe she was Riley's handler.

A more immediate question was what to do next. I'd been right when I told JoBeth I thought Loretta was still alive. I'd also been right that this could change at any moment. Her safe house by the lake had been compromised and she'd need someplace else to stay.

I thought of a solution as I was filling the tank at a gas station in Yonkers and used the payphone to make a couple of calls.

Back on the road, I asked her if she'd been staying at the cabin the whole time since she never came back from Princeton over a week ago.

'Does it matter where I was?' After everything she just told me, she was still keeping stuff to herself.

'I wouldn't ask if it didn't.' I realized I sounded peeved and mellowed my tone a little. 'Look, if I'm going to keep you safe I need to know what you've been up to. You were in New York City looking for Andy Stuivermans, weren't you?'

She made a resigned sigh. 'OK, you got me. I spent a couple of days in Lower Manhattan. I wanted to make sure he was safe, reassure him. I couldn't find him though. That was when I went to the cabin.'

I waited a few beats, then said, 'Andy's the same age as your bother Peter was when he died, isn't he? And suffering the same sort of post-combat mental problems.'

She went quiet again.

'You couldn't save Peter but you're determined to save Andy, is that it?'

'It's not that simple, Wat. And it's not your business.'

'It is my business, Loretta. You made it my business.'

More awkward silence. She flipped on the radio and the car flooded with sounds of the Beatles' *Let It Be*.

The song was righteous but I needed more information – and I had a bone to pick – so I turned it off.

'Why did you lie to me after I'd tussled with Andy and asked you if knew a guy with a mutilated ear?'

'I was trying to protect him.'

'Well, you achieved the opposite.'

'It didn't seem that way at the time. You were – still are – working with a federal prosecutor.'

'JoBeth Medlock isn't my boss.'

'That's as may be.' She sounded prickly. 'But Andy hadn't hurt you any more than you hurt him. And *you* attacked *him*, remember?'

It was a moot point and I let it go.

'Anyway, you were going down a blind alley. I'm sure Andy wasn't the guy did those horrible things to the rabbit and the sheepdog. Andy loved animals. He would never hurt them – even after when he'd been through in Vietnam. And what we put him through at Ramskill.'

I recalled what Erikka told me about Stuivermans' dream of owning a beagle when they'd been together before Vietnam. In my experience, there were things about people that never changed, no matter what happened to them. But that was just my experience. And I didn't know what exactly had happened to Stuivermans in country, still less after he got pumped full of that malfunctioning psychotropic shit.

I took Interstate 87 for New York City and thought carefully about what I was going to say next. Loretta absolutely wouldn't want to hear it, but she needed to know because I needed her help tracking down Stuivermans. So I bit the bullet. 'You should know Andy is in the frame for the campus shootings. Somebody who knew how to use a sniper rifle shot Oleg Bobkov and Gordon Richardson, and a different person killed Boyd Brigstock. Both shooters used guns that weren't issued to the National Guard that day.'

'And you think Andy might have been one of them?' She didn't blow up like I thought she might.

'It's a serious possibility. I'm not saying he was involved. But I can't say for sure he wasn't. That's why I need to talk to him.'

She took a while to consider this. 'Andy had an erratic relationship with Oleg. Sometimes Oleg could be abrupt with all the guys, though I never detected any outright animosity from Andy. And I don't think he even knew the Brigstock boy.'

'The shootings weren't personal,' I said. 'Oleg was shot because, as you said, he was threatening to go public over MPQ-13. Gordon Richardson was collateral. And it seems Boyd Brigstock was hit to put pressure on his mom, who you'll know is a prominent anti-war congresswoman.'

'What sort of pressure?'

'That's unclear. I know Corey Quilton and SLUT have been trying to make her denounce the Cambodian invasion at the UN Security Council. And that may be part of the reason Boyd died. But Harriet Brigstock is also on a congressional committee investigating the research and development practices of big pharmaceutical companies. In light of what you told me at the lake, that would put Kershaw Lefevre – and specifically the MPQ-13 project – directly in her crosshairs.'

She didn't say anything, though I got the impression she was deep in thought.

I wanted to give her time to process this information

herself, reach her own conclusions, so I drove in silence past Yankee Stadium and followed I-278 and the Brooklyn-Queens Expressway.

By the time I exited at Kent Avenue, I figured she needed a little encouragement, so I said, 'Andy has an old grudge against Harriet Brigstock, doesn't he?'

She made a long, despondent sigh. 'Yes he does. And yes he's still withdrawing from MPQ-13, which means he'll be volatile and possibly aggressive. And, yes he's very likely in Lower Manhattan.'

'This thing with Harriet Brigstock, has it gotten worse since he started on the MPQ-13 programme?'

'Worse,' she said. 'A whole lot worse.'

'I have to get to him before he gets to Brigstock.' I kept my eyes on the road ahead but I knew she was staring right at me.

'Are you going to hurt him?'

'I'm hoping it won't come to that.' I tried to sound reassuring. 'I'm sure you know all about the similarities between Andy's background and mine. If stuff had worked out differently, he could have been my brother, my friend. After what happened to him, he deserves some justice.'

'I'm glad to hear that. But I'm really worried.'

I reached for her hand and squeezed it. 'I'll do all I can to get Andy out of this. I promise.'

She forced a smile. 'Where are we going?'

'A place in Andy's old stamping ground – and mine. It'll be your new home until this is over.'

Fifteen minutes later I parked outside Titus Grundy's apartment in New Lots.

My old operations sergeant was standing on the stoop. I'd

called him from the payphone in Yonkers because I couldn't think of anyone better to keep Loretta safe.

With her taken care of, I could resume my search for Andy Stuivermans. And amid all the questions surrounding Ramskill campus, one thing was certain: It wasn't going to be easy.

FORTY-SIX

Early the next morning I went into the *Examiner* newsroom and learned the anti-war rally Harriet Brigstock was addressing had been brought forward – to that afternoon. This meant we had to do something in a few hours that we hadn't been able to do in as many days: Find Andy Stuivermans. I meant what I'd told Loretta about bringing him in unharmed. But the fact was that he had the means, motive and now a perfect opportunity to do to Brigstock what he may well have done to her son. Whether or not he was working with Kershaw Lefevre, or radical activists, or somebody else entirely, was of secondary importance. Our only priority right now was making sure the congresswoman stayed alive. If we were wrong, and there was no assassination attempt, nobody in the Empire State would be happier than us.

JoBeth drove down from Ramskill and met me at Brigstock's office in Lower Manhattan. She agreed to see us but rejected our advice to stay away from the rally. It was scheduled to take place in Washington Square Park at 2.00pm following a protest march starting outside the UN building, with Brigstock billed as the main speaker. She told us she simply couldn't afford to be absent from such a major event at the heart of her own congressional district. I admired her salt but thought she was taking a blinkered approach.

Afterwards we rode the 1 train from South Ferry to Christopher Street and grabbed coffee and cheese blintzes at a place near JoBeth's apartment.

Between bites, I told her what had gone down with Loretta at Pocantico Lake.

When I was done, she gave me an intense look. 'That's an incredible story. I never heard anything like it. And I'm glad she's safe. But I really don't feel comfortable having a triple murderer at large.'

I finished my last blintz and took a swallow of coffee. 'I don't see that we have a choice. We can't have her arrested because we have no evidence – she'd just deny having told me that stuff. Also, the circumstances were truly exceptional and she absolutely won't kill again.'

JoBeth made a dubious expression. 'You can't know that. Not for certain.'

I got where she was coming from. She'd become a federal prosecutor precisely to stop people getting away with murder, then killing again. But the guy she'd gotten off a murder rap as a defence attorney was a very different individual to Loretta Hausinger.

'She won't do any harm, or come to any harm,' I said. 'Not with Titus Grundy minding her. I'd stake my life on it.'

'It's not your life you're staking, though, is it, Wat?'

We went quiet. I didn't want to fight and didn't think she did either.

At last she said, 'It's more black and white for you. I'm not saying that as a criticism, it's just how you are.'

'You're right,' I said. 'I'd have killed those guys myself.

Wouldn't have thought twice if it stopped them giving that mind-bending crap to Stuivermans and guys like him.' I paused and gave her an accommodating look. 'Having said that, I'm not an assistant US attorney. I don't have due process to think about.'

I dropped my voice and leaned a little closer. 'And I know you still blame yourself for what happened when you defended that killer – even though you weren't responsible for what he did afterward.'

Another silence. I knew this was awkward for her.

I tried to sound reasonable. 'Look, why don't we set this to one side for now? Focus on keeping Harriet Brigstock out of harm's way?'

She gave me a fleeting smile. 'You got a deal.'

*

We caught a major break when I called the city desk to check in with Maggie. Erikka, Andy Stuivermans ex, had just called. She'd left a message asking me to meet her urgently at the Bright Day Hotel on the Bowery. This was the flophouse where the guy with the bare-chest and purple fedora gave me Erikka's description.

We took a cab to the Bright Day and arrived fifteen minutes later.

JoBeth agreed to wait outside: Erikka might get spooked by the appearance of somebody she didn't know.

She was waiting in a cubicle room three doors down from Purple Fedora's.

Her eyes were tearful, mascara tracking black lines down her cheeks. 'Andy left thirty minutes ago,' she said. 'I couldn't make him stay. I couldn't get through to him.'

'How did he seem?'

'Laid back. Sober. In fact, totally normal.'

This was more worrying than the opposite, but I didn't say so. Erikka was already upset and my downbeat hunch wouldn't help.

I asked her how she traced him and she said Purple Fedora gave her a call at work. She'd promised the guy five bucks last time she was here if he helped her find Andy.

'I thought he'd be angry with me for hounding him, but he wasn't,' she said. 'We talked about this and that as if everything was back to how it used to be. Then, right out of the blue, he checked his watch and said he had to go. But he wouldn't say where. He made me promise not to go after him. Then he was gone.'

She looked down at the floor. 'That was when I called your office. I didn't know what to do, Wat. I don't want to lose him again.'

'You did the right thing.' I placed my finger below her chin and nudged it upward so she was looking at me. 'I'll do everything I can to make sure he's safe.'

I glanced around the room. 'Mind if I take a look?'

She said no she didn't and I started searching the tiny room for anything that might suggest where he'd gone. There weren't too many places to look: Under the mattress; on the shelf over the bed; under the wooden chair.

I was about to call it a day when I spotted a folded scrap of paper wedged tight in a gap between the plaster wall and the door frame. I used my pocket knife to prise it out. Unfolding the paper, I saw an address: *Kramer Centre* written in a forward-sloping hand.

I knew the place. It was a tall commercial building on

Washington Square South – directly overlooking the spot where Harriet Brigstock would be making her speech.

An ideal location for a sniper.

I looked at Erikka. 'Is this Andy's handwriting?'

She nodded yes and asked what the address meant.

I said I didn't know – which was partly true but less than honest. I guess I hoped I was wrong, that Stuivermans had gone to the Kramer Centre for some innocent reason, even though I knew though this was wishful thinking.

I looked back at the nook: Not the safest place to hide something. He'd either placed it there because the drug had made him sloppy; or because, deep down, he wanted somebody to find it.

*

We hailed a cab to Washington Square Park South and worked out our plan on the way: I'd go into the building to find Stuivermans while JoBeth went to warn Brigstock. This was no longer a theoretical concern, it was a direct and tangible threat to her life.

We left the flophouse a little after 1.00pm – almost an hour before the congresswoman was due to speak. This should have given us plenty of time but the traffic on Houston Street was badly congested. Tempers and engines began overheating. Drivers honked their horns and shouted the odds. I rolled down the window to let some air in, but it was thick with gas and diesel fumes. After crawling a quarter mile along La Guardia Place, we paid off the taxi and went the rest of the way on foot.

By the time we approached the south side of the park

it was 1.40. The surrounding streets were packed with protesters and the park itself was rammed solid. The speakers' platform in front of Washington Square Arch was only 150 yards away, but JoBeth would have a tough time elbowing her way through. Even when she got there, she'd have to persuade Brigstock's security people to let her talk to the congresswoman. It would all take time we couldn't afford.

For my part, I had less than twenty minutes to search a ten storey building. I told the guy on the front desk I was late for a press conference and hurried to the elevator before he could tell me no such event was scheduled. I went to the top floor – Washington Square was surrounded by tall trees so a sniper would need plenty of elevation for a clean shot. I was walking toward the corridor leading to the north facing offices when I noticed the service door to the roof was slightly ajar. This was odd because there was a sign on the door saying: *Strictly no unauthorized admittance – To be kept closed at all times.*

I looked closer. In the dim light behind the door I saw a flight of steel stairs leading up to the roof.

And I wondered if Stuivermans was up there.

I went through the service door and climbed the stairs.

Half way up when the sound of a gunshot snapped the air.

It had to be Stuivermans. He must have shot Harriet Brigstock before JoBeth could reach her.

I reached the top of the stairs in three long strides and came to another door, again slightly open. Edging it open, I stepped outside.

'That you, Wat?'

Stuivermans was in a prone position at the edge of the roof.

He was looking down the sniper scope of an M1C Garand.

There was no point trying to rush him. He was twenty yards away and would have shot me before I'd covered a fraction of that distance. Besides, the damage was already done.

'Yeah, Andy,' I said. 'It's me.'

He turned around slowly, coming to his feet with the rifle pointed right at me.

'I knew you'd come.' He sounded curiously relaxed, even a little elated, like we were the old friends we could have been, reunited after a long absence.

I recalled the scrunched-up paper jammed into the nook between the door frame and the wall; the left-open service door.

I took a few steps forward. 'You wanted me to come, didn't you, Andy?'

'The poetic symmetry would have been neater if you'd been a fellow Ranger.' I saw a faint spark of humour in his pale eyes. 'I guess a Green Beret's fitting enough though.'

I opened my mouth to speak, but he anticipated my question. 'No, Wat, I didn't kill her. Shot went wide. Your partner came out of nowhere and hauled Brigstock to the floor. The round missed by inches.'

This came as a big relief.

But I was also confused. If he'd missed his mark because of JoBeth's last-ditch intervention, why was he so laid back?

He must have noticed my puzzled expression. 'I didn't take the shot,' he said. 'Somebody beat me to it.'

FORTY-SEVEN

'My orders were to hit Brigstock exactly five minutes into her speech,' he said. 'But she hadn't even gotten started when the other guy pulled the trigger.'

I gave him a disbelieving look.

Of course Stuivermans could be lying, though my gut said not.

But why deploy two snipers so close together? Was Stuivermans meant to be a failsafe in case the other shooter failed to make the scene?

I said, 'Where did the other shot come from?'

He nodded to his right. 'Somewhere over there – possibly Judson Memorial Church.'

I glanced at the tall bell tower of the 19th Century church. It was a little higher than the roof of the Kramer Centre and commanded a similar view of the park – as good a location for a sniper, maybe better.

From where I was standing I couldn't see what was going on below, though it didn't take a vivid imagination to picture the chaos. The gunshot would have created panic among the protesters and the bell tower guy would be long gone before the cops could get anywhere near him.

I turned back to Stuivermans. 'Any idea who this other shooter might be?'

He shook his head no. 'First I knew was when he took the shot I was meant to take.'

He tried to sound cheated but I didn't buy it.

'You didn't really want to pull that trigger, did you? That's why you wanted me to find you. Because you're a solder, not an assassin.'

'I'm not a soldier any more. I'm not anything.' He made a whimsical shrug. 'Now that's what I call truly liberated.'

I moved a little closer. 'How did you get to be here?'

He hesitated.

I gave him a prod. 'You said it yourself: Now you're truly liberated. So surely you can tell me your story. I could write it up in the *Examiner*.'

This seemed to pique his interest. 'Would you do that, Wat? Set the record straight?'

'I'd love to, Andy.'

'You feeding me bullshit?' He sounded suspicious.

'You did your research on me. What do you think?'

He appeared to consider this. 'Dr Hausinger said you're one of the good guys. Erikka too. I guess both of them can't be wrong.'

I made a dubious expression. 'Stuff we did in the Circus, Andy, we're not good guys. But we can be honest guys – especially with one another.'

'Sounds fair enough.' He made an easy grin and sat on the low wall skirting the edge of the roof. 'Dr Reese came to me one day when I was working in the grounds. He explained that Harriet Brigstock was a communist subversive working to betray the guys in Vietnam. He showed me evidence.'

'What kind of evidence?'

'All sorts. Secret dossiers, confidential reports, photos of her with Soviet and Chinese agents. Dr Reese proved beyond doubt she's a traitor.'

It came to me that Stuivermans would have been dosed up on MPQ-13 and highly suggestible when Reese disclosed this material. It could easily have been faked and probably was. Stuivermans would have been like a clockwork toy. All Reese needed to do was wind him up, point him at Harriet Brigstock, and sit back.

The rest of the recruitment procedure was predictable: Reese told Stuivermans the congresswoman was above the law and offered him an opportunity to join a special team of patriots dedicated to protecting the country from the red threat. Did Stuivermans want in? You betcha.

I figured he needed another prompt. 'Headley Reese wasn't your handler, though, was he? Who did you report to?'

'I got my orders in phone booths. Never met the caller.'

'According to my intel, Reese was the real traitor.' This was a risky thing to say, but I'd promised to be honest and Stuivermans needed to hear it. Besides, I was confident he hadn't lured me here to kill me. 'He sold out to a big pharmaceutical company called Kershaw Lefevre and they used you and your pals as lab rats. It was Reese, together with Gonzales and Poole who fucked with your head.'

I expected an angry reaction but it never came.

Instead he made a half-assed shrug. 'I just came here to complete my mission – that's what soldiers do, isn't it? Complete the mission, no matter the cost?'

But he didn't seem particularly convinced by his own rhetoric. I sensed his brain struggling against the psychoactive gloop Reese had pumped into it. It was as if the real Andy Stuivermans was trying to punch his way out of a narcotic cocoon. He gave me a quizzical glance. 'You think I been had, Wat?'

'You're a smart guy, Andy. Figure it out.'

More laboured thinking. 'I was never meant to take the shot. That was the other guy's job. I was put up here as an insurance policy, maybe not even that. Maybe just a diversion.'

He spent a few beats staring at the muzzle of his rifle. 'I got suckered, didn't I? *Again*. I don't even know who played me. But I'm past giving a shit. That's all behind me now.'

He was in danger of drifting back into the hazy psychosis that seemed to come and go like mountain mist. So I pressed him again. 'The guy who gave you your orders, did he tell you where to collect the rifle today?'

His gaze wandered down the length of the gun, fixing on the sniper scope. 'Just where to come. The rifle was up here when I arrived.'

I thought about this. The people who manipulated Stuivermans were calculating and resourceful. I'd known that for some while, but this latest revelation showed another dimension to the power they wielded and the threat they represented. 'What about the Ramskill Campus protests? Did you shoot anyone there?'

'No I didn't.' He flashed me a worried glance. 'You do believe me, don't you Wat?'

'We're being honest, aren't we, Andy?'

'Yeah.' His anxiety melted. 'Being honest feels good.'

'This handler, he told you to go out on patrol around the campus that day, didn't he?'

He looked perplexed. 'How did you know that?'

'He didn't want you to have an alibi.'

A hint of anger flickered in his eyes but quickly subsided. 'Man, did I get played.'

'We all get played, Andy.'

'I never hurt the sheepdog, or the bunny, or the National Guard kid.' His tone had become accepting, like this was the type of shit that happened to people like him. 'Some other guy did those things. They knew about my ear. That was part of the put up job too, wasn't it?'

'I'm sorry, Andy, but yeah, it was.'

The way Stuivermans had been manipulated was now as clear to him as it was to me: The guy giving out the orders was setting him up as a both a decoy and a patsy. While Stuivermans was carrying out his nocturnal assignments, his handler was doing the dirty work – cutting ears off the sheepdog, the bunny and Harold Kapp in a way that pointed to a disturbed veteran whose own disfigured ear provided an obvious connection.

He said, 'Remember that night when you and I tussled near the pony paddock?'

I said sure I did. How could I forget?

He chuckled softly, as if he was recalling some fond memory from way back. 'Gotta say, Wat, your close quarter skills were real sharp.'

'No sharper than yours, Andy. You were every bit as good.'

'I used to visit that pony every so often, spend a little time with him. Name's Henry. I'd take a couple of sugar cubes or a carrot. In return, Henry listened to me talking shit about whatever was on my mind.' He made a wistful smile. 'Henry's a very tolerant pony.'

I was getting more and more aware of the circular nature of the conversation and the need to bring it to a close. Setting aside intent, Stuivermans hadn't actually committed a crime and he wasn't going to harm me. If so, he'd have done so before now. He needed help, sure, but there was a way out of this for him. I needed to emphasise this and persuade him to cooperate.

I took a step closer. 'You ready to put down that rifle, Andy?'

'Sorry, Wat, no can do.'

'Come on, man, we can work through this. Get your life back together.'

'We both know that's not on the table.' He chambered a round. 'I really don't wanna hurt you, but I will if you come any nearer.'

I didn't doubt he meant it. 'You're the Man, Andy.'

'Damn straight.' He turned so he was sitting parallel to the wall, placed one foot on the edge.

Then it hit me: He was planning to jump.

'Come away from there, Andy.' I tried to sound relaxed. Like this was just more banter. 'Let's talk some more.'

'Sorry, pal. We're all talked out.'

'What about Junior High 64? You remember Miss Krebbs, the English teacher? She was hot, wasn't she? And Mr Stearns, the math guy?'

'Nice try, Wat, but you're wasting your time.'

I pretended I hadn't heard him. I just carried on talking, as if the longer I talked, the longer he'd live. 'What about the Rockaways? Tell me about your music.'

'The band was great for sure, and writing rock music is the most. But now I gotta leave those things behind.'

'Rock music saved me, Andy. It's still saving me. It can help you too.'

'Nothing can help me, pal. Nothing and no one. Not even Dr Hausinger or Erikka. Even you.'

'That's not true, Andy. We're all here for you.'

He laughed. 'Look at me, Wat. I'm holding a sniper rifle in the perfect location to have taken out Brigstock. My prints are all over it and the real shooter's in the wind. I was the patsy from the get-go. I'll go down for attempted murder and I have no doubt the people who placed me here also have me lined up for the campus shooting.'

'Then help me fight the bastards. Help me take them down.'

'Thanks for the offer, but I have to say no. I'd rather be out of it all.'

The sound of police sirens carried up from the street below. 'Sorry, Wat, seems like you got suckered too. But thanks for being here at the end. I'm real grateful.'

'Andy, for Christ's sake – '

'Look, man, I gotta go. Another life, you and me, we could have done great stuff together … '

He gave me a smile that was real mellow but his face was utterly wiped, drained of everything vital.

He laid the gun on the wall and went backward over the edge without a sound.

FORTY-EIGHT

I looked over the wall and saw Andy lying dead on the street. He might have just laid down to take a nap but for the maroon halo around his head.

Seconds later, a half dozen NYPD squad cars pulled up either side of him, red lights flashing, spewing cops, locked and loaded, ready to bring down extreme violence on anybody who stood in their way.

I lit a cigarette and waited for them to arrive. The people behind this had planned it with impressive ingenuity: The shooter got clean away, tipping off the cops on his way out and leaving Stuivermans to take the fall – though not as literally as the situation played out. Andy had messed with their plan in this respect, although he was still their patsy whether he was in a prison or a cemetery. What would really have pissed them off was JoBeth's life-saving intervention.

The cops burst onto the roof and fanned out, guns raised. I gave them no reason to do anything but cuff and arrest me. They drove me to the 6th Precinct headquarters where I spent less than an hour in the tank before being taken up to the commander's office. JoBeth was waiting with the FBI agent-in-charge of the New York bureau and a senior official from the governor's office. They'd already explained to the NYPD brass what they needed to know about my involvement and, after some formalities, I was free to go.

We went to JoBeth's office at the US Attorney's building in Lower Manhattan and exchanged accounts. She'd gotten through the protesters in the park quickly enough, but had a hard time persuading Brigstock's people to let her talk to the congresswoman. In the end, she barged them aside and launched herself at Brigstock. The bullet went hissing overhead as they tumbled to the floor. Finally, Brigstock accepted the gravity of the threat – and how lucky she'd been to leave the park alive.

I said at least one of our stories ended well, but couldn't keep the sourness from my tone. JoBeth picked up on this. She told me not to blame myself, there was nothing I could have done to stop Andy.

I gave her a fierce look. 'Maybe not, but there is something I can do to make sure his name gets cleared.'

'It won't be easy,' she said. 'The FBI confirmed the gun is a Garand M1C with a Lyman sniper scope. Obviously it has Andy's prints all over it. We're waiting on the lab report, but you and I both know it's one of the guns used to hit Oleg Bobkov and Gordon Richardson or Boyd Brigstock. Why else would they have placed it there?'

'But the round fired at Harriet Brigstock wasn't from that rifle. The feds will know Andy wasn't the shooter when they find the bullet.'

'*If* they find it.'

'But I was up there on the roof. I know Andy never pulled that trigger.'

She gave me a look that was both sympathetic and harsh.

'You didn't actually see him *not pull the trigger*. You were on your way up the stairs when the shot was fired. And nobody saw this other sniper – including you. There's no evidence he was ever there.'

'You don't think the FBI will believe me?'

'I think their view will reflect the verifiable facts.'

'In other words, one that reflects various political agendas.'

She touched my arm. 'Whichever way you cut this, the evidence says Andy was one of the campus shooters and heavily involved in the attempted hit on Harriet Brigstock – whether he took the shot or not.'

She was right, of course. I was being naïve. I'd played games like this often enough to know the rules. I'd also played often enough to know how to break the rules. But that was for later.

I said, 'At least we should nail Gerry Bohannon. We should be able to use that rifle of his daddy's to link him to Boyd Brigstock's death. If we put the screws to him, maybe we can get some answers. Like the name of the guy I heard him taking orders from on the phone at Ramskill Armoury. I got a strong feeling it's the same guy who gave Andy Stuivermans his instructions.'

'OK,' she said. 'I'll ask the bureau about a warrant.'

I walked over to her office window and looked out across to the Federal Courthouse. 'How is Brigstock holding up?'

'She's a tough old bird. I went with her to her downtown office and she insists there's nothing wrong with her that a few cigarettes and a couple of large bourbons can't fix.'

'So she's still planning to attend the Security Council tomorrow?'

JoBeth nodded. 'I also asked her about the congressional committee investigating the R&D activities of big pharmaceutical firms – specifically any names that have come under particular scrutiny.'

I turned back into the room. 'Let me guess: Kershaw Lefevre Laboratories was pretty high up on that list.'

'More than that,' she said. 'Kershaw Lefevre is right at the top.'

FORTY-NINE

Back in the *Examiner* office, I wrote a page-one lead for the final edition. We had lots of colour and detail about the attempted assassination of Harriet Brigstock – especially exclusive quotes from JoBeth as the congresswoman's saviour. But we couldn't print a full account of what happened with Andy Stuivermans without prejudicing the ongoing investigation.

Maggie lifted my piece out of the city desk copy basket and read it. 'This is good stuff,' she said. 'Your partner came up trumps and it'll certainly buy us some time. But I'm getting more and more heat from upstairs. They want the full exclusive, right now.'

'What can I say?' I made and exasperated sound and leaned back in my chair, resting the back of my head in my interlocked fingers. I appreciated Maggie had to answer to the publisher. Even so, this was becoming frustrating. 'Why can't the high-ups ever understand that a piece like this takes time? Don't they get that we don't have the story until we know what's really been going on at Ramskill?'

'They don't think like we do.' She gave me a rueful smile. 'They think about sales numbers and ad revenue, overhead and labour costs.'

She sat on the corner of my desk and regarded me with maternal concern. 'You look dead beat, Wat. You should go home and get some rest.'

I thought this was solid advice and was picking up my coat to leave when the front counter called up to say a guy was asking for me downstairs, name of Corey Quilton.

When I got to the foyer, he was pacing back and forth. The instant he clocked me he came hurrying over. I noted red-rimmed eyes and a leeched complexion. His hair looked like a clump of tumbleweed and fragments of food were stuck in his straggly beard – not so much prophetic as pathetic.

'You gotta help me, Wat.' He looked and sounded desperate. 'Is there someplace private we can talk? I wanna make a deal.'

This snagged my interest. I took him into the conference room and we sat down opposite one another across the long table.

'OK, Corey,' I said, 'tell me what you got and what you want.'

'I got a story for you. *My* story. What really happened the day of the campus shootings. In return I want protection.'

'Who from?'

He leaned forward, features agitated. 'The authorities, man, the apparatus of state oppression, the cops, the feds, the spooks … '

I took out my pack of Camels and my lighter and pushed them across the table to him. 'Tell me what happened the day the soldiers came. Take a deep breath and take it slow.'

He fumbled with the cigarettes and lit one. 'Look, I've done some bad shit. But that's what activists do. I wanna tear down the bourgeois structure and build a new order – '

'I don't need the revolutionary spiel, Corey, I heard it

before.' I made a patient sigh. 'What happened that's freaked you?'

'Will you help me?'

'I can't make promises until I know what you got to say.' I went to the water dispenser, poured two plastic cups and gave one to him. 'Now try to calm down and tell me what went down.'

'When those folks got shot …' He looked down at the table.

There was a fraught hiatus.

Then he was talking real quick and a little garbled, as if he had to get the words out fast, before he lost his nerve again. 'It was me who started the trouble with the National Guard.'

I looked up from my notepad. I'd suspected as much, but the bluntness of his admission came as a shock.

He sucked in some smoke. 'But I'd gotten provoked – manipulated … '

I said, 'Who provoked you, Corey? Who manipulated you?'

'That fascist bastard Bohannon.'

'What exactly did he do?'

He gulped some water. When he started talking again, he seemed less anxious. 'He came up to me on campus the morning the National Guard rolled into town. He said his boys were itching to kick our asses. He was giving out that we were a bunch of pansies, that none of us had the balls to go up against his outfit. He said the soldiers were gonna come onto the campus real soon and when they did we'd turn and run. He said he'd bet me anything I wanted.'

He swallowed more water. 'It was a stupid thing to do. I can see that now. But that guy's a provocative asshole.'

'What did you do, Corey?'

'Told him to put his money where his mouth was. And he did: Said he'd wager a hundred bucks we were gutless pieces of shit. I took the bet, but I didn't think anything of it. I thought the whole thing was just piss and wind.'

He hesitated again, swapped the water for the cigarette and took another long toke. 'A couple of hours later, the protest turned into a full-blown riot. People were breaking windows, starting fires, throwing rocks. And some guys had Molotovs.'

I hunched forward and gave him a piercing stare. 'Those rioters didn't just show up spontaneously, though, did they? They were your people. You brought them in, you jacked them up, told them where to go and what to do. You were their general and they were your troops.'

He gazed at the half-smoked cigarette. He was less uptight now. 'Like I said, it was heavy shit. But like Bakunin said, 'The urge to destroy is also a creative – "

'I know what Bakunin said.' I kept my tone even. I needed information so I couldn't afford to piss him off. By the same token, I didn't have time for his grandiose bullshit. 'What I'm interested in is what went on with you and Gerry Bohannon.'

He crushed the cigarette in an ashtray and looked up at me. 'He showed up with a squad of soldiers about a half hour after the rioting got serious. He marched them over to the front of Stanton Hall, directly opposite where me and my people were. Then he started taunting me – waving dollar bills, flipping the bird, shouting all sorts of shit. The protesters were up for a scrap and it didn't take much to focus their attention on the soldiers. I mean, what right did they have to be on our damn campus?'

He seemed genuinely angry, brimming with self-righteousness.

But I wasn't concerned with the whys and wherefores. I said, 'What happened next?'

'A group of my SLUT people formed a line behind the protesters nearest the soldiers and linked arms. Then we sort of nudged the kids forward.' He made a small grin. His earlier angst had vanished. Now he seemed to be enjoying this. 'You should have seen the faces of those guardsmen when they saw us coming. *They* were scared shitless, not us. We drew back, went again, and again. I tell you, man, it felt so damn good to be sticking it to that bastard Bohannon.'

'I bet it did,' I said. 'But a guy like him, you must have known he wouldn't just sit back and take it.'

He nodded. 'That was when they put on their gas masks. I thought: Here we go, they're gonna lay down CS. But they never did. So we went at them one more time, and another. We had those soldiers cornered and beat. You could smell the fear coming off them. That was when I took out a dollar bill of my own and waved it back at Bohannon. That really made him pissed.'

I struggled to keep the incredulity from my tone. 'You actually wanted them to open fire, didn't you?'

'I thought they'd aim high. Everybody did. But they didn't. Suddenly they were shooting right at us.'

'What did you do?'

'Hit the deck. We all hit the deck.'

'You see what Bohannon was doing while the shooting was happening?'

He shook his head. 'I kept my head down. Then I heard him shouting orders – Cease fire! – something like that. I didn't realize anybody had died or gotten hurt until later. I never wanted that to happen.'

But I wasn't sure this was true. I thought back to the day Sally Newchurch got bayoneted. I recalled how Quilton was raising the ante on one side while Bohannon did the same on the other. I was convinced Quilton wanted to push and push until the Guard opened fire. Again.

'This dick-measuring contest between you and Bohannon,' I said, 'it didn't end that day on campus, did it?'

He refused to meet my gaze.

There was an extended silence.

I said nothing.

At last he looked at me. 'Bohannon's a grade A shit. And don't say you don't agree.'

'I do agree, Corey. Where I don't agree is that it's worth sacrificing innocent kids' lives to prove it.' By now I couldn't keep the contempt from my voice. 'Three people got killed and a half dozen wounded that day, and yet you and Bohannon were still playing the same crazy game three weeks later. I saw the pair of you. You wanted violence as much as he did. And Sally Newchurch got bayoneted as a direct result.'

'That was on Bohannon.'

'She nearly bled to death.'

'I'm sorry about what happened to Sally, really I am.' He gave me a beseeching look. 'But I didn't shoot the Brigstock boy, or Bobkov or Richardson, or any of the kids who got wounded on campus. And I didn't start the fire at the Biomedical Centre.'

'Maybe not, Corey, but you got blood on your hands, one way or another.'

'You gotta help me, Wat. I gave you my story. I owned up

to what I did. Now you gotta talk to Chief Ducey. He'll listen to you.'

I recalled what Gene Ducey said to me after the Biomedical Centre fire about wanting to question Quilton. Clearly this had taken place and whatever Ducey said had scared Quilton bad.

'I can't go to jail, Wat.' All the bravado had fallen away and he was back to being a freaked-out punk. 'I didn't do any of that stuff Ducey says I did.'

'Sorry, Corey, but I can't get involved in police business.' I watched him stew awhile.

Then I added, 'However, my partner JoBeth Medlock just may be able to help – if you're prepared to give her a sworn deposition detailing what you just told me. Plus those anonymous notes you sent to Harriet Brigstock.'

'I'll do it,' he said.

I thought about Gerry Bohannon. Quilton's testimony on its own might not get JoBeth a conviction, but it would play a big part in any case against him.

FIFTY

'We need to question Colonel Riley.' JoBeth was talking between bites of potato kugel. 'He's the link between the National Guard and Kershaw Lefevre.'

'Agreed,' I said. 'Let's finish eating and go brace the bastard.'

We'd bought some lunch from Yonah Schimmel's Knish Bakery on East Houston Street and eaten in Sarah D Roosevelt Park. Earlier that morning I'd visited Erikka at her apartment on Eldridge Street and told her what happened on the roof of the Kramer Centre. I emphasized that whatever the authorities announced, I didn't believe Andy would have pulled the trigger on Harriet Brigstock. I also told her I was also convinced he had nothing to do with the Ramskill shootings, or the ear mutilations. She stayed stoical throughout and thanked me for trying to bring him down off the roof. She even gave me a quote for the *Examiner*. The moment the door closed behind me, though, I sensed she'd give full vent to her grief. I felt gutted too – a perverse achievement for somebody with stunted emotions. The closest me and Andy came to knowing each other had been up there on the roof. But guys like him and me, we were used to making friends fast and losing them even faster. So my sense of loss was real enough. So too was my desire for revenge.

JoBeth spent the morning taking a statement from Corey Quilton at the US Attorney's office. Plea-bargaining was a way off, though it seemed likely Quilton would escape prosecution in return for giving evidence against Gerry Bohannon. As a result, the FBI had gotten a search warrant to seize his dad's M1 Garand – the rifle Lenny Lesniak saw him using to shoot Boyd Brigstock.

When we were done eating we went direct to the 55th Regiment Armoury and asked to see Riley.

The desk clerk told us the colonel was busy. I said he'd want to talk to us: We were on urgent business concerning a young woman named Park Ahnjong. The clerk picked up the phone and five minutes later we were shown into Riley's office. Unlike last time, there were visitor chairs and he was wearing civvies.

The hippo man gave me a look someplace between aggressive and browbeaten. 'What is this, Tyler, some sort of shakedown?'

'You tell me, Colonel.'

He gave me a bullish frown. 'You turn up out of the blue, demanding to see me about Ahnjong, this sure isn't about military business. And I already know you aren't who you said you were. You never resigned your commission and you weren't sent home in disgrace.'

'I never said I had, or that I was.'

'Even so, you joined my outfit under false pretences.'

'You were commanding it under false pretences.'

I saw him flinch at that.

All the same, he stood his ground. 'Whatever you're up to, you're not on the level.'

I shrugged. 'You'd need to take that up with your adjutant general. Because he's the guy I'm reporting to. Having said that, technically I'm on detached duty on Laurence Westerby's staff. So you could take this up with the National Guard brass or the Pentagon brass. Either way, though, you'd be wasting your time.'

'You're a glib bastard, Tyler.'

I said nothing.

He turned to JoBeth. 'Who's your partner?'

JoBeth leaned forward. 'JoBeth Medlock. I'm an assistant federal attorney for the Southern District of New York. I can't arrest you, Colonel, but I can ask the FBI to swing by and I'm sure they'd oblige because I'm investigating this case for the Department of Justice.'

'OK, I get you're not here to blackmail me. So why bring Ahnjong into this?'

He was clearly puzzled.

Which made three of us.

I glanced at JoBeth and she gave me a don't-ask-me look.

Then she turned to Riley. 'We have compelling evidence that you've been meeting secretively at various Manhattan hotels and restaurants with Ahnjong, a Korean national young enough to be your daughter. You represent a significant prima facie risk to national security. Why wouldn't we bring her into this?'

'Because she *is* my daughter.'

Not often I saw JoBeth lost for words, but this was one of them. Like me, she was stopped in her tracks.

She recovered quickly though. 'Colonel, you should

know you're the subject of an FBI enquiry. So I'd suggest you talk to us now because it's all going to come out anyway.'

He moved his big head from side to side as if admitting to himself there was no way out of this. 'My family in the US doesn't know about Ahnjong.'

'Tell us.' This was JoBeth.

He made a heavy sigh. 'I had an affair when I was serving in Korea. Ahnjong's mother wanted an abortion, but I'm Irish Catholic so I couldn't let that happen. But nor was I prepared to abandon them. I sent money, visited on the rare occasions army business took me back to Seoul. I tried to do right by them. Sadly, Ahnjong's mother died five years ago and she came to New York. She'd become a promising biochemist but lacked the funds to finish her PhD.'

JoBeth said, 'So, what, you agreed to pony up the money for her doctorate?'

He walked over to a burr wood cabinet, took out a decanter of brandy and poured himself a tumbler. 'I should have known I couldn't keep it quiet. Big Apple my ass, New York is a village. It was just a question of time before they found out and started turning the screw. But I never expected to get investigated by a federal prosecutor, along with the Special Forces' finest. You see, until this morning, I believed Tyler here *had* gotten busted and sent back in disgrace. That was why I thought you'd come as part of some double shakedown.'

'Hold on, Colonel,' I said. 'What do you mean by *double* shakedown? Who are 'they'?'

He sat down in his desk chair and took a mouthful of brandy.

He said, 'Kershaw Lefevre.'

This didn't surprise me.
Then he said, 'And Edison Phipps.'
This did surprise me.

FIFTY-ONE

JoBeth reacted first, 'What does Edison Phipps have to do with Kershaw Lefevre?'

Riley made a resigned shrug. 'Phipps' family owns a big equity stake in Kershaw Lefevre, which invested heavily in a new wonder-drug under development up at Ramskill. But the research programme was being threatened by this pinko scientist, Oleg Bobkov. He was trying to sell the drug to the Soviets. Phipps said he had to be stopped – '

'Phipps told you Bobkov was involved with the Russians?' JoBeth gave me a quick sideways glance.

The hippo man nodded yes. 'He said the FBI didn't have enough evidence to act and some of their high-ups were taking kick-backs. So a communist traitor was going to get away with handing a critically important asset to our enemies – unless somebody did something about it.'

'That somebody being you and Phipps?' JoBeth raised an eyebrow.

He made a dry chuckle. 'That somebody being Phipps. He was calling the shots. I was over a barrel. He knew about Ahnjong and was threatening to tell my wife unless I cooperated. If she finds out, that will mean the end of my marriage, my career, everything.'

JoBeth pushed ahead with the questions, 'What form did this cooperation take?'

Riley drank more brandy. 'After what happened at Kent State, places like Ramskill were tinderboxes waiting for a spark. Phipps knew his unit would be deployed if there was serious trouble. He said he'd worked out exactly how and where he could make that trouble happen. His plan was to provoke a riot and take advantage of the chaos to eliminate Bobkov. Nobody else was supposed to get hurt. I didn't like it one bit. But Bobkov was a traitor and Phipps had the power to ruin me if I didn't do as he asked.'

I asked, 'Which was what?'

'Not much different to what I would have done anyway if the 55th had been asked to handle serious civil disorder. It all began as Phipps told me it would: The protest became a riot and the Guard was ordered to Ramskill, then onto the university campus. Shortly before noon, I gave Phipps orders to disperse the campus protesters. He knew Bobkov walked from the Biomedical Centre to the faculty cafeteria every lunchtime at 1.00pm. This would give him plenty of time to deploy his men and get into position himself.'

I hunched forward. 'What sort of position?'

He guzzled more brandy as if it was water. 'What do you think?'

'You mean a firing position?' JoBeth sounded astonished. 'Are you saying Phipps was the sniper who took out Bobkov and Richardson?'

'He'd served in the regular army in the late 50s and fancied himself as a marksman.' Riley gave me a knowing look. 'You'll be well aware, though, that there's a big difference between the firing range and a live target in a fluid situation.'

He looked down at his brandy glass and swirled the amber liquid. 'When the deed was done, I was supposed to confirm whatever Phipps said in his report. This would be something like: His boys came under intense provocation so he ordered them to shoot over the protesters' heads. But one bullet went astray and tragically killed Bobkov.'

Downing the remaining brandy, he made a throaty cough and continued in a weary voice. 'Of course I never made that report because the plan collided with reality. Phipps missed Bobkov with his first shot and killed Gordon Richardson instead. He hit Bobkov with his second round, but by that time the Brigstock boy had also taken a bullet to the head and six other students were wounded. For my part, it was too late to do anything except what Phipps told me to.'

Riley went to refill his glass.

I traded anxious looks with JoBeth and guessed she was thinking the same as me: A little booze would lubricate Riley's vocals; too much and he'd start rambling.

He came back to his desk real slow, as if he never wanted to get there, and dropped into his chair with a limp thump.

Before he could sink more brandy, I said, 'Tell us about the second shooter.'

Riley's stubby fingers encircled the tumbler, but he didn't pick it up. 'That would have been Master Sergeant Gerald Bohannon. He was the only guy in Phipps' unit who knew about the plan, which was a big mistake.'

I could understand why. An operation as intricate as this, the last person on earth I'd have picked for a vital role would have been Gerry Bohannon. But then Phipps probably didn't have much of a choice.

Riley continued unprompted. 'Bohannon was tasked

with stirring up trouble among the protesters – the one thing he could be relied on to do. He'd already got the needle into a leftie agitator named Corey Quilton who was organising a protest that morning in front of Putney Hall. Phipps exaggerated the level of unrest in order to get a squad onto the campus. I advised the governor accordingly and, somewhat reluctantly, he approved my request. The appearance of Phipps' men on campus really kicked the hornet's nest and Bohannon soon got the protesters even more fired up.'

Now Riley seemed eager to talk – apparently the brandy was doing its work. 'The master sergeant's next job was ordering his guys to put on their gas masks. This was intended to restrict their vision – but crucially, not to lay down any gas.' Riley turned to JoBeth, sensing that although I didn't need an explanation, she might. 'CS gas hanging over the campus would have made Phipps' sniping job almost impossible.'

She sat back and gave him a studious look. 'So the masks meant the soldiers were unlikely to see Phipps moving to the groundskeeper's store to use his sniper rifle. And their limited vision also made the stray shot story more plausible.'

Riley made a tight smile. 'You got it, ma'am. Phipps gave Bohannon a hand signal to indicate he was in position. Then, when Phipps had taken his shot, Bohannon was meant to order the squad to fire high, masking the report from Phipps' rifle.'

She tilted her head to one side. 'But Bohannon came off the rails, didn't he?'

'You got it again.' Riley drank more brandy. 'The big lump turned up with his own rifle. The instant the squad had opened fire, he looked around for a target. He spotted

Boyd Brigstock in the parking lot and deliberately shot him. This was absolutely not part of the plan. And it was where it all started to unravel. The Polish kid Lesniak saw Bohannon bring the rifle out of the armoury, then use it to take aim and fire low.'

I thought back to the one-sided phone conversation I overheard between Bohannon and the guy ordering him to make sure Lenny kept his mouth shut. After what Riley had just revealed I had no doubt Phipps had been at the other end of that line. And there was something else. I recalled Bohannon's words: *I'm sure Captain Phipps saw nothing. He might as well not have been there. As usual he left the decision-making to me.* It was now obvious that Phipps was making Bohannon repeat what he needed to tell the authorities in order to absolve Phipps of all blame. I also remembered that seemingly tripped-out moment after Sally Newchurch got bayoneted and Phipps snapped at Bohannon, the way Big Gerry acted cowed and somewhat intimidated by Phipps as we drove back to the armoury. What I'd seen wasn't a rare display of backbone from Phipps, but the real Phipps, the ruthless Phipps, Phipps the killer, Phipps in command.

I said, 'Phipps must have been mightily pissed off when Bohannon went rogue and smoked the Brigstock boy.'

Riley made another bitter laugh. 'He was furious beyond words. The accidental shooting of Richardson was bad enough, but killing Boyd Brigstock was cruel, stupid and hugely counterproductive.'

JoBeth asked, 'So why did Bohannon do it?'

Riley finished his brandy and I was relieved when he sat back rather than going for more. 'He knew Harriet Brigstock was causing problems for Kershaw Lefevre. For reasons known only to himself, the master sergeant thought shooting her son would send a message: Somehow make her back off with the congressional investigation. But clearly Bohannon hadn't done his due diligence on Harriet Brigstock. All he did was make her more determined and add another futile death to the butcher bill. When he squeezed that trigger, though, the knucklehead really did believe his boss would give him a big pat on the back.'

I cast my mind back to my first meeting with Riley, when he'd described Boyd's death as 'thoroughly rotten luck'. At the time I thought this was because Riley was a self-obsessed asshole who saw this as a career obstacle. Now I could see he was angry because the kid wasn't supposed to die.

This show of basic decency, along with his loyalty to his Korean daughter, made me think again about Riley. Maybe he wasn't the nasty piece of work I thought he was when JoBeth and I walked into his office a half hour ago.

She wasn't ready to let him off the hook just yet though. 'What's the connection between your daughter and Kershaw Lefevre? I gather she recently took up an internship at their head office here in Manhattan.'

Riley ran his fingers through his bristly hair and gave JoBeth a dead-beat look. 'Phipps came to me with a combination of threat and incentive, though there wasn't much carrot and a whole lot of stick.'

JoBeth gave him a wary look. 'So the internship was a sweetener?'

The hippo man nodded. 'If she does well, they'll consider her for a permanent position. That would be a significant career boost. But of course it depends on me continuing to play ball. And in the meantime my daughter is working inside a company controlled by Phipps' family. He's implied more than once that if I step out of line, Ahnjong's employment prospects wouldn't be her – or my – only concern.'

I said, 'So even this apparent sweetener tightened Phipps' grip on you?'

'You said it.'

JoBeth was still curious. 'How does his family control Kershaw Lefevre?'

'As I said earlier, the Phippses own a big slice of equity in the business – enough to put his step-father on the board as executive vice president and his brother-in-law as chief finance officer.'

JoBeth threw me a sidelong look, then turned back to Riley. 'The step-dad and the brother-in-law have surnames that aren't Phipps, right? So the company's shareholder list wouldn't reveal any obvious or direct link to Edison Phipps?'

He made bleak smile. 'The Phippses are more of an organization than a family – you could call them an Ivy League version of the mob. They know when to strut their stuff and when to fly under the radar. As far as Kershaw Lefevre is concerned, the Phippses dictate corporate strategy and make all the major investment decisions.'

I said, 'Like the funding that went into the super-drug project at Ramskill?'

'That was their baby.' Riley examined the bottom of his empty tumbler, appeared to think about another drink, then placed it back on his desk. 'It was going to be the investment so big and bold they'd never need to make another. That was why they insisted on financing and controlling the research directly.'

The fog around another mystery began to clear.

I said, 'They went behind the back of the university president, didn't they? They set up their own private programme with their own finance?' I didn't need Riley to confirm this, but he did anyway.

JoBeth pressed him some more. 'They must have pulled some pretty powerful levers to make that happen.'

Riley shrugged as if this was no big deal for people like the Phippses. 'Edison's aunt, Antonia Langdale is a trustee. I've been doing business with her for years and know her socially. She always was domineering and devious and I can't imagine she'd have had too many problems getting her way with the other board members.'

This, I thought, explained why none of the trustees could be linked to pharmaceutical companies. Phipps' aunt was yet another under-the-radar relative – her name wouldn't have appeared on any Kershaw Lefevre documents because there was no formal connection.

JoBeth and I went quiet for a while. I was figuring out the implications of what we'd just learned and I guessed she was doing the same.

At last Riley cleared his throat. 'Might I ask, what's going to happen to me?' He didn't sound uptight, though. Just the opposite. He might have been asking if we thought it might rain later.

I decided he deserved some honesty, so I gave it to him straight. 'Hard to say right now, Colonel. Miss Medlock will report to the US attorney and I'll be in touch with Adjutant General O'Hara. But your openness and frankness today will certainly be taken into consideration. I must tell you, though, that there's no version of events where your wife and family don't discover what's happened – including about Ahnjong.'

His tone remained laid back. I even picked up a note of relief. 'I've known that for some time. I've known it since 1950.'

JoBeth came to her feet and said we'd be in touch.

We were half way to the door when Riley called from his desk.

'I was wrong about you, Tyler. You're not a jumped-up hillbilly. And I shouldn't have criticized your field commission. For what it's worth, you've been a better officer than me throughout this goddamn business.'

This was as close as I was gonna get to an apology – not that I wanted one.

Even so, I thanked him for his remarks.

I'd been as mistaken about him as he was about me. Sure, he'd made some catastrophic decisions, but he'd acted to protect a daughter whose welfare he'd placed above his own. If I'd gotten half that much commitment from either of my parents, I'd have considered myself truly blessed.

*

We went back to JoBeth's place and she cooked a righteous lasagne for dinner.

Not long after we finished eating, she got a call from one of the FBI guys she was working with: They'd recovered a bullet from the trunk of a tree in Washington Square Park and were confident it was the one that narrowly missed Harriet Brigstock. Just as crucially, they'd executed the search warrant at Bohannon's place and seized his rifle. The firearms lab test was being expedited and the master sergeant was a very worried man.

FIFTY-TWO

JoBeth had a six-pack of Rheingold beer in the refrigerator and we took one each into the living room. Riley had given us a lot to take in so we waited until we'd done eating before discussing the minefield of implications. JoBeth said we'd enjoy the lasagne better if we weren't talking between mouthfuls, but I sensed she also wanted some time to allow the weight of new information to settle in her mind.

Sitting on the couch with our beers, though, we went straight to business.

I said I had no doubt Phipps was the sniper in the Judson Church bell tower. It was his operation and he'd been the designated shooter on Ramskill Campus – even though he missed Bobkov with his first round. He missed again yesterday at Washington Square Park, though at least he had the excuse of JoBeth's last-ditch intervention. After seeing the shot go wide, I figured he bugged out fast and used a payphone to tip off the cops about suspicious activity on the roof of the nearby Kramer Centre. That way he created misdirection and a fall-guy in one move.

'What about the more obvious possibility?' she said. 'That Gerry Bohannon was the bell tower shooter. We know the feds are analyzing the bullet along with his rifle. The calibres match and I think we can predict the lab results.'

'Agreed about the gun and the bullet.' I sipped my beer. 'The whole scene was set up to mirror Ramskill Campus – two shooters, two M1 Garands – in a way that no investigator could possibly overlook. But Phipps would never have trusted Bohannon with a job so important. Big Gerry already messed up bad when he shot Boyd Brigstock on campus. That must have jeopardized Phipps' entire plan. Then he overstepped again when he put Lenny Lesniak in the hospital. Phipps wouldn't risk a third screw-up. He'd have taken the shot himself.'

She drank some beer. 'So, what? He got hold of Bohannon's rifle and used it to shoot at Harriet Brigstock? Then drove back to Ramskill and returned it to Bohannon so the feds could snag it?'

I nodded yes.

She wasn't convinced. 'Bohannon would have to be incredibly loyal or incredibly dumb or both.'

'He's not a deep thinker,' I said. 'And loyalty is probably his only virtue. That makes him putty in Phipps' hands.'

She still wasn't buying it. 'But surely, Andy Stuivermans was Phipps' dupe, not Bohannon.'

'Phipps doesn't do things by halves. Andy was set up for sure, but I don't think he was the only one.' I took out a Camel and lit it. I'd go back to the delayed action routine tomorrow. 'Why settle for one red herring and one fall-guy when you can have a pair of each?'

She made a baffled frown. 'Why would Phipps want Bohannon to get caught?'

'He's a liability Phipps can no longer afford. Not with

the whole MPQ-13 programme and millions of dollars of investment on the line.'

She seemed to catch my drift. 'Phipps realized we could use Bohannon's rifle to link him to the campus shooting. So he devised a plan to finish off Harriett Brigstock while also framing the two guys already under suspicion for the campus shootings and the other violent incidents at Ramskill.'

'You said it.' I took a pull on my cigarette. 'For very different reasons, Bohannon and Stuivermans had become major problems for Phipps: Big Gerry couldn't be kept under control and Andy was living evidence of everything wrong with MPQ-13. So Phipps laid breadcrumbs at Washington Square Park that would lead first to Andy, then – when the feds dug the bullet out of that tree – to Bohannon. They'd inevitably conclude that Bohannon took the shot, with Andy as back-up. And firearms forensics would connect both rifles to the campus shootings.'

'There's something else.' JoBeth leaned back, resting the back of her head on the couch and gazed at the ceiling. At last she said, 'Tom Pickles, my FBI liaison said they found other things at Bohannon's place – stuff that was interesting but not necessarily incriminating.' She turned to looked at me. 'I'm sure he mentioned a far-right newsletter.'

'That's not altogether surprising for a guy like Bohannon. He's not exactly liberal-minded.'

She shook her head. 'I got the impression it wasn't run-of-the-mill racism and anti-immigration stuff. I should have gotten more details but I was focused on the rifle.'

She went to the phone and picked up the receiver. 'I have Pickles' home number. I'll ask him.'

It was almost nine and a little late to be calling somebody

about work, but this didn't seem to bother JoBeth. She spoke with the agent for a few minutes and hung up with a satisfied expression.

'They found pamphlets from an organization called Nazi Eagles of America.' She gave me a knowing look. 'Ring any bells?'

I shrugged.

'The Nazi Eagles are under federal investigation for fomenting violence against a number of left wing politicians. Ring any bells now?'

I thought back to our first meeting with Harriet Brigstock, when she said SLUT was a bunch of show-off campus kids and produced what she believed to be a much more menacing threat from a Nazi group.

'Bells are ringing loud and clear,' I said. 'The Nazi Eagles sent that threatening note Harriet Brigstock showed us at her office. As I recall, there was a big swastika at the top. It said something along the lines of her being a commie bitch, knowing where she lived … and where her faggot son went to college.'

'Remember the sign off?' She gave me a hard look. '*We gonna kill you both.*'

I leaned forward to flick some ash. 'The fact that a hard-nosed politico like Brigstock took those people seriously says a lot.'

She gave me a crooked grin. 'But not as much as the fact that the feds found their pamphlet at the top of a pile right next to Bohannon's rifle rack.'

It took a couple of beats for the penny to drop. When it did, I returned the smile. 'You think Phipps planted the Nazi Eagles stuff?'

'Why not? The rifle in itself is damning enough. But like you said, Phipps doesn't do things by halves.'

'Makes a lot of sense.' I stubbed out my Camel. 'You got a clear demonstration of motive and intent right there. What more could a prosecutor ask for?'

She finished her Rheingold and went to bring two more from the refrigerator. When she came back, she seemed perplexed. 'What concerns me is Bohannon's ability to turn state's evidence. He cops a rap for murder one, he'll work out Phipps has set him up and won't need any encouragement to start ratting out his boss. Phipps would know this from the start, so why take the risk?'

'Because there is no risk.' I popped my can and took a swig. 'OK, *we* don't know exactly what Bohannon knows, but dollars to dimes it's not much. If Big Gerry had any real damaging skinny, Phipps wouldn't have served his balls up on a silver platter. Bohannon may know Phipps' family controls Kershaw Lefevre, but that's not a state secret. He may also have been aware that Harriet Brigstock's congressional committee was causing the company some concern. But Bohannon would have serious problems if he tried to play the conspiracy card in front of a jury. There's an unbelievable leap from Phipps' family getting grief from Brigstock to Phipps asking Bohannon to shoot her son, then assassinate the woman herself.'

She thought about this and nodded slowly. 'Put like that, it does sound like a ridiculous allegation.'

I lit another cigarette. I needed to cut down, just not now. 'Big Gerry has another major credibility problem. From what I heard of his phone conversation with Phipps at the armoury, he's already told the National Guard brass that Phipps wasn't really in control of the unit on Ramskill Campus. The message Bohannon repeated back was something like: Phipps was useless as usual and left all the decisions to Bohannon. The master sergeant is over a barrel in more ways than one.'

She opened her beer and said, 'That leaves Riley as our only credible witness. And there's nothing on the forensic side linking Phipps to the shootings at Ramskill or Washington Square Park.'

'There's Loretta Hausinger.'

She gave me a careworn look. 'How can she help? Unless Chief Ducey knows something he isn't sharing, we can't pin the Biomedical Centre fire on Phipps. Same goes for the shot that missed her out by the lake.'

'I get why you're sceptical,' I said. 'But we both know Phipps was behind that fire and the lakeside attack on Loretta. And unlike you, I don't need to follow the rules of evidence.'

'So, what? You're going to publish and be damned? Go vigilante?'

I detected an edge of irritation in her tone and kept mine even. 'I didn't say that. But I can go after him as a reporter in ways you can't as a prosecutor. More to the point, though, Loretta represents a massive threat to Phipps and Kershaw Lefevre because her allegations about MPQ-13 will be taken seriously.'

'Unless she gets charged with the triple murder at the Biomedical Centre.' She gave me a suspicious look. 'You trying to get me to let her off the hook?'

I tried not to sound terse. 'No, JoBeth, I'm trying to point out that Phipps has already tried to kill her twice because he knows how much damage she can do. For starters, her disclosures would punch a big hole in Kershaw Lefevre's balance sheet. Then there'd be question marks over corporate reputation, customer loyalty and regulatory compliance. And of course, Brigstock's congressional investigation into pharmaceutical R&D practices. Those folks on Capitol Hill would just love to hear what Loretta has to tell them. Upshot is there's very little Phipps wouldn't do to get to Loretta. And that could make him vulnerable.'

She sipped her beer. 'You sure she's safe with your buddy?'

'No one in New York City I'd trust more.' This was true, but even as the words came out, I began to realize my faith in Grundy might not be enough – not with a guy like Phipps.

I set my beer on the table. 'I need to use your phone.'

Grundy picked up quickly. He told me Loretta was fine and seemed a little put-out that I should think any different.

Even so, I reminded him not to let her out of his sight, no matter what.

When I hung up with Grundy I turned to JoBeth, 'You and I need to stick together too. Riley can't rat us out without ratting himself out. But Phipps is a resourceful bastard. If he finds out you're on his tail, you'll be competing with Loretta for a spot at the top of his to-do list.'

She threw me a dubious glance, 'And you won't be?'

'Of course I will.'

'But you're a tough man and I'm a weak woman, that it?'

'It's not a gender thing.' I leaned close and smiled. 'But I am a badass snake-eater, remember?'

She kissed my mouth, then drew back a fraction. 'I don't need taking care of, Wat.'

I stood up, scooped her up and carried her to the bedroom.

I said, 'We'll see about that.'

FIFTY-THREE

I waited in the Skylark outside the US Attorney's Office while JoBeth went inside for a meeting with her FBI liaison Tom Pickles. She thought I was paranoid and she was probably right. But my nose for danger had kept me alive more than once and right now it was telling me to be ready for anything. True, this state of mind has persisted over the weekend and neither of us had come to any harm. Nor, for that matter, had Loretta. But in light of the stuff Edison Phipps had pulled off, I'd have been plain stupid to underestimate his capabilities.

I'd already called Westerby and Maggie. The *Examiner's* publisher was pressing even harder for my exclusive but I couldn't make the piece stand up until I had all the facts. I did, however, sweeten my message to the top floor with a confident prediction that we wouldn't have too long to wait.

Maggie told me to be careful and I said sure I would – wasn't I always? But whatever I said I knew she'd worry.

JoBeth came out of the building and slid into the passenger seat.

'We got the lab results,' she said. 'As we thought, Bohannon's M1 fired the bullet aimed at Harriet Brigstock *and* the round that killed her son.'

This was a relief. Sure, I'd have bet my bottom dollar on

this result. But until you had something in the bag there was always a nagging doubt.

I pulled onto Centre Street and headed toward Brooklyn Bridge.

As we eased into the traffic, she said, 'The firearms experts found something else: Bohannon's rifle had been modified so it could be used with a Lyman sniper scope – the model with the threaded adjustment cap you found in the groundskeepers' shack.'

I thought about the logic of this. 'According to Lenny Lesniak, Bohannon didn't use a scope when he shot Boyd Brigstock. In fact, he was already taking a significant risk by bringing his own rifle. Even a lame-brain like Gerry would have known he couldn't get away with a scope as well – not out in the open. So Phipps must have taken the one he used for the assassination of Bobkov, then fitted it to Bohannon's M1 for the shot at Harriet Brigstock.'

'That's what the firearms experts figure.'

'Smart move,' I said. 'The scope would obviously boost Phipps' chances of hitting Harriet, while at the same time creating extra evidence to frame Bohannon.'

'Again, that's the expert opinion.'

'And presumably the rifle Andy Stuivermans had when I arrived at the Kramer Centre was the one used to take out Bobkov and Richardson?'

'I'm sorry, Wat.' She gave me a sad smile. 'Andy was a good guy caught in a bad situation.'

'He was manipulated into a bad situation.' I watched the Lower Manhattan skyscrapers roll by on the right as we crossed Brooklyn Bridge. 'I guess that means mission accomplished for Phipps' set up job.'

'You can't blame the FBI for being sceptical about what happened between you and Stuivermans. Until we have proof positive that Phipps was the other Ramskill shooter, Andy will remain in the frame for the Bobkov and Richardson shootings – and complicit in the attempted hit on Harriet Brigstock. But they *are* looking for Phipps.'

'They won't find him,' I said. 'But they won't need to.'

'How so?' She sounded baffled.

'Because he'll come looking for us.'

She sounded even more baffled. 'Surely he'll know we'll have reported to our bosses: That taking us out won't put him in the clear.'

'Of course he will, and my bet is that he'll have plans to leave the country. But first he'll want to even the score. Old money aristo like him, he'll make damn sure he doesn't come off second best to anyone – especially a pair of hardscrabble hillbillies.'

She said nothing and I got the impression she thought I was overstating the threat from Phipps. But the fact that it had taken us all this time to finger him spoke for itself.

She turned away and changed the subject. 'The lab people also confirmed the bullets that wounded the six protesters at Ramskill were from rifles issued to the National Guard. As your friend Lenny said, they thought they were firing high, but actually weren't. With their vision impaired by the gas masks, I guess it's understandable.'

'So you're not going to prosecute Lenny or any of the others?'

'We'd have a hard time proving the case against any individuals, so no.'

'What about Loretta Hausinger?' I gave her a sideways

glance as we entered the Brooklyn-Queens Expressway and went north. 'Had any further thoughts about prosecuting her?'

She said nothing.

I kept my eyes on the highway.

At length she said, 'You know what I think about turning a blind eye while a murderer goes free.'

'She's not a murderer. Her life was in danger from the people who assassinated her friend Bobkov, and who were planning to drive thousands of veterans crazy with a defective drug. She reacted to an extreme situation.'

'Maybe you're right.' She made a long, wistful sigh. 'Also, the case would be impossible to put before a jury. We have no material evidence so even if I subpoenaed you, it would be your word against hers.'

Even with a subpoena I wouldn't testify. I was a news reporter as well as an investigator and Loretta was my source. I'd have gone to jail myself rather than give her up. But I didn't want to provoke JoBeth so I kept my mouth shut.

Another long pause. The Skylark ate up more highway. She turned to look at me. 'Are you absolutely sure you ever had that conversation with her, Wat?'

I glanced back, read her look.

I said, 'No, JoBeth, I'm not at all sure.'

FIFTY-FOUR

Lenny Lesniak opened the front door of his parents' house. The kid was clearly anxious, which was good – any other sort of response to an unexpected visitor would have made *me* anxious.

I asked if he was OK and he said sure he was.

One of the reasons we'd driven up to Ramskill was to check on Lenny. He'd eyeballed Bohannon shooting Boyd Brigstock, which meant he was JoBeth's star witness. Problem was, it also gave Bohannon every reason to shut Lenny up permanently. So far, Phipps had exercised some level of control over Bohannon, but there were no guarantees this would last, which was why Phipps wanted rid of the big fella.

As if to prove my point, Lenny threw a wary glance up and down the street. 'You should watch out for Bohannon, Wat. Word is, he's batshit.'

'So what's new?' I tried to sound upbeat, but I was fooling no one.

'Seriously, man. He's pissed about having his place tossed by the feds. He's blaming you.'

'The feds will be back for Gerry all too soon,' I said. 'And this time they'll be arresting him for the murder of Boyd Brigstock.'

'You better hope they find him before he finds you.'

I peered over his shoulder. The TV was on and I could smell food on the stove. 'Your mom and dad at home?'

He nodded and told me dad knew about Bohannon. He'd gotten his old 12 gauge from the attic and knew how to use it.

'That's good,' I said. 'You see any sign of Gerry, you call 911 right away.'

Having satisfied ourselves about Lenny, we went to Putney Hall to deal with another reason we came to Ramskill: Blair Murdoch.

The university president saw us in his office. He told us how grateful he was for our assistance and assured us Phipps' aunt would be immediately removed from the board of trustees – along with the others who had gone along with the covert funding for MPQ-13.

I went into the men's room while JoBeth waited in the lobby downstairs.

I'd just finished at the urinals and was walking toward the wash basins when Gerry Bohannon launched himself at me from a toilet stall.

I'd gotten ambushed a lot of times, but never like this. Nothing came close.

There was just enough time to register the thought before 240 pounds of apeshit Irishman hit me side-on.

The momentum knocked us both into the wash basin counter. I winced as my outer thigh crashed against the hard laminate surface. Shifting behind me, he grabbed my collar and yanked my head back, ready to slam my face into the stainless steel fawcett.

This was his first mistake: He should have smashed my head down right away. That would have been the smart play. But smart plays weren't a big part of Gerry Bohannon's thought process.

My nostrils were invaded by the beer and onion stink of his breath hit as he pressed his face close to mine. 'Last time you're gonna see that pretty boy face of yours, Tyler. I'm gonna mess you up real bad.'

Talking this shit was his second mistake – though I sensed he had an uncontrollable need to savour the moment, to say something to mark the occasion.

Upshot was he gave me all the time I needed. Pivoting my left leg at the knee, I swung my heel up and drove it hard into his groin.

In the mirror, I saw pain crumple his fleshy face. He let go of my collar and staggered back, clutching his crotch.

Most guys would have folded under a blow like that, but Big Gerry stayed upright. He must have had big balls, or maybe very small ones. Whatever, he somehow got his fists back up, ready to go again.

We stood there, watching for the other to make a move.

I'd counted maybe a half dozen beats when he sucked in a sharp breath and came at me with a powerful right hook. I raised my arms in a cross-guard and felt the impact on my left forearm. It was gonna hurt when the adrenalin went, but I didn't care because it left the side of his head exposed to my right elbow. I smashed it into his jaw and sent him juddering sideways.

I moved away from the basin counter to give myself a little more space. 'You should give it up, Gerry. It was Phipps who set you up with the feds. He's been playing you from the get-go.'

‘You’re a lying chickenshit, Tyler.’ He moved toward me, fists still raised. ‘That’s why you don’t understand loyalty.’

‘Loyalty’s a two way deal, Gerry. You gave Phipps all you had and got nothing back except mightily shafted.’

We waited some more: Another half dozen beats. A globule of sweat formed on his brow and slanted along the jagged scar that ran diagonally from his hairline to his jaw. The little eyes were still misted with rage, but there was frustration there too.

He came in with a barrage of blows, arms flailing, feet kicking. But it was a wild attack, easy to block and dodge. And while he was expending energy, I landed a couple of hard jabs that cut his cheek and lip.

He stepped back, wiped away a string of bloody saliva with the back of his hand.

‘C’mon, Gerry, let’s call it a day.’ I tried to sound reasonable. ‘The feds are looking for you right now. You don’t want to add assault, or worse to the rap sheet you’re already looking at.’

He made a contemptuous snort. ‘Rap sheet I’m looking at, it don’t much matter what I add to it. But I’ll gladly do the time for another murder if it means offing you, you pansy-ass piece of crap.’

I watched his face muscles twitching, like he was using them to massage his brain, make it work better. For a dumb schmuck like Gerry, making it work at all would have been a start.

He glanced to one side, clocked the heavy steel fire extinguisher and snatched it from the wall.

Raising it above his head, he lunged forward, bringing it down on mine.

I moved toward him, sidestepping his bulky frame. Then I leaned my shoulder under his armpit, shoved him sideways and kicked his back foot off the ground.

He went down fast and heavy. I saw a welter of spit spray from his mouth as his chest hit the floor.

The fight had gone out of him, but I didn't feel inclined to taking any chances. So I knelt on his back and levered his right wrist between his shoulder blades, pinning him down.

It was at that point that the door swung open and a uniformed security guy appeared.

'You better call Chief Ducey,' I said.

FIFTY-FIVE

Bohannon said nothing as he was arrested, cuffed and taken to a squad car.

Gene Ducey asked me to go along to the station and give him a statement. First, though, I needed to talk to JoBeth. I asked Ducey if he'd seen her on his way in. He said no.

I went downstairs to the lobby area. She wasn't there. I asked one of the girls in the back office to check the women's room. She went in an came out shaking her head. I called the Journalism School, but she wasn't there either. I called JoBeth's campus apartment. No answer.

By this time my irritation was turning to concern. A half hour had passed since Ducey and his boys arrived. Sure, JoBeth had insisted she didn't need a guy like me to look after her. But she wasn't stupid. She wouldn't have vanished without telling me.

I tried the young woman on the reception desk. A lot of people must have come and gone in the last twenty minutes, but it was worth a shot.

When I'd described JoBeth, the receptionist gave me a curious look. She was a sharp-looking girl with an alert expression. 'This lady, is her name Medlock?'

I told her yes.

'I got a call from a guy who asked me to give her a message. Said he was with the FBI.'

I frowned. 'Did he give a name?'

'Special Agent Pickles. I remember because it was unusual – sort of funny, don't you think?'

Tom Pickles was JoBeth's FBI liaison. But she'd met with him in Manhattan only two hours ago. What was he doing in Ramskill?

I said, 'What was the message?'

'He said he had urgent information in relation to some guy Miss Medlock was looking for. I wrote it down.' She glanced down at a notebook next to the switchboard. 'Yes, here it is: Phillips.'

My frown deepened. 'Are you certain it was Phillips?' All sorts of alarm bells were ringing now. 'Might the caller have said Phipps?'

She thought about this. Then she said, 'I guess so, yes.'

'What was the rest of the message?'

'This Agent Pickles said he needed to speak to Miss Medlock. He said he'd be right outside. I passed on the message and she left the building.'

'Did you see where she went?'

'Not really. There was a dark-coloured panel van parked near the payphone opposite. I suppose she might have gotten into it because when I looked again it was gone and so was she.'

'And you didn't see the guy she was with?'

She shook her head no.

I called the FBI field office in Manhattan and asked for Tom Pickles. He sounded as worried as I felt. He had no new information on Phipps and no reason to talk to JoBeth so soon after they met. Nor did the bureau have anyone on campus. He said he was going to drive up right away and asked me to wait until he arrived. I agreed, but had no intention of hanging around if I picked up a lead.

Next I went to the campus cop shop. I explained everything to Ducey and asked for five minutes alone with Bohannon. Ducey was hesitant and I appreciated why. I said I was almost certain Phipps had abducted JoBeth. Her life would be on the line unless I found her fast. And Phipps would be well outside Ducey's jurisdiction by now.

He made a deep sigh and took me into a room where Bohannon was waiting to be questioned.

'Five minutes, Wat.' Ducey looked me in the eye. 'And no funny stuff. You dig?'

I dug. He closed the door behind him.

Bohannon was cuffed to a metal table. He didn't look at me as I stood opposite him.

'You can tell me to fuck off and I will but – '

He told me to fuck off. I said I would, but only after he heard me out. He had very little choice, and maybe an opportunity to help himself, so he agreed.

'I get that you hate my guts, Gerry. But you got nothing against JoBeth Medlock and you got plenty against Edison Phipps. If it wasn't for him, you wouldn't be here.'

He looked up, his battered features expressionless. 'Phipps grabbed your gal, didn't he?'

I said, 'I need to know where he might have taken her. Anything you can tell me, I'll make sure Gene Ducey and the feds know you did what you could. And you'd be helping to even your own score with Phipps.'

He said nothing, stared back at the table.

I counted to ten.

I counted to twenty.

Then I turned to leave. My hand was on the door handle when he called across the room.

'Phipps has a sailing yacht – *Tomahawk* he calls it – moored on the Hudson.'

I turned back into the room.

He kept his eyes on the table. 'Little place called McIver's Yard, mile or so north of Tarrytown. I never went there, but he'd sometimes talk about it as his bolt hole – a place where he could cast off and be alone on the water. My guess is, that's where he's taken her.'

*

I found an address for McIver's Yard in the phone book. I drove north on Route 9A then east on 117, past Pocantico Lake, and south on US9. The place I was looking for was on a spit of land that extended maybe a hundred yards into the Hudson. The yard comprised a tin roof repair shop, steel frame boat hoist and two timber jetties where two dozen sail boats were tied up. The yard was deserted, the repair shop locked up, and nobody on any of the yachts.

I jogged along the smooth timbers of the jetties, glancing at the names painted on the sterns. None of them was called *Tomahawk*.

I was beginning to suspect Bohannon had sent me on a wild goose chase, that I'd misjudged the doggedness of his loyalty to Phipps. Or his hunch was plain wrong. He wasn't the most insightful guy.

I looked out across the river, about two miles wide at this point. The water was smooth and grey under dense overcast. Three freighters and a pair of pleasure steamers were moving slowly upstream in the centre of the channel. Closer inshore a speedboat was churning a V of foam.

But there were no sailboats.

I tried to imagine what Phipps was planning. I had no doubt he snatched JoBeth as a hostage. And it made sense to use his boat to escape. The Hudson was a big and busy river and he could go anywhere, hide up in some isolated inlet nearby, sail north toward Canada or south to New York Bay and then the open sea.

It made a lot of sense. Except it didn't because neither Phipps nor his yacht were here.

On the drive over, I calculated that I was forty-five minutes, maybe an hour behind him. I didn't know much about sailing yachts, but I did know it look time to rig the sails and shove off. Even if Phipps' vessel had an engine, it would be an auxiliary one, not designed for speed. I doubted he could have sailed out of sight.

I hadn't told Gene Ducey where I was going, or called Tom Pickles' office, because I knew how heavy-handed cops and feds could be. Delicate situation like this, I didn't want choppers and patrol vessels swarming around. Seemed I was wrong though. Instead of helping to rescue JoBeth, I'd given Phipps as much of a head start as he could wish for. He could have driven to Manhattan. He could be half way to Philadelphia or a good way to Boston. He could be anywhere.

Then I saw a pale triangular sail nudge slowly from behind a stand of trees on the northern side of the spit. The boat was a sleek white craft, maybe a thirty-footer. It was perhaps a quarter mile out. Too far to make out any detail. Hustling back to the car, I brought my field glasses and trained them on the boat. At first it was sailing parallel to the shore. After a few minutes though, it turned. I read the name on the stern: *Tomahawk.*

FIFTY-SIX

Spotting Phipps' boat was one thing; reaching it, another.

There were plenty yachts moored alongside, but I had no idea how to rig the sails, still less operate them. Even if I did, he'd be out of sight before I could get underway.

I wondered again whether I should have involved the cops and the feds. But experience taught me to stay in the game at all costs. Waiting for Tom Pickles to drive up from Manhattan would have given Phipps a massive advantage. This way, I'd located him – even if he was out of reach. And I still had the option of calling Pickles. At least now I could give the feds a positive sighting and an actual location.

Unless that was somebody else sailing the *Tomahawk*. Maybe one of Phipps' buddies? I could see a guy at the helm, but he was sitting with his back to me and could have been almost anyone. I was also assuming JoBeth was aboard. What if he'd handed her over to somebody else? Or left her bound and gagged someplace?

I reminded myself that what-ifs were costing me crucial seconds. I focused on what I could do here and now.

Once more, I scanned the boat yard. Nothing.

Again.

And again.

This time, though, I noticed a set of steel ladders fixed to the far end of the jetty. They seemed to lead somewhere, or to something. I went to take a look. As I got closer, I saw a small fibre glass dinghy bobbing in the water. Mounted on the stern was an outboard motor – one piece of water transport kit I did know how to operate.

I climbed down the ladder and moved to the stern, then levered the propeller into the water, inserted the fuel pipe and yanked the pull-cord. The engine sputtered and wheezed, but didn't fire. I adjusted the choke and tried again. This time there was a little more life, but the end result was the same. I looked across the river. Phipps had completed another turn and was even further out into the channel. I pulled out the choke some more, squeezed the hand-primer to pump extra fuel into the engine, and hauled the pull cord. The engine coughed, stammered and finally came to life. I removed the mooring lines, gunned the throttle and watched the water churn in my wake as the little craft gathered headway. The motor wasn't powerful, but I was able to steer straight for where I was going, unlike Phipps who was having to complete a series of zig-zags to work his way out into the river.

Even, so progress was slow. Each time I thought I'd closed the distance, he let out his big sail and put on a spurt of speed. At least to start with he didn't seem aware that I was chasing him. After twenty minutes, though, I was less than one hundred yards behind him. That was when he gave me a second look, and a third. Then he disappeared into the cabin and came back with some binoculars. Now he was in no doubt. I saw him put the helm over and surge deeper into the middle of the channel. I was already at my top speed and had no idea how much fuel was left in the tank. The farther out I went, the more choppy the river became and the little dinghy started to buck and vibrate as it hit successive swells. My big advantage, though, was my direct line of approach against his need to tack back and forth.

Gradually, I got nearer.

At fifty yards, he took out a snub-nose revolver, took aim and fired. The round hit the water six feet to my left. That sort of range, in these conditions, he'd have to be damn lucky to hit me. He seemed to grasp this too and waited until I was much closer – around twenty yards. This time his shot punched a hole in the hull. It was high above the waterline and too small to make me worry about taking on water, but it was a sign that his accuracy would only improve as I approached.

I manoeuvred closer still. The *Tomahawk's* wake made the dinghy even more unstable. I looked up and saw the yacht's main sail towering overhead. If I had any doubts about the skipper's identity, they vanished when I saw Phipps looking straight at me from his steering position at the stern. I thought he smiled, though it was hard to be sure as I bounced from one swell to the next.

I realized that if I got any closer, he wouldn't miss. So I opened the range, staying parallel to the yacht and nudging slightly ahead so that its big sail gave me cover. My tactic worked real well – until he altered course and the thirty foot yacht was suddenly bearing down on my flimsy craft. I pushed my tiller away, mirroring his turn, but I was going way too fast for such a violent manoeuvre. The dinghy heeled right over on one side. Instinctively, I shifted my weight to the opposite side. For a half dozen beats I clung to the edge of the hull, pushing my upper body out over the water to counteract the tipping motion. I seemed to hang there for ever, on a knife-edge, almost standing up straight over the murky water. I glanced up and saw the side of the yacht shoot by. Six feet closer and my dinghy would have been pulped. Another pistol shot rang out. But I was too busy trying not to capsize to notice where the bullet went. Then the bottom of my hull slapped back down on the water. The dinghy lost headway, rocking and bobbing like crazy as it was butted side-on by the wash from the *Tomahawk*.

When my boat eventually settled on an even keel, I let the range widen before resuming the chase. Now, though, I was more wary about my angle of approach. I tried to figure out a way of using the wind to give me an edge. I didn't know much about sailing, but I did know Phipps couldn't sail straight into the wind, so I steered to a position directly upwind of him. By approaching head-on, I could keep the length of the yacht between me and Phipps, who was steering from the stern. Coming at him this way would also hinder his visibility because he couldn't easily see me over his cabin roof.

Getting to grips still wasn't going to be easy.

I steered this way and that, always keeping dead ahead of him, and closed the distance slowly, watching the trim of his sail for signs of a change of course. Finally, I worked the dinghy to a position in the cover of Phipps' sail and waited as he came closer.

Closer yet.

Fifty yards, forty, thirty –

I let out the throttle and moved the tiller to make a tight U-turn. It brought me level with the bow of the yacht, just twelve feet away. The dinghy was buffeted hard by the *Tomahawk's* bow wave but I anticipated this and steered head-on to reduce the pitching. My vision was filled by white hull and sail as I went crashing toward the yacht. With seconds to spare, I turned parallel and locked the tiller. The hulls were almost touching, a pale mash of water between them. I moved to the middle of the dinghy, focused on the chrome guard-rail at the very front of the yacht. There was no going back now. The dinghy began to roll. I launched myself across the narrow sluice of water.

FIFTY-SEVEN

My fingers closed around a horizontal section of the guard-rail. I tried to haul myself up to the deck, but couldn't get enough purchase. My whole body slid backward along the hull. I braced myself for the cold drench. Then my right hand struck a vertical support. My legs swung toward the stern but my grip held.

I got my chin level with the foredeck and glanced around. Phipps was nowhere to be seen. But he could appear at any second.

What was he up to?

As if in reply, the bow tilted and dipped, dunking me chest deep in the river. I caught my breath against the sudden chill.

I hung on.

Muscles burned, vision blurred, breath came in sharp gasps as the water tried to suck me down.

Still I didn't let go.

I waited until the bow began to come up again, levered myself higher, hitching my right knee on the deck. Next I got my left hand higher up the guard-rail and hooked my right elbow around a stanchion. Finally, pushing my knee behind a mast stay, I rolled sideways onto the deck.

Now, all I had to worry about was a psychopathic killer with a gun and no place to run.

I came to my feet in a low crouch. I figured Phipps was right astern in the cockpit, concealed by the sail and the cabin roof. This was a streamlined structure, two feet higher than the deck, with a narrow gangway on each side. Not much cover, but better than nothing.

I started moving along the right hand gangway toward the stern. Peeking around the edge of the sail, I saw him looking right at me.

'Welcome aboard, Wat!' He made a toothy grin. 'Gotta say, there were times when I didn't think you'd make it.'

I stepped out from behind the sail and closed the distance between us to around twelve feet.

'That's close enough.' He raised the snub-nose.

I nailed it as a Smith & Wesson Model 36 with a five-shot chamber and two-inch barrel. He'd fired three rounds, which left two. I'd kept a close eye on him most of the time, but he could have reloaded when he was out of sight behind the sail. It didn't take long. My gut told me he didn't bring spare ammo. The fact that he was still wearing suit pants and a tie suggested he'd come here in a big hurry, probably straight from work. But he could have picked up a box of bullets. That didn't take long either.

I was also counting on the lack of accuracy that came with a short barrel. Even at twelve feet I wasn't an unmissable target, especially on the constantly tilting deck. Nor was I planning to stand still when he made his move. And Phipps' track record meant he wasn't as good a marksman as he seemed to think.

Despite all that, the odds were very much in his favour – even with two rounds.

By the look on his face, though, I didn't think he intended to shoot me right now. Guy like him, he'd want to crow over the situation before finishing me off.

'I got your partner in the cabin,' he said. 'She was surprisingly easy to snag. I drove right up to Putney Hall, called reception from the payphone opposite, and she came straight out. I was waiting with my van and my little friend here' – he indicated the revolver – 'and before you could say Agent Tom Pickles, I'd gotten her in the back. All very straightforward.'

I made a what-can-I-say? expression. 'Looks like you're in control, Edison.'

He sat back, seemingly relaxed. 'You play ball, Wat, and there's every chance the pair of you can walk off this boat in one piece.'

I raised an eyebrow. This was probably bullshit, but worth exploring. 'How so?'

'I sailed *Tomahawk* across the Atlantic once, no reason I can't do it again. Or go some other place. Canada, the Caribbean, Latin America. You and JoBeth are valuable assets. Not much your bosses wouldn't do to get you back. That means you're my ticket out of the USA. Once we're clear of American waters I could put you ashore wherever you want: Bermuda, Bahamas, Jamaica.'

'I need to be sure JoBeth is unharmed.'

'You're hardly in a position to make demands, Wat.' He made a generous expression. 'But go ahead. If you step back onto the companionway, you can see her through the cabin windows.'

I did as he suggested and peered through the nearest window. It was sheathed in specks of brine, but JoBeth was there all right, on an upholstered bench seat with a cord around her ankles, hands bound behind her back and duct tape over her mouth. She looked up at me and made a sharp nod, as if to confirm she was OK.

I glanced around the cabin: Not much to see except the two bench seats facing each other, a bolted-down table, cupboards and a little galley stove. I wondered if there was something she could use to free herself, though it was unlikely Phipps had left anything to chance.

I returned the smile and made a thumbs-up sign. I didn't know who I was trying to kid, but I couldn't think of anything better.

Turning back to Phipps, I said, 'OK, so she's fine. But assuming you reach international waters, what's to stop you putting a bullet in our heads and dumping us over the side?'

'I'm a man of my word.'

'You're a killer.'

'So are you.'

'I'm a soldier.'

'So am I.'

'You're not fit to wear the uniform.'

He shook his head as if I'd totally misunderstood him. 'I know you went to see Phil Riley and most of what he told you was probably true. Bobkov gave me no choice and Richardson was an accident. The other deaths were down to the stupidity of others.'

'Meaning Gerry Bohannon?'

'Mainly, but not entirely.'

I gave him a knowing look. 'Working with Bohannon can't have been easy.'

'You said it.' He glanced up at the sail, shifted the tiller slightly. 'Taking his daddy's rifle on campus was dumb beyond comprehension. If he hadn't done that, we wouldn't be here now.'

'He did it for you.'

'He did it for himself. He was determined to use that protest as his own private firing range, with live targets. A twist of fate put the Brigstock boy in his sights and he didn't think twice before pulling the trigger. It was only afterward that he convinced himself he did it to help me out. What he was really doing was zapping the offspring of a woman he considered to be a vile pinko bitch.'

Maybe he was right about Bohannon's motives, but I didn't want to interrupt his flow.

'I realized at this point that Gerry had outlived his usefulness – or rather uselessness. He'd become a major liability. This was confirmed when I told him to lean on Lenny Lesniak to keep him quiet, but instead he put the kid in the hospital.'

'So you decided to set up Bohannon and Andy Stuivermans for Ramskill as well as Washington Square?' I gave him a curious look. 'That must have taken some planning.'

Again, he glanced at the sail and altered course a few degrees. 'It wasn't conceived, it evolved over time, in response to changing circumstances. But, yeah, eventually I worked out how to use Bohannon's stupidity in a way that resolved issues rather than complicating them.'

'I'm enthralled,' I said.

He gave me a dark look.

'Really,' I said. 'I'm not being sarcastic.' And I wasn't.

He went quiet, peering over my shoulder at some aspect of the yacht's trim. Then he leaned to one side of the cockpit and operated a stainless steel winch to wind in a rope and tighten the sail.

I still needed to find out how he'd played Andy Stuivermans, so I said, 'Must have been a big challenge – making it all come together?'

He made a what-the-hell shrug. 'I had eyes and ears inside the biomedical place. Investment that big, we needed an internal perspective.'

'One of the three scientists who got shot?'

He nodded. 'They were all cooperative – hell, we were paying them enough. But Headley Reese was our main man. A few months ago, we were having a general conversation and I mentioned how Harriet Brigstock's congressional probe was starting to cause problems at Kershaw Lefevre. That was when Reese told me about Andy Stuivermans having a bee in his bonnet for Brigstock. He thought it was ironic. I thought it was a potential opportunity. I took a gander at Stuivermans' file and quickly realized I was looking at a gift from God: one of our own volunteers with a longstanding grudge against Brigstock – plus special ops sniper skills. I mean, what were the odds?'

FIFTY-EIGHT

It wasn't a gift from God for Andy, but I kept quiet. I wanted more information more than I wanted to say my piece.

Phipps continued in a more sanguine tone – as if it was helpful to get this off his chest. 'Soon after the campus shootings the MPQ-13 programme hit severe turbulence. Blair Murdoch instigated his enquiry into the funding source and Harriet Brigstock was getting increasingly vocal – despite what Bohannon had done to her son. We were told by a friendly congressman that she was targeting Kershaw Lefevre in particular. There were whispers of the business having gotten infiltrated, folks on the board losing their nerve. Anyway, the rumour mill got cranked up and our share price didn't look so healthy. We needed to silence Brigstock and fast, but in a way that wouldn't implicate the company.'

'And Andy Stuivermans was the perfect dupe.' I didn't even try to disguise my disdain.

Phipps didn't appear to notice. 'He was our get-out-of-jail-free card. Reese agreed to increase his dosage of MPQ-13 as well as using subliminal stimuli to get him in a state of mind where he was ready to assassinate Brigstock. By the time Reese was done with him, Stuivermans really believed he'd been selected for a government-sanctioned black ops mission. He'd call me on a payphone for instructions and I sent him out at night to sharpen up his recon techniques.'

I said, 'You were never going to use Andy to hit Harriet Brigstock, though, were you?'

He shook his head. 'Stuivermans was ideal misdirection. I could utterly depend on him to arrive at the Kramer Centre and take up a sniping position at exactly the right time. I could also count on him to stay there until the cops arrived to find him in possession of the same rifle I used to kill Bobkov and Richardson.'

I thought: *You devious bastard.* But I didn't want to inflate his ego, or rile him. So I said, 'Then JoBeth arrived in Ramskill, closely followed by me. That can't have been good news.'

He made a bitter laugh. 'We thought we'd gotten through the worst phase of the investigations, but we couldn't have been more wrong. With the two of you poking around, it became even more urgent to produce a version of events that would tie up the campus fatalities as well as the Washington Square shooting.'

'Sorry to have pissed on your parade.'

He made a *c'est la vie* gesture.

Then he went quiet and I sensed he needed another push. 'Did Bohannon know what you were planning for Harriet Brigstock when you asked to borrow his rifle?'

'Yeah, I told him the whole deal and he was happy to go along with it – including the modification of the gun to take a Lyman scope. He said he'd help out in whatever way he could if it meant taking out Harriet Brigstock. And he was ever so grateful when I returned the rifle, minus my fingerprints. Even when I told him I'd missed, he remained ridiculously enthusiastic – said he was sure I'd nail the bitch next time.'

'That was when you planted the Nazi Eagles stuff?'

'I hardly planted it. I just tossed it there by the rifle rack.' He made an almost embarrassed smile. 'Framing Gerry was absurdly easy. He even agreed to do a few hours of Bravo Company paperwork at his place while I was at Washington Square. He lives alone, so that meant he had no alibi. When the feds found the bullet I knew it would be linked to Gerry's rifle, the killing of Boyd Brigstock and the attempt on Harriet. To cap it all off, Bohannon will be charged with the attack on Lesniak, and Stuivermans will be blamed for the ear-themed attacks on the animals and Harold Kapp.'

I was appalled and didn't try to hide it. 'You sliced up Chip Amelsfort's sheepdog, the little girl's bunny and maimed Harold Kapp just to lay a trail that would specifically lead *me* to Andy Stuivermans?'

'You were the guy with the Vietnam ear-trophy knowledge. You were the guy I could depend on to find out about Stuivermans' ear.'

He spoke as if what he did to the dog, the bunny and Harold Kapp, were my fault. I couldn't find the words – not often you could say that about me.

'I didn't enjoy doing those things, you know.' He sounded somewhat defensive. 'I'm not some sadistic freak.'

That was exactly what I thought he was, but couldn't afford to anger him. Not yet, anyway. So I kept my mouth shut.

Besides, I had another avenue to explore. I said, 'Loretta Hausinger threw a wrench in your works too, didn't she?'

He altered course again and made a frustrated grunt. 'Like I said, Gerry Bohannon was the worst culprit, but he wasn't the only person who made catastrophically bad decisions.' He pushed his fingers through his thick hair. 'I knew she was going to be a problem from the outset. That was why I asked Reese and the others to freeze her out, force her to find another job someplace else.'

'Hence all that sexist crap?'

'I didn't like it, but my hands were tied.' He threw me a give-me-a-break look. 'Hey, I'm a liberated guy. For her own good, Hausinger had to go.'

I realized then that the eager-to-please, easy-going Edison Phipps wasn't entirely an act. He really did have a genial side, he really did like to be liked. And he was remarkably thin-skinned. Problem was, the other Edison Phipps called the shots. The psychopath only wheeled out the nice guy when circumstances required his presence.

I said, 'But Loretta didn't quit, did she – even after you killed her friend Bobkov?'

He looked genuinely hangdog. 'She dug her heels in – partly because she'd bonded with Stuivermans. Gotta say, though, I never thought she had the salt to do what she did. That took courage and audacity.'

'It didn't stop you torching the Biomedical Centre when you thought she'd be inside.'

'Hausinger sealed her fate when she killed Reese and the other two.' His tone hardened. Mr Nice Guy had been replaced by the scheming killer. 'But that wasn't the only reason I set light to the place. We'd taken all the research data we needed to resurrect the programme, but we had to destroy the remaining physical evidence.'

'You did a good job tailing me to the lake,' I said. 'But you fouled up with your shooting – again.'

He winched in a little more sail. 'Doesn't matter. In fact, there could be a way out for her too. Maybe she doesn't need to be eliminated. But her credibility does.'

'That your next line of attack? Go after her reputation like you tried to do with Bobkov's? It was you who mailed those compromising pictures to Blair Murdoch, wasn't it?'

He made a whimsical sigh. 'Looking back, that may have been a better approach from the start. Scientific research at that level is all about reputation. If we'd gotten Bobkov fired for gross misconduct, he and the others would still be alive. But hindsight is a wonderful thing, wouldn't you say, Wat?'

I didn't reply. I was thinking where this dialogue was leading, and about how I could move close enough to take him down.

'You got any sailing experience, Wat?' His voice was suddenly upbeat, even jaunty.

I said no I didn't.

He looked to the top of the mast, then back at me. He was smiling. 'Well, this boat is sailing on what we nautical sorts call a broad reach on the starboard tack. The wind is coming across our starboard quarter, which is to say over my right shoulder. It's a nor-nor-easterly, five or six knots. Nothing exhilarating, but plenty to get you from A to B.'

He loosened a rope connected to the heavy wooden boom, to which the lower edge of the sail was attached. It swung even wider over the water, almost ninety degrees to the hull.

'We're going to do a manoeuvre known as a gybe.' He sounded like a teacher talking to a dim kid. 'Any idea what that means?'

I said no I didn't. But I could tell from the change in his tone that it meant nothing good.

He put the helm over.

The stern shifted counter-clockwise. The sail went limp – but not for long.

I felt the wind shift from the right of the stern to the left.

It filled the sail.

And suddenly the boom was sweeping over the cabin roof – straight at me.

FIFTY-NINE

I'd hit the deck fast and hard plenty of times, but never so fast and never so hard. A half second later, I heard the boom whoosh close overhead. The sail whacked it far out across the water on the opposite side of the yacht. Then the rope went rigid and the whole rig jarred to a halt. Down in the cockpit, Phipps was using a winch to haul in the rope and bring the sail back under control.

He glanced up, with the gun still on me. 'That was quick work, Wat. I expected to be dealing with a man overboard situation. Not that there'd have been much point turning the boat around. The boom would have broken your legs and you'd have drowned in considerable pain before I could reach you.'

'That would have been too bad.' I got off my belly and came to my hands and knees, weighing up my options. This didn't take long because I didn't have any. I was confronted by a guy with a gun on a thirty foot yacht, with no weapon and no cover except the sail and cabin roof.

'I didn't want to have to shoot you, Wat.' He sounded reluctant, almost apologetic. 'It'll be messy. And I have my paintwork to think about. But your interview didn't go so well and, after surviving my surprise gybe, you've left me with no choice.'

I gave him a puzzled look. 'Interview?'

He locked the tiller so the boat would hold its course and came to his feet. 'The conversation we just had could have gone a number of ways. But it became clear from your attitude that keeping you aboard would be more trouble than it was worth. I have JoBeth as my hostage.' He made a resigned shrug. 'Sorry, pal, but I don't have room for another.'

I couldn't imagine anything I could have done or said that would have resulted in him deciding not to kill me. But there was clearly no point debating the issue.

I said, 'That's a Smith & Wesson Model 36 with a two inch barrel and five-round chamber. You've laid down three rounds already and I'm willing to bet you haven't reloaded. That gives you two rounds to finish me off with a weapon not noted for accuracy.'

He started coming toward me. 'I don't need two rounds, or accuracy, Wat. Not this close. I got one for you and – when the time comes – one for your friend JoBeth.'

I shuffled backward on all fours.

He followed me, staying on the starboard gangway.

When I reached the end of the cabin roof I placed my feet on the deck and took cover behind the sail.

But he kept on coming and there was no place I could go. I was seconds away from becoming a point blank target.

As I moved back toward the bows, my heel kicked some sort of object. I looked down and saw a yellow plastic mooring fender. It looked like an elongated football with a short length of nylon cord attached to one end. The yacht tilted and it rolled a few inches across the deck but in an odd, lopsided way. I picked up the cord and felt the weight of the fender. Water seemed to have leaked into it, hence the unusual rolling movement.

It wasn't much of a weapon, but the water inside would give it some heft.

And it was better than nothing.

I wrapped the cord around my fist and felt the weight: No more than a couple of pounds. Not heavy enough to hurt Phipps, but enough to distract him. I gave myself five seconds to think. Then I started moving toward the starboard gangway, to the point where Phipps would emerge from behind the sail.

It wasn't much of a plan, but Phipps would not be expecting me to come at him.

And it was better than nothing.

I heard his footfall on the wooden deck.

He was real close now – six feet, maybe less.

I stooped to peer under the gap between the boom and the deck. I saw his legs moving in short, cautious steps.

He came from behind the sail quicker than I anticipated, gun in a two-handed grip and ready to shoot. I swung the fender the instant he clocked me. A lot happened in the next few seconds. I let go of the cord and the fender bounced off his right shoulder. I glimpsed a look of surprise on his face. Then the gun went off. I felt a sharp sting as the bullet hit the top of my left arm.

We both retreated.

I stepped back to the guard rail. The round must have gone through my upper arm without hitting bone or the brachial artery. But I was losing blood. It was streaming down my arm in a warm tide. And it hurt like hell. I could ignore the pain, but not the blood loss. Not for long anyway.

On the plus side, he was down to a single round.

This was going to be touch and go. If I could keep moving, I had a chance to overpower him.

He appeared again from behind the sail, much more wary this time.

He stood facing me at a distance of nine or ten feet. Close enough to be fairly sure of hitting me; distant enough to be able to shoot before I could rush him.

'That was a cute move, Wat.' He took one slow step forward, staring right at me.

This was a mistake because he wasn't aware that he'd placed his left foot in a loop of rope lying on the deck. The other end was tied to the guard rail to my right, out of his line of sight. One wrench might unbalance him just long enough for me to close the gap. But I'd have to get the timing just right. If he cottoned on he'd shoot me on the spot.

I let my right hand fall to my side, as if I'd accepted the inevitability of what was coming. I twisted my upper body slightly, moving my hand real slow. I fumbled for the rope, didn't find it. Fumbled some more, still nothing.

'It's been a blast.' He pulled back the hammer. 'But this is the end of the road.'

I tried again for the rope. This time my fingers closed around it. I was sure he'd nail what I was doing. And one more step would take his foot out of the loop. But he didn't see and he didn't move.

I gripped the rope, prepared to yank it.

I heard a noise from the deck behind the sail. Sounded like something rolling from one side to the other.

He tilted his head – he'd heard it too.

If I could divert his focus, even for a split second, it could make all the difference.

'Sounds like you didn't secure your gear so well, Edison.' I made a lazy smile that absolutely did not reflect how I felt. 'I thought you were a regular deep sea mariner.'

'The boat's secure enough, Wat.' He lined up his sights. 'You won't get me with a trick like that.'

I braced myself. He was still looking directly at my face, unaware I'd gotten hold of the rope.

This was it. Shit or bust. I counted to three: One, two –

Phipps' expression changed from assured to astonished. His chest thrust out, shoulders drew back.

I yanked the rope. The noose snared his ankle, dragging it toward me. He lost his balance as he pulled the trigger. The round went somewhere out over the river. Then he dropped the gun, stumbling sideways and snatching a mast stay with both hands.

I was puzzled. I'd hauled hard on the rope, but the idea was to trip him. Somehow I'd completely disabled him.

Only I hadn't.

He dropped to his knees, still gripping the wire stay with both hands. Then he swung through 180 degrees and I saw an axe with a red handle embedded in his spine.

JoBeth was standing behind him.

Phipps tried to haul himself to his feet, his face twisted in an alloy of pain and determination.

He looked at JoBeth, then back at me. His expression was difficult to read: Someplace between defiance and disbelief.

Then he went over the side, vanishing astern, face down in a welter of pink-grey foam.

SIXTY

My plane came in to land at Pleiku airbase and I glimpsed the foothills of Vietnam's Central Highlands. I was back in the fast lane of harm's highway, the meanest and spookiest place in the Nasty – with or without the war. Nobody sane would want to be here. But I knew this now. And I accepted that one day, perhaps soon, I'd have to quit.

A lot had happened in the week after Edison Phipps died, though it took three days to recover his body.

Luckily for us, he'd been in such a rush to cast off that he didn't do a great job of binding JoBeth's wrists. She managed to work her hands free and grabbed the axe on her way out of the cabin. It was stowed for nautical emergencies, though nothing like this one. JoBeth said she didn't think twice about using it, but I knew she'd thought a lot more than twice about it later. Split a guy's spine with a heavy blade, that's not something you come to terms with quickly, perhaps not ever.

Would I have avoided Phipps' last bullet without JoBeth's intervention? Maybe. But I was much happier not to have rolled the dice. I was still losing blood from the bullet hole in my arm and JoBeth used her belt as a makeshift tourniquet. She knew enough about sailing to steer the yacht and we were back on shore in less than an hour. First stop was the hospital at Tarrytown, where a surgeon fixed my wound and reluctantly agreed to discharge me.

Second stop was a meeting with Laurence Westerby, New York National Guard chief Almerin O'Hara, and Mike Seymour, the US attorney for the Southern District of New York, who was JoBeth's boss. We each gave a verbal report and left the high ups to their deliberations. We never mentioned Loretta Hausinger, still safe with Titus Grundy. We simply – and truthfully – said there was no evidence to justify an arrest or secure a conviction for the Biomedical Centre homicides.

Then I wrote my exclusive for the *Examiner*. I led on Phipps assassinating Bobkov to stop him exposing the defective drug that Kershaw Lefevre wanted to dole out to thousands of veterans. In my second paragraph I revealed the attempted murder by Phipps of Harriet Brigstock because she, too, was a threat to MPQ-13. And I cited Andy Stuivermans as an innocent victim of Phipps' conspiracy. Soon after my paper hit the streets, the entire board of Kershaw Lefevre resigned in the face of a plunging share price and looming insolvency.

A few days later, JoBeth told me Philip Riley had fully cooperated with her office and been allowed to resign his National Guard commission without prosecution. Of course he still had to tell his American family about his Korean daughter, but I had a feeling he'd make things work out. He and I would never see eye to eye, though I did respect his guts and his loyalty. Corey Quilton was in the process of making a deal with Jo Beth that would see her overlook his threats to Harriet Brigstock in return for his giving evidence against Gerry Bohannon. Big Gerry was certainly going down for the murder of Boyd Brigstock, though his lawyer was trying to plea bargain a rap of second degree murder, rather than first. In exchange, Bohannon would spill all he knew about Phipps' conspiracy. Either way, he would spend a very long time behind bars.

I picked up Loretta from Titus Grundy's place and we took a cab to the mid-town Manhattan hotel where she was staying while she figured out what to do next. She didn't want to return to Ramskill, though she was determined to continue her career in biomedical research. She didn't say where this might take her and I didn't ask. I wished her well, though. What she did took true courage and I meant it when I told JoBeth I'd have done the same in her shoes.

Saying goodbye to Maggie wasn't as easy. I knew she worried about me on a daily basis when I was in Vietnam. I tried to reassure her. I promised to take care, to stay safe. But we both knew taking care and staying safe weren't a big part of what I did as a Special Forces captain.

I last saw JoBeth on the doorstep of her apartment on Sullivan Street. I was due to fly out of JFK later that morning.

She said, 'I won't see you again, will I?'

I gripped her hands. 'I have to go back. I always had to go back.'

She made a faint smile. 'Look me up when you come home?'

I said sure I would.

'You will come home, won't you? Even if you don't look me up, make sure you come home.'

'I'll do both.'

I kissed her mouth, slow and damp, then turned and took the first steps of my journey back to the Nasty.

This book is printed on paper from sustainable sources managed under the Forest Stewardship Council (FSC) scheme.

It has been printed in the UK to reduce transportation miles and their impact upon the environment.

For every new title that Matador publishes, we plant a tree to offset CO_2, partnering with the More Trees scheme.

For more about how Matador offsets its environmental impact, see www.troubador.co.uk/about/